ALSO BY EMILY WIBBERLEY
AND AUSTIN SIEGEMUND-BROKA

Always Never Yours

If I'm Being Honest

EMILY WIBBERLEY

AUSTIN SIEGEMUND-BROKA

VIKING

VIKING
An imprint of Penguin Random House LLC, New York

First published in the United States of America by Viking,
an imprint of Penguin Random House LLC, 2019

Visit us online at penguinrandomhouse.com

LIBRARY OF CONGRESS CATALOGING-IN-PUBLICATION DATA IS AVAILABLE

ISBN 9780451481092

Printed in the United States of America

Design by Kristie Radwilowicz
Set in Elysium STD

3 5 7 9 10 8 6 4

To the shrews who won't be tamed

One

"BITCH."

I hear the word under Autumn Carey's breath behind me. I guess I earned it by daring to walk ahead of her to reach the dining hall door. I cut her off while she was examining her reflection in her phone's camera, trying to decide if her new bangs were a bad choice. Which they were. Part of me wants to whirl around and tell Autumn I don't have the *entirety of lunch* to walk behind her, but I don't.

Instead, I tilt my head just enough to tell Autumn I heard her, but I don't care enough to respond. I have things to do. Autumn's not remarkable enough in any way to hold my attention, and I've been called that name often enough, under enough breaths, for it not to hurt. Not from a girl like her. It's hardly an uncommon thought here. *Cameron Bright's a bitch.*

I throw open the door and walk outside. The sun sparkles on the fountain in the heart of the courtyard, encircled by low hedges and lunch tables. It's about a billion degrees out because it's September, when Los Angeles gets apocalyptically hot. I head for the stairway to the second-story patio, under the red-tiled roofs and cream-colored arches of the school's mission architecture.

I notice heads turn in my direction. The girls watch me with half worship and half resentment, the boys with intrigue. In their defense, I do realize I'm . . . well, hot. I'm a natural blonde, and I have the body that comes with running six miles a day.

A sophomore girl stares from the railing with the undisguised interest of someone who doesn't realize she's been noticed. I give her a *what?* glance, and she drops her eyes, her cheeks reddening.

I'm popular. I don't entirely know why. I'm hardly our school's only hot girl, and it's not like I'm rich. I'm not. My dad is, but he's lived in Philadelphia since the year I was born, which is not a coincidence. He sends a check for my tuition and my mom's rent, and nothing else. And I'm not popular because my parents have won Oscars or played for sold-out stadiums or were groupies for Steven Tyler. My mom could be considered an actress, but strictly of the washed-up, C-list variety. She had roles in a couple of commercials and stage plays when I was in elementary school. From there, it's been a downward trajectory to watching daytime soaps on the couch and job searching on the internet.

I'm uninteresting among my classmates, honestly. Beaumont Prep—the top-ranked, priciest private school on the West Coast—is full of the children of the rich and famous. Actresses, entrepreneurs, athletes, musicians.

Then there's me. I live forty minutes away in Koreatown. I drive a Toyota I'm pretty certain predates the Clinton presidency. I don't set trends or post photos of myself on Instagram that get thousands of likes around the world.

2

Yet I'm popular. Undeniably and unquestionably.

I find our usual table overlooking the courtyard. Everyone knows the second-story patio is ours, the best view to see and be seen. No one's here yet, which gives me the opportunity to pull my notebook from my bag and write down a quick list, organizing my thoughts.

To Do 9/8
1. Pick up peer-reviewed Wharton essay

2. Conditioning run

3. Econ homework

I know there's a fourth item. I'm itching to remember it, and it's not coming. I use lists to unwind because I get edgy when things feel disorganized and out of my control. The way I feel right now, trying to remember the final thing I have to do today—

"You could come over tonight . . ." croons an obnoxious male voice, unmistakably Jeff Mitchel's. Two bags drop to the ground at the table behind me. I roll my eyes as a female voice replies.

"You're not going to Rebecca's party?" The girl's tone is bashful and obviously flirtatious. I wince. Jeff Mitchel is the worst. Rich, spoiled, and just attractive enough to make him insufferably entitled. He gets straight Ds, smokes pot instead of going to class, and enjoys impressing girls by "treating" them to five-hundred-dollar dinners at Daddy's restaurant.

"Not if you're coming over," Jeff replies. I hear fabric rustling, telling me there's been physical contact. Of what form, I don't want to know. But I have a list to finish, which won't happen with *this* playing out behind me.

Gritting my teeth, I round on the two of them.

I find Jeff in his popped-collar glory, one hand on the white-jeaned knee of Bethany Bishop. Bethany, who's had her heart broken by nearly every one of Beaumont's dumbasses of record, a string of careless rich guys and philandering athletes. I have neither the time nor the inclination to watch this one cross the starting line.

"Really?" I drag my eyes to Bethany. "You're flirting with *him* now?"

Bethany flushes, glaring indignantly. "No one asked your opinion."

"You just got dumped." I ignore her. "The whole school knew. You ugly-cried by your locker for *weeks*. I'm not interested in having to walk past that again on my way to Ethics every day, and Jeff's a worse guy than your ex—"

"Hey," Jeff cuts in.

I fire him a glare. "Don't get me started on *you*." I turn back to Bethany. "Honestly, you're decently attractive. I mean, your wardrobe needs updating, and you have a really annoying laugh. But all things considered, you're a six-point-five for Beaumont. Jeff"—I fling my hand in his direction—"is a two. You could be doing way better," I tell her encouragingly.

Bethany grabs her bag. "Screw you, Cameron." She walks off in a huff, not realizing the huge favor I've done her.

Nobody ever does. When they're not calling me *bitch*,

people have told me I'm overly honest. I know. I know I am. When you grow up with a dad like mine, whose unwaveringly direct commentary came with every one of the rare visits and phone calls we've had throughout my childhood, it's just an instinct. He's never wrong, either, even when his words hurt. Which they do—I know he's a jerk. But he's a successful jerk, with Fortune 500 profiles and penthouses on two continents. With every critique he's given me, I could wither under his words and feel inferior or I could rise to them and become a better version of myself. I've always appreciated his honesty for that.

Bethany clearly sees things differently.

"What the hell?" Jeff asks, irritated. "Bethany was one hundred percent going to put out. You owe me."

"Please. *You* owe *me* the ten minutes of my life I'll never get back."

He eyes me, his expression changing. His raised eyebrow makes me gag. "I could give you ten minutes," he says in a voice he must imagine is seductive.

"I'd rather die."

"Damn, Cameron," he says. "You need to loosen up. Do the world a favor and get yourself laid. If you keep up this ice-queen routine, eventually there won't be a guy left who'd do the job."

"As long as you're first on that list." I'm ready for this conversation to be over.

"You don't mean that. Come on, you're coming to Skāra tonight, right? I'll be there. We could—"

But I don't hear whatever it is Jeff Mitchel wishes we could do tonight, because his offer, while thoroughly disgusting, reminds me of the missing item on my list. I return to my notebook and start writing.

4. Find out if soccer team is going to Skára

I may be a renowned "ice queen" on campus, but I won't be for much longer. Not if a certain member of the soccer team comes to the North Hollywood nightclub where one of the cheerleaders is having a huge party tonight.

"Are you even listening to me?" Jeff whines, demanding my attention.

"Of course not." I look up in time to see my two best friends approaching. Elle Li levels Jeff a look of such pure disgust she doesn't even have to utter a word. Jeff picks up his backpack and *finally* gets out of my sight. I swear, she has a gift.

"Permission to rant?" I hear characteristic exasperation in Elle's voice. She drops down across from me, Jeff entirely forgotten. I close my notebook as she and Morgan place their lunches on the table.

Morgan has her brilliantly blonde hair in an elaborate braid. She's wearing a Dolce & Gabbana dress, but Morgan LeClaire could wear sweatpants and she'd look like a movie star. Because she pretty much is one. Her mom's a record executive, and Morgan's hung out with the Donald Glovers and Demi Lovatos of the world her whole life. She decided she wanted to act when she was ten, and a year ago her agent began booking her roles in local indies. On the bench next to Elle, she looks bored, and I get the feeling she heard the first half of Elle's rant on the walk over from the dining hall.

Elle flits a perfectly manicured hand through her short, shiny black hair. She's five foot two, and yet everyone—teachers included—agree she's the most imposing person on campus.

Which is why I'm not about to interrupt her. "Permission granted," I say, waving a hand grandly.

"MissMelanie got the Sephora sponsorship," Elle fumes, her British accent coming out. She grew up in Hong Kong until she was ten and learned English at expensive private schools. "I made multiple videos featuring their lip liner. I even did a haul video where I spent seven hundred dollars of my own money on makeup I don't need. I wrote kiss-ass-y emails to their head of digital promotions—for nothing. For them to go with an idiot like MissMelanie, who mixes up 'your' and 'you're' in her comments."

Ellen Li, or Elli to her 15 million YouTube subscribers, is one of the highest-viewed makeup artists for her online weekly tutorials. Every week she creates and models looks for everything from New Year's Eve parties to funerals. She's been on *Forbes*'s Highest-Paid YouTube Stars list twice.

Despite my complete and utter lack of interest in makeup or internet stardom, Elle and I are remarkably alike. She's the only other person I know who understands how desperate and careless 99 percent of this school is. Elle's unflinchingly honest, and she'll do anything to achieve her goals. It's why we're inseparable.

And it's why I know she can handle a little attitude in return. I cut her a dry look. "You know you're acting incredibly entitled, right?"

Elle hardly even glances in my direction. "Obviously," she says, hiding a smile. "I'm *entitled* to the Sephora sponsorship because of my hard work, just like I'm *entitled* to have you listen to me unload without complaining because I've come to every one of your interminable cross-country races."

To be fair, this is true. Elle and Morgan have come to pretty much every race I can remember. They're often the only people in the bleachers for me. They first came when I was a freshman, when I'd invited my dad because he happened to be in town for the week to woo investors for an upcoming stock offering. I'd gotten my hopes up he'd come and see me win. When I crossed the finish line, he wasn't there—but Elle and Morgan were. They surprised me by coming, and it was the only thing that kept me from being crushed.

"You two are terrible," Morgan says, shaking her head. "I don't know why I'm even friends with either of you."

Elle and I don't have to exchange a look. We round on Morgan in unison. "You're an honor student, you're nice, you have cool, rich parents," I start.

"You're an actress, and you're gorgeous," Elle continues.

"You're too perfect," I say.

"No one *but* us could handle being friends with you," Elle finishes flatly.

Morgan rolls her eyes, blushing. "You guys really are the worst."

I shrug. "But you love us."

"Debatable," she delivers with a wink. She pulls out her phone, probably to text her boyfriend, Brad.

I catch the time on her screen. *Shit*. There's only ten minutes left in lunch. I have to drop off the essay I peer-reviewed and pick up mine from the College and Career Center. I shove my notebook into my bag and stand. "Morgan," I say, remembering the final item on my list. "Would you ask Brad if he knows if the soccer team's coming to Skāra tonight?"

Two pairs of eyes fix on me immediately. It's a reaction I knew well enough to expect. "What do you care about the soccer team?" Elle inquires. "You're not considering ending your two-year streak of lonely Friday nights with a hookup, are you?"

"What's wrong with a little window shopping?" I reply lightly. I throw my bag over my shoulder and leave, eager not to be interrogated.

I head in the direction of the College and Career Center. Passing the courtyard fountain, I pointedly ignore Autumn Carey and her friends glaring in my direction. I could not care less. If every glare I earned, or didn't earn but received nonetheless, bothered me, I'd drown in the judgment.

I quicken my steps to cross campus in time to pick up my essay. The College and Career Center pairs up seniors to read and review each other's college essays. It's mandatory, unfortunately, given the utter disinterest I have in my classmates' opinions on my college prospects. I was paired with Paige Rosenfeld, who's outstandingly weird, but luckily I don't have to talk to her. Her essay was about feeling like she couldn't help a classmate who was being bullied, and I gave her only a couple comments. Learning about Paige's personal life isn't exactly item number one on my priority list.

I have *my* essay to worry about. It needs to be perfect. I

worked for the entire summer on the draft I submitted to the CCC. Writing, rewriting, reviewing. I even had Morgan's boyfriend, Brad, who's on track to follow in his dad's footsteps to Harvard, edit it with permission to be harsh, or as harsh as Brad's capable of.

Because I need it ready, polished, and perfect by November 1. The deadline for the Early Decision application for the University of Pennsylvania's Wharton School.

It's my dad's alma mater. Even though we've never lived together, even though our relationship is admittedly dysfunctional, I've long wanted to go where he went. If I got in, he'd know I could. If I got in, we'd have Penn to share.

I walk into the College and Career Center with minutes left in lunch. It's empty, and I cross the carpeted, overly clean room to the student mailboxes. I drop Paige's essay off, then head to my box. The envelope with Paige's comments on my essay sits on top. Hurriedly, I slide the pages loose and start scanning the red ink in the margins.

Which . . . there's plenty of. I feel my heart drop, then race. I didn't plan on particularly caring what Paige Rosenfeld had to say about my essay, but faced with this treatment, it's hard to ignore.

I flip to the final page, where I find Paige has written a closing note. I force myself to focus on each sentence, even when I want to ignore every word.

This just reads as really, really inauthentic. Anyone could write this with a couple Google searches on UPenn. There's no "you" in here. Whatever reason you want to go there, tell them. Try to find a little passion—and then start over.

I frown. Who is *Paige* to tell me what's "authentic"? She doesn't know me. It's not like her essay was brilliant either. If I'd cared, I could have written her a note criticizing her trite choice of topic and overdramatic descriptions. Beaumont hardly has a bullying problem.

It's embarrassing, reading feedback like this on writing I was proud of. The worst thing is, though, I know she's right. I was so wrapped up in being professional that I didn't get to anything personal.

But I refuse to be discouraged. I'm not like Bethany. If I could be broken by harsh words, I would have given up a long time ago. I *will* rewrite this essay, and I *will* get in to UPenn.

Inside my bag, my phone buzzes. I pull it out on reflex and find a text from Morgan.

> **The soccer team will be there. Looking forward to whatever you're planning . . .**

With half a grin, I flip my essay closed. I drop it into my bag, my thoughts turning to tonight.

Two

I'M LATE TO SKĀRA BECAUSE FRIDAY-NIGHT TRAFFIC on Highland is horrendous, and I had to hunt for half an hour for parking because I didn't want to pay seventeen dollars for the garage. The club is on the top floor of a huge mall on Hollywood Boulevard, between tall apartment complexes and art deco movie theaters. I have to dodge tourists clogging the curb chatting in languages I don't recognize and taking photos of the Hollywood Walk of Fame.

I finally reach the door, and the bouncer waves me in. The club is typically twenty-one and up, but tonight Rebecca Dorsey's dad rented the place out for her birthday. They won't serve us drinks, obviously, but people find creative ways to raise their blood alcohol content.

Under the erratic lighting, I spot him immediately.

He's leaning on the velvet couch near the edge of the dance floor, laughing with the rest of the soccer team. He's the picture of perfect carelessness. The picture of perfect hotness, too. He's tall, built like the varsity athlete he is, and his smile stands out in his corner of the club. I watch him reach up with one arm to rub the back of his neck, pulling up the hem of his Beaumont soccer polo, exposing the strip of dark skin above his belt. It's a nice strip, a really inviting strip.

This is my moment. I just have to walk up to him, join the conversation, and then lead him to a place where it's just the two of us.

But I can't.

The music pounds uncomfortably in my ears. I can't even walk past the kitschy sculpture by the door.

I've wanted this for a year. I've planned for it. Why can't I do this? It's possible I've forgotten how to flirt. I've been rejecting guys for two years while developing this crush in secret. What if I've forgotten how this particular game is played?

I watch him roll his eyes at whatever idiotic thing Patrick Todd's saying, and I know what's coming next. His eyebrows twitch the way they do every time he's preparing one of his effortless comebacks. He's wonderfully no-bullshit.

It's the first thing I ever loved about Andrew Richmond. Even when he was new to Beaumont, I noticed his quick and imperturbable humor. Our friendship deepened because we both felt out of place among our wealthy, glamorous class-mates. Andrew had the added difficulty of being black in our predominately white school. For one reason or other, we both entered Beaumont feeling like outsiders.

I've talked to him countless times, but never in this con-text. Not even crappy pickup lines are coming to mind. I need help.

Feeling my heart race with frustration, I sweep the dance floor for my friends. People I know and people I don't fill the crowded, darkened room. Morgan, dressed like a hipster on a Beverly Hills budget in a strappy gold dress with a beaded headband, perches on one of the L-shaped white couches near the balcony. She's eyeing Brad with that eagerness I've learned to recognize—and avoid. I know where their night's headed, and I won't be interrupting *that*.

But in front of the bar, Elle's running a finger down the arm of Jason Reid. Ugh. I have no problem interrupting Elle's completely indefensible hookup plans. Before she can pull Jason into a dark corner, I cross the room and grab her by the elbow.

"Cameron!" she protests.

I ignore her and usher us both into the ladies' restroom. I close the door, and Elle walks past me. I give the restroom a once-over. It's filthy, and the dimmed lights don't hide the spilled drinks and littered tissues on the floor. In one stall a girl in a sequined dress holds her friend's hair while she dry-heaves over the toilet.

"I hope there's a very good reason you pulled me away from Jason," Elle says, raising an expectant eyebrow.

"Other than the obvious?" I reply, my goal momentarily forgotten. I've explained to Elle a dozen times why I disapprove of Jason. He's an annoying, airheaded actor who adores nothing more than his own reflection. He has a girlfriend, who I'm guessing isn't here—and who I have to hang out with every day during cross-country after school. "You know I don't condone this."

"If I wanted your opinion I would have asked for it," she replies. "Why'd you pull me in here?"

My nerves catch fire. Andrew's out there only feet away. I

pace the disgusting restroom floor, running a hand through my hair in frustration. "Do you have a shade of lipstick that's, like, seductive?"

Understanding dawns in Elle's eyes. "You *are* interested in one of the soccer players. Tell me who."

"Andrew."

"Andrew *Richmond*?" Elle starts to smile.

"Do you have any lipstick or not?" I ask loudly, crossing my arms.

Elle's watching me with skepticism and a hint of humor. "For your information, I don't just carry around a complete color palette wherever I go. If you're going to borrow my makeup, you're going to need to text me beforehand what you're wearing and how much sun you've gotten that day. I don't just *have* lipstick for you."

"Fine." I level my gaze with hers. "I'll go borrow Morgan's. I have plans for the night, and if you won't—"

Elle sighs. "Come here," she orders. "You'd look awful in what Morgan's wearing."

With a swell of satisfaction, I lean on the counter, facing away from the mirror, and watch Elle pull out no fewer than four shades of lipsticks from her purse. She proceeds to mix them on her hand and then dab the color on my lips with one finger. Elle's a professional and a perfectionist. I knew she'd have something.

"For years you have me do the dirty work of discouraging every guy interested in you," she says, holding my chin while she paints my lips. "Now you're chasing Andrew Richmond. Would you care to explain?"

"No, I would not," I reply shortly. I could explain if I wanted to. For months I've had a list of reasons to break my no-dating rule for Andrew. *He makes me laugh. He's objectively gorgeous. We're both runners. He's committed. He's proven he has goals and works hard. I don't want to die a virgin.*

"It's because he's new blood, isn't it?" she goes on, ignoring me. "He's new to the popular crowd. He just made varsity soccer, he's the only guy here who hasn't dated every blonde within reach—he's exciting. And you haven't had enough time with him yet to know he's as lame as every other guy."

"I've known Andrew for years," I fire back. "I'd know if he was lame. Like I know with Jason." I cut her a pointed look, which she brushes off. "Andrew's . . . different."

"*How* different?" Elle presses, her voice heavy with skepticism.

I don't reply right away, because I'm remembering a rainy afternoon in December of junior year. We were in my bedroom because our moms were having dinner downstairs, but we couldn't go for a run with buckets pouring from the sky. We'd been working on homework, and I was panicking about a group project on which I'd been paired with none other than Abby Fleischman, who'd unacceptably decided dressing in a ridiculous costume and going to a comic book convention was a worthwhile use of her weekend. Which it obviously wasn't, and we'd gotten nothing done on the project. I was five minutes into a world-class rant about Abby's objectionable life choices when Andrew glanced up from his history textbook.

"People are starving, Cameron," he said dryly. "You'll survive."

I blinked, too thrown to be angry, and burst out laughing. And then Andrew was laughing, and the panic in my chest eased. I noticed he was cute when he laughed. I noticed the dimple in his right cheek. I noticed the way his eyes lit up, and the whole room with them.

"We work. We just do," I tell Elle.

She doesn't reply. "If I'm going to finish your lipstick," she says after a moment, "you'll have to stop smiling like an idiot."

I can't help it. I smile wider.

Elle flicks my nose in return. "Okay." She steps back to scrutinize her work. "You're ready."

Every memory of Andrew and me dances through my head—every conversation, every run, every laugh. Every private, perfect moment. Why was I nervous? Tonight isn't about looking perfect or saying the perfect flirtatious thing. It's about him and me.

"I am," I say, not bothering to check my reflection in the mirror. Andrew knows me better than everyone except my closest friends. All I need is to be myself.

Three

I TAKE A DEEP BREATH AND PLUNGE back into the club.

The crowd is a battle. There's a football player grinding on a petite redhead in my way. I send him a withering glare, and he backs off, looking chagrined. Nimbly I dodge Sara Marco and Ben Nguyen halfway to third base. When I'm nearly to the lounge, an elbow hurtles perilously close to my face.

Jerking away instinctively, I round on the idiot responsible—and my eyes widen.

Paige Rosenfeld is *drunk*. She sways sloppily over the shorter girls, her badly dyed red hair a sweaty mess. She's dancing with the composure of an alcohol-fueled teenage giraffe. Her ugly yellow body-con dress reveals curves I didn't know she had. She usually comes to school covered in the frills and lace of her obviously and inexplicably homemade garments. I watch her almost spill a nearby girl's drink, her eyes not registering me.

I kind of can't believe she's here. Paige Rosenfeld isn't exactly a member of the rather wide circle that comes to Beaumont parties. I didn't think dancing, fun, or human contact was her thing. She's on scholarship to Beaumont, not that being one of the school's few scholarship kids is a barrier to popularity. It's that she has a new terrible hairstyle every month, she wears incomprehensible clothes, she listens to droning, depressing music, and—probably worst—she's the older sister of Barfy Brendan, the kid who throughout middle school threw up in the cafeteria, on the bus, and on his classmates too often to be well liked. I started calling him BB, for Barfy Brendan, and it sort of caught on. I don't know why Paige is even here.

I have my answer when Jeff Mitchel walks onto the dance floor carrying two drinks. Both of which nearly spill on everyone within a five-foot radius when Paige spots him and flings herself at him.

I try not to gag too obviously. Two Jeff Mitchel encounters in one day? I must be cursed. Why Paige, who openly denigrates our classmates' BMWs and Birkin bags, would have any interest in Jeff is beyond me. If I cared even a little bit, I might try to figure it out. But I don't.

Out of the corner of my eye, I catch Andrew heading toward the club's open-air terrace. Leaving Paige to the hookup she'll inevitably regret, I follow him. The terrace runs the length of the club, with modern chairs and patio heaters and an outdoor bar interrupting the view of the city. Over the commotion inside, I hear horns honking and the hum of traffic from Hollywood Boulevard.

I find my eyes drawn to the glittering skyline of downtown Los Angeles. The cluster of skyscrapers, the parallel lines of white and red headlights streaming in from the freeways. The colors contrast beautifully, the brilliant lights against the black night sky.

They'd be perfect for a website I'm working on. I take a picture on my phone.

The terrace is full of my classmates, everyone holding red plastic cups. While I'm walking toward the railing, a couple water polo guys call my name.

"Want a drink?" Kyle Cretton calls, flashing me a flask in his sport coat.

I wrinkle my nose. Even if every other girl out here is drooling over the water polo captain, I'm interested in *nothing* involving Kyle Cretton and his hidden booze. Perfect abs and a Speedo are all well and good, but Kyle's no different from every guy I've rejected. He's content to ditch class for doughnuts and spend every Friday plying underclassmen with drinks. He's not interesting. He's not driven. He's not worth the effort or the risk.

"With you?" I call back. "Definitely not."

Kyle cringes, and with hollers of "Burn" and "Damn, dude," the other guys jostle him. Bored, I continue past them.

I find Andrew leaning on the balcony overlooking the skyline, the only person out here not sneaking drinks or ogling drunk girls. His posture's rigid, like he doesn't know what to do with himself. He's in his still-creased short-sleeve Beaumont soccer polo, and the bright green stands out against his skin. I pause a moment, drinking in his appearance. The way the fabric outlines his muscular shoulders. The close shave of his fade, his hair contoured tightly around his ears. The perfect amount of stubble on his jaw.

"Andrew Richmond," I say, walking up next to him. Confidence looks good on me.

When he hears my voice, he visibly relaxes a little. His lips curl into a faint grin, his eyes remaining on the view.

I drape myself over the railing, facing the terrace. "Enjoying the party?" I ask.

He turns to me, his eyebrows knitting together. He looks like he's not certain if he's dreaming or I'm crazy. "What are you doing?" He's not being critical. His voice holds genuine curiosity.

"Talking to the newest starter on the Beaumont varsity soccer team, I thought." I notice the way his chest puffs up with pride, but some of the light leaves his eyes. A cloud passes in front of the moon, casting us in shadow.

"Yeah, you just . . ." he starts haltingly. "You don't usually talk to me."

"What?" I lean in, our shoulders close to touching. "We hang out."

"But not, you know"—he throws his head in the direction of the club—"not at school stuff."

Guiltily, I know he's not entirely wrong. When Andrew first came to Beaumont in the middle of sixth grade, he and his family knew no one. His mom and mine became fast friends, bonded over a shared love of *The Bachelor*, which they watch together religiously. Andrew's mom, Deb, brought him with her when we were both in sixth grade, hoping he'd make a friend. By the time we were too old for forced hangouts, he'd become her designated driver.

As a result, Andrew and I have spent a good amount of time together across high school, doing homework, watching TV, or just talking. We run together every now and then.

I didn't really notice Andrew when we first hung out, other than his occasional humor. He never had a sense of himself. With his uncertain fashion sense, his mediocre grades, and his tendency not to talk in groups, he never knew who he was. I didn't consider him romantically because he was too adrift to risk tying myself to. If I was going to commit to someone, I wanted him to be worth the worry, worth the part of me I was going to give to him. It was a lesson I'd learned from my unfortunate first relationship, in which I went to obscene lengths to get a guy without bothering to wonder whether he was worth the effort. He wasn't. We broke up almost immediately.

Then Andrew filled out. He didn't care about organized sports, but his long legs and lithe frame had become perfect for dribbling a ball down a field.

I noticed. I noticed potential.

A year of hints, and Andrew finally committed to a training regimen and took the initiative to try out for the team a few weeks ago.

I place a hand on his arm, which is goose-bumped even in the warm Hollywood night. His eyes follow, narrowing in on where my fingers rest on the bend of his elbow. "Now that you're on the team, I think our social circles will be . . . intersecting." I give him a meaningful look.

He has to swallow before he can speak again. I'm not surprised his mouth is a little dry. When he looks up, he's recovered his cool. "Intersecting?" he says evenly. His pupils engulf his dark eyes. "What do you mean, exactly?"

I hear a shriek behind us. Andrew and I both look in time to see a girl furiously wiping the amber stain down the front of her dress, while a couple water polo guys laugh behind her. *Idiots.*

It's time I take this somewhere more private.

"Follow me and I'll show you," I whisper in Andrew's ear.

I withdraw quickly. Feeling his gaze burning into my back, I head inside, his footsteps behind me.

Andrew being on varsity soccer isn't why I like him. He's not like the guys I refuse to date. He's smart, and he's unfailingly kind, and he's proven himself driven and talented. I can imagine having something real with him in a way I never could before. Him making the team was just the final necessary piece.

I lead him past the crowd toward the VIP booths in the back. They're curtained off with a velvet rope in front, which I'm guessing means we're not supposed to go inside. But nobody's watching, we're far from the dance floor, and the club is rented out. It'll be fine. I undo the velvet rope and slip inside the curtains. It's empty, and I turn and wait.

Only moments later, Andrew rushes in. He looks at me. And I look at him. I walk forward, and his eyes widen when I run both hands up his chest. Whatever he was expecting from tonight, it wasn't this. In the next instant I'm kissing him, and, finally understanding where we're going with this, he wraps his arms around my waist. He has a natural talent for this, I find myself realizing.

I draw him by the hand toward the couch and recline on the pillows. "I really like you, Andrew," I whisper, pulling him down to me.

"Funny." He pauses short of my lips. "I always got the opposite impression. We've been friends for years, and you've never—"

I cut him off with a long kiss. "I am now," I say, pushing down the frustration in my voice. "Isn't that enough? We could talk about it more, or we could . . ." I trail my hand down to his waistband.

He kisses me this time. There's no trace of hesitation in the way his mouth meets mine. Nothing but the momentum of months of wanting this, momentum I know he feels with me. I pull off his polo, exploring the stretch of skin I find underneath. He runs a hand through my hair, down my chest, and breathes, "You're so beautiful."

It's perfect. It really is.

Until there's a crash behind Andrew, and something heavy falls onto him. He's rocked forward, his forehead ramming into my nose. My eyes water before I even feel the pain burst through my face.

"What the *hell*?" I yell, standing up sharply and pulling my dress up over my now-braless chest. Andrew looks similarly stunned. When my eyes recover from the flash of light of the curtains parting, I realize there's now a third person in this booth.

Paige Rosenfeld.

"Are you drunk or just severely stupid?" I snap. If she looked horrible before, she's an abject mess now. Her too-heavy mascara runs in gunky black spiderwebs down her cheeks, and when she hauls herself off the edge of the couch, I notice honest-to-god snot on the front of her dress.

I hear my dad's voice in my head. *Pathetic.*

"Sorry," Paige says with a violent sniffle. "I didn't think someone would be shameless enough to be screwing in a club with only a flimsy curtain hiding them."

I narrow my eyes. Paige isn't as drunk as she seemed. What right does she have to say I'm shameless when she was flinging herself at Jeff in front of everyone? "Jealousy looks bad on you," I sneer. "I guess it didn't work out with Jeff, huh? Why don't you find someone as *pathetic* as you are to hook up with?" I'm staring Paige down, but in the corner of my vision I catch Andrew's eyebrows go up. It's possible my resentment over her scathing review of my essay is seeping into my frustration over her intrusion. I don't care, though.

Fresh tears well in Paige's eyes. "I've wondered . . ." she says, her voice shaking, "I guess you really are as awful on the inside as you act." She strides past the curtains without giving her tears the chance to fall.

I roll my shoulders, shrugging off the insult. Reclining on the couch, I place a hand on the cushion to invite Andrew. "Where were we?"

He doesn't move. His lips slip into a quizzical frown. "You want to go back to making out after that?"

I still, working out what he's just said. "I know she spoiled the mood," I say, struggling to keep my voice light. "But I've waited too long for this to let *Paige Rosenfeld* ruin it." I sit up, hugging my dress to my chest.

Impossibly, his eyes never leave mine. "She was obviously upset. You didn't have to insult her." His voice is gentle, but not without a critical edge.

"*Excuse* me," I say. I'm honestly in disbelief we're still discussing Paige. "She insulted *me* first. Remember? But really, the insult isn't even the point. I don't have much sympathy for girls like Paige." I know I'm not exactly helping the mood, but this is what I'm feeling, and I'm not going to push it down. "Reduced to tears because it didn't work out with some douchebag she barely knows? Please. It *is* pathetic."

I burn with defeated expectation when Andrew pulls on his shirt. "You know," he says, "you're really beautiful, and sometimes when it's just the two of us, I feel like you might be worth it. But the truth is"—he pauses at the entrance—"you're a bitch, Cameron Bright."

The curtain flutters closed behind him. I sit in silence.

I'm a little shocked how harshly the insult stings. I've never been called that word by someone I care about, someone whose words have the power to hurt.

I'm not going to cry, though. Crying *is* pathetic. It won't help.

It never does.

Four

I'M WOKEN UP THE NEXT MORNING BY my phone ringing, ruining my usual Saturday morning plans of sleeping in. I glance over to check the name on the screen—Elle. With a twinge of guilt, I hit mute, and she goes to voicemail. I hope she enjoyed her night with Jason. But I'm not ready to hear the gory details right now.

Get up. Run. Deal with Mom.

The list is enough to get me out of bed.

I'm hurt by where Andrew and I left things, by what he called me. The thought chews the corner of my mind while I make my bed. What I said to Paige sounded bad—honestly, I could have been a little nicer. Andrew knows me, though. He'll come around.

Or he won't, and I will have lost what I waited a year for. There's nothing I can do now. Nothing but wait.

I need a run.

I keep my running gear exactly where I want it, the way I do everything else in my room. It's impeccably organized, which I'm proud of. My room isn't big—nowhere near the colossal square footage of my friends'—and I hear my neighbors fighting through the wall on a regular basis. The paint's peeling from the cream-colored walls where I've hung design boards for websites I'm working on. But nothing's out of place. Every scarf has a peg on the rack by my door, every sheet of homework a place on my desk. Every issue of the *Economist* is in order on my bookshelf.

I put on my Beaumont cross-country shirt and pick up my shoes from next to the door on my way into the hallway. Inevitably, I wince.

While I keep my room neat and organized, the opposite is true of my mom's treatment of the rest of the apartment. I walk by her room, where piles of laundry—dirty or clean, it's impossible to say—cover the floor. She's left pairs of shoes in the hallway, pink plastic heels and slippers she stepped out of and didn't pick up.

I collect the shoes and take them into her bedroom. When I glance over at the bed, I'm thrown to find the sheets unfurled and the bed empty. Mom's not usually up until closer to noon. I quietly reorganize my list.

Deal with Mom. Run. Find opportunity to sneak into her bedroom and sort laundry.

I find her behind the counter in the tiny kitchenette, stirring a spice of some kind into the blender. My hope she might be out of bed for a productive reason disappears when I take in her bathrobe and the foil folded in her hair. If she's bleaching it, she's not leaving the house for hours.

Her hair's blonde like mine, which is where the resemblance ends. My mom has round, full features—like a young Renée Zellweger, she'd say. She *does* say. I've caught her modeling expressions in the mirror with pictures from *Jerry*

Maguire pulled up on her phone. I, on the other hand, have my dad's long, sharp features, his blue eyes and thin lips. They're the only things he's given me other than tuition and the *Economist* subscription, which he seemed genuinely surprised I'd wanted for my sixteenth birthday. It's one of the rare birthday gifts he's given me. Generally his financial contributions to our family are only those that make him look good to his colleagues.

"Is that cayenne pepper?" I ask Mom while I lace my shoes.

"I'm trying something new," she says brightly. "Lemonade, cayenne, and kale. Deb lost fifteen pounds on it! Which reminds me," Mom glances up, looking surprised herself to remember, "Deb cancelled on coming over tomorrow."

"Wait, why?" I ask, pausing in the middle of knotting my shoe. There's no way Andrew's mom cancelled because Andrew doesn't want to see me. Right?

"She said something about her in-laws still in town," Mom says, hitting the switch on the blender, which lets out a horrific whine. I nod in relief. I remember Andrew saying something about his grandparents not having a flight home to New Jersey. It's probably a good thing Monday night's not happening. The idea of sitting in stony silence with Andrew while our moms hoot and hiss over school-board gossip puts the kind of knot in my stomach only a run will release.

Mom shuts off the blender, and it grinds to a shuddering stop. It's a small miracle the machine still works, considering my mom's had it since my dad lived in L.A. before I was born and she's subjected it to innumerable cleanses in the past eighteen years. I finish lacing my shoes and eye the vomit-colored drink she's pouring into a chipped glass.

She must detect the skepticism in my look, because she meets my eyes. "This cleanse is different," she says, continuing triumphantly, "Jared Leto uses it."

"Oh-kay . . ." I put my heel on the back of the couch and bend over to stretch my hamstring. "But you always start these cleanses and give up two days in. I just don't see the point."

Mom's smile vanishes, replaced by a hard and defensive frown. It's one of the fundamental truths of my mother's existence. There's insecurity behind every smile. "I can start a cleanse and quit it if I want, Cameron," she protests. "What does it matter to you?"

"Nothing," I say glumly, and switch the leg I'm stretching on the couch. This is the difference between her and me. My mother gives up on everything. First it was acting, the dream she moved to Los Angeles from Indiana for twenty years ago. Now it's whatever kind of job she can get, whether it's catering, cutting hair, or waitressing. Our lives might have been different if it hadn't gotten harder to get roles when she hit forty. But aging isn't welcomed in Hollywood, and my mom couldn't take the repeated rejections. When the going gets tough, she's gone—on to the next job or onto the couch. Rejection cripples her. I watched it happen after countless auditions, and I watched it happen throughout years of her trying to get my dad to marry her.

"It's not like everyone has your metabolism," she goes on. "Have some sympathy for the rest of us."

Seriously? I swing my leg down out of my stretch, knowing she's oblivious to how I'm *in* my running clothes *about* to go for a six-mile run. Instead of arguing with her, I change tactics. "What are you doing today?" I ask, even though the bathrobe and foil give me a pretty good idea.

Mom's quick glance to the side confirms my hunch. "You know I'm between jobs," she says with clearly forced nonchalance.

I recognize the edge in her voice, and I decide to walk it. "Yeah, but what about interviews? I could help you look—"

"No thanks!" She picks up her drink, her cheery expression tight. "I'm not ready yet. Next week." Glass in hand, she shuffles to the couch and eases herself down, pulling her favorite leopard-print blanket over her lap and flipping on the TV.

I take a deep breath. I'll have to email Dad for money, I know in the pit of my stomach. Even though he pays our rent—enough for us to live forty minutes from the school he pays for, no closer—he probably won't respond well to emails requesting more. I can't even blame him is the thing. It'd be different if Mom were looking for a job. But what incentive does he have to help her when she won't even try to help herself?

"Hey," I venture, knowing before I say it that it's a terrible idea, "what about the acting school Morgan took classes at over the summer? I bet you could teach there."

"Teach?" Mom echoes, her eyes not leaving the screen. "Teach *those* spoiled kids? No thank you."

I ignore the slight to my friends, even though I'm pretty sure she intended it. "But you're good, Mom, really." I overheard enough auditions and watched enough rehearsals to know that. "Morgan said you were the first to point out how she overused her lip twitch. I think you'd be great—"

"Enough, Cameron," she cuts me off, her voice hard and petulant again. "I said I'm not in the mood. You think I need to be reminded every day of how I failed as an actress? No thank you," she repeats, definitive this time.

"Sitting on the couch all day *doesn't* remind you?" I snap, unable to contain myself any longer. I hate her on mornings like this. Mornings when I'm just trying to get to tomorrow and she's trying to go nowhere. "Fine. Don't try. Let me know when I should write to my dad to beg for more money."

I grab my keys and head straight out the door.

Every time I have the urge to cry, I run instead. Tears reach your nose first, not your eyes. If you're good, you can quench them before they ever touch your eyelids. You breathe in from your mouth once, then out.

You get good eventually.

I run in the opposite direction I usually do with Andrew, up the hill on sidewalks dotted with old gum. The apartments in my neighborhood have wrought-iron fences, and the billboards above them advertise dentists and DUI lawyers. I run onto Sixth and pass Chungmuro, the restaurant where Mom and I went for my birthday. Koreatown's not a rough neighborhood—here I am, a seventeen-year-old girl running by herself on the street—it's just not the nicest neighborhood. It's certainly a far cry from the polished sidewalks and perfect lawns of Beverly Hills, where I run with the cross-country team on school days.

I push hard into the second mile of the run, the pain in my chest changing from heartache to exertion. Mom never tries hard. Never. Not even when I've told her how fears I feel too young for—healthcare, rent, making ends meet—clutch at my throat when I drop my guard.

I don't want to ask Dad for money. Every time things get rough, it's him she depends on. It's not like there are no repercussions either. Begging him is bad enough, but in the instances he decides to come and check in on things, everything gets . . . worse. I'm no saint, but Dad has half my patience with her. He's not kind. They've had an on-and-off relationship for years, off the great majority of the time, and the expectation of nights together when he's in town for business does nothing to weaken the withering criticism he heaps on her.

I stumble on an uneven curb but catch myself before my knees hit the sidewalk. My parting remark to my mom went too far, and now I feel guilty. I know the truth can hurt, even when you need to hear it. Which she does. She just refuses to listen. Every time she hears she's unmotivated and flippant, she gives up a little more. She sinks into the couch, or she doesn't leave her laundry-littered bedroom for days.

Never does she think of me. Of what I need from a parent. Of the cross-country races and open houses she's bailed on, the bills she's neglected—the things I need to feel secure and cared for. I've never hidden from the truth of our relationship. The cold, hard reality is that I'm just her meal ticket, her excuse to wring my father for what she won't work for herself. I'll always resent her for it.

The thought burns into me like fuel, and I push myself up the next hill. I'll never understand why she doesn't try to prove my dad wrong. He tells her she's lazy and helpless, and she takes it, and then she puts herself right back in the position where she'll inevitably hear it again. It makes me so mad sometimes I snap, and I find myself echoing the harsh words of my father.

I stop on the corner of Sixth and Oxford, my side splitting. While I catch my breath, I pull my phone from my armband and write an email to my dad.

From: c.bright@beaumontprep.edu
To: db@brightpartners.com
Subject: Carol

Sorry to bother you. She needs help again. It's been four months and she's not even looking for a new job.

Once I hit send, I start running. It's times like these I wish I could live with my father. He's been very clear about that, though. He legally acknowledges I'm his daughter, he just doesn't have room in his life for that kind of relationship. His firm boundaries were made apparent to me when I was six and asked if he could come to Disneyland with us for my birthday. He told me he was too busy for that kind of thing.

I'll never forget his exact words: "that kind of thing." As if everything his daughter wanted and hoped for and needed could be casually compacted into "that kind of thing" and dismissed.

Only when I was older did I learn that "busy" wasn't a made-up excuse. He runs a venture capital firm in Philly where he handles a worldwide portfolio of technology investments. He graduated from Wharton at the top of his class, and his firm's invested in over two hundred companies with a market value of $2 billion. I'm taking Economics in the Entrepreneur's Market this semester to be eligible for his firm's internship this summer. While working with my dad won't be like living with him, it'll be something. It'll be a chance to follow in his footsteps, hopefully in the direction of success like his. It'll bring me into his world, if not his life.

Which I can't help wanting. I'm not naive—I know he's a jerk. But he's the only other parent I have. To my mom, I'll always be a tool to extort my father. To him, I could be worth more. I just have to earn his respect.

I run through crosswalks and past parked cars, from Oxford to Olympic. I know the way home by heart. I've run probably every block of the neighborhood since my dad moved Mom and me into our current apartment six years ago, when I started at Beaumont Middle School. I pass two dumpling restaurants next door to each other, the smell wafting invitingly through the doors. Someone's spray-painted a mural of Seth Rogen looking wistfully at what I think is meant to be a female Yoda. Three girls are taking selfies in front.

I feel tired when I reach the elaborate Korean Baptist church, but I keep going. Near the end of the run, my phone buzzes, and I come to a halt, scuffing the toes of my shoes into the curb. I open my email to find a message from Chelsea Wyndam, a name I vaguely recognize. She's one of my dad's personal assistants. Because Daniel Bright rarely writes his own emails, obviously. Never to his daughter.

From: db_asst@brightpartners.com
To: c.bright@beaumontprep.edu
Subject: Re: Carol

Mr. Bright said he'd handle it.

A little of the pressure eases off my chest.

When I get home a few miles later I find Mom on the computer, her eyes red and puffy. Though she hasn't changed out of her bathrobe, she has job listings up on the screen.

I don't need to ask what happened. I know. Dad *handled it.* He called and threatened to withhold the rent if she doesn't get a job. He probably told her she was pathetic, told her she was fortunate to have been beautiful enough to win a night with him eighteen years ago. He probably reminded her that the second I'm out of the house, she's on her own, and she'd better hope I take care of her because no one else will.

I've heard it before.

"I'm sorry. I don't know what's wrong with me," she says as I walk past. I know what's going on here. Whenever Dad tells her she'll depend on me, she's unusually contrite. She knows if she loses me, she loses the roof over her head. Part of me wants to fire back something nasty at her. But I know better.

"It's okay. Just try, Mom," I say from the hallway. "Try to prove him wrong."

I walk into my perfectly orderly room and out of the uncertainty of my mom's life. I can't change her, can't control any of it. All I can do is make sure I don't end up the type of person who gives up in the face of a challenge. Who lets other people tell her who she is.

I peel my shirt off over my gray sports bra. Before I toss it in the hamper, I recognize the grass stain on the sleeve and remember when I fell in the rain and landed on my shoulder. Andrew was running with me. He helped me up, and we walked home even though it was pouring.

You're a bitch, Cameron Bright.

Andrew's wrong, and I won't just sit here and hope he comes around. I won't be my mom, waiting on the couch for things to go her way. I want him too much for that. I'm going to prove to him exactly who I am. I'll do whatever it takes.

Five

BEAUMONT PREP *REALLY* WANTS TO BE ONE of the venerable prep schools of Connecticut or New Hampshire or wherever. We have a coat of arms, and wooden tables in the dining hall give the school a historic character. But we're in California, where historic isn't Gothic or colonial. The architecture is mission-style, the buildings beige and the roofs red-tiled. We don't have uniforms either. Thank god.

I walk up the steps and between the precisely trimmed rose bushes flanking the front entrance, earning more than a couple of admiring stares from my male classmates for my clingy T-shirt dress. I parted my hair on the side, and it all hangs down on my right shoulder. I duck directly toward my first class.

Walking into Ethics, I finalize the plan in my head. I need to prove to Andrew that I'm a good person. When I know he's watching, I'll walk up to Paige and offer the most generous apology humanly possible. I only have to wait until fourth period, when I have class with the two of them. Andrew will understand he had me wrong, and he and I will be an item by the end of the day.

While Mr. Chen hands out today's thought experiment—

the Trolley Problem—I find my seat next to Morgan. I turn, wanting to be certain Paige is here today, and a momentary panic fills me when I don't find her.

Until the girl in the back in a knee-length black dress and scuffed Converse raises her head. Paige has re-dyed her hair into a mildly less offensive shade of red and chopped it into a messy bob. I can't imagine why. If she thinks a crappy haircut will catch Jeff Mitchel's attention, she's in for a rude awakening.

She pulls a pair of fishnets from her Hello Kitty bag, unbelievably, and begins mending the giant hole in them on her desk.

"Tell me I don't have a cold sore," Morgan says next to me. I notice she's holding her hand over her lips. I pull it down, revealing a cluster of bright red blisters beneath her bottom lip.

"You don't have a cold sore," I pronounce, repeating her request. She eyes me skeptically. "But in a more truthful sense, yes, you have a gigantic cold sore," I go on. "What have you and Brad been up to? Or what have *you* been up to? Or what—"

"Cameron!" she hisses with a giggle. She covers her mouth in mortification and shoves me lightly. "This is *tragic*."

I hear someone snicker from behind Morgan and me. I don't need to check to know it's Paige. On other days, I would call her out. It's bullshit for a girl who looks like Edward Scissorhands styled her hair to mock Morgan, who's not only gorgeous but whose gorgeousness is part of her career.

But today, I pretend I didn't hear. I playfully return

Morgan's shove. "You're friends with one of the most popular makeup experts in probably the world. You don't think it'll be fine?"

"But—"

"No buts." I give her a stern glance. "Why don't you focus on more important things—like the design board I sent you yesterday?"

Morgan's eyes light up instantly. Her hand drops from her mouth, and she grabs my arm. Morgan's a very grabby person. "It's *incredible*, Cam," she gushes, and I feel a swell of pride even though I already knew it. I've put the past couple weekends into redesigning Morgan's professional website with her headshots and highlight reel. "You could do this professionally," Morgan goes on. "For real."

I shrug. Web design's a good hobby. I'm meant for Wharton and econ, though.

"Well, I don't know where you learned to do that," she says, shaking her head. "Brad's totally going to want you to update the Mock Trial site, too."

"Only if he can prove he didn't give you herpes." Morgan giggles loudly this time. Mr. Chen cuts her a reproving glare.

I bend down to pull my Ethics book from my bag. Without intending to, I lock eyes with Paige. She's staring daggers at me. In just a couple hours, I'll be apologizing to this girl, regardless of how hard I know she'll make it.

Of course, the apology's not for her.

I have Economics and then Calculus, and then Elle and I get Morgan looking like herself in an emergency concealer session before fourth period. I don't cross paths with Andrew the entire morning—a shame, given the care I've put into my outfit, but I guess not a surprise. He was right when he reminded me he and I never hung out except outside of school. I don't even know where his locker is.

I walk past the fountain in Beaumont's inner courtyard, where the student body president, Lisa Gramercy, is publicizing this year's winter formal, which will be held on her father's yacht. I like Lisa, but I ignore her today. I've barely survived waiting for fourth period. Finally, I have the chance to fix what I broke between Andrew and me.

In the history of the known universe, I've never arrived early to English. Ms. Kowalski watches me in undisguised surprise. Andrew walks in a few minutes later, and I feel a familiar heat rise in my cheeks. He looks *uh-mazing*.

I don't know if it's possible for a person to become objectively better looking over one weekend or if it's the memory of our recent romantic entanglement, but there's something different about him. He's not wearing anything special, just jeans, black Adidas, and a black T-shirt, but there's a casual ease to his look that's just . . . hot. He looks like a young John Legend. I'm finding it extremely difficult to tear my eyes away.

Paige follows right behind him, ruining my Andrew-related reverie, because the world is an unforgiving place. Her eyes narrow when they find mine. I don't engage. Instead, I pretend I'm reading the whiteboard behind her, where Ms. Kowalski has written instructions for the new unit we'll be forced to endure for the next six weeks.

And it's Shakespeare. *The Taming of the Shrew.*

Wonderful.

I hate this class. Literature is frustrating. It's counterintuitive. You're supposed to get into the mind of a character, to experience his or her world and thoughts, but writers do everything they can to get in the way. Figurative language, symbols, meter, and rhyme—everything we write essays about only ever obscures the point of the book. Truths don't become more true when delivered in metaphors and metonymy. It's stupid. Except the Hemingway we read in AP junior year. He did his characters the favor of describing their real emotions. Too bad they're whiny failures.

Shakespeare's, for what it's worth, aren't. They're just the worst offenders in hiding everything they want to say in floral wording, *whences* and *whereofs*. Characters, and people for that matter, should say what they mean.

Ms. Kowalski asks Andrew to hand out a Shakespearean English glossary. I try to catch Andrew's eye while he passes the pile down my row. He pointedly refuses even to look in my direction. It hurts. A week ago we were on a run together, laughing about the number of French bulldogs we passed on our route (there were seven). Three days ago he had his hand under my bra. Now he won't even look at me.

While Kowalski goes over the handout, I can't help glancing over my shoulder at him, even resorting to tactics like dropping my pen and pretending to rearrange my hair. The minute she gives us time to read aloud in groups, I'm out of my chair and walking toward Paige before she can partner up with anyone.

On the way, I purposefully walk close to Andrew's desk. My dress brushes his paper onto the floor. I pick it up and put it on his desk, but I don't linger. While he's still looking up, I continue on to Paige.

Here goes . . . everything.

"Hi, Paige," I start, my voice overly gentle, the way I talk to my mom when she gets depressed and won't leave the bedroom. Paige glances up warily. Her haircut really is terrible. "I owe you an apology for Friday," I continue, glancing toward Andrew, whose head is tilted in our direction even though his reading partner is loudly declaring the opening lines of the play.

"Oh yeah? For what?" Paige asks, her expression flat.

I size her up for a moment. Paige continues to surprise. I know what she's doing—she's forcing me to repeat what I said to her. Now is not the time for retaliation, however. I take a breath, schooling my features into remorse.

"What I said to you was uncalled for," I go on. "You were obviously having a rough night"—to put it generously—"and I'm sorry I made it worse." It's time to play the extenuating-circumstances card. "I was having a bad day. Honestly, my mom lost her job. I'm not making an excuse," I rush to say. "I just hope you'll forgive me."

Andrew starts to smile. I feel a flush of excitement, and I have to bite my cheek to keep from beaming in the middle of my heartfelt apology. It worked. Andrew's looking at me the way he used to. I can tell—

"Why are you apologizing now?" Paige's voice rips me from my already forming fantasies.

I turn back to face her, finding her watching me carefully. It takes me a moment to reply. "What do you mean?" I ask, controlling my composure.

"You saw me in first period. Why didn't you apologize then?"

The excitement rushes out of me, and anger rushes in. For a moment I can't marshal my expression. I know exactly where this is headed, and I'm certain I'm not the only one who knows Andrew is watching. I narrow my eyes, feeling my nostrils flare. "We didn't have any free time in Ethics. I've been waiting for a chance like this," I get out.

Infuriatingly, Paige grins.

"Huh," she says. "You had time to talk about your friend's *tragic* cold sore."

I don't know how to respond. I know how I'd *like* to respond. I'd tell her helping my friends with literally anything comes before apologizing to a girl who's done nothing but glare at me. I know Andrew's watching, though, and I hold in the retort. Aware I'm losing ground, I say desperately, "I want to make this right."

Paige reclines in her chair, crossing her arms over her chest. She's enjoying herself. "Make this right while Andrew Richmond is watching, you mean," she says, and I feel my cheeks flame. "Because I can't imagine a different reason why you wouldn't have apologized in first period or even during break. You can't fool me with your charm and your perfect blonde hair, Bright," she says, her voice turning low and ugly. "I see through you. By now, I imagine Andrew does, too."

Her mouth curls in an acidic smirk. For a moment I'm almost impressed. "I guess this means you won't be accepting my apology." I have to muster every ounce of calm in me to get the words out.

"You guess right," Paige says.

We hold each other's glares. Then I turn on my heel. When I walk back toward my desk, I notice Andrew watching me without bothering to hide it.

Earlier today I would've given anything to have his eyes on me. Now I'd give anything to erase the disgust in them.

Six

I SIT BETWEEN ELLE AND MORGAN ON the patio for lunch. Elle's trying to catch up on History homework, while Morgan pokes her kale salad disinterestedly. "I don't get it," I grumble. Morgan nods understandingly. Elle's eyes flit up in acknowledgment, then return to her homework. "I know he likes me. He's liked me since freshman year. And now he writes me off as a bitch?"

I wait for reassurance. I tried to talk to Andrew today in the wake of the disastrous apology attempt. He won't even look at me. Won't walk in my direction in the halls. Won't anything. It pisses me off, honestly. I don't know why he thinks he has the right to judge me—as if he's better than I am, as if he's never insulted anyone in anger, as if he's perfect. If I weren't really, really into him, I'd give him a piece of my mind about it.

Morgan only nods. Her eyes wander to the burger on Brad's plate. Brad's examining his fingernails, but I know he's listening.

"If he doesn't see you're in no way a bitch, he's not worth it. Who even cares what he thinks? Don't let other people's opinions get in your way," Elle says finally. She closes her textbook with a short sigh. "I'm never going to finish this."

"*Brad . . .*" Morgan glances indicatively at his plate. He rolls his eyes and pushes his burger in her direction. Morgan, pleased, grabs the burger and looks up at me. "We're your friends, Cameron. If you were a bitch, we'd tell you."

I nod, unconvinced. What my friends don't understand is that I'm not only upset about a guy. Andrew is—was, it hurts to realize—a friend. He knows me as well as Morgan and Elle do, and I can't just disregard his judgment. If Morgan or Elle thought I was a bitch, I'd want to prove them wrong. I'd *need* to prove them wrong. If I couldn't, what would that say about me? I'd be my mom, refusing to disprove my dad's criticism.

Elle shoves her textbook into her Prada bag, then stares at Brad like she's just remembered something. "I need you," she declares, "for a video."

This gets Brad's attention. His head pops up, his eyes wide. "We've discussed this," he says, sounding scarily like his dad. "*No.* Get a model or an actor or whoever."

Imploringly, Elle places both hands on the table. "But you're so beautiful!" Morgan snorts. Elle goes on, "I *need* to do a video on male makeup . . ." I tune out while she pleads her case, my mind churning over the Andrew question. I can't have him out there thinking badly of me. It feels like a bruise I can't help but touch, hoping it's healed and instead bringing on a fresh wave of pain.

When the bell rings, I head to Computer Science, a class held in the newly refurbished science and technology building someone's mom funded a couple of years ago. The stainless steel curves of the Frank Gehry–designed building rise in contrast to the school's adobe arches, making our campus honestly cooler than 90 percent of college campuses in the country.

I was scared to sign up for AP Computer Science at the beginning of the year. I thought my meager-to-moderate web building and design experience wouldn't compare to the smarts of a bunch of scholarship geniuses. I hold my own, though. Coding takes creativity, but it's clear and organized. If you watch for mistakes and don't lose focus, you're good to go.

I walk in behind Abby Fleischman and Charlie Kim talking eagerly over each other. I hear words like "paladin" and "orc knights' guard" and have to restrain myself from rolling my eyes. I don't understand why people like Abby and Charlie bother with video games, especially when this class has proved to me they're way good enough with computers to be designing apps and coding operating systems.

I sit in the far left corner of the room, where I have space to tune everyone out except the teacher and concentrate on my own work. The Computer Science room is no less impressive on the inside than outside. Under the high ceiling run rows of widescreen iMacs and those ugly-as-hell yet impossibly comfortable mesh chairs. On the board is the assignment I finished Friday.

Which is perfect. On the walk over from lunch, I decided what to do about the Andrew problem. I have to take the direct approach.

While the rest of the class opens Python to finish writing

a hangman game, I log into my school email account—not the account I would have used to write a long apology to my crush, but the school blocks access to Facebook and Gmail on school computers, and I don't want to be caught on my phone in class.

Dear Andrew, I write.

No. Too formal.

I go with just *Andrew* and then write from the heart. *I hope you'll give me a chance to explain. I don't know how things got so messed up so quickly, but you're important to me, even as just a friend. I hope you'll give me a second chance—*

I'm interrupted by someone tapping my shoulder firmly, like I've annoyed them. "You're supposed to be working on the assignment from Friday," I hear a low voice say.

Over me stands Barfy Brendan—no, looms, because he's about six and a half feet tall. The way he's looking at me, the blend of ambivalence and assertiveness in his brown eyes, is eerily reminiscent of how his sister stared me down a couple of hours ago. He's a year younger than Paige, and he shares her freakish height and curly hair. His is brown, not red, and unlike his spindly sister, he has broad shoulders and some-what muscular forearms. There's a universe in which he's cute, if you could overlook his social-pariah status. He's the TA for Computer Science because he got a perfect score on the AP exam when he was a sophomore.

"Wait, what?" I ask, distracted by his T-shirt. It's modeled after the Evolution of Man but shows four robots labeled DALEK, R2-D2, CYLON, BORG. For whatever reason, there's a hot blonde on the end labeled CYLON, too.

"The assignment?" he repeats.

"I finished it on Friday." I turn back to my email. "Thanks though, BB." Before I get through a couple more words, he reaches down and force-quits out of Safari, and the draft is gone. I blink in indignation. "Hey! What was that for?"

"If you're done with the assignment, you should submit it and start working on tonight's problem set," he says, almost with disinterest. Without another word he walks to the front of the class. I have no choice but to gape behind him. BB and I haven't interacted often over the years, mostly because he avoids social situations like Elle avoids swim P.E.

I didn't know he could be so commanding. I would be impressed if I weren't annoyed.

Whatever. I wait until he's busy with another student, then reopen my email to rewrite what I had to Andrew. Instead, I find a new message in my inbox.

From: db_asst@brightpartners.com
To: c.bright@beaumontprep.edu
Subject: Re: Re: Carol

Dear Cameron, Mr. Bright has arranged for your mother to take a waitressing job at one of his associate's restaurants. She starts next Monday. Don't hesitate to write me if you should have any more difficulties!
Best,
Chelsea

I have to keep myself from letting out a rueful laugh. I

think about writing her back. *Yes, Chelsea, I'm having more difficulties.* I'm going to have to talk Mom off a ledge over the prospect of a job that's an embarrassing handout from her ex. I might have lost the one guy who saw me as more than a pretty face. And it'd be nice if my dad could even pretend to care about his daughter so I don't believe the ugly words said about me.

He'd never understand, of course.

Instead of writing that, I close out of my email and submit the assignment. When the bell rings, I run straight out the door to cross-country and keep on running.

Seven

I'VE FINALLY FOUND ANDREW'S LOCKER. IT ONLY took complimenting a suggestible sophomore on the soccer team who told me the right hall and then spending the whole lunch on Wednesday waiting and watching which locker Andrew went to. I duck out of Calc five minutes early, claiming a stomachache, and wait out of sight at the end of Andrew's hall. From yesterday's recon, I know he'll stop by his locker before English. I pull the letter from my bag and run my finger nervously along the crease, feeling the soft fold in the paper.

Write letter. Find Andrew's locker. Deliver letter.

I spent hours yesterday writing. I decided on Monday that email wasn't right, and I spent Tuesday stuck. But I don't give up easily. People who give up don't deserve what they want. People who give up end up like my mother.

Whereas people who pursue their goals end up like my father. And while I might live with her, I've done everything not to repeat my mother's choices. Even in Hollywood, a city practically built on broken dreams, and a school like Beaumont full of aspiring everythings, I've remained on the periphery of fame and fantasy. I'd rather struggle through the dense, sometimes impossible homework for Economics in the Entrepreneur's Market in hopes of earning a practical internship and not ending up on the couch with nothing but dead-end dreams.

Once I'd finished reading three *Economist* articles for class, I wrote the letter to Andrew. I stayed up late working, explaining the night I yelled at Paige, how I was scared because I'd never had a relationship I cared about and nervous he wouldn't want me the way I wanted him. I wrote how I screwed up the apology to Paige because I panicked, how his friendship means too much to me. I labored over it until two in the morning, rewriting it twice. When he reads it, he'll understand how much of a bitch I'm not.

The bell rings. I hear snatches of conversation while people walk past me in the hall—winter formal, service projects, dates, and breakups. I just stand there, watching Andrew's locker with an eager anxiety I haven't felt on campus since I was a freshman.

I want to hand him the letter in person, ideally. And it can't be in English. Paige would undoubtedly glare obnoxiously and spoil everything. But as the minutes pass without sign of him, I settle for sliding it into his locker. He has to read the letter today, one way or another. I walk to the locker and start to push the letter under the door when, of course, I catch his broad frame coming toward me.

Our eyes meet, and his gaze drops. With it goes my hopes for repairing things. After a moment's pause, he approaches the locker, his eyes avoiding mine.

"You won't even give me a chance to explain?" I ask, working to repress the indignation in my voice.

He drops in his cleats and pulls out a hefty Classical Philosophy textbook. "Cameron, I'm not really looking for an explanation right now," he says, sounding weary.

He closes his locker with a clang and walks past me. I have no choice but to follow, my Nikes squeaking on the linoleum. "But on Friday you wanted to be with me," I argue. "I'll admit I acted badly, but you *know* me." I struggle to keep up with his long stride. "You know who I am. I'm the girl who runs with you, who watches shitty MTV movies with you, who—"

"Cameron." He rounds on me. "I've liked you pretty much since the day I met you." I feel a smile springing to my lips. Andrew stares at me hard. "But you only wanted to be with me once I'd passed some popularity test."

My smile fades.

"I don't know if making the team made you see me in a new light or if you always wanted to date me and only felt you could when I made the team. I don't know which is worse. Either way, I don't want to be with you."

I open my mouth to refute him, but he talks over me.

"I wish I had reason to believe that beneath everything, you're nice or decent or something. But right now, I don't." Turning his back, he walks into class without giving me a chance to defend myself. As if he knows I can't.

I could run to the bathroom right now. Could conceal myself in a stall instead of going to class. But I'd just come out of that bathroom in forty-three minutes knowing I'd have to face him eventually.

I walk into class.

When we're in our desks, Kowalski holds up her copy of

The Taming of the Shrew. "You've all had a chance to digest the first two acts," she says, giving us a meaningful yet somehow threatening look. "Let's discuss our title character, the shrew—Katherine. How does Shakespeare treat her?" Perched on an open desk, Kowalski calls on the girl in front of her.

I don't listen to what Lisa Gramercy has to say. And when Kowalski calls on someone else, I don't listen to them either. The discussion continues around me, but I stare at my notebook. I made a mistake somewhere. That much, I can easily admit. Maybe I should've gone to his house to talk. Or I could've worked up a couple tears in the hall. Really, I should have found a room with a door to pull him into at Skāra. If Paige had been kept out, none of this would have happened.

I glance over my shoulder at her—the girl who ruined everything. Paige notices me watching her and shoots me a sardonic look as she covers the front of her book so that only *Shrew* is visible. She nods in my direction with a smirk.

I turn to my notebook, too tired to muster even a haughty expression. On the open page I've jotted down my list of ideas for winning Andrew back—*apologize to Paige while he's watching, email him, write him an old-fashioned letter*—each of them now crossed out. But I never give up, and I definitely won't on Andrew. He's not just a guy I could date. He's *the* guy. He's everything I want. We're *right* together. I've planned for him and me on countless lists of goals for my senior year.

The class discussion is empty noise around me as I stare at my notebook, willing a new idea to appear.

"Andrew," I distantly hear Kowalski say, and his name is enough to lift my head.

"Sure, she's not treated great," Andrew says, "but I can't exactly feel bad for her either. Regardless of how she's viewed, Kate doesn't give the audience reason to believe she's anything but terrible on the inside."

I blink, his words to me from moments ago still echoing in my ears. I can't help but notice the familiar phrasing. *I wish I had reason to believe that beneath everything, you're nice or decent or something. But right now, I don't.* I sit up straighter, suddenly interested in this discussion.

Elle doesn't wait to be called on before responding. "You're just upset because Kate doesn't conform to her patriarchal society." Her tone is uncompromising, her expression a mixture of passion and disgust. "She shouldn't compromise who she is because of some guy or because she's expected to find a husband."

"Yeah," I find myself saying. Kowalski's eyes dart to me. It's rare I participate in this class, but I'm fueled by every time I've had to listen to Andrew tell me I'm not good enough. "Just because she doesn't fit your or Petruchio's notion of a well-behaved woman doesn't mean she has to change."

Andrew appears startled to have attracted such a strong reaction. He raises his hand and waits until Kowalski nods for him to reply. "This has nothing to do with being a well-behaved woman," he argues. His posture's rigidly defensive. "You guys honestly think smashing lutes over people's heads and insulting them at every turn is acceptable for *anyone*, regardless of gender?"

I glance down to the open page in my book, rereading. Baptista's criticizing Katherine for insulting people who didn't deserve her anger. *Why dost thou wrong her that did ne'er wrong thee? When did she cross thee with a bitter word?* With an unexpected churn of my stomach, recognition dawns. The quote could be about me, about how I treated Paige the other night and how I've dealt with everyone who's frustrated me. I'm undeniably Kate-like.

"Forget about having a husband," Andrew goes on. "Kate wouldn't have *friends* if she continued acting the way she does. *I* wouldn't choose to spend time with her. It's a good thing for her that Petruchio helps her—"

Elle cuts him off, her face red. "You mean *tames* her, like she's some kind of animal!"

Andrew turns to Kowalski, refusing to engage directly with Elle. "Is it actually a bad thing to be *tamed*"—he darts a glance in Elle's direction, acknowledging the word choice— "when it makes you a better human being?"

I hear Elle's disapproving snort, but by the time she starts speaking again, my attention's left the discussion. Andrew said he needed an indication that I'm nice on the inside, and here he is, arguing that Kate's transformation redeems her. I flip to a blank page in my notebook and start scribbling down the ideas sprinting through my thoughts.

If he can accept Katherine after changing, then he'll accept me. The only difference is that I won't wait for some Petruchio—some *guy*—to "tame" me.

I'll do it myself.

Eight

FOR THE FIRST TIME, I DECIDE TO get ahead in English.

I redirect every ounce of my anger over Andrew's words and holier-than-thou attitude into proving him wrong. I read the whole play, scouring every line for ideas. I cut through *twixt*s and *ne'er*s and *doth*s, not to mention hundreds of overly complex and circuitous phrasings like *to make mine eye the witness* just to say *to see for myself*.

The problem is that all of Petruchio's methods of taming Katherine are terrible.

Moral ramifications aside, starving myself or keeping myself sleep-deprived would hardly make me a *nicer* person. I toss the play aside and try to think for myself. If Katherine were to work on being a better person, what would she do? The first answer is obvious: be nicer to people. Easy.

And too slow. Holding doors for people and complimenting them on their hair or whatever might get Andrew's attention eventually. But how many months of observing little daily kindnesses would it take?

I need more than that. I need something that'll catch his attention while making myself look good *and* helping others. I come up with and cross out a dozen possibilities.

It's not until I remember Andrew's exact words in class that I begin to have an idea. Andrew mentioned Kate smashing the lute over her tutor's head. If Kate wanted to redeem herself, she would apologize. But apologies don't repair real damage, and as I've learned through recent personal experience, it's hard to make them genuine enough to work. Kate would have to bandage the tutor's wounds and replace his broken lute before anyone really thought she'd changed.

That's it.

Apologies alone won't be enough. But I won't only apologize. I'll make amends with people I might have wronged. Whatever I did to hurt them, I'll undo. It's perfect. Performing grand gestures has a much higher visibility factor than mere compliments and politeness. It won't take long for word to reach Andrew about what I'm doing, and then he'll know I've changed, just like Katherine.

As much as I'd rather not, I'll have to start with Paige. Even if I don't particularly like her, Andrew won't believe I've changed until I've made it up to her. The problem is, I haven't the faintest idea what I could do for her.

I spend the next week following Paige everywhere, hoping for clues. I lurk on her hallway conversations, flip through last year's yearbook to find out what extracurriculars she's in, and stalk her movements during lunch. While my friends sit on the patio at our usual table, I tell them I'm working in the library and instead watch Paige and her friends in the dining hall. Nobody's the wiser.

But I find nothing. Paige never complains about a class she's failing or a project she needs help with, which means I can't help her academically. I thought I might join one of her clubs and thereby help its stature, but amazingly for a Beaumont student, she isn't involved in a single school activity. And despite her relative lack of popularity, she spends every lunch with a decently sized group of friends who appear to adore her.

I got momentarily excited last night when I realized I'd read her personal statement. I wracked my brain for everything I could remember—which wasn't much. Admittedly, I didn't really care when I read it. But I knew she wrote about feeling like she couldn't be herself because she had other people to worry about. There were parts about bullying, about how difficult it is to watch without being able to help. Nothing specific, though. Nothing I can use.

She doesn't have a boyfriend. I know that. Setting her up with someone would definitely be doable, but I haven't overheard her talking about anyone she's interested in. There's always Jeff. At Skāra she was obviously into him, and considering how she had been sobbing when she stumbled into Andrew and me, I know whatever happened between them didn't work out the way Paige had hoped.

But he's *Jeff*.

In English I wait for the bell to ring, gazing out the window to the parking lot. Sure enough, the windows of Jeff's Mercedes are fogged up with an unmistakable pot-smoke haze. I can make out his aggressively pink polo—with the collar popped, of course—through the cloud.

Even if Paige likes Jeff, I don't think setting anyone up with him could ever qualify as a good deed.

I sigh and turn my attention back to Kowalski, who's giving some impassioned lecture about the ways Bianca and Katherine serve as foils for each other, highlighting each other's differences. Yawn.

In following Paige, I have noticed one thing. She and her friends are not completely honest when asked their opinion. Between their heated discussions of TV shows I've never heard of and whatever RPGs are, they'll ask each other for advice. *Does this hat make my hair look bad? No one saw my underwear when my skirt flew up, right? Do you think Jason Reid will ever like me back?* These questions have obvious right answers: yes, no, and definitely not. But each time, Paige and her friends parrot whatever it is the asker wants to hear.

I didn't understand it at first. Wouldn't a person be a better friend if they told the truth? I'd want my friends to tell me if I had a hideous hat on or if I was wasting my time on an unrealistic crush. Or if I had, say, a blindingly bad cold sore. I've always thought of honesty as helpful even if it's hurtful.

But reading *The Taming of the Shrew*, I'm beginning to doubt that. Katherine's honesty helps no one and leaves them hating her. Her honesty is everyone's main complaint with her. Katherine's honest to a fault—like when she tells Petruchio he's an ass within the first couple lines of meeting him. Even if "ass" for Shakespeare means donkey, it's still a pretty savage insult. It happens again and again. Katherine doesn't hide a single negative thought or opinion, which is why people come away convinced of her reputation as a shrew.

If I'm going to be less like Katherine, I'll have to work on reining in my honest opinions some.

The bell *finally* rings, and I take my time collecting my things, waiting for Paige to leave. She shoves her copy of *The Taming of the Shrew* in her bag, pulls on a weird purple beanie with cat ears sewn on top, and walks to the door.

I'm about to follow her when Andrew cuts me off.

"Cool hat," Andrew says, passing by her.

Paige holds the door for him. "Thanks," she replies.

I frown. It's not the first casual display of budding friendship I've observed over the week. Every day there's something—a wave in the hallways, a brief conversation about the night's readings, a shared glance when someone says something particularly stupid in class. I don't like it. Not that I'm jealous in a romantic sense. I'm reasonably confident Paige isn't Andrew's type, considering he's had a crush on me since freshman year. However, the better friends they become, the more important it will be I win over Paige before she further turns him against me.

I get into the hallway to find Paige already finished with her locker and heading to the dining hall. I hate that I know exactly where her locker is and where she sits for lunch.

"You're working on your Econ assignment *again* today?" I hear Elle ask behind me. She walks up next to me, scowling at the couple of junior boys who cross her path.

I've been telling Elle I have an Econ project not because I think she'd be judgmental about what I'm really doing. It would just take plenty of explaining. I don't enjoy being dishonest with my friends—and once when I told everyone I was spending spring break in Avignon like the rest of my classmates, I ended up running into Elle and her entire family in a restaurant near my house. That didn't feel great.

Desperate times, however.

"Unfortunately," I lie.

"How much longer is this assignment going to take?" Elle asks. I recognize the playfulness under her pointed tone. It's a distinction I've picked up over years of overhearing her peeved conversations with vendors and promoters versus having her pester me about hanging out and helping with videos. "Why do you *care*?" she goes on without waiting for my answer. "I know you hate Econ."

"I don't hate Econ," I protest. I don't *love* the late nights and eye-watering spreadsheets. It's worth it, though.

Elle eyes me. "How much longer?" she repeats drolly.

"Today," I say. "I promise." I've devoted nearly a week to the Paige project. If something doesn't come along in the next couple hours, I'm going to need a new strategy.

"Good," Elle says emphatically, opening the door to the dining hall. "I don't know if I can take two more lunches with nothing to do but watch Brad and Morgan eye-bang each other."

"Please. You didn't practically walk in on them," I reply, remembering a uniquely unpleasant encounter in Morgan's bathroom at the end of the party. "Puppy-dog eyes in the dining hall is *nothing*."

Elle laughs. We walk together toward where Morgan and Brad are—of course—gazing goofily at each other. "Oh boy," Elle mutters. She shoots me a stern look. "For real, Cameron.

Finish this Econ project." It's not a question.

"I will. Promise," I repeat. "Do you . . . you know"—I nod toward Morgan and Brad—"need a barf bag? I have a Ziploc from my lunch . . ."

Elle rolls her eyes. "Get to work, Cam."

With a grin, I pull away. I enter the dining hall as Paige is leaving the kitchen. Instead of heading for her usual table, she turns toward the science wing. Walking against the crowds coming from classrooms to the dining hall, I follow her. She stops in front of the robotics room. I linger a distance away while she pulls open the door and goes inside.

I wait for her to finish her errand, not looking forward to another day of eavesdropping on her friends' conversations about video games and Japanese TV and probably learning nothing. There's a new episode every Thursday of one of the group's favorite shows. They'll probably be preoccupied with that today.

Ugh. I feel like a psycho. Except instead of Beyoncé or Ryan Gosling or someone reasonable, my stalkee has weird taste in hats and an anime obsession.

I check my phone, realizing it's been over five minutes since Paige went in. That's way longer than you need to drop off homework or pick up a test. There are only a limited number of reasons a person would want to be in an empty classroom during the middle of lunch, chief among them: hookups.

If it's Jeff, gross. If it's not, it might be someone I'm less morally opposed to helping her with. It could be the first useful piece of information I've learned. While I don't exactly want to witness whatever's going on in there firsthand, I have no choice. I have to peek.

Pulling my bag over my shoulder, I walk nonchalantly to the window. I notice a poster on the door for BPR—Beaumont Prep Robotics—over a design resembling men's and women's restroom identifiers, except the figures have square heads instead of round. Robots. *Clever design.*

I press my face to the glass, preparing for the worst.

Okay, this *would* be a morally objectionable pairing.

I have only an obscured view from the narrow window. The room is dark. On one end, a bare bulb dimly illuminates a table and a desk chair, with heaps of old robotics equipment and extension cords in the corner. In the chair sits Barfy Brendan.

Paige lingers by the desk. I watch the two of them. BB's busy with the computer, typing, his face turned from his sister's. On hers is written a complication of emotions I don't recognize from Paige. Not the exhilaration and skepticism that wage war when she's geeking out about whatever she and her friends geek out about. Definitely not the ire I exclusively earn.

She looks hopeful, and hurting. Like she's putting on an enthusiastic face.

I watch her talk to Brendan, prodding his shoulder and craning over him to check out whatever he's doing. While I can't understand the conversation—even with my unnervingly excessive surveillance of Paige this week, I haven't learned to lip-read—I catch one word that falls unmistakably from Paige's mouth. *Please.* From her imploring expression and the way she waves in the direction of the door, I infer she's trying to get Brendan to have lunch with her outside the robotics room. He gestures toward the computer, and Paige's face falls. I instantly translate what I read in her expression. Worry.

Which is when it hits me. Worry, like in her essay. I am an *idiot* for not realizing the person she was writing about. The person she worries about often enough to feel like she's losing herself. The person she watches get bullied with nothing she can do to help.

Nothing *she* can do. But maybe there's something *I* can do.

She turns, and I don't step away from the window in time. We lock eyes. Her expression hardens in surprise. Recognizing me, it fills with fury.

I know I have no chance of retreating and having the whole incident forgotten. I wait, and in seconds Paige charges out and faces me. "What the *hell*, Bright?" she spits. "You're *spying* on me now?"

If only you knew. I remind myself not to go in a retaliatory, lute-smashing direction. I cannot be Kate right now. I need Paige's *forgiveness*, not to mess things up worse. "It's not what you think," I finally say.

"Oh no? What is it, then?" she sneers. "Interested in joining the robotics team?"

"Of course not." I feel my nose wrinkle and realize I probably don't want to be denigrating robotics in front of Paige. I school my expression into understanding. "Not that I have a problem with the robotics team, I just—" I begin to recover.

"Cut the crap," Paige interrupts. "'Popular girls'"—she forms finger-quotes—"don't care about robotics, and they certainly don't spend school lunches following people like me. You're up to something."

"What would you know about popular girls?"

Paige's eyes widen. She gives a bitter laugh. "Good one. That was funny"—her voice comes out heavy with sarcasm—"if characteristically mean."

"No," I say, conscious of how horribly this is going. "What I'm trying to say is not everyone who's popular is just a one-dimensional, popular-girl stereotype. *I'm* not a one-dimensional, popular-girl stereotype."

"Could've fooled me." Paige is stone-faced.

Finally, I feel anger flare up, and it's out of my mouth faster than I can contain it. "Could you knock it off with the woman-scorned act for just, like, a couple minutes?" I hear myself say. Paige startles. "Look," I go on. "I want to . . . I don't know, fix things. I followed you here—" I notice Paige become smug, and I sigh. "Yes, okay? I followed you. I followed you because . . . I wanted to do something nice for you."

Her eyes narrow. With confusion this time, not anger. It's progress.

"I want to make things right," I say. "After what happened at Skāra."

Paige's eyebrows rise. She gives an indignant huff of a chuckle. "Well, you can't, Cameron. You can't *make it up* to me. Not that it's a gaping wound in my self-esteem, what you said to me. I'm just completely uninterested in forgiving you."

I feel my heart plummet.

"There's nothing you could do that I'd possibly be interested in," Paige says, turning to leave.

"What about your brother?" I call to her.

Paige pauses. I can practically feel how much she wants to walk away warring with . . . what?

She rounds on me.

"What about him?" she finally says. "Why would *you* having anything to do with my brother *ever* be a good idea?"

"I remember your essay," I say, the reply ready on my tongue. "He's the person you worry about." When Paige doesn't say anything, I continue. "What if I apologized? You're right to say I *of all people* have nothing to offer your brother. What if I could fix that? What if I went into the robotics room right now and apologized for the nickname I gave him?"

Paige's eyes dart to the robotics room. I go on, unwilling to lose my focus.

"I might be 'mean'"—I return the finger-quotes and earn the hint of a raised eyebrow—"but I'm not unobservant or unintelligent. Who's to say if I went in there and apologized, Brendan wouldn't . . ." I gesture to the robotics room. "Who knows? What if an apology gets him out here, having lunch with his friends instead of hiding in there?"

I probably come off desperate. But I don't care, because I've got the wheels turning in Paige's head.

I watch her consider. Her expression softens, her eyes moving from mine to the door. Her hard frown eases nearly imperceptibly. After a moment she purses her lips. Not in consternation—in what feels like grudging, reluctant agree-ment.

Hardened, her eyes return to mine.

"Fine," she says.

"Really?" Until I hear it from Paige, I won't accept I've actu-ally found the answer to the problem I've wrestled with for the entire week. What I really *don't* want is for Paige to decide in a couple of hours that it was a horrible plan for me to apolo-gize to BB and I'm a horrible person for even having the idea.

Paige nods. "Apologize to Brendan—fix things with him—and I'll forgive you for what you said to me. You know where to find him." She crosses her arms. "He's in the robotics room every lunch." From the smugness in her expression, I have a hunch she doesn't think I can pull this off. Doesn't think Cameron Bright, bitch extraordinaire, can get through even one apology.

I don't care. Finally, I permit excitement to well in my chest. If Paige forgives me, I'm one giant step closer to her telling her new BFF Andrew about how the incident at Skāra was no big deal, how I went out of my way to be thought-ful to her brother, and how I'm really not the person she thought I was.

"Done," I reply.

Without a word, Paige walks off. I gather my composure and open the door.

Nine

THE ROBOTICS ROOM IS CLOSER TO A warehouse than a classroom. A thick wooden table down the length of one wall is piled high with what appear to be pieces of metal bolted together in half-finished forms and wires running from motors to electronics with little blinking lights. On the other wall is a row of computers, new Macs next to old desktops someone's halfway done repairing.

I walk between the tables toward where BB sits in the back of the room, my footsteps swallowed by the sound effects coming from the computer on his desk. I pause a couple feet behind him and glance over his shoulder. He's playing a computer game on a desktop he's hooked up to an external hard drive and intricate keyboard with extra keys that must be designed for gaming. Furiously, he punches his fingers on the keys.

I watch the screen for a couple seconds. The two-dimensional character isn't moving despite Brendan's clicking and typing. What I'm guessing is a sorceress, dressed in a dramatic black dress and with blonde hair, closes in on the stuck character. I notice the color palette of the game is all over the place, pastels combined with neons without rhyme or reason.

I watch the sorceress reach the unmoving boy and promptly chop off his head. The words GAME OVER flash on the screen.

Brendan sighs exasperatedly and types in more commands. I figure this is the best window I'm going to have. "Hi, B—Brendan," I say, my voice echoing oddly loudly in the enormous room. "What are you doing?"

BB whirls. He searches the room, suspicious, like he's looking for some explanation for what I'm doing here. The dim light plays shadows on his features, which have a definition to them you wouldn't expect on a junior boy's face.

"Do you want help with the problem set or something?" he asks.

"What?" I'm thrown until I realize the problem set is, in fact, the likeliest reason I'd come find him. "No. I'm, um, here to talk to you."

He narrows his eyes. "Why?"

I sit on the stool next to him. His shirt, I notice, reads THOROUGHBRED OF SIN in big block text under a picture of a horse. He keeps his eyes on me like he's expecting me to pounce.

"I realize I might not have been the nicest person to you over the years," I say sincerely.

BB watches me for a second longer. I hope—in an illogical part of my brain—it's going to be this easy, and Brendan will shrug and say, "Whatever," and bygones will be bygones.

Instead, he turns back to the computer. "I don't know what you're talking about," he says unemotionally. "We don't even know each other." He glances toward me a second later out of the corner of his eye. "If you're worried I'm going to tell Mr. West you were emailing in class, forget about it."

"Why would I—" I begin to point out West wouldn't care, then cut myself off. I have to give BB a genuine apology—the quicker, the better. "Remember when you first moved here in sixth grade and I was in seventh?" I say hurriedly. "You, like, threw up at school a bunch of times? It was, like, every week, and we'd know not to eat in the cafeteria when you were in there and not to go near the second-floor boys' bathroom?"

I'm rambling. I never ramble. But Brendan is no longer facing the computer. His eyes fix on mine skeptically. His attention is suddenly making me self-conscious.

"No," he says dryly. "I'd completely forgotten that *wonderful* period in my life. Thank you for reminding me, Cameron."

I wince. I'm doing exactly what Kate does. I'm being too blunt, too honest. But what do I say instead? My inexperience with apologies means that I have no idea what I'm doing. "I'm terrible at this," I tell Brendan. I study his nose and his brown eyes, noticing that when you look up close, he doesn't really look very much like Paige. I don't know why, but the thought brings me a fresh bout of nervousness. Only remembering why I'm here keeps me from throwing in the towel and getting out of here. *Andrew.*

"Here's a tip," Brendan replies, an edge entering his tone. "Whatever *this* is, don't. Just don't. Go take selfies with your friends or whatever."

"Hey," I fire back, hardly caring I'm not keeping my cool. "You don't have to go and insult me when I'm in here trying to apologize."

BB's eyebrows bounce up. "You're trying to *apologize*? Wow, you're *really* terrible at this."

His words smother my anger. It's not even worth it to try to defend myself. He's 100 percent right. My breath leaves my chest in a frustrated sigh. "I *know*," I say. "But, Brendan, I'm sorry I started calling you BB. And I'm sorry it's what the whole school's called you for the past five years."

It's not like I didn't have a reason, to be fair. In seventh grade, I was just minding my own business, reading in a second-floor hallway during recess. I didn't want my friends to know, because reading was obviously uncool, but my dad had sent me one of the few birthday gifts I've ever received from him—*The Lion, the Witch and the Wardrobe*. On the one hand, it was a completely tone-deaf gift, not something in which I'd ever expressed interest. On the other, it was from my dad. The thought of him going to the store, picking something out, and wrapping it meant the world to me.

I was reading in the hallway, unfortunately near the bathrooms. Brendan rounded the corner, clutching his stomach. I had no time to react. In the next second, he'd puked voluminously on the ground, sending spatter onto my backpack, my shoes—and the book.

From his stool, BB's staring, taking in my apology. I'm not expecting his harsh laugh. "Okay, great. Thanks."

I study him, trying to figure him out. "I feel like that wasn't totally genuine."

He shakes his head. "Everyone knows I have celiac disease," he says, weary again. *I* didn't know—or did I? I could've forgotten if I ever heard, admittedly. "Everyone knows I *barf* when I have gluten," he continues, and I don't miss the emphasis. "When I was in sixth grade I had to do these painful and embarrassing tests because nobody knew what was wrong with me. It could've been fine when they found out—except, thanks to you, my entire high-school experience has been defined by your catchy nickname for me." His voice has gathered momentum, his dark eyes unexpectedly fierce. "Do you know how hard it is for me to make friends? To know that everyone in every one of my classes immediately thinks 'barfy' in connection with my name?" He turns back to the computer. "Of course you don't."

I have no idea what to say. I have *nothing* to say. I sit in stunned silence, trying in vain to come up with a reply. "I—I'm sorry," I stutter. "Tell me how to make it right. I'll do anything."

"There's nothing I could ever want from you," he replies quickly.

I stand sharply, having finally had enough. My face burns. Screw holding in my opinions. "Fine, stay hidden in here and blame your complete lack of a high-school social life on me. It's *definitely* because of the nickname and not because you're antisocial and choose to spend your time playing mindless video games with a color palette it looks like a third-grader picked instead of talking to a girl, or a guy, or whatever."

I collect my things to storm out of the room.

Before I have the chance, I hear BB behind me.

"I'm not *playing* a mindless video game," he says quietly. "I'm making one."

I turn and glance toward the computer screen. For the

first time I notice the notebook sitting next to it. The open page is filled with sketches and models of what I recognize to be the boy and the witch from the game. I remember my words from a moment ago with a twinge of guilt. *A color palette it looks like a third-grader picked.*

I stare at the screen with new respect. "You're making that?" I repeat.

By way of reply, Brendan brusquely turns off the monitor. He shoves his notebook in his backpack and pauses in front of me. "You want to know how you can make amends?" he asks. "Stay out of my life." He gathers his things and walks out of the room.

Ten

I'M DREADING FRIDAY MORNING.

I know I'm going to run into Paige. And I *know* she's going to come at me hard for what happened with BB—*Brendan*—yesterday. I'm expecting harsh language, name-calling, a full recount of how I epically screwed up.

Which won't be the worst of the fallout. Worse will be what she says to Andrew—how I ended up driving her brother deeper into his insecurity while trying to win her over, because *I* couldn't handle the consequences of having called *her* horrible things.

What a bitch Cameron Bright is.

While I'm prepared for the disaster I have coming to me, I'm not exactly looking forward to the confrontation. I do everything in my power to avoid Paige in the morning. I'm hoping I can skirt into the hall as close as possible to the start of class and slip into the classroom after Paige is already inside.

Instead, of course, Paige finds me when I'm grabbing my notes from my locker. Dumb mistake.

What I'm unprepared for is how casually she comes up to

me. She's wearing a purple striped top, a floor-length skirt, and a black beanie with dragon ears. She slouches against the neighboring locker, watching me.

I don't pretend I don't notice her, or the hard line of her mouth, lipsticked an unspeakable purple. I wait for the outburst. I'm definitely *not* going to initiate this conversation.

"Well," she finally says, "calling my brother an antisocial loser wasn't exactly what I had in mind when you said you'd apologize."

I grimace, drawing in a deep breath. "In fairness, I never used the word 'loser'—"

I pause. Because the look I catch on Paige's face is not entirely furious. In fact, I wouldn't even call it moderately furious. Mildly furious, possibly. What catches me short is what I glimpse under the questionable level of furiousness. She looks . . . amused.

"You're not mad," I venture.

Paige shrugs. "A little," she says.

I wait, confused. Where I left off with BB was *definitely* worse than where I began. I unquestionably hurt his feelings. Which unquestionably found its way back to Paige. What am I not getting?

"You know," she says casually, pretending to study the chipped black polish of her nails, "I didn't think you'd go through with it. Apologizing to Brendan. Or trying." Her eyes find mine, and the hint of mirth hasn't disappeared. "It was very non-one-dimensional-popular-girl-stereotypical of you."

She pulls her shoulder off the locker and walks toward Ethics. I follow behind her, hardly comprehending what I'm hearing. "Are—are we good?"

"Please." She rolls her eyes, pulling open the door for me. "Of course not. You called me pathetic and now my brother a loser. We're far from *good*, Bright." As I pass her, a corner of her purple lips slips up into the first sign of something resembling a smile she's ever given me.

Paige is . . . weird.

Eleven

FOR THE SECOND TIME THIS MONTH, I'M bringing a handwritten note to school for a boy. I don't remember ever using physical pieces of paper to communicate with my classmates before—I'd prefer to text, obviously. We're not first-graders putting identical fakey Valentines in the boxes on each other's desks. But in this circumstance, the note is the only way.

I hustled to school ten minutes early—not easy given the unpredictable traffic on Olympic Boulevard on Monday mornings. In the halls, I head in the direction of the far end of campus, clutching the note. The hall outside the robotics room is empty when I reach it.

I know BB told me to stay away from him. This is for his own good, though. When he finds out why I've ignored his request, I have a feeling he'll understand.

I wrote the note on Sunday in a rush of inspiration.

Dear Brendan, please join me, Elle Li,
Morgan LeClaire, and Brad Patton for
lunch today. We sit on the second-story

patio. I know you don't like me, but I trust you understand that sitting with popular seniors would immediately elevate you out of obscurity. I'm confident that one lunch, possibly two, would undo the damage of the unfortunate nickname I gave you. Once again, I'm sorry about that. I promise you won't have to talk to me if you don't want to. Some of my friends are genuinely nice. You might even enjoy it.

BB's reclusive, not dumb. He'll know I'm right.

The robotics room is empty when I pull open the door. I find my way through the tables and piles of equipment to Brendan's bulky gaming computer in the back. His notebooks are exactly where I saw them the last time I was in here, and I get the impression he's the only person who uses this station. I place the note on the keyboard, and I'm out of the room before the bell rings.

The first half of the day passes without incident. We compare our course reading to episodes of *The Good Place* in Ethics, which actually is kind of fun. In Econ we work through the diluted-earnings-per-share problems I finished yesterday, except for the final two. I half listen in English while Kowalski lectures on Lucentio trying to win Bianca in *The Taming of the Shrew*. Instead, I work on a new list.

People I Need to Make Amends with, and How
1. Paige Rosenfeld, for calling her pathetic—fix
   things with Brendan

2. Brendan Rosenfeld, for giving him the nick-
   name that allegedly ruined his life—

It's a work in progress.

Elle's typing intently on her phone when I reach our table for lunch. Next to her, Brad pores over his AP Government textbook. Morgan watches the courtyard, eating an apple.

Just them.

That's okay, I remind myself. BB's probably grabbing lunch. He'll be here.

Except then the minutes pass. I finish my lunch with no sign of him. Elle notices my repeated glances in the direction of the stairway and gives me a probing look. I force myself to continue listening to Morgan's explanation of why her entertainment lawyer wants her to find a new agent. I feel growing frustration with every minute lunch inches closer to over.

Finally the bell rings. Brendan didn't come.

Pulling my bag over my shoulder with brusque good-byes to my friends, I work the problem over in my head on the way to Computer Science. It's possible he didn't get the note, I guess. It would have been easy for the paper to fall off the keyboard and wind up underfoot, or for a teacher to throw it in the trash. In class, I'll have the chance to talk to Brendan and find out what happened.

I walk in, and BB's behind his desk, working on the computer. His features register nothing when I pause in the doorway, reading the board for instructions on today's new problem set.

I'll talk to him when class is over. I walk to my computer, getting my mind in gear for today's assignment. Dropping my things, I pick up the hefty packet of coding instructions.

On the front of mine, in handwriting unmistakably matching the hard-edged characters on the board, I find two words.

Not Interested

Well, I guess Brendan got the note. I feel fire in my cheeks. Glancing up from my packet to where he sits in the front of the room, I wait for him to meet my eyes. Instead, he remains determinedly working on the computer.

He's given me every reason to leave him be. To take the hint.

I went into this project with one intention, though. If I give up, I won't deserve his forgiveness and I won't deserve Andrew.

Which is why I won't give up.

When I get home, I wipe my running shoes off in front of the door. NAMASTE IN BED reads the doormat. I roll my eyes every time I read the idiotic inscription. Today, I pointedly rub off a clump of dirt on "bed."

I'm in a terrible mood, thanks to Brendan. Even placing second in today's cross-country race couldn't keep my head from returning to BB's harsh rejection. It's rare when running doesn't distract me from whatever's bothering me. I like the clear and definite objective of a race. You put in the time and the effort, and then you win. In today's three-mile course in Runyon Canyon I beat my personal record and finished in under eighteen minutes, though to be fair, I was expecting to hit a new personal record. We train every weekday from three to four thirty, and every day this week I kept my paces exactly to schedule. Today was the beginning of the competitive season, and I want to cut down my time in every one of our weekly races.

I unlock and kick open the front door, then pull off my shoes to examine the pain in my big toe. It's bleeding once again, I discover, right through my sock. I have to grab a Band-Aid—

"Cameron! Hi!"

I abruptly drop my bloody foot, glance up, and realize I'm not the only person in my living room. Deb, Andrew's mom, watches me from the couch. Here I was, performing triage on my toe, which could've booked a guest role on *Grey's Anatomy*. I flush what is probably not my prettiest shade of pink.

It's Monday night. *Of course* it's Monday night.

Mom's stirring something on the stove, and Andrew's lingering by the counter. Normally he'd have a textbook open, but today I notice his keys in his hand.

I can't believe I forgot he was coming over. I've been so

focused on impressing Andrew, I managed to forget about . . . Andrew. I would've remembered if I hadn't had half a billion plans in my head about Paige, Brendan, everything.

"Andrew," my mom says, "you really can't stay for dinner?"

I glance up, hoping to meet his eyes. He won't look in my direction. "I'd like to, but I have practice."

I know for a fact he doesn't have practice. Not this late.

He's never not stayed to work on homework or go for a run with me on a Monday night. I guess it's not enough for him to avoid me in the Beaumont courtyard or the halls. Now he's avoiding me in the one place we were really friends. Of today's two unmistakable rejections, this one hurts worse.

He walks out, passing me without a glance, and I wince when the door closes. Instead of fixating on Andrew, however, I look at my mother, who shouldn't have had time to prepare the meatloaf sitting on the counter.

"I thought today was your first day, Mom," I say evenly. I know she knows what I'm hinting at, because her eyes flicker before she gives me the world's phoniest smile.

"Why don't you shower? Dinner's almost ready." I hear the strain in her singsong voice.

I walk to the stove, where I can mutter to her without Deb overhearing. I know she's trying to hide behind her guest, and I'm not about to be distracted by her cheerful act. "I thought you weren't off until seven," I say, letting an edge into my tone.

"Today was only a training day. I got off early." She looks

away and watches the gravy boil. I know she's lying. The slippers next to the couch, the dishes in the sink, the plate covered in crumbs, and a half-empty coffee mug. Typical.

Frustration forces its way into my throat like bile.

"Fine," I say with a hard stare. "I have to make one phone call, then I'll be right out." I catch Mom's grimace. She understands it was a threat.

I leave the room before she has a chance to reply.

When I step out of the shower ten minutes later, she's waiting in my room. I recognize the combination of dread and defiance in her eyes. She's leaning on the corner of my desk, fiddling nervously with my pen, even though I've told her a million times not to move things in my room. I honestly don't know if she's messing with me or if she just doesn't remember.

"You don't have to call your father before dinner, you know," she whispers bitterly. "I don't need him yelling at me while I'm having a nice evening with friends."

"You didn't go into work today, Mom. Don't bother lying." I drop my running clothes in the hamper.

"He already knows, Cameron. You can bet the company called him," she fires back. She puts the pen down on my homework pile instead of in the Venice Boardwalk mug, where I know she found it. I cross the room to the desk and very deliberately replace the pen in the mug.

"Why didn't you go?" I say, gentler. I'm upset, but I know there's a point where resentment and accusation no longer work on my mother. "We needed this job. How are we going to pay the bills?"

"We'll be fine," Mom replies, brashly confident. "I got a loan from my sister." Her head jerks up quickly, like the loan wasn't something she meant to tell me. I'm impressed Mom wore Aunt Jane down, honestly. My mom's only sister lives in Connecticut with her lawyer husband and openly disdains her family. I can only imagine Aunt Jane wrote her a check to hold her off for the next decade. "But don't tell your father," Mom rushes to say. "It's better if he thinks we're a little harder pressed for money."

I feel my mouth go dry. I'm not often disgusted with my mother. Frustrated, yes. Pitying, on occasion. The moments when her behavior stoops low enough for me to wish we weren't related come few and far between.

Right now is one of them. "You did not just say that." I hear my voice darken.

I expect her to wither or cringe. To have enough dignity to recognize the *indignity* of her little scheme. Instead, she holds my gaze. "Don't pretend I'm the villain here," she says defiantly. "That man's done nothing but the minimum when it comes to bringing up his daughter. If you think he'll just let you and your mother starve, you know nothing about the circles he runs in. He'll send money." She nods like she's convincing herself. "I know he will."

"He pays our rent. He pays my tuition—"

Mom cuts me off. "He only pays for Beaumont because he wants to tell his friends his daughter goes to the fanciest private school in the state. You know he doesn't do it for you."

I flinch and hope she doesn't notice. I know she's right, but she said it to hurt me. I have no delusions about my father. I know he's not a perfect dad. He's probably not even a good dad. The fact remains, though, he's done more for my future than my mother ever has. Paying for Beaumont isn't nothing, regardless of his reasons. My mom's only interest in my future is how it benefits *her*.

"You'd really rather sit on the couch all day and collect money from the man who knocked you up and didn't even want to marry you?"

Her eyes flash. "Don't lecture me about things you don't understand. I'm going back out to our *guest*." She emphasizes the final word as if to pretend I forced her in here. "If you want to call your father, fine." The door half-open, she gives me a final spiteful glance. "Good luck getting him to pick up your call."

I reach for my phone once she's gone, trying to figure out how I'll explain the loan to my dad. If I tell him, he'll probably never send money again, which, aside from issues like rent and insurance, would make college next year impossible. There's no way my mom will be able to contribute to my tuition. But if I don't tell him . . . he'll write a check and my mom won't have to find a job for who knows how long. She'll get everything she wants, even if it comes with him telling her she's pathetic. And she'll continue to see me as financial leverage instead of a daughter.

I shut off my phone screen. For once, I'm not going to

involve him. For once, my mom is going to have to fend for herself. If she doesn't want a job, let her be the one to go begging to her family. I'm done playing into it.

Fuming about my mother and hurting from Andrew's departure, I plaster a smile onto my freshly glossed lips and follow Mom into the kitchen. I hate feeling helpless. I hate how she's trapped me. Everything about my life depends on two people too wrapped up in their own lives to spare a thought for my place in the middle.

I sit next to Deb, who looks to be on her second or third glass of wine, and try to make conversation. But I'm hopelessly distracted by my mom's slippers next to the couch, where I have no doubt they'll remain.

When dinner's over, I retreat to my pristine room without a word to Mom. I pull off my cream cable-knit sweater and fling it onto the bed. I hate leaving things out of order, not where they belong. I just don't have the energy to fold it and put it in the drawer. Instead, I drop into my desk chair. What I really want to do is go for a run, feel the wind in my lungs, clear my head. But I'm risking injury if I run now after having already run today.

I pull out my Economics in the Entrepreneur's Market textbook and muddle through about five minutes of reading before "present-value calculations" and "consumer surplus" blur in front of my eyes. Frustrated, I flip open my laptop. If I can't go running, web design is the next best thing, and I think Morgan might have been serious about designing a concept for Brad. I find the perfect font pretty quickly, a lightweight serif with a Futura feel.

I'm working on finding a complementary blue when I have an idea.

I open my email. Everyone's addresses are programmed into the school email client. I type in one I never have before.

From: c.bright@beaumontprep.edu
To: b.rosenfeld@beaumontprep.edu
Subject: You probably won't open this but . . .

Brendan, I know you're NOT INTERESTED in anything having to do with me, but I thought you might want to check out this website on color palettes. Video games are probably way more in-depth than a website, but the same principles might apply. I like number 27. Cameron.

Twelve

I'M RUNNING ON NEXT TO ZERO SLEEP. It's Wednesday, and I haven't had more than three hours the past couple nights since the conversation with my mom in my room. The familiar worries keep me up—finances, my mom's job. And yesterday, I found out I got a C on our first Econ exam. I'd worked hard, too. I'd pored over the diagrams in the textbook for days. Yet when I got to the exam, I felt like I'd read the wrong pages. The problems were completely foreign.

Which is not good. I need an A in Econ. This was only the first exam—there'll be plenty more opportunities to improve my grade. I'll ace the next exam, double-check every homework problem, take notes on every reading. If I don't do well in Econ, I won't get the internship. I'll lose the chance to work with my dad. I *definitely* won't be cut out for Wharton, for a life close to his.

Fortunately for my walking insomnia, there's a Student Government coffee fund-raiser in the courtyard during lunch. Normally, I wouldn't waste half the lunch period on badly brewed coffee. It's a testament to my desperation that I've been waiting in line with Morgan and Elle for twenty minutes.

"Ugh," Elle groans. "This line is *endless*."

"I know," I say. "But I'm not going to make it through the day without heavy caffeinating. Look at the bags under my eyes."

She studies me. "You're right," she replies. "They're horrendous."

I'm not usually bothered by Elle's unflinching commentary. I'm used to it. I enjoy her remarks and return them with equal frequency. I don't know if it's the worry or the exhaustion, but today they hurt a little.

I smile hollowly, feeling uncomfortably self-conscious. "You don't have to wait with me if you don't want," I reply, keeping my tone judgment-free.

"In that case," Elle says unhesitatingly, pulling out her phone, "I'm going to go find Jason."

I say nothing.

Elle waits until her phone vibrates in her hand, and her mouth flickers in the hint of a grin. Her eyes flit up to mine. "Hey, but we're still on for milkshakes tonight, right?" she asks. I nod. We're planning to stuff ourselves with shakes and animal-style fries from In-N-Out. "Great. See you then."

She eagerly darts out of the line to meet Jason. I feel certain they're going to spend the remainder of lunch in an empty classroom. I sigh. "Between Andrew and this Jason-and-Elle thing," I say to Morgan, "I'm beginning to feel like I should just give up on romance. Is it really worth the trouble?" I don't mention the really glaring example of a wasted, unhealthy relationship in my life—my parents.

"Elle and Jason do *not* count as romance," Morgan replies.

I laugh and walk up to the counter, where I proceed to order the greatest number of espresso shots they'll put in one cup. Morgan deftly reaches in and hands the barista her card, ordering her own espresso and paying for both before I can pull out my wallet. It's a generosity I no longer resist. My friends know I have nowhere near the spending money they do.

"But yes," Morgan says while we wait with the crowd. "It is worth it. With the right person." Her eyes get the happy, faraway look they do whenever Brad's around. I feel a pang of envy.

The barista, whom I recognize as a senior in Student Government, holds up a cup behind the counter. "BB," she calls out.

Brendan pushes past me to the front. I hadn't noticed him in the crowd. "It's Brendan," he says gruffly to the barista.

"Sure, BB," she chuckles. A couple other Student Government seniors laugh with her.

I feel an unexpected twist in my stomach and level the barista a glare. "You heard him," I say, hardening my voice. "His name is Brendan."

The barista blinks, thrown by my sternness. "Oh, um, yeah," she fumbles, wilting. "Yeah, Cameron, you're right." She hands over my triple cappuccino, as if in a gesture of goodwill.

I can't help it—I turn, hoping Brendan heard my correction. Instead, I'm faced only with a wall of under-caffeinated Beaumont students waiting for their orders. Finally, peering over their heads, I find Brendan's retreating back halfway across the courtyard. I deflate.

"That was really nice of you, Cam," Morgan says beside me. "Huh?" I'm distracted watching Brendan.

"Helping Brendan," she clarifies. "You were being nice."

We leave the crowd. "Don't sound so surprised," I say, sipping eagerly on my coffee and ignoring the sting of its too-hot temperature on my lips.

"*I* know you're nice. It's just a side you don't often show others." Morgan gives me a wry look. "See you tonight," she calls over her shoulder as the bell rings.

I walk to the computer lab, Morgan's words unfurling into an idea in my head. I know how I can help Brendan and earn his forgiveness. He hates me for the nickname I gave him, but I have the social clout to undo it. If I can erase "BB" on campus, I'll repair his reputation and make amends with Paige.

When I walk into Computer Science, Mr. West's busy with a group in the back and everyone's beginning to unpack and work on today's project. It's the perfect opportunity. Determined, I walk right up to Brendan's desk. He's on his computer, his half-finished iced coffee next to the keyboard. Written in sloppy Sharpie, BB faces outward incriminatingly.

"Brendan," I venture, "could you help me with my homework? I got stuck on the last task."

Without sparing me a look, he wordlessly follows me to my station. I repress a small surge of frustration that he's not even acknowledging what I did for him at the coffee cart. Loading my program on the computer, he starts testing the scenarios.

"Did you get the email I sent you?" I ask, annoyed at his continued silence.

"Yeah." His eyes remain firmly on the screen, and he continues clicking through my work.

"Was it helpful?" I prod.

He shrugs. "I didn't open it. Your homework is perfect, by the way." Finally, he looks up, glaring. "Which you already knew."

"I need help on today's assignment," I reply, undeterred.

"Which part, specifically?" he asks evenly.

"Um." I give the board a quick glance. "The . . . first part?"

The hard line of his mouth curls in a frown. "Why don't you get started," he says, "and you can raise your hand if you get stuck. I'll send Mr. West over."

He starts to walk away, and everything pent up in me for the past week forces out my next words. "Come on," I say. "That's it? I defended you today. I'm going to keep doing it, too. By the end of the week, you'll be Brendan. Not BB."

Brendan walks back to me, and I'm caught for a moment by the commanding intensity in his expression as he looms over me. "I don't need or want you fighting my battles for me. I can stand up for myself. Here, watch: Cameron Bright, return to your assignment and don't bother me again."

He returns to his desk, leaving me in the middle of the aisle, a little stunned. I know I should be frustrated, offended, demoralized.

I'm not. I'm impressed.

I sit down in front of my computer, an approving smile forming on my lips.

Thirteen

I'M ON FAIRFAX THE NEXT DAY, TAKING photos on my phone. I had the time today when cross-country ended—I finished my Econ homework yesterday, I checked ahead in the Ethics textbook and wrote this week's paper over the weekend, and of course I'm way ahead of the class in *The Taming of the Shrew*.

I don't want to go home. Not with my mother and me pretending to ignore each other. Hours to myself to photograph are exactly what I need.

I don't love Fairfax. It's dirty and noisy. It's like the music in every restaurant and trendy store is turned up ten notches too high. It's crowded—people wait outside some of the stores with literal camping equipment, prepared to stay overnight in hopes of grabbing a jacket or pair of sneakers. While parking in Los Angeles is never easy, only varying degrees of frustrating, parking on Fairfax is a crime against humanity.

I wouldn't be here if it weren't better than nearly everywhere in the entire city for inspiration. It's where I come every time I want web design ideas, and it never disappoints. Parts of the Arts District give it competition, but when it comes to design, Fairfax is unparalleled.

I grab a quick photo of the juxtaposition between the hard, industrial font of a gym on the corner and the jagged, indecipherable pink graffiti on the outer wall. It's a great combo. If I ever design a website for a musician or a club or something it would be perfect.

Not that I ever would. Not with Penn or Economics in the Entrepreneur's Market. Web design is only a hobby, not the kind of thing I could do professionally. Not the route to a life resembling my dad's—

I cut off the train of thought. I can take a day for a hobby. I'll return to Econ tomorrow, to my almost-finished Wharton application and worrying about the internship.

Today, I'm taking one afternoon to cut myself loose from the thick cords of my life pulling me down—pulling me apart. The helpless positions my mom puts me in. The accomplishments I need to achieve to prove I'm worthy of my dad's pride. The inadequacy of my entire personality to a friend I respect, a problem I can't figure out how to remedy right now. For one afternoon, I need to escape it all.

I wander down the block, passing advertisements for concerts and movies—identical posters copied over and over in a nonsensical row. Sweet and spicy air wafts over me from the churro cart. I'm about to go over and grab one when I'm drawn by my camera to the sign over a coffee shop. It's lettered in swooping, old-school font on a blue background. It's a nice blue, heavier than sky blue, but more complicated than American-flag blue.

I could photograph *everything*, honestly. The billboards that are more art than advertisement. The graffiti spray-painted onto the sidewalk. The coffee shops neighboring delis from the thirties.

I'm about to cross the street to check out a café when I hear my name. "Bright!"

Nobody calls me that. Well, *nearly* nobody.

Reluctantly, I glance back to find Paige Rosenfeld climbing out of a car as crappy as mine. She's illegally parked in front of the red-painted curb for a fire hydrant.

"You want to make it up to me, right?" she calls. From the trunk of the car she hefts a cardboard box over to the curb.

"Um," I say, confused. "Right?"

Paige grins. "Carry this into the Depths of Mordor for me."

I frown. "Excuse me?"

She nods in the direction of the storefront windows behind me. Following her eyes, I find THE DEPTHS OF MORDOR written over a display of dusty paperbacks with elaborate fantasy covers.

I cross my arms. "You know," I call, "wanting you to forgive me doesn't make me your personal slave."

Paige's grin never falters. She shrugs. I notice a meter maid driving up the street—and I guess Paige does, too, because without a word she climbs into her car and pulls away from the curb.

I gaze at the box.

I just wanted the afternoon off. But . . . I don't *have* to go home for a couple of hours. I doubt my mom would bother calling even if I didn't come home for dinner. I *do* want to work on getting Paige to like me.

I pause for a moment in front of the bookstore, taking in

the hideous design. SECONDHAND SCI-FI AND FANTASY reads the cardboard sign in hasty permanent marker under the name of the store. In one window hangs an unbelievably detailed replica of a dragon, transparent wire around its neck and scaly tail. Wooden bookshelves packed with fat paperbacks fill the front of the store, covers decorated with indecipherable scenes of moons rising over shimmering cities, spaceships firing their weapons, and scantily clad elves and sorceresses squaring off with long-haired knights.

Whatever. With a half sigh, half grumble, I walk over to the box, reach my fingers under the cardboard, and heave.

It's *heavy*. I glance under the lid. The contents only heighten my curiosity. Paige wants me to carry into the bookstore . . . a sewing machine, chunky and antiquated. No wonder the box weighs a hundred pounds. Other than the sewing machine, the box contains swatches of colored fabric, purples and reds, and a couple of pieces of black lace.

I walk into the Depths of Mordor and nearly drop the box on my feet. Because there's my one ex-boyfriend, Grant Wells, perched on a faded green armchair between stacks of books, in fishnets.

And a corset.

And lingerie.

I freeze in the doorway. The shop's nearly empty, but in the chairs around Grant, in what I'm realizing is a reading area in the sci-fi section, I notice a couple people I know from school. Abby Fleischman and Charlie Kim are doubled over laughing and cheering Grant on. The bookstore's only other patron, a ponytailed middle-aged man in a WINTER IS

COMING shirt, watches Grant with confusion and concern.

My eyes meet Grant's. Like someone's just kneed him in the balls, he emits a strangled squeak and hops off the chair.

I really don't want to go over there. Not only is the visual of Grant in that outfit deeply disturbing, he inevitably reminds me of the utter disaster of my only previous attempt at dating.

It was an *extraordinary* lapse in judgment, the kind of regrettable mistake I'll wish I could forget every day until I'm eighty. Grant Wells is the reason I swore off boys for two years. I went into the relationship without carefully considering the decision—without weighing the guy in question's practicality, his rightness for me, his possible *current* girlfriends—and it ended horribly.

We dated for two months during sophomore year. I had flirted aggressively with him while he was dating Hannah Warshaw. Why? I honestly don't know. He was Brad's best friend, and it made a certain amount of sense for me to date him while Morgan dated Brad. Morgan specifically didn't invite Hannah to her sixteenth birthday party, and my white string bikini was too much for Grant to handle. We hooked up in the Jacuzzi. I told Hannah the next day, she dumped him—and he was mine.

The problem was, he never really got over her. I could tell, and it's possible I reacted badly. I flirted with his friends, I ignored him, and I paraded him in front of Hannah so she'd never want him back. I was pretty much the world's worst girlfriend. By the time I very publicly dumped him, I didn't even recognize myself. I'd become my mother, who clings to her hopeless attachment to my father despite everything, playing petty mind games and pining for affection from a guy with whom it would never work out. After Grant, I decided I would carefully plan the guys I date, to protect myself from obsessing over someone who's not worth it.

Grant, for his part, fell out with the popular crowd and landed, I guess, with Paige's friends.

In a corset. And fishnets.

I hope I live to forget the image. I need to make a hasty retreat. I don't care if Paige wants to press me into indentured servitude in return for her forgiveness.

I'm searching for coffee table space for the sewing machine when the bell over the door rings and Paige hurries in. Before I have the chance to put the box down, she begins rummaging under the lid and pulls out a piece of lacey fabric.

"Okay," she calls to her friends. "I found the perfect—"

From over my shoulder I hear Abby's voice, affronted. "Why's Cameron Bright holding your costume box?" She says my name with a disgust I don't often hear. Whatever cachet I have with my classmates generally is absent among Paige's friends.

Paige eyes me, as if realizing I'm an unexpected guest. "Relax, Abby," she says with an authority I wouldn't have expected. "She helped me avoid a parking ticket."

Abby doesn't reply. I get the sense Paige is kind of the ringleader of her gang.

"You mind plugging that in?" It takes me a moment to realize Paige is talking to me. I guess the tremendous aftershock of the image of Grant hasn't entirely worn off.

I clear three books off the table—*Dune*, the covers read—and place the box down beside a figurine of a wizard. I open the lid, then pause. This can't be cool with the shop. I check behind the counter or in the back for a clerk, but the place is practically vacant.

"It's fine," Paige says, noticing my hesitation. "The owner's used to us."

She walks over to her friends, past the towering bookshelves lining the left wall. I give the inside of the store a closer look. The back is crammed with oddly angled bookcases, a tight maze of black-painted wood and colorful book binding. On the ends of the rows of hardcovers and paperbacks sit dusty bookends in the shapes of skulls and mythical creatures. Covering the walls are murals of scenes like the books' covers, but bigger—red and green planetary landscapes, medieval hunting parties, robots and monsters. It's probably the nerdiest place I've ever seen.

Paige pulls a newly reluctant Grant out of his chair. His eyes catch mine, and he blushes an unflattering pink. Paige steadies him with one hand and holds the lace up to the hip of his corset. I have no idea what's going on.

But I find myself plugging in the sewing machine.

I watch Paige and her friends. Charlie and Abby have a comic book open between them, Charlie craning his neck to read while Abby thumbs the pages. Under Paige's ministrations, Grant recovers a little of his confidence. "You guys," he addresses Abby and Charlie, sashaying lightly as Paige pins the lace to the corset, "does this lace make my package look big?"

I look away, my discomfort increasing by the minute. The

group laughs, and Paige pokes him in the hip with her pin. "Stop trying to get everyone to stare at your junk, Grant."

"What's one more wizard's staff in a place like this?" Grant replies.

Paige and Charlie laugh. In the same moment, a girl walks out from the back. I recognize Hannah Warshaw, Grant's ex. I understand Grant's former infatuation with her. She's pretty, if in an understated way, with round cheeks, straight dark hair, and a beauty mark under her eye.

Her eyes fall on Grant, and I watch her give his body a quick once-over. Her cheeks redden. Her voice, however, comes out cold. "You can't wear that in here," she calls to the group.

Grant pushes away Paige's hands and steps closer to Hannah. "What do you think, though?" His expression becomes painfully eager. "I know I'm no Tim Curry, but the costume's pretty good, right?"

"You need to change," Hannah orders, unwavering. "Or Russell will kick you guys out. For good this time." I'm guessing Russell is the owner of this place. Hannah retreats behind the register, where she starts sorting receipts, and while she doesn't glance over at Grant again, I notice that the blush hasn't fully faded from her neck.

Grant wilts. He grabs his sweatshirt and jeans and walks dejectedly toward the bathroom in the back.

Paige drops into the green armchair. "Thanks, Bright," she says.

I nod, remaining undecided whether I'm going to follow my initial instinct to get out of here.

"In return for your labor," Paige offers expansively, "I can pay you in"—she looks around and picks up some sort of trading card off the table—"this sexy alien card."

I try not to look, but I catch a glimpse of tentacles and boobs. "I'm good," I say.

"Good call." Paige frowns, examining the card.

She punches the sewing machine's on switch. Ignoring me, she slides fabric under the needle. I understand it's probably my cue to leave, not unaware that Charlie and Abby are continuing to eye me disdainfully.

If I leave, I have to go home. I have to confront my mom—or confront the ugly, quiet *non*-confrontation that could occupy home for days.

"What, um . . ." I begin. "What's going on here? Why's Grant dressed in . . . whatever that is?"

Paige laughs—a genuine laugh, not the scornful sound I've come to expect. "*Rocky Horror*," she says, like those two words clarify everything.

"Is that . . . the school musical this year?" I know Grant played trumpet in orchestra, but I don't remember him doing musical theater. Besides, I thought I overheard Jason crowing the other day about playing Tony in *West Side Story*.

Hannah comes out from behind the register. She walks past Paige and picks up the three *Dune* books I placed on the floor. With an accusatory glance in my direction, she pointedly puts them on a shelf. Paige continues sewing, unperturbed. "No, just the movie."

"You need a costume for a movie?"

Paige's eyes flit up to mine. "Wait, have you never been to

Rocky Horror in a theater?" She sounds scandalized, like I'm the one who was just strutting her stuff in a bookstore wearing only a corset and fishnets.

"In a theater? Isn't the movie kind of old?" I shoot back. "And, like, *bad*?"

Paige's gaze is withering. "It's called *camp*. Even though the movie's old, theaters and drive-ins and conventions and other places play it every weekend, and audiences dress up and participate and everything. It's this whole thing. I can't believe you've never done it." She deftly snips a thread with a pair of bright pink scissors. "Hannah got us into it. We're going to a screening for Halloween this year."

Just like that, everything fits into place in my head. Grant's costume, his eagerness toward Hannah, her blush, his disappointment when she distinctly didn't care. "I know what's happening here. Grant's trying to win Hannah back by thoroughly embarrassing himself for a night while doing Hannah's favorite thing."

Paige falters in mid-stitch. She eyes me doubtfully. "What? No," she scoffs. "Grant wouldn't try to get back together with Hannah. Because of, you know, you." I'm about to point out that when Grant and I were together, he was obviously still hung up on Hannah, when Paige continues. "Even if he did try, there's no way Hannah would consider it. It took her forever just to let him hang out with us."

I nod, unconvinced.

"What are you doing here?" Paige interrupts my train of thought.

"What?" I give her an incredulous glance. "You forced me in here, remember?"

"It was *not* force, Bright," she says, grinning. "It was *gentle* coercion." Her eyes gather a glint of inquisitiveness. "I didn't mean here in the first place. I meant why haven't you left yet? Don't you have popular-girl things to do?"

"No," I say shortly, chafing at the reminder of what I *do* have waiting for me when I get home. From the way Paige's grin catches, I know she hears the frustration in my voice.

"It looked like you were photographing the graffiti on Café Casablanca when I drove up," she says, inspecting her fabrics. I hear the hint of hesitation in her voice.

I nod, appreciating the change of subject. "I like the way the lettering interacts with the typography of the café. It's a good juxtaposition," I say, finding myself elaborating. "It's for a website I'm working on."

Paige glances up. She studies me for a moment. "Huh."

"What?" I feel a flare of indignation. If Paige thinks I'm too dumb or too "basic" for web design—

"It's just not what I would have guessed," she says.

I hear a door open, and Grant comes out of the bathroom, now dressed acceptably in jeans and a hoodie. His eyes instantly dart to the register. He takes a couple of steps and then pauses, looking torn, like he's searching for something to say.

"Well, I told you you didn't know anything about popular girls," I tell Paige.

I watch Grant, whose face brightens. He eagerly takes a half step before he halts abruptly. The excitement in his expression fades, and he retreats to the chairs near Abby and Charlie. He broods as he folds the costume in his lap and doesn't laugh along with whatever conversation Charlie and Abby are having.

And an idea begins to form in my head.

I owe Grant for ruining his relationship with Hannah. He deserves a place on my amends list no less than Paige and Brendan, and I can't cross Paige off my list until I've repaired things with her brother.

I thread the handles of my bag over my arm.

"You going home?" Paige asks, sounding surprised.

"Yeah," I say. I glance back and find Hannah behind the counter, working too hard to keep her eyes off Grant. "Good luck on the, um, *Rocky Horror*."

"Thanks, Bright."

I'm parked a few blocks away, on a residential street near a high school, and the entire way I start sketching the edges of my new project. I don't care if I have to fight with my mom or ignore her in shared resentment. I know what I have to do next, and I'm going to need time to plan.

I'm going to right two wrongs at once.

I'm going to get Grant and Hannah back together.

Fourteen

FRIDAY CLASS DRAGS BY. I WATCH THE minute hand shift on the clock over the whiteboard and force myself to focus on Grant. English will be over in twenty minutes, and then I have lunch to implement the first part of my plan. I have everything figured out. I emailed Paige last night and learned that Grant's spent lunches this week in the library researching for an essay. She wanted to know why *I* wanted to know—I didn't write back.

When I got home yesterday, I went directly to my room. I avoided my mom the rest of the night. Which was exactly what I'd planned. I had work to do.

Instead of revising my UPenn essay per Paige's peer-review comments, I edited my amends list. Brendan remains impossible. I added Grant and Hannah and my plan for repairing their relationship. Following the complete failure of my attempts with Brendan, I know better than to expect it'll go flawlessly. But I have to try.

When Kowalski finally dismisses us after rambling seven whole minutes into lunch about the *Taming of the Shrew* term paper we have due before winter break in December, I run down the stairs, painfully aware of how little time I have left.

I've prepared a whole pitch for Grant, and if I don't—

I round the corner and hit the brakes hard enough I almost fall over. In front of the entrance to the library, Andrew's talking to a group of guys from the soccer team. He hasn't noticed me. I watch him leaning on the locker, looking more confident than I remember ever seeing him.

I know I need to talk to Grant. But in this moment, I'm caught, watching. Remembering. We were in middle school the first time Andrew ever came over to my apartment. He was wearing jeans and a T-shirt three sizes too big, and he laughed nervously at whatever I said. I thought we'd have nothing in common, but after a year of tortured silences while we worked on homework in my room, he noticed my running shoes.

Things started to change after that. We would run together as the sun was setting, and our silences weren't tortured anymore. They were comfortable. I got used to the sound of his even breaths, the rhythm of his shoes and mine on the pavement. We ran what felt like every street, every hill, miles in every direction. And I remember the day I noticed he would always run one step behind me so he could watch me. Once when I tripped on a curb, his hand was on my elbow before I could fall.

I almost kissed him right then and there.

But I couldn't be certain he and I would work out. I knew who he was, but I didn't know who he wanted to be. With the whole Grant Wells pileup in my rearview mirror, I wasn't ready to commit to a guy I couldn't be confident would commit to his own life. Commit to his goals, commit to me.

"Cameron!" the soccer captain, Patrick, calls from the lockers.

Pulled from the memory, I walk over, my eyes on Andrew hopefully. He's reading something on his phone, and unsurprisingly he doesn't look up when I reach them.

Patrick flashes me a dazzling smile, and I restrain myself from rolling my eyes. I wonder how many girls get that smile every day. "You're coming to the game tomorrow, right?"

It's on the tip of my tongue to express bluntly my disinterest in the prospect. But Andrew's watching me warily. Expecting me to do exactly that.

"I'll try to be there," I say encouragingly, earning looks of astonishment from Patrick and the other guys. I glance at Andrew, hoping he'll say something, smile, anything. He doesn't. "See you guys later," I say, trying to keep disappointment from my voice.

I walk past them toward the library, returning to the pitch I have to give Grant. But as I step through the library doors and catch sight of Grant standing in the stacks, my uncooperative mind returns to Andrew.

That day on the run, I should have kissed him when he was watching my every step. Because now he doesn't watch me at all.

It makes me want to give up, just a little. I might never win Andrew back. Even if I accomplish every apology on my list, even if Paige begs him to reconsider.

I pause by the reference desk. Grant doesn't know I'm here. I could walk out of the library, spend lunch with Morgan and Elle . . . eventually find someone new.

But I'd be no better than my mom if I did, I remind myself. If I were to give up on making amends, on Andrew, it'd be no different than every time she gives up on a job, or on us. I have to go through with everything I have planned.

I find Grant in the history section. He's hunched over a thick textbook, and I remember one of the only real things I learned about Grant while we were dating. He goes ahead of the readings in every history class, he likes history that much. The Civil War in particular.

The library is nearly empty, thankfully. In the back, a couple of freshmen work on the computers under windows throwing bars of sunlight on the floor. There's a table strewn with binders by the history section, but nobody's there. I walk across the hardwood floor and join Grant in the stacks.

"Hey, Grant," I say at library volume. His head springs up, his eyes wary. "Could I ask you something? I know you're working on homework. I just wanted to catch you when Hannah's not around."

His eyes narrow, and I realize how bad that probably sounded to the guy I persuaded into cheating on his girlfriend. "I'm not falling for that one again," he says dryly, confirming my guess. "No offense, but kissing you was the worst decision of my life."

"I know," I assure him. "I want to apologize. I'm sorry I pursued you when you had a girlfriend, and I'm sorry I told Hannah about us and she dumped you."

Grant gives me a careful look. I know what happens next. He's trying to decide where to begin in his list of grievances with me. I brace myself for the outburst, the resentment and anger I've come to expect every time I apologize to someone.

Instead, Grant shrugs. "It's okay."

I wait for the other shoe to drop—the sarcasm, the spite. When neither comes, I watch him, dumbfounded. "It is?" I ask.

"It's nice of you to apologize and everything," Grant replies, closing the textbook. *Brother Fighting Brother* reads the cover, I note with the tiniest twinge of gratification. "But it's my fault," he goes on. "I cheated on Hannah. I don't know why I did. No offense," he hurriedly adds, looking me up and down.

I feel doubly guilty. I ruined his relationship, possibly his life, and now he's being nice to *me*?

It makes what I say next genuinely heartfelt. "I want to help you win her back. If it weren't for me, you'd probably be together right now, cowriting comic books and cosplaying as Zelda and . . ." I reach. "Boy-Zelda. I know you both still care about each other."

Grant flushes, exactly like in Mordor. "I don't know what you're—"

"Don't bother, Grant," I cut him off, waving a hand. "I know she has feelings for you, too. *You* didn't see the way she checked you out when you were in that corset." I raise a provocative eyebrow.

His cheeks flame redder, probably for a couple reasons. He looks pleased, though. "Wait, how exactly did she check me out?"

"Let's just say she had a definite answer to your question of how big the lace made your package look."

His expression brightens. For a fleeting moment he looks like I've given him every dream he's ever had. The next moment, his face crumples. He collapses into one of the chairs near the stacks, his eyes elsewhere. "She's just . . . amazing, you know?" he asks, not like he's expecting a reply. "She works really hard at everything she does, and when she's fangirling over something like *Rocky Horror* or *Doctor Who* it's like her passion is . . . I don't know. Uncontainable."

I smile softly. Grant is sweet. Even while we were dating I knew that. His words leave an ache in my chest, though. If only Andrew thought of me with that devotion. I'd even be content with half.

But that'll only happen if I stay focused.

I sit opposite Grant. "If you want this to work, you're going to need to give me a couple weeks where you leave Hannah be," I order him. "Don't flirt, don't go out of your way to talk to her, don't flaunt your junk. Nothing."

He looks skeptical. "How will that help?"

I weigh how to answer. There's really no nice way to say what Grant needs to hear. But telling him he's too pathetic to be desirable might be a little harsh. It's the kind of thing Kate would say. I settle for a milder version of the truth. "You're an overeager puppy dog when it comes to Hannah," I tell him gently. "You need to cool it and let me take over for a while. Just two weeks. If it doesn't work, you can unleash everything you've got at this *Rocky Horror* thing."

Grant pauses, looking unconvinced but like he wants to believe me. "You really want to help me?" he finally asks.

I nod. "I do."

Grant gets up and pulls his backpack over one shoulder. He glances to the door, and my hopes deflate. Who was I kidding? Of course Grant wouldn't want my help. "I would have to be pretty desperate to put my fate in the hands of Cameron Bright, the girl who wrecked my life in the first place," he says, avoiding my eyes.

"Grant," I try hopefully. "You passed desperate when you were modeling lingerie for the innocent bystanders in a bookstore."

Grant grins, and a little of the discouragement eases in my chest. He finally looks me square in the eye. I hold my breath.

"Fair enough," he says, and I feel a rush of relief. "Two weeks." He walks past me. I give myself mental congratulations before turning my thoughts to how I'm going to handle Hannah.

I hear Grant's voice behind me. "By the way"—I turn, startled he's still here—"it's Link," he says, like I should have any idea what he's talking about.

"What?"

"Boy-Zelda," Grant clarifies earnestly. "His name's Link. Thought you might want to know." I roll my eyes, and he heads for the door. "And, Cameron," he adds, pausing once more, "thanks."

With that, he gives me a genuine smile. Unexpectedly, I find myself returning it.

I'm heading toward the entrance to the library, sneakers squeaking loudly on the hardwood, when I catch sight of somebody at the table next to the stacks—right where Grant and I were talking. Walking toward Grant, I'd noticed the binders and books on the table, and it takes me a moment to register who's returned to them.

Watching me with open interest is BB. *Brendan.*

I feel my face redden. I didn't hear him sit down while I was talking to Grant. From the look on his face, however, I'd guess he heard everything. "You're not in the robotics room," I blurt.

He tilts his head. "Why would you think I'd be in the robotics room?"

"You're in the robotics room every lunch," I say before realizing it's not something a non-stalker would know.

"That's a really invasive thing to know about me," Brendan confirms.

"I know," I sigh. "Sorry."

He studies me, and I find myself curious what he's going to say. "They're holding the freshman Math Olympiad in the robotics room," he says after a second. "That's my reason for being here," he continues. "I'm interested in yours. I guess I'm not the only person you're apologizing to."

"Or trying," I reply. There's less of the hostility I was expecting in his expression. He's looking at me with amusement, and something else. It might be intrigue. "*Some* people are more cooperative than others," I say lightly.

Brendan gives half a laugh. I feel my shoulders loosen. "Well, let's not give Grant too much credit. You hardly even insulted him in your apology." His mouth twitches, like he's on the verge of grinning, but he doesn't yet.

"I could apologize for that, too, if you want. I was just trying to undo damage to your reputation," I tell him.

Some of the levity fades from Brendan's face. He looks like he's genuinely considering what I said. For the second time in the past hour, I feel an unexpected punch of nervousness. Brendan could open his mouth and tell me I've totally misread him, or tell me to get lost for the four hundredth time.

Instead, he shrugs. "Believe it or not, I don't really care whether you or anyone else think I'm a loser. I'm just curious"—he closes his book—"why the personality change? 'Apologetic' isn't exactly the word that comes to mind when I think of Cameron Bright."

I raise an eyebrow. "And how often is that?"

A funny noise comes out of the back of Brendan's throat. "Not that—just—when I grade your homework in Computer Science," he finishes, thoroughly flustered. "Really, though," he recovers, "why bother apologizing to people like me and Grant?"

I decide to let him off the hook for that flimsy cover-up. *Computer Science homework*. Ha. "Is being a better person not reason enough?" I ask with feigned innocence. It's good he's talking to me. Wherever this conversation is going, it's a far cry from our last exchanges.

"Not for you." Now Brendan grins. I have to suppress a laugh of my own. He's blunt, but he's not wrong.

"Fair," I say.

"Then why?" Brendan's watching me curiously, and I have an idea. I walk up to the table and place a hand on his textbook.

"I'll tell you if you let me help you," I offer.

He slides the textbook out from under me with a wry expression. "Unfortunately, there isn't some girl I'm interested in who you could fix me up with and thereby solve my problems."

"How about a boy?" I realize the second I've said it, I should have put it a little more delicately. It's not that I'm inclined to think he's gay. I don't know him well enough to have an opinion either way. I haven't seen him with guys in a romantic way. Then again, I haven't seen him with girls, either. I wonder if that'd be different if I hadn't given him his nickname.

His eyebrows go up. "You think I'm gay?"

"I hadn't thought about it," I reply.

"I'm not," he tells me. "Well, as far as I know I'm not. Either way, Cameron, there's nothing I want from you."

He runs a hand through his curls and reclines in his chair, his eyes lively. I know that look. He was stubborn, possibly intrigued, when we started this conversation. Now he's daring me to reply.

"Bummer." I straighten and cross my arms. "I guess you'll never know my motivations, then."

Brendan eyes me evenly, weighing his response. "I guess not," he finally replies.

In Computer Science, I sit down to find I have one unread email in my school inbox. It's from—Brendan Rosenfeld. With a small rush of excitement, I open the message while the bell rings and Mr. West writes the day's coding exercise on the board.

How bout this? I would ask you to give your honest opinion, but who am I kidding? You always do.

He's attached three screenshots to the email, the files titled *The Girl's a Sorceress*. Catchy.

I recognize the sorceress and the boy character from Brendan's video game. Only this time, he's working with an elegant blend of blacks, blues, and silvers. I'm flattered to recognize the one I suggested, palette number 27.

I open a reply. I'm beginning to write when I catch Brendan's tall frame coming toward me as he walks down the aisles, checking on everyone's work. He reaches my row, pauses by the edge of the desk, and gives me an exaggeratedly stern look.

"You wouldn't be writing a personal email in class, would you, Cameron?" he asks.

"Of course not," I reply.

Brendan waits a moment more, then nods with that faint half smile of his. I open the day's assignment, still smiling to myself.

Fifteen

I RUN, FEET POUNDING THE PAVEMENT. THE perfect hedges and big Beverly Hills houses fly by, and I draw breath after even breath, weightless. With everything on my mind, *weightless* is what I need right now.

It's the third week of October, though you wouldn't know it from L.A.'s unchanging heat. I'm three miles into the course for cross-country practice, miles I've used to force from my head the *Taming of the Shrew* act 4 reading worksheet I have waiting for me when I get home. I've run past Cañon Gardens and the talent agencies, and I have only a stretch of Camden Drive left until I reach school.

The Christina Perri on my playlist fades out, replaced by my ringtone. I hit answer on my earphones since my phone is strapped into my armband. It's probably Elle or Morgan wanting homework help. Elle despises History like I do English, and—

"Cameron?"

I can actually *feel* my knees weaken. I never knew that really happened to people. I stop so hard I stumble momentarily, because the voice on the line is my dad's, cold and direct. "Can you hear me?" He knows I can hear him. He's impatient, and he wants me to acknowledge him.

"Yeah," I say. I irrationally sweep a strand of hair out of my face. It's not like he can see me, but talking to him feels like a formal occasion. I feel very out of place in my running shorts and tank top.

"I don't have time for this, Cameron," he charges on, like I expected. "You have to speak with your mother." I practically hear his frown.

I struggle to steady my breathing. He won't like it if he realizes I'm in the middle of something, even though he's the one who called me without warning. "What about?" I ask.

"You know full well what. I'm extraordinarily busy. I cannot check on her every day. She's a grown woman, and she needs reminding to remember to go to work? It's out of control."

I know, I admit to myself. It's been a week since she didn't go to the job he set up for her. I say nothing. I have no idea what she said to him to prompt this call.

"It's not my job to babysit her," he finishes.

"And it's mine?" The words fly out of my mouth, and instantly I know I should have pushed them down. But on the rare occasions when we talk, I'm always the one who calls him. I have time to prepare, to choose my words carefully in anticipation of what he's going to say. Today, he caught me off guard. He's the one person I never—*never*—speak my mind to. For good reason.

His voice cuts through the speakers, carving into me.

"Of course it's your job. I go above and beyond when it comes to that useless woman." I feel myself getting smaller with every word. "She's spoiled. *I've* spoiled her. And you—you go to the expensive school I pay for and waste time with your bratty friends. You're ei—seventeen years old, and you can't get your mother out of the house. It's pathetic, Cameron."

I feel tears searing my eyes. Footsteps sound behind me, and I distantly realize the rest of the team is catching up to me. I want nothing more than—nothing *other* than to run. But while my dad is on the phone, his voice holding me in place, I can't.

A tear trembles on my eyelid. I blink it away.

"I'm sorry," I say, hating the tremble in my voice. "I'll do something."

He doesn't skip a beat. "You'd better. I ask for nothing in return for the comforts I give you."

"I know," I say weakly. "I appreciate it. I'm sorry," I repeat.

I want him to hang up. I want to run, to go home—even my Economics report feels like shelter. I want to begin what I know will be the evening-long fight to forget the words he's called me. *Waste. Pathetic.* But from underneath how beaten down he's left me, I feel a flicker of hope. The flicker I feel every time I talk to him. If I could just say one right thing, he'd see who I really am. How I'm worth his time. How I'm nothing like my mother.

"By the way," I keep my voice even, a fight in itself, "Mom probably didn't tell you, but I'm in an upper-level Economics course this semester. We're studying your company next week." I fly through the sentences, figuring he'll cut me off if I pause.

The moment I finish, exactly like I expected, he's rushing to reply. "Cameron, were you even listening? I don't have time to *chat* about your *day*." The patronization in his tone is heavy. I feel my mouth go dry. "If you need a quote or something," he goes on, "email Chelsea."

He hangs up.

I stare at the phone a moment longer, until the sound of footsteps stops behind me. I feel my teammates waiting, watching me. "What happened, Cameron? We thought you'd beat us," I hear Leila behind me, gently teasing.

I hurriedly wipe my eyes and take out my earphones. *If there's one thing that could make this moment worse.*

"Were you on a *phone call*?" Leila chides. She comes up next to me. "You know Coach will make you do sprints for that."

I hate how they're catching me like this. With tears in my eyes, with a pallor I know hasn't vanished from my cheeks. Still hurt and afraid. I round on Leila. "Don't tell her, then."

Her expression falters. "I'm the team captain," she says, uncertain. "I have to tell her."

I put my earphones back in. "Fine," I say nonchalantly, looking Leila right in the eye, feeling all that smallness and hurt turning into armor. Turning into anger. "If getting me in trouble makes you feel big and important, go for it. I *really* don't care. You probably need it, what with how your own boyfriend's barely interested in you."

Leila recoils like I've struck her. Her face turns pink, and her lower lip wobbles like she's going to cry. It's a reaction I'm not entirely proud to have caused.

But instead of apologizing, I turn and run, letting the wind dry my eyes.

I get home to find my mother on the couch, wrapped in her blanket. Sleeping. There's a box of tissues and a glass containing what I'm guessing is a completely un-drunk cleanse on the coffee table. The grainy green drink is congealed and completely disgusting.

I drop my bag, knowing the three textbooks I brought home hitting the floor will wake her up.

Her eyes open groggily, finding me in the doorway. "Cameron, hi." Propping herself up, she says, "I've been thinking of what to fix for dinner."

Her voice is casual, even cheery, like this is normal. Like my mother sleeping on the couch in the middle of the day in her pajamas could possibly be *normal*. Like I haven't been responsible for picking up the pieces of our life when she won't.

I've had enough. "I don't care if you get a job or if you find some other family member to write you a check. But I won't let you extort *my* father while you sit on the couch all day." The edge in my voice catches her off guard. I watch her eyes focus and a flush rise in her cheeks. "If I find out you've tried to trick him into giving you more money, I'll move out."

She hauls herself off the couch and plants her hands on her hips, a vain effort to look imposing undercut by her rumpled sweats and knotted hair. "Where will you go?" she challenges.

"I'll live with Elle," I reply, having thought this through on the final leg of the run. Her older sister goes to Princeton and moved out two years ago, leaving a bedroom empty. I watch Mom's eyes flicker, panicked, and I go on. "You'll be completely alone, and without me, Dad won't pay your rent. I'll have him send the checks to Elle's parents—not that they need them. They don't spend their days doing nothing on the couch." I know I'm throwing her worst fear in her face: losing the financial security I provide.

Mom's mouth works like she's searching for words and finding none. "Cameron, I don't—" she finally tries.

I cut her off. "I'm not interested, Mom. Do whatever you want. I just thought you should know my plans." I collect my bag and head for my room.

The second I'm in my room, I drop the façade of confidence and control. I sag against the door, my hands on my knees, my breath shallow. I feel sick, like I might throw up. I'm angry at everyone. At my mom, my dad, at Andrew for being stubborn and writing me off. At myself. I feel like I could scream until my throat is raw and it wouldn't be enough.

I hate how my father, who just called me pathetic, is the only impossible flicker of hope I have for a parent to care about me. To consider me a person, not just a checkbook. I hate having to dismiss whatever kindness I receive from my mother because I know it's just her final performance for an audience of one.

I pull out my computer and quickly log into the Common App portal. Unhesitatingly, I upload my UPenn essay. I wracked my brain for days trying to incorporate Paige's comments and got nowhere. There are two weeks remaining until the application's due, but this essay is as good as it's going to get.

I hit submit.

I force an even breath into my lungs. Neatly, I unpack my bag and organize my folders into their tray. Everything I've planned for, the entire future I've constructed in hopes of bringing myself closer to my father, is out of my hands now and on the desk of an admissions officer somewhere in Philadelphia. I can't think about it.

In hopes of distraction, I try to do the *Taming of the Shrew* worksheet. I flip to a scene in the play where Petruchio torments his new bride, Katherine.

But it's impossible to concentrate. Not just because of UPenn or my parents, either. I keep replaying what happened with Leila. I know what I said was cruel. It's just unbearable sometimes. It's like there's this horrible thing eating me from the inside, and the only way to let it out is to fall apart—or to lash out. To leave someone else with hurt and doubt and insecurity just to know *they know how it feels*.

Because I couldn't let myself fall apart, not in front of those girls. My chest may be hollow, but my eyes are dry. That's what's important.

But I owe Leila an apology. I add her name to my amends list.

Katherine deserves every bit of the mistreatment she gets.

I'm beginning to fill in the worksheet when an email notification pops up in the corner of my computer screen. It's a confirmation of my Common App submission. Quickly, I move it to a college folder to keep its reminder from stressing me out and find Brendan's email back at the top of my inbox.

I absentmindedly click open the images again. Drawn in for a closer look, I can't help noticing the details in the characters. The boy stands strong in the face of the imposing sorceress, who's scowling with her scepter raised.

Without thinking, I hit reply.

From: c.bright@beaumontprep.edu
To: b.rosenfeld@beaumontprep.edu
Subject: Re: Less "third grade"?

1000x less. Question: does the evil sorceress have to be blonde?

I hit send, not expecting a response. None comes for half an hour, while I'm working on my response paper. I'm halfway done when I'm distracted by a ding from my computer.

From: b.rosenfeld@beaumontprep.edu
To: c.bright@beaumontprep.edu
Subject: Re: Re: Less "third grade"?

Um, yes.

Just, "um, yes"? He knows how to be cryptic, I'll give him that.

From: c.bright@beaumontprep.edu
To: b.rosenfeld@beaumontprep.edu
Subject: Okay, Mr. Unhelpful

Why, though?

Now he replies immediately.

From: b.rosenfeld@beaumontprep.edu
To: c.bright@beaumontprep.edu
Subject: Better, Ms. Persistent?

Because blondes are infinitely scarier than everyone
else. It's a law of the universe.

I look closer at the sorceress, with her golden hair. For
whatever reason, I remember the stunned hurt in Leila's eyes.
From the way the sorceress is menacing the young hero, I'd
guess she comes to some gruesome defeat in the end of the
game. Even though my legs are aching from the afternoon's
run, the pressure in my chest has me reaching for my running shoes. Until a second email from Brendan appears.

From: b.rosenfeld@beaumontprep.edu
To: c.bright@beaumontprep.edu
Subject: Re: Better, Ms. Persistent?

Besides, it's kind of a thing for video games to have hot
girls in them.

I can't help it. I grin. I drop my shoes and sit down to write a reply.

From: c.bright@beaumontprep.edu
To: b.rosenfeld@beaumontprep.edu
Subject: What are you implying?

Because it *sounds* like you're saying blondes are hot. If it's a blonde you want, Brendan, I could probably make something happen. In the interest of making amends, of course.

I reread the email once I've sent it. *What did I just write?* Before I can think too hard about it, I write him again.

From: c.bright@beaumontprep.edu
To: b.rosenfeld@beaumontprep.edu
Subject: You do have a phone, right?

Text me. This conversation is quickly leaving behind the school-approved subjects of homework and homework.

I include my number and try to return to *The Taming of the Shrew*, telling myself there's no reason to expect Brendan Rosenfeld would want to text *me*. It's useless. I'm distracted, waiting for my phone to ping. Which it does. I unlock the screen before I read his message.

SOME people MIGHT find blondes hot. I wasn't speaking personally.

I lean back in my chair, my run forgotten.

Good. I hate it when guys look at a blonde and write her off in the "hot" category.

I know what you mean. I hate when girls look at a teenage computer nerd/gamer and automatically think "stud." We're so much more than that, you know?

I laugh out loud. I never knew Brendan was funny. I guess I knew nearly nothing about him. It's just that a sense of humor is one of the things I definitely wouldn't have predicted from someone who ensconces himself in the library and the robotics room every chance he gets.

I'm glad you told me. I'll correct the error of my ways.

No problem. Even though I'm definitely 100% not in the slightest the kind of guy who finds blondes hot or whatever, I'll make sure no one gets the wrong idea from my game. The sorceress has depth, I promise, in addition to being the kind of girl SOME people MIGHT find hot.

I'm surprised how long this conversation has gone on,

how much he's saying. He has surprising charisma and charm for a guy with an antisocial reputation. I'm starting to suspect he doesn't socialize not because he can't but because, for reasons I don't know, he just doesn't want to.

Yet here he is, texting me like we're old friends.

I feel like this means he possibly doesn't hate me.

> You might want to decrease her cup size.
> People won't see depth if they're distracted
> by her double Ds.

I would expect an embarrassed smiley, except I'm not convinced Brendan's discovered emojis.

> Damn. Noticed that, did you?

> Don't worry. I DEFINITELY believe you when
> you say she's not your type.

> Good. I DEFINITELY wouldn't want you to get the
> wrong idea.

If I didn't know Brendan better, I'd think he was trying to flirt with me. If I didn't know him, I'd think he was doing a pretty great job.

It feels like a natural place to pause the conversation. I let his reply be, even though a very unfamiliar part of me wants to keep talking. Putting my phone down, I feel how the stress and frustration I carried home have almost dissipated. It's something I never would've expected, but it's been an awful day, and Brendan Rosenfeld made it feel okay.

Returning to my response paper, I find myself rewriting. Katherine has her flaws. Why do they only ever earn her isolation and pain? I refocus my thesis and write a new draft. Katherine deserves to be held accountable for the horrible things she does. But underneath the nasty exterior, it's possible she's a person and not just a problem. A person who needs to change but deserves a chance.

Sixteen

WE'RE IN THE DINING HALL TODAY BECAUSE it's raining. We're packed into the wood-paneled room, elbows touching at the long oak tables. Morgan prudently went for a burger today. But she hasn't taken a bite because she's busy expounding on every detail of the role she landed in an indie horror movie.

I would be in a pretty good mood right now, even though rainy days usually frustrate me—L.A.'s not a city built for running in the rain. When I left for school in the morning, my mom wasn't home. The black pumps she wears to job interviews were gone from the pile of shoes in her closet where I left them a week ago. It's a start.

What's bothering me is Leila. If we weren't in the dining hall, I wouldn't have to watch her with her friends. Wouldn't have to be reminded of how guilty I feel.

Which . . . is weird. I didn't expect to feel bad about what I said, not when I'm right about her and Jason. Not when it's not even in the top ten worst things I've said to people. But I do.

She's working hard to flirt with Jason next to her. I know she's upped the PDA because of what I said. Every other second she's draping herself on him, resting her head on his shoulder, or ruffling his hair.

"We're shooting during the college fair. I don't care. It's not like I'm planning to go to college," Morgan goes on. "The producer already loves me, and my costar wants to—"

I want to listen. I really do. I'm excited for Morgan—she's a good actress, and this is the first role where she has a chance to show it. But I'm distracted by Jason, who gingerly removes Leila's arm from around his neck, plants a peck on her cheek, and gets up from the table.

And walks straight toward ours.

He taps Elle on the shoulder. "Hey, want to help me with that . . . thing?" He's wearing a winning grin, the one I remember from his *Cyrano de Bergerac* performance junior year.

Elle turns, her expression a combination of eager and wary. She chews her lip and glances at Leila. Who, unsurprisingly, is watching their interaction with undisguised displeasure.

"You know you guys aren't being even a little subtle, right?" I ask abruptly. Elle's eyes flash to mine, and she frowns.

"You told your friends?" Jason hisses over her shoulder.

Elle's frown deepens, and she redirects it to Jason. "They're my friends, Jason. What were they going to think when you and I disappeared from lunch? That I was helping you with your makeup?"

Brad stifles a laugh behind me. "Everyone knows anyway, dude. Half the football team saw you yesterday in the student lounge."

With that, I watch the anger ebb from Jason's face. He straightens his shirt, changing easily from indignant to arrogant playboy. "Whoops," he says. I have to restrain myself from grimacing in revulsion, which I do for Elle's sake.

I have to work harder when Jason forces himself between Elle and me and plants himself on our bench. I pointedly lean away from him, turning to face Morgan.

"What are you doing?" Elle's voice is prickly with annoyance.

"Sitting with you at lunch," Jason replies, clearly pleased and pretending this is normal.

Elle drops her voice, but her impatience with Jason is unmistakable. "That's girlfriend-boyfriend territory. I'm fairly certain your girlfriend is over there."

Elle doesn't dance around what she wants. It's the same when it comes to her YouTube career and her personal life, and it's why she has the success she does in the former—and, honestly, very little in the latter. She never compromises. I've known her long enough to know Jason's seriously getting on her nerves. I glance over and, sure enough, I recognize her stony expression and the deepening line in between her eyebrows.

"Come on"—Jason nods in Leila's direction—"it won't be long before that's over." He looks at Elle with what appears to be earnestness. "We could have all the girlfriend-boyfriend territory. Just say the word."

Elle avoids his eyes, her voice unwavering. "We talked about this, Jason."

He places his hand on top of hers. "Elle—"

She yanks her hand away. "Just don't," she says dismissively.

The arrogance falls from his face, replaced by something almost vulnerable. "So I'm good enough for fifteen minutes at lunch, but I'm not good enough for a relationship?" I hear the hurt in his voice hidden under indignation.

"I told you what I wanted from the beginning," Elle replies furiously. "You have no right to be surprised."

Jason gets up abruptly, nearly knocking my soda onto Morgan's lap. "You know," he says, "you're the one who found me at that party, while *I* had a girlfriend. You convinced *me* to cheat. What, did you only want to screw up my relationship with Leila? Because you obviously weren't really interested in me."

"I wanted what I wanted. I don't have to explain it." Elle's expression is flat, disinterested. "Go away, Jason."

Jason waits for a moment, probably hoping she'll reconsider. But when Elle doesn't even look up, he finally walks off without a word. With a nonchalant flip of her hair, Elle returns to her lunch.

I watch her, feeling an unfamiliar unease. I've never cared about Jason and Leila's relationship. I don't even *like* Jason Reid. I just can't help noticing how devastated he is, and it's obvious how little Elle cares. How . . . content she looks to ruin his relationship because she wanted him and then didn't.

It's not only the ruthlessness of Elle's behavior that bothers me. It's the recognition I felt watching her wreck someone without a thought except for herself.

It's something I would do. Something I *have* done, with Grant and Hannah.

I don't know if it's because I want Andrew to think I'm a decent human being or because consciously admitting and cataloguing my misdeeds has me seeing them in a new light, but the idea of treating people like Elle just did twists my stomach in a knot. I'd never known it for what it is, never known Elle and myself for what we are.

Selfish.

Elle peels an orange, digging her perfect nails under the skin. One by one, she places pieces of the rind in a discreet pile. "Brad, you're going to the college fair, right? You have to talk to Harvard," she says, every trace of Jason forgotten.

I finish today's hill run in a minute over my usual time. I'm distracted, and now it's even affecting my cross-country performance. I walk in the gates to Beaumont's back field, wringing my headband in frustration. The sun's come out, because once again, the California weather can't make up its mind. The cheerleaders are constructing a human pyramid on the field for practice, and next to them is the soccer team, which I avoid looking at.

When I reach the girls' locker room, I'm greeted by the sight of Jason making out with Leila against the concrete wall of the gym. I know he's hoping I'll run and tell Elle, and she'll become insanely jealous and want him back.

Not going to happen. I walk into the locker room without a second glance.

As I'm collecting my bag, I hear Leila come in. She opens her locker next to mine. "Good run today," she says, sounding unsurprisingly chipper given the five solid minutes she just spent enmeshed with Jason.

"Yeah," I reply. I don't know what to say. Zipping up my bag, I head for the door.

But with one hand on the handle, I pause, remembering for the hundredth time today when I was cruel to her about Jason. How the pain bled into her eyes. Why she's thrilled Jason's paying attention.

Leila's on my amends list. Better now than never.

I take a breath and walk back to her locker. Her eyes flit up to mine, questioning. "Hey," I begin. "I'm sorry for what I said on Tuesday, about your boyfriend not being interested in you. It was a shitty thing to say, and I want you to know I regret it."

Leila's smile slips. "Thank you," she says. "It's big of you to apologize. Besides"—she nods toward the door—"I think it's pretty obvious you were wrong." She puts her hands on her hips, but her voice is thin, like she's not convinced.

I nod, conflicted. It's on the tip of my tongue to tell her everything. Except that'll only hurt her worse. It's the kind of brutal honesty I could imagine Katherine dispensing just to twist the knife.

Then again, I'm not known for being nice. Telling Leila feels like the right thing to do, whatever it says about me.

"I know you're going to think I'm trying to hurt you or stir up shit with Jason," I say in a rush. "But I don't care. You deserve to know. Jason's been cheating on you for the past couple weeks."

Leila flinches. She stares at me for a hanging moment, her expression unreadable. I know I'm not the one who hurt her. Jason is. But like on Tuesday, I want to escape how I know she's feeling. I want to give her space, or maybe I selfishly want to avoid watching her cry.

"I knew it," she finally says, her voice nearly a whisper. She sits down heavily. "It's Elle, isn't it?" Her eyes find mine, but they don't contain the accusation I anticipated. Her expression is closer to defeat. "It's why she's been avoiding him."

"Um." I'm caught off guard. I won't betray Elle even if I'm not exactly comfortable with what she did.

"Actually, don't tell me. I don't want to know." Leila's talking to herself now. She rubs her eyes, and her voice comes out choked. "He's such a dick."

"He really is," I reply, relieved we've found something to agree on. Leila gives a teary laugh. "I honestly don't get what everyone sees in him."

Her face falls. She glances toward the door. "Well, he used to have a really sweet side. Before he got obsessed with attention, with everyone treating him like a celebrity."

I nod, not knowing how to contribute to the conversation. It's hard to imagine a Jason who doesn't strut his way into every party, who's not interested in girls *plural* hanging on his every word, whose number-one goal isn't everyone knowing his name. I wonder if I never knew that Jason *because* he wasn't interested in those things, because the quiet, sweet guy wouldn't have been on my radar.

Leila stands up. I follow her to the door. She hesitates, and I realize it's because she's remembered Jason might be waiting. Reaching past her, I push open the door. I've never been good at comforting, but I hope she understands I've got her back on this.

We step outside, and he's not there. Leila's eyes scout the field. Wherever Jason is, he's nowhere to be found. I don't know if it's a relief or a final slap in the face. "You didn't deserve this," I say haltingly. "He should have been honest with you."

"He should have," she says, her eyes fixed on some point in the distance. Then she turns to me. "But you were. Thank you."

Seventeen

I FIND A PERFECT PARKING SPOT IN front of the Depths of Mordor. It's definitely a good omen.

I drove to the bookstore flush with purpose after walking Leila to her car. Before I go into Mordor, I open my notebook and edit my amends list.

People I Need to Make Amends with, and How
1. *Paige Rosenfeld, for calling her pathetic—fix things with Brendan*

2. *Brendan Rosenfeld, for giving him the nickname that allegedly ruined his life—find a way to undo his unpopularity*

3. *Grant Wells and Hannah Warshaw, for the worst two-month relationship in history—get them back together*

4. *~~Leila, for being cruel about her relationship with Jason—tell her the truth about what her boyfriend did behind her back~~*

I'm confident I can continue to make progress on the Grant-and-Hannah project. I have news for Paige, too. I texted with Brendan. That's certain to earn me points, if not Paige's forgiveness altogether.

There's a mirror propped up on a lamppost on the sidewalk, and an elderly gentleman is snapping selfies in a red coat in front of it. I'm about to walk into the bookstore when the door opens—and Paige walks out.

She pauses when she recognizes me. "What are you doing here, Bright?"

"Um. Looking for you," I fumblingly reply.

At that, Paige cuts me a grin. "Careful," she says. "If I didn't know you better, I'd think you wanted to be my friend."

I recover. "'Friend' is a strong word." Paige laughs. "Where are you going?" I ask.

She nods in the direction of Mordor's tiny parking lot. "Andrew's. I completely forgot I said I'd help him on a History presentation." She skirts around me. "I was supposed to meet him at his house fifteen minutes ago," she adds apologetically.

A pang of jealousy hits my chest. *I* used to work on homework with Andrew, not Paige. *I'm here for a reason*, I remind myself.

"Hey," I say, catching up to Paige in front of her car. I notice a couple dings it didn't have when I helped her with the sewing machine a few days ago. "Brendan gave me his number," I say.

Paige pauses, hand on the door. She arches a suggestive eyebrow.

"It's not like that!" I go on. *Or I'm fairly certain it's not.* "I just—" I don't know what I planned to tell Paige other than that. "Did you know he's really funny?" I hear myself ask, then remember I'm talking to his sister.

"I did know that, Bright," she says and smiles.

Not the coy, catlike smile I get every time she's decided I've said something overly honest or unintentionally incriminating. I've never gotten this smile—happy, real, even proud, possibly.

It lingers for only a moment before it catches a touch of humor. "Is that why you're here?" she asks. "To inform me my brother knows his way around a joke? You could have told me that at school. Or would you be ashamed if your friends knew you and I are practically BFFs by now?"

"I'm not ashamed!" I protest. Paige opens her car door, throwing me an unconvinced glance, droll and tinged with something else, something like resignation. "Really!" I say. "I wouldn't be."

"Prove it, Bright," she replies. I notice the inside of the car's an abject mess. School books, gum wrappers, yerba maté cans, and actual CDs have collected in a chaotic pile on the passenger seat. I don't know what I expected. "Hang out with me at the college fair tomorrow," Paige says. "Everyone's going to be there."

"Are you asking me on a friend-date?"

Paige shrugs. "Are you accepting?"

I echo her nonchalance. "Why not?"

Paige closes the car door and starts the engine. She rolls down the window as she's pulling out of the space. "Don't stand me up," she calls from the window, and winks. I roll my eyes in return and find I'm smiling. I shake my head.

Paige's sense of humor is really growing on me.

I guess she's got that in common with her brother.

In the parking lot I weigh whether to drive home. I have to redo a problem set I messed up in Econ, and I have to finish putting together my internship materials to submit to Human Resources tonight. But I drove thirty minutes out of my way to get to the bookstore, and I guess I had my heart set on hanging out here for a while.

But before I begin walking to the front of shop, the back door opens onto the parking lot. Hannah, in a Depths of Mordor T-shirt, comes out carrying a pile of empty cardboard boxes. She hauls them in the direction of the dumpster.

I don't know if she doesn't notice me or if she's ignoring me. There's a very good chance of either. The parking lot is empty, and even though I'd rather go inside and put this off, I can't give up the opportunity to talk to her on her own. From what I can tell, Grant's done admirably with my orders to avoid bothering Hannah with his constant flirtation. It's time for me to begin my part.

"Hey, Hannah," I say, schooling friendliness into my voice. Whatever I can do to earn her goodwill. "Can I help?"

Hannah doesn't reply. I don't know if she's heard me. It's hard to imagine she hasn't—Fairfax isn't *that* noisy, even with the distant thrum of hip-hop from a car window or sidewalk sale. Hannah hefts the cardboard boxes into the dumpster and slams the lid with more force than the job probably required.

"No," she says harshly.

Well, I know she heard me. "Hannah," I start gently, "I wanted to talk to you. I need to apologize—"

Hannah rounds on me, fury in her eyes. "Don't, Cameron," she utters. "Don't. I know what you're doing here. Paige explained you wanted to earn her forgiveness or whatever. If you're about to apologize for hooking up with my boyfriend—don't."

No longer a rookie with apologies, I expected this. "I'm sorry, Hannah," I press on. "I wanted you to know I'm sorry. I deserve your anger."

"That's just it," Hannah replies. "You don't. It's *Grant's* fault. Obviously, what you did was shitty. It was a thousand times worse coming from Grant, though." Hannah runs a hand through her hair, releasing a frustrated sigh. "It's his fault—and mine, for dating a worthless dirtbag like him in the first place."

I wince. *Worthless dirtbag.* This is not going to be easy.

"He feels horrible, Hannah. If you—" I tentatively begin.

"Whoa," Hannah interrupts me, her eyes finding mine again. They've lost none of their menace. "I don't hold a grudge for what you did. But I *definitely* don't want you giving me relationship advice. You're not a good person," she says. "I don't care if you and Paige braid each other's hair now or whatever. You and I will *never* be friends, and I will *never* want your opinion on Grant or me or anything."

Without waiting for a reply, Hannah heads for the door. Not that I have anything to offer in my defense.

She swings the door shut with enough force to knock over the LOT FULL sign next to the entrance to the lot. I replace the sign upright. It's tempting to follow Hannah inside just to needle her, but it wouldn't further my agenda. I guess I'm going home after all. Walking to the curb, I hardly remember where I parked, a pair of thoughts completely consuming my head. One, I'm really getting tired of people reminding me how crappy a person I am.

Two, this "taming" is proving to be harder than I expected.

Eighteen

MOM IS ECSTATIC. SHE HAS A NEW job. Not just a job—an "opportunity," she says in singsong whenever I'm near enough to hear her. She serves coffee in the Director's Guild of America. She's explained in the same slightly manic voice that she's just *certain* Michael Bay or Christopher Nolan or whoever will come by to pick up his triple-shot Americano and notice her, his next leading lady.

I don't know how to deal with this new mood swing. I don't know if she even remembers I gave her an ultimatum a couple days ago or if she's conveniently "forgotten." I do know things are definitely a little weird in the apartment. She's gotten out of bed early, cooked real meals—not smoothies—and started going to yoga. Which would all be great if she hadn't also begun talking a mile a minute and playing music until two A.M.

She waltzed out the door this morning, calling over her shoulder that she was going to gangsta rap yoga in Lafayette Park and she'd be gone until ten. I'm taking the opportunity to do a long-overdue cleaning of the apartment.

I guess her newfound focus doesn't extend to picking up dirty socks off her bedroom floor. I gingerly place them in the hamper. Under the bed I discover a small pile of junk food wrappers. Ruffles, Reese's Peanut Butter Cups, an empty bottle of Sprite. I know she tends to binge eat when she's depressed. But with the yoga and the cooking, I'm hoping she's giving it a rest for the time being.

I'm folding laundry next to the washer and dryer when I hear the door open and close. Mom walks in a moment later with a bottle of water, her face flushed. Without sparing a glance at the unfolded pile of shirts I'm working on, she closes the lid on the toilet and sits down.

"How was your workout?" I ask patiently.

Mom exhales a contented sigh. "It was *amazing*. My energy is completely refreshed." I hold back a request that she channel that *energy* into folding some shirts. She goes on. "Know how I can tell?"

"No, Mom." I pointedly pull the GRIFFITH PARK 5K shirt from under her elbow. She remains oblivious. "How?"

"I had—it must have been four men whistle at me from the parking lot. I haven't had it that good since before I met your father." She takes a satisfied drink from her water. I hide my gag face behind the shirt I'm folding. "Michael Bay," she says confidently. "I'm telling you, one of these days Michael Bay's going to walk in, and I'll be there. Everything's going to change for us, kid. Just wait."

I focus on the precision of my folding to keep from pointing out that Michael Bay probably has assistants get him his coffee. His assistants probably have assistants to get them *their* coffees.

"And the next time your father's in town . . ." She gives me

146

a suggestive look I wish I could un-see. "You and I both know he has a soft spot for me, no matter how hard he resists."

I can't dispute her there. Unfortunately.

"Wait until he sees the new me." She admires her reflection in the mirror.

I've had enough. "Why would you even want Dad back?" I ask, dropping the shirt I'm holding onto the washing machine. "He just upsets you, and he made it clear he doesn't want to marry you. Even when you guys were together."

Mom hops up from the toilet. She throws me a patronizing look, like I'm just a teenager who wouldn't know the first thing about her unfathomably mature love life. "We have a really complicated relationship, Cameron." She emphasizes the "complicated." "Real love is never easy, you know."

She bounces out of the room. I want to follow her. To convince her she shouldn't waste her time pining for my dad.

Except it hits me how hypocritical I'd be. How can *I* tell someone to give up on the person they want? Don't I spend every day hurting over Andrew, wishing he would take me back?

In a weird way, my mom is right. Real love *is* never easy.

It's just worth the hard work.

Nineteen

IT'S SATURDAY NIGHT. THE COLLEGE FAIR.

I'm a collection of frayed nerves wound up in a white button-down and black pants. I have to impress the Wharton rep, who's a real admissions officer for California and will be reading my application and determining my entire future. With my 1440 SAT score, which is on the low end of what Penn accepts, my current B in Econ, and the internship with my dad's company not official yet, I have to *distinguish myself* somehow. *Make an impression. Individualize my application.* I hear the words of Beaumont's painfully overqualified college counselors ringing in my ears, over and over.

I don't usually get nervous about school stuff. Econ's the exception. Otherwise, I'm imperturbable. But the college fair is different. It's not a competition of how much I've studied, how hard I've worked. It's a dog-and-pony show, where every dog's wardrobe is more expensive than mine, every pony's tutor more exclusive, everyone's summer "service program" experiences more impressive.

Elle and Brad find me on the front steps. Elle once-overs my outfit admiringly, allaying my nerves a little. "Very preppy, Cam," she says. "I love it." I glance at my shoes and smooth my shirt, and I know Elle reads the self-conscious-ness in the gestures. She slips off her blazer and holds it out. "Here, add this."

I spare her a grateful smile. "You don't need it?"

She laughs. "Please. I'm only here because my parents forced me. I *have* my plan for the next four years, and it does not involve college."

Elle's been saying she's not going to apply to college since sophomore year. I know her parents, though. I know they're going to force her to, and I know without a hint of jealousy that she's going to get in everywhere. I've watched her compile revenue spreadsheets for her endorsements, overheard her negotiate her partnerships over the phone. Her business is every bit a *business*.

Regardless, she looks amazing without the blazer.

"I wish my parents understood." She rolls her eyes. "Morgan's lucky hers don't care."

I glance at Brad, who's evaluating the SUVs and sports cars dropping our classmates off in front of school. "How's Morgan's shoot going?" I ask.

"Fine, I imagine," Brad mutters. He thumbs the collar of his Brooks Brothers shirt, visibly bothered. "With the costar."

Elle and I share an amused glance.

"You've really *never* seen the costar?" Elle prods. "You haven't IMDb-ed him?"

"Not yet," Brad grumbles. "I would have. But I don't know his name. Morgan only ever calls him 'the costar.'" He adopts a Morgan voice, which is pretty convincing. "The costar forgot his lines. The costar bought everybody lunch. The costar and I had fake sex in front of the whole cast and crew."

Elle's in stitches. "Why didn't you ask his name?" she gets out.

"How could I? I would have come off crazy jealous and insecure."

Elle erupts in a peal of laughter. "I've seen him," I jump in. "Morgan sent me a couple images from the movie for her website. You have nothing to worry about, Brad."

"Thanks, Cam." Brad touches his perfectly combed hair, looking endearingly unconvinced. "I know it's stupid of me to worry. I want Morgan to achieve her dreams, one hundred percent. But what's going to happen when she's filming with, you know, Chris Pratt? She loves Chris Pratt!"

"Everybody loves Chris Pratt," Elle contributes thoughtfully.

Brad throws up his hands.

We walk up the front steps, down the hall, and into the quad, where within the impeccably manicured hedges, it's a wall-to-wall crush of people. Crowds press right up to every table. If I were near the ornate octagonal fountain in the center of the quad, I'd be afraid of getting pushed in. Even walking is going to be a challenge.

Lisa Gramercy, in class-president mode, is passing out programs, reveling in every moment of looking like a student leader in front of reps from Harvard, Princeton, Penn. I'd hate Lisa if she weren't just obscenely nice.

"*Ugh.*" Elle collapses against Brad in indignation. "Better get this over with. I have to talk to Princeton for my dad. He's going to check if I have a program or a bookmark for proof. He hasn't *said* he's going to. But I know he's going to. Brad, you headed to Harvard?"

Brad nods once. His dad went to Harvard Law with Obama.

"And Cameron's doing Penn," Elle concludes.

"The Ivies will be in the back of the quad," Lisa says out of nowhere. I don't know how she emerged from the crowd to come up to us. But here she is, black curls bouncing from her ponytail, pearls in her ears. Before I can get annoyed by her eavesdropping, she gives me a glance of friendly envy. "That's a *great* blazer on you, Cameron."

I smile. Elle does, too, I notice out of the corner of my eye. "Thanks, Lisa," I say. "You look really pretty."

Lisa beams and disappears.

"Of *course* they're in the back," Elle deadpans.

We're heading into the crowd when I catch sight of Paige—and with her, Brendan. They're tightly compressed in line for a school whose banner I can't completely read. *Something* University. Mr. Keeps to Himself doesn't look uncomfortable the way I would have expected, and I remember his confidence in our texting conversation the other day. Brendan's eyes flit up occasionally from the brochure he's reading, seemingly sizing up the booth's representative and eavesdropping on other students' conversations. He's in a dark gray suit stretched over his huge frame, his curly hair just the right level of combed.

He looks . . . good.

"I'll find you guys later," I call up to Elle and Brad.

Elle pauses. Glancing over her shoulder, she cocks her head when she notices Paige. "Do you want us to wait for you?" she asks uncertainly.

"Um. It's okay," I reply. "I promised some people I'd hang with them for a while."

Something crosses Elle's face, something hard and inquisitive. She opens her mouth like she's about to say something then closes it, and her features relax.

"Okay," she says. "Break a leg. Not that you need any luck, what with your dad."

I nod, glad she understood about Paige and wishing she hadn't mentioned my father. It's not like he'd *ever* provide even a kind word to his alma mater about his own daughter, and on the other end of the equation, if I'm *not* admitted . . . I'm worse than a disappointment. I'm unworthy.

When it comes to my father, legacy's not a gift. It's a prison.

Shaking off the familiar fear, I join Paige and Brendan. "Wow," I say, walking up. "Here it is. Conclusive proof that Brendan ever ventures outside."

"I'm here because my dad forced me," he replies, his expression tight. Paige's eyes flicker with unconcealed concern.

"You could check out schools other than MIT," she offers. "If you wanted to."

Brendan glances over the heads of the crowd from his extraordinary height. I can, tell he wishes he were elsewhere, and I know Paige can, too. He turns to his sister, his expression softening. "Yeah," he says. "I will."

He and Paige share a look. I'm left wondering if I've

stumbled into something private, until Paige pokes my arm. "Ready for our date?"

Brendan jerks up, obviously wondering if he heard right.

Paige and I exchange glances. "Don't I look ready?" I eye Paige invitingly, straightening my lapels. "I got dressed up for you and everything."

"This . . . really throws things into a new light." Brendan's watching the two of us curiously.

"Relax, Brendan." Paige stretches to perch her chin on her brother's NBA-height shoulder. "We're joking."

"For the most part," I chime in.

Brendan blinks. "I'm glad you guys have each other. *I'm* going to the MIT booth." He affectionately prods Paige's hair. "Please feel free to continue your non-date without me." He leaves, and Paige and I share an amused look.

"I don't really want to wait in this line," Paige announces. "They have a computer-aided design program I thought Brendan would be interested in, but, well . . ." She gestures in the direction he disappeared into the crowd.

"Where to?" I ask.

"I want to check out RISD and Tisch. What about you?"

I dodge the question, deferring to Paige's choices. "Art school, huh?"

Paige shrugs. "I guess. I don't know. I'm not like Brendan, who's brilliant enough he could probably pick whatever school he wants."

"But you're here on scholarship," I reply. "You have to be *kind* of brilliant."

Paige shakes her head. "Not like Brendan. Believe me."

Once again, I can't completely read the combination of emotions in her voice. I hear . . . not jealousy. Closer to pride churned together with protectiveness.

We push our way into the crowd. Without completely avoiding trampling our classmates' toes, we finally reach RISD. I wait while Paige collects a couple brochures, feeling my stomach clench—RISD's a few tables over from Penn. I'm practically right under the blue banner emblazoned with the Penn crest.

I guess Paige notices me looking at the banner when she returns from the RISD table. "You want to check them out?" She nods upward, following my eyes.

"Uh," I demur. "Not right now."

Paige nods once. I'm grateful for her not remarking on the obvious unease in my voice. I follow her once more into the crowd, figuring we're probably headed to Tisch or possibly CalArts. I've read their program measures up to the East Coast schools.

While we walk, I glance through the crowd and catch a glimpse of Brendan. He's reached the front of the MIT line, and I watch him talking to the representative. Not just talking—charming. His shoulders back, a rakish confidence on his features, Brendan finishes some sort of story or explanation, prompting a real laugh from the representative. If I hadn't seen Brendan spending every lunch in the robotics room for myself, I'd never believe this collected, charismatic boy in front of me is the same person.

I'm starting to say something to Paige when, without

warning, she ducks behind a display. Her cheeks burn bright enough to match her hair.

I look around, confused, until my eyes alight on Jeff Mitchel. And it is a miracle—a mercy—I didn't notice him before. He's wearing a horrible pink blazer and green striped tie, the type of outfit intended to tell college reps he couldn't care less what they think of him because Daddy's donations will get him in wherever he wants.

I give Paige an uncertain glance. "Tell me when he's gone," she says.

I watch Jeff while Paige hides. The only college prep he's getting here is practice for an inevitable career of harassing girls at fraternity parties. I watch him ogle a group of juniors. When they relocate, obviously uncomfortable, he follows.

I beckon Paige out.

"Care to explain?" I ask.

Paige is incredulous. "Do I need to? It's *Jeff*. He's a loser."

"But you wanted to hook up with him," I point out.

"I *did* hook up with him," Paige corrects me bluntly.

Surprised, I privately wonder why she ended up in tears that night. But it's not my place to ask. I cut her a droll glance instead. "I can't believe you actually hooked up with *Jeff Mitchel*. What, did he show you the sensitive side he hides behind his asshole exterior? You probably helped him with a school project, and he realized you're not the weirdo everyone thinks you are, and you learned he takes care of his sick grandma or something when he's not trying to be cool in front of his friends."

Paige laughs.

"Was I right?" I press.

"No," she says. "I only know the Jeff Mitchel everyone else unfortunately does. I've hardly said two words to him."

"Then why?" I ask, genuinely curious. "Why'd you hook up with him?"

"Because he's hot," she says slowly, like she's explaining something to a child. "Did I need any other reason?"

I laugh. "Fair enough. I can respect that. I just thought someone like you would have less shallow reasons than the rest of us," I tease.

"Weird artsy girls can be plenty shallow," she replies assuredly.

"I'm getting that."

I'm about to ask Paige where we're headed when I notice her face brighten. For a moment of fleeting hope, I wonder if Jeff Mitchel just got slapped by one of the junior girls and Paige watched it happen. Until I follow her eyes to . . .

Andrew.

Paige waves, obviously completely oblivious to how I'm on the verge of a nervous breakdown. I don't *not* want to talk to Andrew—I've wanted to talk to Andrew for days—just not here. Not in this pressure-cooker crowd, not without a clue what I'm going to say or how I'm going to guide the conversation to how hard I've worked to right the wrongs he hates me for.

"Paige," I begin feebly.

"Hey, Andrew!" she calls out, ignoring me. I don't know if she's forgotten Andrew hates me or if she knows and wants to watch me squirm. He gives Paige a friendly nod, the way guys do, and continues toward the two of us.

I can tell the moment he notices me, because his expression freezes over.

Not exactly a confidence-builder.

But Andrew continues the next couple feet up to us, threading through a cramped line for one of the Ivies. Paige gives him a friendly hug. "Hey, Paige," he says, discomfort heavy in his voice. "I was just going to"—he nods over our heads, eyes never meeting mine—"check out Berkeley. I'll be back in—"

"Oh, wait for me?" Paige implores. I don't fail to notice the flicker of frustration in Andrew's eyes. "I wanted to hit Berkeley, too, but we're right next to Pratt." She gestures to the booth beside us. "I'll be gone two minutes, I promise."

Andrew looks like he wants to protest. But he only nods, and Paige darts toward the Pratt display.

Leaving just me and Andrew.

"Hey," I say, and it comes out high and hopeful and completely obnoxious.

"Hey," Andrew says.

I wince. Off to a great start. We're the only people in this crowd not chatting, and it's really awkward. I don't know whether to look at him or nonchalantly pull out my phone or what.

"I'm on a friend-date with Paige," I blurt. Hearing instantly how that was probably the weirdest conversation opener in history, I begin to ramble. "I just . . . we're here together. Like a date. Except we're just friends. You know."

Andrew gives me a look. He *definitely* doesn't know.

"You guys are friends?" he asks, obviously reluctant to be engaging me in conversation.

"I don't know," I answer truthfully.

Neither of us has anything to add to that. The pause yawns on into awkwardness, until finally Andrew declares, a challenging edge in his voice, "You and Paige are nothing alike."

I pick up on the implication. Andrew's definitely *not* referring to my blonde hair and Paige's multicolored stylings, nor to how out of place her *Invader Zim* sweatshirt would appear in my closet. It's, *Paige is understanding. Paige helps me on my homework. You're judgmental. You're a—*

I know, Andrew. I know.

I remember *The Taming of the Shrew* and bite down what I have a feeling Katherine would say. "We're not that different, actually, Paige and I," I offer. "We have a pretty similar sense of humor." Besides, she's not exactly gentle with her commentary every now and then either. I remember the excoriation of my UPenn essay and a hundred often-deserved clap-backs since. We have that in common.

"Except Paige doesn't care about appearances." Hardened in accusation, Andrew's eyes find mine.

I bite back a retort—Paige called *herself* shallow. "I don't really care about appearances either," I say instead. Andrew frowns, and despite the doubt it gives me, I continue. "I know you think I only liked you when you made varsity. But it had nothing to do with the team, I promise. You could've gotten a perfect score on the SAT or the lead in the spring musical." Andrew's mouth twitches, and I have a hunch he's recalling telling me he peed his pants while playing an elf in *The Elves and the Shoemaker* in second grade. "I was just waiting for an indication you would commit to something. I wanted to know you would really try," I continue.

The defiance in his eyes fades a little. If I didn't know better, I'd think it was replaced by interest.

"You didn't really have hobbies or aspirations when we met," I say. "And then we started running together, and I realized you were really athletic. I just wanted you to try hard at it."

"And succeed," he adds.

"Hard work is good," I reply, unabashed. "Success is better. You've met my mom. You know who my dad is. Can you blame me for caring about that?"

When I find Andrew's eyes, his expression is gentler. In a swell of hope, I feel his guard weakening, his resistance beginning to ebb. He lets his crossed arms drop. The crowd shuffles around us, and he ends up closer to me. "Speaking of running," he says, "I heard you beat a school record at your meet the other day."

And just like that, it's easy. I'm telling him how I had a tough first mile because it was windy, how I picked up half a minute in the final stretch when everyone else was tired. He's bragging about being the fastest guy on the team, detailing for me a new route he's found near his house. It feels instinctive, like the runs I've longed for the past couple weeks.

I'm working up the courage to brush my arm against his when a curly-haired head emerges over the crowd.

Brendan weaves his way through the courtyard. I watch

him elbow gently past our classmates, hardly registering them. Not a single person waves him over. He's solitary, a person-shaped space moving through groups of junior girls laughing excitedly and guys swapping stats on athletic programs. Gone from his face is the enthusiasm of his conversation with the MIT representative, and I'm left wondering again why he's forever isolated if he has such charm in him. Wondering whether it's entirely my fault.

"I thought you said you don't care about appearances," Andrew says, his voice a razor. I turn back to him, uncomprehending. He nods in Brendan's direction, and I realize I've been watching Brendan with a frown on my face.

I round on Andrew. "You know, by saying that you've made it clear what *you* think of Brendan. I wasn't thinking that at all."

Andrew pauses, caught off guard. "He's Brendan now?" he asks after a moment. "What happened to BB?"

"He's Brendan now," I repeat firmly, realizing I haven't thought of him as BB in a while. It gives me an idea. Andrew's not going to dictate who I am, and I want him to know who I'm becoming. With a quick look at Andrew, I wave and catch Brendan's eye. He's confused, I can tell, but I beckon him over.

With what looks like reluctance, Brendan navigates the crowd over to us. I press into the back of the person in front of me to make room, earning a grumble from ahead of me, which I ignore. While keeping Andrew in the corner of my eye, I face Brendan and put every ounce of enthusiasm I have into my voice. "How was MIT? Looked like you were killing it with the rep," I say.

Brendan watches me warily, though not without a hint of humor. "Were you spying on me?"

"Get over it." I roll my eyes. "I'm giving you a compliment."

"That's a first," he replies. "MIT was . . . fine. My dad's decided I'm going there regardless of what I want. I just wish they had a program for"—he glances quickly at Andrew—"what I'm interested in."

"Video games?" I ask.

Brendan nods. "Video game *development*," he corrects lightly. "It sounds more professional that way."

"You want to study video games in college?" Andrew interjects doubtfully.

Brendan goes quiet, his features growing guarded. I speak for him. "Brendan's designing his own video game. It's, like, really impressive." Brendan flushes, but not, I have to guess, with embarrassment. "I can't imagine the initiative, the hard work . . ." I give Andrew a pointed look I know he notices.

"It's really not—" Brendan begins.

"What will you do with the game when you're done?" I interrupt before he can downplay his project.

"There's this, um, contest at UCLA," he says haltingly. "The winners get internships with Naughty Dog."

This time I'm the one puzzled. Andrew, however, looks impressed. "Whoa, dude, that's cool."

"What's Naughty Dog?" I butt in. "Please tell me it's not porn."

Finally, Brendan smiles. "It's not porn," he confirms, sounding a little more at ease. "It's a video game developer. Their games are really innovative while being fun in traditional ways. They've pioneered in-depth narratives, they've won every award . . . Working there would basically be a dream come true." He's rambling a bit. It's kind of cute. But his eyes close off, as if he's just remembered where he is. "It probably sounds geeky to you guys," he mutters.

"No," I rush to say. "It sounds incredible." I mean it, too. I didn't even know Brendan made video games weeks ago. Now I find out he's kind of legit.

I realize the instant after I've said it, I'd actually forgotten Andrew was next to me. Brendan smiles again. The crowd pushes in on us suddenly, and Andrew's arm is pressed into mine. I wait for him to step away. Instead, he remains, and a pleased flush heats my cheeks.

"How's it going with Grant and Hannah?" Brendan asks.

I'm jolted from the happy daze of Andrew's skin on mine. "Um," I say, recollecting myself. "No progress yet." I look at Andrew, whose face is almost irresistibly close. "I'm going to get Grant and Hannah back together," I inform him. "I won't be deterred, though," I tell Brendan. "You may not know this about me, but I'm very persistent."

"Oh, I know," Brendan says wryly.

Andrew's head jerks in his direction, like he's startled by the familiarity in Brendan's voice. I wonder momentarily if Brendan's going to bring up my repeated efforts to apologize to him.

Instead, he continues, "I remember when I was in eighth grade, you got mandatory swim P.E. cancelled for the entire school."

I laugh, a little pleased Brendan remembers, until I hear Andrew chuckle coldly next to me. "Yeah, because you didn't want your perfect hair and makeup wrecked."

"No." I round on Andrew. "It was because *Elle* didn't want *her* hair and makeup wrecked. She was just starting her channel then, and her parents wouldn't let her wear makeup when she was home. She had to film everything at lunch. Think she would've hit fifteen million subscribers if she'd had chlorine hair in her first videos?" Andrew falls silent, and it occurs to me I might've come on a little harsh. I'm just sick of him judging every word I say. "It wasn't entirely altruistic, I'll admit," I add. "I didn't want my perfect hair and makeup wrecked either."

Both boys turn to me, amused admonishment on their faces.

"What?" I protest jokingly. "Like aspiring to hotness is criminal."

"That reminds me," Brendan speaks up, "I took your feedback into account. The sorceress in my game now has proper, um, proportions."

"Wait." I grin. "How did my hotness remind you of your sexy sorceress?"

Brendan rolls his eyes, but he's blushing, like I've caught him red-handed. "It was the abstract concept of hotness," he fumbles to say. "I thought we established that the"—he clears his throat—"'sexy sorceress' wasn't my type."

"And that extends to anyone who might or might not resemble her," I ask leadingly.

"Naturally," he replies.

"You're such a liar."

"Am not."

Andrew's watching us curiously.

Paige emerges from the crowd, holding a handful of flyers. Noticing Brendan with Andrew and me, her eyes light up. "Cameron," she says, holding a program out for me. "I got you this."

I take the program. Flipping it over to the front, I read, UCLA DESIGN MEDIA ARTS. The text is imposed over a photograph of a big, beautifully modern building.

"I know you want to go to UPenn. But check out this design program," Paige goes on. "You know, if you ever want to do web design in college."

I feel my mouth working, but I find nothing to say. To be honest, I'm touched by Paige's completely unexpected thoughtfulness. Web design in college—I never even knew you *could* do web design in college. For the briefest moment, the idea rushes into my head of spending days in front of layouts and color palettes instead of spreadsheets and algorithms.

Then it's gone. Paige, no doubt noticing my dumbstruck expression, gives me a quick grin.

"We're doing Berkeley, right?" she asks Andrew, who nods a confirmation. "We have to get in line," she says. "The fair's practically over."

I check my phone—she's right. It's ten minutes to nine. "Crap," I say under my breath. It's now or never. "I have to talk to Penn," I tell the group. "Um . . ." I find Paige's eyes. "Thanks. For the UCLA thing," I get out.

"Of course." Paige nods.

I try to pass through the group in the direction of UPenn. The crowd contracts, and momentarily I'm pressed chest-to-chest with Brendan. I glance up at him. He's averted his eyes, but I'm fairly certain I feel his breath catch. I inch past him, not entirely knowing why my face flushes once more.

I get out into the crowd. By the time I turn to tell the group good-bye, the line for USC's formed in my way. I'm walking up to the Penn table when I feel my phone vibrate. I pull it out to find a text from Andrew.

> I hear our moms are doing their dinner thing this week.
> Want to run?

I reply immediately, feeling excitement tingle into my fingertips.

> I'd love to!!

While the person in front of me talks to the rep, I'm unable to hold back a smile. Talking to UPenn feels a little less daunting. Before it's my turn, I find myself writing a text to Brendan.

> You are too a liar.

I pause when his typing bubble appears.

> Am not.

Okay, I might be.

Just a little.

I reply with the blushing emoji.

I walk up to the UPenn rep, a silver-haired man in a navy blazer. "I'm Cameron Bright. I'm a senior," I say.

"Good to meet you, Cameron." He shakes my hand. His expression is warm, easy, welcoming. It does a little to calm the cold tingle of nerves in my chest and fingertips. "Do you know what you're planning to study in college?"

"I'm interested in the Wharton School," I declare, reaching for the Wharton pamphlet.

"Wharton is, as you know, a top-flight program for business," he tells me. "I hope you're ready for a schedule filled with business credits. Wharton students have very demanding course loads. I tell prospective applicants to be certain of their interest in the program before committing."

Committing. Be certain. The words wind an unexpected twist in my stomach. I open the Wharton pamphlet and find the coursework list, which confirms what the rep's saying. Courses line the length of the page: Statistics, Advanced Mathematics, Financial Analysis. Economics.

I feel the twist in my gut tighten, reminded of my Economics in the Entrepreneur's Market homework. Of bleary-eyed nights spent unraveling the complicated concepts and problems, or trying. I'll be confining myself to years of nights just like them if I go to Wharton. To a lifetime of them.

From behind the Wharton brochure peeks a blue corner of the UCLA pamphlet Paige gave me. The image flits behind my eyes again of days devoted to design instead of derivatives.

"Hold on." The representative blinks, breaking me from my thoughts. He studies me. "Did you say your name was Bright?"

"Um," I say. "Yes."

"You wouldn't happen to be Daniel Bright's daughter, would you?" His expression's taken on a new interest.

I force a smile. "I am."

"Wonderful!" he exclaims. "I had no idea Daniel's daughter was a senior. Well, a Bright would certainly excel at Wharton. I look forward to mentioning it to your father. I hope to see your application in my pile."

The idea of doing design in college collapses in my head. Replacing it is what I've known for what feels like forever. Wharton is my father. Economics is my father. He's the reason I'm doing this, why I'm committing to this life. The opportunity to live in his world, to never worry about unpaid bills or borrowed blazers, to have a future of my own, is worth every endless night.

"You will," I promise. "I already sent it in."

I thank the representative for his time and walk away from the table. The crowd is emptying from the courtyard now, everybody heading for their cars. I don't find Brendan's tall frame in the throng. He and Paige have probably already left, I realize with a touch of disappointment.

I pull out my phone, where I find a reply from Brendan. A pleased flutter runs through me, enough to calm my nerves.

Wait. Did I, video game nerd Brendan Rosenfeld, make you blush?

Don't be ridiculous.

Okay . . .

Just a little.

I reply, thoughts of Wharton thousands of miles away.

Twenty

PAIGE HAS NEWLY PURPLE HAIR. IN THE reading nook under the SCIENCE FICTION sign in the Depths of Mordor, I watch her intricately hand-stitch an apron to what appears to be a French-maid costume. Even with her fingers decked in the cheap plastic rings you get from a vending machine, she deftly passes the needle through the fabric, not wincing when the point hits her thumb. She completes ten, twenty stitches in seconds.

It's impressive. Kinda cool, even.

She explained to me the other day what "cosplay" is, how she devotes days and weeks to recreating the costumes and props of her and her friends' favorite characters from video games, TV shows, and the Japanese comics they're always reading. She's proudest of the Effie Trinket character she designed from *The Hunger Games* a couple years ago. Personally, I can't understand putting that many hours into a costume you'll wear for one day, but I caught the pride in Paige's voice when she described her pink Effie suit, and I held my tongue.

In the chairs opposite us, Abby and Charlie play a game I don't recognize. It's got dice and a board and decks of cards with pictures of grotesque creatures. They're focused on the board, wordless. The shop's predictably empty otherwise, except for Grant on a couch near the register trying to do homework, his nose in a book, and the WINTER IS COMING dude, who I'm convinced lives here and never changes his shirt.

"Andrew didn't say *anything* about me?" I press Paige. "For the whole rest of the night?"

"Oh my god," she groans, not skipping a stitch. "For the hundredth time, no. I didn't even know you were still into him."

I collapse onto the armrest. "I've liked Andrew for a year! You're the one who ruined everything." I find myself not hesitating to confide my crush in Paige, even though it's definitely friend territory. I guess our friend-date went well.

"You ruined it on your own, Bright." It's exactly what she would have said a couple weeks ago. Except this time, she's giving me a teasing grin.

"I know . . ." I sigh.

Paige notices my dejection. Her eyes flit to me before returning to her needle and thread. "He's having a hard time with the team," she offers. "We pretty much just talked about that after you left. He probably would have said something about you otherwise."

I pull my head up off my hand. "What's happening with the team?"

"Oh, you know," Paige says easily, "he just feels like he doesn't fit in with the other guys." I *didn't* know. Why didn't I know? "Those guys are more interested in partying and hookups," Paige continues. "They don't exactly want to come over and watch *Sherlock* with Andrew."

"Sherlock?"

Paige glances up from her costuming, openly aghast. "Come on. You can't be too cool to know what *Sherlock* is."

"I know what *Sherlock* is," I reply. Honestly, I've long had a thing for Benedict Cumberbatch. He's definitely gawky and nerdy, with his bushy hair and narrow frame, but I'm into it. "I didn't know Andrew was a fan."

She snorts incredulously. "Haven't you seen Andrew's room? It's practically a shrine to the BBC."

I feel a pang in my chest, the way I did when Paige went to help Andrew with his History homework. Paige and Andrew have only just become friends, and she's been in his room? I haven't in over three years of friendship. Or what I thought was friendship.

"Hey, did Brendan have a good time last night?" I ask, eager to change the subject.

Paige brightens. "I think he actually did!" she enthuses. "I was kind of amazed he didn't leave after he talked to MIT. Do you know how rarely he hangs out with people?"

"I don't know why," I say. "He's plenty socially capable. And he's really talented. He's definitely going to get that Naughty Dog internship. *The Girl's a Sorceress* looks amazing. He sent me a few images the other day . . ." I trail off, noticing Paige's expression. Her eyes hold questions alongside a knowing glint.

"Wow. You know more than I do," she says.

I blush, not entirely knowing why. It's not like being friends with Brendan is an embarrassment. But I feel like friendship isn't exactly what Paige is suggesting. "I just mean

Brendan's really cool, and he must have friends in his grade." Or he should. But I guess I haven't seen him hanging out with people.

Paige gives me her characteristic *you're-an-idiot* look. "Your nickname certainly didn't help," she says pointedly.

My face falls. "It's really because of me?"

Picking up her needle, Paige pauses for a long second. "It's not entirely your fault," she says eventually. "Truthfully, it's Brendan's choice. He doesn't try to have friends. Home stuff is . . . hard on him. If it weren't, the nickname would've only been a bump in the road." From the way she says it, I understand she doesn't want to elaborate. I leave the conversation there and let Paige return to her stitching.

Hearing the thud of the back door, I glance behind me. Hannah walks out in her Depths of Mordor shirt and goes to shelve paperbacks on a robot-themed display. She comes no closer to Paige and me. Ever since the talk I had with Hannah in the parking lot, she's done a remarkable job of remaining just far enough from me that I'm unable to start a conversation. She pointedly keeps her eyes on the books, never glancing in Grant's direction or mine. She finishes shelving and retreats behind the counter.

Paige scratches her head and winces violently enough to drop her thread. I grab it before it tumbles off the coffee table. "Thanks," she says.

I give her a sympathetic glance. "Cracked scalp?" I remember my mom furiously itching over breakfast every time she'd bleach her sandy blonde hair a couple shades lighter, trying to imitate Reese Witherspoon or Cameron Diaz. She'd twitch in pain and spill milk on the counter or coffee on the floor.

"Cracked and now seared to a crisp because of the bleach," she replies. I nod understandingly. Paige pushes her hair behind her ear, and I can't help noticing how stiff and frayed it is. I'm honestly surprised she still *has* hair, what with her dyeing it every two weeks.

"Why do you do it?" I wonder out loud. "Change your hair so often, I mean."

"To express my inner pain."

She gives me a dramatic look. It's pretty convincing, and it's Paige. She's probably serious. I restrain myself from gagging over the teenage-cliché factor.

"Just kidding," she says, winking and cutting her thread. "I do it to piss off my parents." She tosses the costume to Abby, who doesn't catch it. The dress knocks a deck of cards to the floor, and I hear Charlie groan.

Paige rolls her eyes. Collecting the dress, she pulls Abby from her chair and ushers her into the bathroom, ordering her to try on the costume.

I'm left with volume one of *Saga*, the comic Paige dropped in front of me when I got here and ordered me to read. I'm enjoying the plot, I have to admit. On the couch, Grant has his book open. *Romeo and Juliet*, I read on the cover. But he's not turning the pages, and every couple minutes his gaze darts to Hannah, who's talking to WINTER IS COMING guy.

It's unexpected, how at home I feel here. I couldn't have imagined myself weeks ago in this dusty bookstore with this group of people. It's nothing like the afternoon would have looked with Morgan and Elle, whom I realize with a touch of remorse I haven't hung out with in a while. We'd probably be in Starbucks, ordering Frappuccinos, and I'd be listening to Elle detail her newest sponsorship and Morgan rave about her weekend on set. Instead, I'm reading a comic book next to a sewing machine and a board game I've never heard of—and I'm enjoying it just as much.

Hannah cheers when Abby comes out of the bathroom. Abby's in the French-maid costume, and she spins, showing off how perfectly it fits. I catch Grant scowling, evidently jealous of Hannah's enthusiasm.

"Paige," Hannah squeals, "you're amazing. We're definitely going to win."

Paige gives a dramatic bow. Despite the exaggeration of the gesture, I read genuine pride on her face. "I'm devoted to the cause," she tells Hannah. She returns to our corner and drops into a chair.

"Win?" I ask.

"Yeah, for *Rocky Horror*," Paige replies. "There's a costume contest. The winners get to go on stage for 'Time Warp,'" she adds, like I have any idea what she's talking about. "Hannah's *really* into it."

"Does everyone dress as a character?"

"Yeah, well, not exactly. People sometimes just put on whatever outrageous, sexy stuff they can find. Whatever's *Rocky*-worthy." Paige pauses, her eyes finding mine. "Wait. Why do you want to know?"

I look at Hannah, fussing over Abby's costume, and feel a grin forming on my face.

Twenty-One

I'M HEAVING MY ETHICS TEXTBOOK FROM MY locker on Monday morning when I glimpse two words on a piece of paper under my books. *NOT INTERESTED.* I blink. I'd forgotten I kept the note inviting Brendan to lunch.

I pause in front of my open locker. People pass me in the hallway, heading toward their classes, conversations ending in classroom doorways. I have a few minutes. Biting my lip, I impulsively remove the note from under my book pile and pull a pen from my bag.

Below Brendan's *NOT INTERESTED*, I write, *How about now?*

Throwing my locker closed, I walk quickly toward the other end of campus. The robotics room is still empty when I open the door and dart to Brendan's desk. I neatly place the note on his keyboard.

I pass the first half of the day in anticipation. It's a different kind of anticipation from the last time I left the note on Brendan's computer. I'm not just eager to accomplish a goal, to check an item off a list. Honestly, I enjoyed hanging out with Brendan. I hope he enjoyed hanging out with me enough not to *hate* the idea of joining me and my friends for lunch. I've had enough of him hiding his pretty outgoing personality in the robotics room.

Ethics, Economics, English—the morning drags by while I think of what I can talk to him about and how I'll explain this development to Elle. When the bell rings for lunch, I hurry to collect my lunch from my locker and head to our table on the patio, irrational excitement pumping in me the whole way.

Elle describes her concept for a new video. Brad tries to enlist her and Morgan in being bailiffs for his mock-trial competition. I wait with growing frustration, watching five, ten, fifteen minutes go by on my phone's clock.

He's stood me up. Again.

I know I shouldn't care. I hardly know Brendan. Yet in the next instant, I'm grabbing my bag in a huff and getting to my feet with a hasty explanation to my friends. "Excuse me. I have to go set an idiot straight."

Elle perks up. "Need backup?" she asks sympathetically.

"I got this," I mutter, already on my way.

I head down the stairway, thread through lunch tables in the courtyard, and walk with purpose through the science hall until I'm in front of the robotics room. Without hesitation, I fling open the door. Brendan's hunched over the computer, his back to me. He's the only person in here, and he's working half in the dark.

"Brendan," I call. "Seriously?"

He whirls, looking startled. Finding only me, he relaxes. Not a reaction I'm used to provoking, but whatever. "Oh, hey, Cameron," he says.

"That's it?" I stride up to his desk. "Did you not get my note? I left it right on your stupid keyboard."

"I got it." He sounds bewildered. He pats the journal next to the computer, where the note sits on top of the cover.

I stare for a moment, waiting for further explanation. "*And?*" I demand when none comes. "What, you're too cool to have lunch with me and my friends?"

Brendan grins, impossibly. He's *enjoying* this. "I had no idea it mattered this much to you."

"Oh, shut it." His eyebrows flit up in amusement. "We hung out at the college fair. We text," I charge on. "It's obvious you don't hate me anymore. Why won't you just have lunch with me?"

His features cloud over. "Did you only ask me because you think it'll make me more popular?"

I expected the question. "Maybe," I reply. "Or *maybe*, despite my expectations, I actually enjoy talking to you, you weirdo."

Brendan laughs once, genuine and involuntary. "Thank you?"

"You're welcome," I huff.

He pauses a moment, like he's weighing his words. "You're . . . not the worst to talk to, either," he eventually says.

"Obviously," I say, hiding how pleased I am by his admission. Pulling a stool over from one of the tables, I take a seat beside Brendan. Easily, like I belong here, I unwrap my sandwich.

"What're you doing?" He watches me uncomprehendingly.

"Eating my lunch," I reply. "You've given me no choice." I

reach into the brown paper bag resting on my knee. "Carrot?"

"I'm . . . good." He hesitates, his eyes wandering to his computer. He opens his mouth, and I realize he's going to ask me to leave.

Which I have no intention of doing. Not when we're having our fourth halfway normal conversation. I preempt him. "Show me what you're working on," I say, nodding toward his game.

Clearly caught off guard, he stares for a second, a combination of emotions I can't decipher in his eyes. "I'll do one better," he finally declares. "Want to play it?"

The offer surprises me. "Video games aren't really my thing," I say, realizing a moment later it didn't exactly come out gently. "No offense," I add hurriedly.

But Brendan pulls my stool forward. Our knees briefly touch, the skin of my leg brushing the worn denim of his jeans. Before I have time to wonder if the contact was intentional, he's pushed me in front of the keyboard. "Here." His voice is low.

He places his hand on mine. I hadn't realized how cold my hands were until I feel the warmth of his. Gently, he moves my right hand to the mouse and guides my left to the keyboard. Stunned, I don't resist. His fingers linger a second on mine, and I find I'm holding my breath.

Okay, video games might not *not* be my thing.

"Now try not to die," Brendan tells me.

"Wait, what?" The question has hardly passed my lips when the computer screen comes to life. I find my character in the hallway of a school, wearing a black baseball hat and toting a ridiculously hefty sword. Helplessly, I watch what look to be zombie teachers come out of the room marked TEACHERS' LOUNGE. They circle my character, and he flashes red when they bite into him. In under a minute, I'm dead. "That was totally unfair," I complain, rounding on Brendan—who's holding in laughter.

"Use the keys to move. Click to use your sword," he says gently. "Here, try again."

I do. This time I manage to run away for a minute before I get killed. On my fifth try, I kill one. I give an involuntary whoop, which echoes in the empty room. Brendan cheers with me. A mummified basketball player pops up behind me, and I dispatch him easily. "Okay, I sort of understand the appeal," I say. "The virtual stabbing is oddly satisfying."

"I don't know if you're aware how disturbing you just sounded," he replies.

I pull out my sandwich while Brendan takes my place in front of the keyboard. He opens up a toolbar, and I watch him fiddle with the settings. It's quiet for a few minutes, a restful, comfortable quiet. "See?" I say. "This isn't terrible, is it?"

"What?" He faces me.

"Having lunch with another human being."

His smile fades. "No, it's not terrible," he says.

"Then come sit with me," I implore.

"I want to. It's just . . ." His eyes return to his computer. "I really do have to work on my game. I'm not allowed to when I'm home."

"What do you mean?"

"My parents—my dad, really, doesn't love my interest

in game development. Computer games won't get me into colleges with good financial aid. They won't get me scholarships," he continues. I remember he's on scholarship here at Beaumont, too. "When I'm home, I'm expected to study. If I were caught doing this . . . I don't know, he'd be pretty upset. It's just easier if I work on the game here. Besides, getting scholarships *is* important."

"Not if you can't study what you're interested in," I find myself replying almost instantly. I start to tell him scholarships and finances aren't worth giving up his passion, but I stop myself. Sometimes choosing financial security *is* responsible, like I'm doing with Wharton. Even if you might have other interests, too. Other dreams.

He shrugs. It's not a carefree gesture, rather one weighted with resignation. "I make time," he says simply.

I say nothing, realizing, for the first time, that I understand Brendan. Understand why he confines himself in here even though he could easily have friends. It's like Paige said: it's his choice. A choice he's been forced into, but a choice he's made to pursue his passion.

"Well, surely you can have fun occasionally." I bump his shoulder playfully.

His lips twitch. "Occasionally."

"Good." I reach for the controls. "Because I want to kill more zombie teachers."

Brendan laughs, his features brightening. He leans over me to reload the game, and I notice that the tension normally in his shoulders is gone. Then, grinning, he takes a carrot from my bag.

Twenty-Two

I WALK INTO MY MOM'S CLOSET IN my running clothes after school. I have only a few minutes before Andrew and his mom get here for dinner—and much more importantly, for Andrew's and my run.

The closet's a mess. I push past dresses and jackets smelling of mothballs, packed way too tightly, and falling halfway off the hangers. I shove aside empty shoeboxes, remove old shopping bags and fling them onto the floor outside the closet. I ignore the unopened carton of Healthifex cleanse powder in one corner.

Finally, I find what I'm after. The cardboard box is pushed deep into the far end of the closet, its corners flattened from years of having things piled on top. I have to wrestle it free. When I do, a cloud of dust follows me out into the bedroom.

I fold open the cardboard flaps, holding my breath because I know I'm going to sneeze. I recognize immediately the white feather boa on top of the box's contents. I remember putting it back in the box when I was ten years old. I'd play dress-up with the clothes inside, parading through the living room pretending to be my mom while she got ready for performances. I feel a wave of longing—to be younger, to want to be my mom, to watch her chasing her dream before she decided it was behind her.

I pull out the boa, and with it I put aside a flapper dress and a pair of ruby slippers. I have something specific in mind. I spent the afternoon researching *Rocky Horror* on the internet. I'd planned on watching the movie itself, and at lunch I asked Hannah if I could borrow her copy. Part of me hoped it might be the thing to get her to have a conversation with me.

It half worked. She looked me up and down, hesitating, her expression conflicted. I knew her desire to avoid me was warring with her intense fandom for *Rocky Horror*.

"If you really want to do this," she said finally, "your first viewing has to be with an audience. It's the only way to really understand *Rocky*."

I'm curious what exactly I'm getting into, but I didn't want to ignore the first thing Hannah's said to me since the parking lot. I dutifully avoided the movie and kept my research to Google, which in turn led me to some admittedly disconcerting fan forums. In a couple hours, I had a good idea of how I could put together a costume.

From the box on my mother's bedroom floor, I remove what I'm looking for: a woman's tux jacket with tails, complete with a frilly dress shirt. My mom wore the outfit on a kick-line ten years ago. She let me try the jacket on in the dressing room while she did her makeup. I hardly remember the performance. I do remember the cherry lollipop Mom got me in the lobby on our way in, and I remember the way the actresses would bustle in and out between acts for quick changes and retouches. It had felt unbelievably grand and glamorous at the time.

"Cameron?"

My mom's voice pulls me from the memory. I fold the jacket in my arms and turn toward the doorway, where she's waiting with one hand on the frame. Her eyes move from me to the box on the floor, and she frowns.

"What are you doing with that?" she says. "Andrew and Deb will be here any minute."

"Can I borrow some of this stuff?" I ask.

Mom walks into the bedroom, eyeing what I have in my hands. "I don't know why you'd want to," she says, an edge entering her voice, "but okay." She stares into the box on the floor for a long second, then the boa on the bed. Her frown deepens. Finally, she averts her eyes. "Throw everything away when you're done."

I turn to face her quickly, stung by her resignation. "Come on, you don't mean that," I implore. Reaching into the box, I take out the black satin dress she wore for her only starring role. She played an heiress in a small, critically acclaimed short film. "This stuff is great."

She reluctantly places a hand on the dress I'm holding, fingering the fabric, her eyes straying like she's remembering. "Your father came to the screening we had in L.A.," she says after a moment. "It was our second date." She drops her hand from the dress. "For all the good that brought me."

I blink, pushing down her painful implication. "You can't get rid of all this," I try again. "You were really great. Remember this play?" I hold up a 1940s evening gown. The play was

And Then There Were None. I remember the murders even if I wasn't old enough to understand the plot.

I'd thought my mother, under the lights in her gown and pearls, was the most beautiful woman in the world. I was six.

"I remember. Your father was in town," she replies, her voice turning cold. He was, and I was dropped off for a conveniently timed sleepover with Morgan following the play. I only realized why a few years ago, once I'd come to expect the extra layers of bitterness and depression I'd find in my mom every time I came home after. Every time he rejected her after briefly rekindling whatever screwed-up semblance of a relationship they had.

"Your father said I wasn't right for the part," she reminds me.

"He was wrong. I remember," I say. I don't know how often I've wished I could just erase from the fabric of time every awful thing my dad's said to her.

She laughs ruefully. "What did you know? You were just a kid." She walks to the door. I will her to pause, to retract her words, to say she's proud of her past on stage. To grow a spine. "Take whatever you want. I'll toss the rest," she says instead. "No use holding on to that dream. Your dad was right. He always is," she adds and leaves the room.

I hear her walk down the hall to the kitchen.

I stare down into the open box.

Before I've even decided what I'm doing, I'm packing every scattered piece of clothing back into the box. The feather boa goes in on top of the slippers and the satin dress. I'm charged with defiance—defiance of my mother, who let her dream die, and defiance of my father, who crushed the life out of it with a million cruelties.

I fold the flaps closed and haul the box to my room, where I push it under my bed, hiding it behind old yearbooks and shoes I inherited from Elle and Morgan. I stand upright, looking for something in my room to straighten, to dispel my stress. I shuffle the small pile of recent homework on my desk, revealing the Wharton brochure from the college fair. I hastily close it and put it in a drawer, not wanting to dwell on the future the representative laid out for me—the future I'm beginning to doubt my place in.

I'm pulling my hair into a high ponytail when I hear the front door open. Deb's voice echoes down the hall, greeting my mom.

I fly into the front room and find Andrew waiting in the doorway, dressed in his running shorts and shoes and a Beaumont shirt. He's holding a plastic bag I know contains clothes to change into before dinner. When he catches sight of me, he smiles.

Day made.

"Want to go?" he asks.

The moms have moved into the kitchen, where they're gossiping at full strength. I hear mention of Laura Walter's dad drunkenly hitting on waitresses at a fund-raiser. "Definitely," I tell Andrew, and we're out the door.

It feels exactly like I hoped it would. We leave in the direction of our normal route. It's sunset, and the sky, behind a tangle of telephone wires and streetlights, is breathtaking. Even this far from the beach, the light paints the evening a vibrant gradient of oranges and violets. To warm up, Andrew and I jog the hill from my house to the corner.

When we hit flat ground, I pick up the pace. I'm expecting Andrew to fall in step behind me. Instead, he matches my stride, catching me off guard. We run side by side in the direction of Olympic Boulevard. I push the pace, forcing myself to run faster and faster.

I keep waiting for him to drop back. He doesn't.

Finally, I notice I'm winded, and we're running much faster than we usually do.

"Damn, you really haven't slacked off," Andrew says, echoing my thoughts.

Wondering what it means that he's not running behind me, I ease off the pace, and we come to a corner where we have to wait for the light. "What?" I chide. "Don't tell me you're out of shape. Doesn't your coach have you do distance runs?" I glance at him when I bring up the team, nudging the conversation in the direction of what I know he's told Paige.

He laughs, and I feel a thrill of hope. "Oh, he loves distance runs. The rest of the team not so much." I wait for him to go on, to elaborate.

We jog in place until the light changes. "Do you like your teammates?" I ask after a minute. I jump sidewise to avoid a fallen palm frond.

"Yeah, well enough," he says.

A three-word response. I'd sigh in frustration if I weren't winded. "I know some of those guys can be hard to be around," I offer. "Sometimes I think they only care about the next party."

"I guess," Andrew says neutrally. "They're all right. You should come to a game," he adds, and I feel my heart jump.

"I'd love to," I say enthusiastically.

"You could try to get Paige to come," he goes on. "She's made some vow never to attend an organized sporting event."

"Oh," I say. My heart crashes to the ground like a dancer who's lost her footing. "Yeah. That would be fun. We could maybe watch a movie or TV afterward," I suggest, recovering. "I just started *Sherlock*, and I'm dying to watch the next one."

I watched the whole thing, actually. When *Doctor Strange* came out, I went on a pretty bad Benedict bender. But Andrew doesn't know that.

"*Sherlock*'s pretty cool," Andrew replies, not even glancing in my direction. I feel frustration rising in my chest again. What does he want to hear? Why does everything he's interested in bringing up to Paige fall flat when it comes from me? "Or we could hang out at another party," he suggests.

I feel my stride falter. "You'd want to?"

Andrew's steps slow. "As friends for now," he says carefully. "But . . . I'm beginning to feel like I misjudged you, Cameron. I'm not saying I'm ready for something more. Not yet. But . . . sometime. I hope." He gives me a smile, which I find myself returning.

We run in silence, passing palm trees on our left. It's a few moments before I notice he's running behind me, the way he used to.

But the frustration hasn't entirely subsided. I should feel happy, satisfied, validated. He's almost ready to give me a second chance. It's exactly what I wanted. Exactly what

I've planned for. Instead, my mind circles on unanswered questions. If what we have is real, or if it's ever going to be, wouldn't he want to share his worries, insecurities, and interests with me the way he does Paige? Why doesn't he want to know what interests me, what worries me? And, if we're going to be more than friends, why is it always me working my hardest to be enough for him?

Real love is never easy. I remind myself of my mother's words.

They're more hollow comfort than they were the day she said them.

I struggle to find my stride, my breath pinched and feet heavy. We only get half our usual distance before I tell Andrew I want to turn back. We head for home, the sun dipping into twilight.

Twenty-Three

I CROSS THE FINISH LINE IN FIRST place in our Wednesday cross-country meet. For the first time I can remember, there's no one in the stands waiting for me.

I wipe the sweat from my face, feeling it stick to me in the uncomfortable October sun. Finishing my stretches on the red rubber of the Beaumont track, I fight wishing my friends were here. It feels juvenile, and I know they have good reasons. Morgan's out of town for the week, filming on location in Vancouver. Elle told me she had to work on her next video—which I'll admit was an unusual excuse. She's never skipped one of my races, not even the time she got mono. Part of me twists uncomfortably, wondering if Elle resents the time I've spent with Paige's group instead of her and my other friends. I have to find a way to bring them together.

I won't pretend I'm not a little lonely without Elle and Morgan here. I pull off my gray sweatband, a birthday gift from Andrew a couple years ago, along with the thoroughly worn Nikes on my aching feet. Wringing the band in my hands distractedly, I watch my teammates join up with family and friends for congratulatory hugs. Wrestling down resentment, I walk in the direction of the locker room, unable to keep myself from searching the bleachers in irrational expectation of finding my friends. I recognize Leila's younger sister, who's a sophomore, and—

Brendan?

He's sitting on the bottom bleacher, right behind the low green chain-link fence separating the stadium concrete from red rubber. Our eyes meet, and he grins. He's not on his phone or watching other runners. He's sitting on his own, expectant. Like . . . he's waiting for me.

I walk up to him. "Are you here for me?" The question comes out blunter than I intended, and I'm struck with self-consciousness. If he's not here for me, this isn't a good look.

"Of course not." Brendan watches me, running a hand through his curls. "I'm a *huge* cross-country enthusiast. I'm amazed you didn't know that about me."

A winded laugh escapes me. "You do constantly surprise me." I'm joking, yet the moment the words leave my lips, I realize how true they are. First his quiet but unwavering confidence when he was rejecting my apologies, then his sense of humor, then his easy charisma with the MIT rep.

"I stayed after school to work on *The Girl's a Sorceress*," he explains. He stands up from the bleachers, and we walk together toward the locker rooms. "I had time before my dad expects me home and decided I'd come watch. You're fast," he says, eyeing me. "I'm trying not to be intimidated by your obvious athleticism."

"A girl has to do something to impress the boys who stay late to work on their video games," I reply without thinking.

Brendan raises an eyebrow. I meet his gaze evenly. Flirting

with Brendan just . . . happens, and it's not worth fighting. It's harmless. I know I like Andrew. I view flirting with Brendan as practice for him, for when he's no longer unpopular—thanks to me—and he needs to know how to handle himself with girls drawn to his tall frame and defined jaw.

"Well, thank god you're good at running," he says. "Because before I saw this, I really felt bad for you. You're thoroughly unimpressive otherwise."

I shove him playfully. We round the corner, and a clash of colors catches my eye. On the bulletin board beside the door to the boys' locker room, flyers posted on top of each other in explosive hues create an unexpected collage of lines and lettering. Intrigued, I pull my phone from my armband and take a picture.

Brendan follows when I continue in the direction of the girls' locker room. "If I'm so unimpressive, then explain why you've hung out with me three times now," I say, staring up at him challengingly.

"Wait, what was that?" Brendan asks, his brows coming together with curiosity. "Why did you take a picture of the bulletin board?"

"Oh, it's nothing," I say haltingly. I didn't expect he'd be interested. "I just thought the fonts and textures were cool. I sometimes draw inspiration from stuff like this when I design websites."

"Websites?" Brendan's eyes light up. We're in front of the locker room now, but I don't go in.

"Really, it's boring," I say. "I do web design as a hobby is all."

Brendan looks at me with new interest. "Can I see one?"

I toe the concrete uncomfortably, my cheeks heating. I'm not used to sharing my design work outside my closest friends. "It's really not a big deal."

"God, Cameron," he says, shaking his head. "Like I said. Thoroughly unimpressive."

I laugh. The discomfort drains from me in an instant. "Hey," I say, wringing my headband in my hands. "Thanks for coming to my race." There's obviously no way he knows what it meant to me, with my friends not here and everything. But he chose to come here with his extra time, without knowing if I'd even want to hang out with him. It means something. I don't know what.

He shrugs. "You played my game."

"Yeah, but that was fun. This was just a boring race."

"Believe me," Brendan says, "I wasn't bored." He heads back toward campus, leaving me chewing my lip, trying to stop the stupid smile spreading on my face.

Twenty-Four

THE BELL RINGS HALFWAY THROUGH ENGLISH ON Friday. Kowalski cuts off her exhilarating lecture on essay thesis statements and reluctantly instructs us to walk down to the gym for a pep rally.

I'm out of my seat immediately. Elle flew up to San Francisco for the day to film a collaboration video with a YouTuber she describes as frustratingly popular. While everyone begins to pack up and file out, I wait for Paige by the door. Andrew walks past me, dressed in his Beaumont soccer polo, his chest a little puffed up in a way he doesn't try to hide.

"Don't let the fact that the entire school is required to celebrate you go to your head," I say to him. I meant the comment to come out flirtatiously, but there's something empty in it. I don't know if Andrew hears it.

He doesn't seem to. "I won't," he says, smiling over his shoulder and leaving the room to a smattering of applause from the class.

Beaumont is generally terrible when it comes to sports. We have a student body of two hundred, and we don't have athletic scholarships. We're not exactly a powerhouse. The one exception is boys' soccer. They went to the California championships last year, and while they didn't win, they might as well have for how excited everyone was. They're the only team on campus that inspires school spirit. To celebrate the kickoff of their season this year, the headmaster declared a school-wide pep rally.

Paige meets me in the doorway. We walk into the hallway together, joining the mob of everybody filing out of their fourth-period classrooms.

"*Rocky* this Sunday," she reminds me. "You really don't need help with your costume?" She holds open the hallway door.

I shake my head. "I'm good," I say. "Have you, um, told everyone I'm coming?"

We file into the gym. It's chaos, our two hundred classmates crammed into the echoing, high-ceilinged space. "Everyone loves you," she reassures me. "It'll be fine."

I give her a look.

"Okay, Hannah hates you," she corrects herself. "But it's all worked out."

We push toward two empty seats on an aisle near the front of the bleachers. The school settles in, the collective sound of a hundred conversations about college and Halloween and hallway gossip coming to a clamor. The cheerleaders form a line on the court, where the teachers and the soccer team sit. Andrew watches the crowd, his eyes bright. He looks better than ever. I find my gaze wandering to the bleachers, to everyone fighting for seats, before it comes to rest on a tall figure on the opposite end.

Brendan's looking at his phone, ignoring everything going on around him, or trying. He pockets his phone and turns to survey the crowd disinterestedly. I wait, wondering what he's looking for.

His eyes find mine, and a slight smile lifts the corners of his mouth. He glances down, and a moment later, I feel my phone vibrate.

Hi.

I roll my eyes *very* obviously. Fighting the pleased flush rising in my cheeks, I reply.

Hi.

The band erupts into the fight song, which no one knows, and Brendan faces front. I notice Grant playing trumpet in the second row. The soccer coach walks up to the podium, and conversations change into whispers.

"Ugh," Paige groans next to me. "I do everything I can to escape the inanity of campus athletics, and yet I get pulled out of my favorite class to witness *this*. Sports are the worst. No offense."

The cheerleaders start a "Go Beaumont" chant, and I join in, pointedly cheering in Paige's ear, earning a scowl. "Get over yourself," I reprimand her jokingly. "Sports are fun."

Paige shakes her head, unable to hide the grin behind her grimace. "Sometimes I don't understand how you can be friends with me and my brother," she says.

"I question it, too, sometimes," I reply, and Paige punches me in the shoulder.

The coach leaves the podium, and the captain replaces him. I half listen to him hype the team's prospects for the season until he brings up their impressive new talent, and the crowd begins a new cheer. *"Rich-mond."* They're chanting Andrew's name, which he evidently notices, looking surprised if not entirely displeased.

"Go Andrew!" I hear next to me. I round on Paige, my eyebrows flying up. She doesn't meet my incredulous gaze, her eyes fixed on Andrew and written with feelings I can't decipher. I've never seen this side of Paige before, this eager, unironic enthusiasm.

"Andrew told me you and I should go to one of his games," I say, watching her carefully.

Her eyes don't leave Andrew. "What? Oh, uh, yeah," she says distractedly. She turns to me, her expression shifting. She studies me with an uncomfortable seriousness. "I know you like him, Bright," she says. "I respect you, and I wouldn't want to—" She cuts herself off, her cheeks heating, and a knot forms in my stomach. Paige's feelings are obvious.

"Did you just say you respect me?" I ask, wanting to steer this conversation onto safer subjects. But instead of punching me in the arm again, Paige drops her eyes.

"I'm not an idiot, Bright," she says. "I know you're trying to repair things with Andrew, and I know he'd probably be impressed by you fixing things with people like me. But tell me one thing," she continues. "You're not just being my friend, being Brendan's friend, to win over Andrew, right?"

I can hear her hesitation, her fear. The knot in my stomach

clenches. Paige has figured it out. Of course she has. She saw right through me when I botched her apology in English. I should have guessed she'd know I had a purpose in righting my wrongs toward her and her brother.

I don't want her to think our friendship is only for Andrew, though.

The thought hits me with unexpected force. This all began with Andrew . . . but I'm no longer *only* doing it for Andrew. I don't want Paige to doubt whether I genuinely like her, or her brother, because truthfully, we are friends, however unimaginable the thought would've been to me months ago.

"I *like* being your friend. And Brendan's," I say carefully. "Whatever happens with Andrew, that won't change. I promise." It's the honest truth, even though it's not a direct answer to her question.

Paige nods, her expression guarded, no doubt understanding what I didn't say. Whatever she's thinking, she doesn't press it. "I don't hate being your friend, either," she informs me, and I know we're okay, or the weird kind of okay I've found with Paige over the weeks.

"Hey, Paige." Andrew's voice cuts between us. "Lunch?" he asks.

I turn, yanked from the conversation—which I'm realizing I was focused on enough not to notice that the pep rally is over. Everyone's getting up, heaving backpacks and Kate Spade bags onto their shoulders. The rest of the soccer team is still on the court. Andrew must have leapt up two rows of bleachers to reach us this fast.

Or rather, to reach Paige. His eyes find me and flicker with surprise.

"Oh, hey, Cameron," he says stumblingly. "You want to come, too?"

It's an afterthought. I hear the reservation in his voice. I've been on the inviting end of enough insincere lunch plans to recognize he's reluctant to have me join him and Paige. Uncomfortable, even.

Which . . . bothers me, but it's not crushing.

I stand, waving off the offer. "You guys go," I say. "I'm going to hang with Morgan. Then I might drop in on Brendan."

"You sure? You're welcome to come," Paige replies, and at the same time, Andrew says, "You're having lunch with Brendan now?" He sounds slightly . . . jealous?

I don't give myself the chance to dwell on it. "I'm good," I say to Paige, then turn to Andrew. "From time to time. Turns out I kind of like video games." His eyebrows twitch up. "Want to run again on Monday?" I continue evenly.

"Definitely," he says.

I climb down the bleachers, Paige and Andrew a few feet behind me. We file out with the crowd, and I can't help glancing over my shoulder, watching them together. Paige laughs at something Andrew says, her cheeks flushing a pleased pink. I face forward, leaving them to whatever joke they're sharing.

Paige likes him, and I have no idea how I feel about it.

Twenty-Five

PAIGE'S HOUSE IS ORDINARY. IT'S IN CULVER City, on a wide street lined with enormous trees. Their hulking limbs have littered the pavement with endless brown leaves. It's quiet here, way quieter than Hollywood or where I live. I notice half a dozen cars in front of the curb, including Paige's beaten-up black sedan. The house is one story, with chipping paint and overgrown hedges.

It's nothing like the rest of my classmates' homes. Refreshingly, I have to say.

I walk up the paved path to the front door on Sunday night, the bag containing my costume under my arm. It's Halloween weekend, and trick-or-treaters prowl the streets. I knock on the door next to a gaggle of Elsas from *Frozen*.

"I'll help you with your corset in a minute, Grant," Paige's voice calls from inside, followed by footsteps. She opens the door dressed in a black suit jacket and white button-down unbuttoned enough to reveal her nude-colored bra. I feel my eyebrows rise when I take in her wig. It's pale and stringy with a big bald patch on the top of her head. I vaguely recognize the costume from my *Rocky* research. She drops a couple pieces of candy in the Elsas' pillowcases, and they run off giggling.

"Wow, your wig is incredible," I say. "It looks so real."

Paige holds the door open for me. "It is," she says.

In the entryway, I round on her. "What?" She's grinning like this is the response she hoped for. "You shaved a *bald* patch on your head?"

"It's going to be the next big trend," she says easily. I gape. Paige bursts out laughing. "Oh my god, it's for Riff Raff. The character," she clarifies. "I'm going to shave the rest of my head when we get back from the movie."

"Okay, when I said I wanted to be a part of this," I warn, "you know I wasn't volunteering to permanently change my appearance, right?"

Laughing, Paige leads me into the living room. The house is impeccably tidy, the shelves dust-free, nothing except a book of photography on the coffee table. I follow her into the hallway, past framed baby pictures of her and Brendan in perfectly coordinated outfits. We reach what could only be Paige's bedroom door—there's a poster on it of two vampire guys gazing lovingly into each other's eyes, one dark-haired and brooding and the other peroxide blond. I hear weird accordion music from past the door and a nasally voice singing about urchins in a priory.

"Don't worry, Goldilocks," Paige says, hand on the door. "Cameron Bright without blonde hair would upend the order of the universe."

Paige opens the door, and my comeback dies on my tongue. Four pairs of eyes find mine. Grant's, Charlie's, and Abby's hold open confusion, and it dawns on me that Paige didn't tell them I was coming. I knew she was full of it when she said it was all "worked out."

In Hannah's expression I find only fury. "You're joking, Paige," Hannah says harshly. "Please tell me this is a prank and not Cameron Bright in your bedroom right now." She drops the glue gun onto the costume she's working on repairing in her lap. I can't help noticing that Paige's room is a complete mess. Clothes piled on top of and around a hamper, her dresser covered in papers and empty water bottles and figurines I don't recognize, a sewing mannequin adrift in a pile of shoes in the corner. I cringe in spite of myself, checking the impulse to organize and declutter.

"You're the one who told me to experience *Rocky* live," I remind Hannah.

"I didn't mean with *us*," she fires back.

"Cameron's coming with us," Paige says. I recognize the authority in her voice from when she first brought me into the Depths of Mordor. "She's got a costume and everything."

Hannah gets up from Paige's bed abruptly, the glue gun and a handful of sequins falling to the floor. "If you think I'm hanging out with *her* tonight, you're crazy. I'll drive over by myself," she declares.

I'm hard to perturb, but the intensity of Hannah's glare makes me uncomfortable. I never wanted to ruin Hannah's event for her. Exactly the opposite. I reach for something I can say, a justification or a compromise or even a plea. Before I open my mouth, I hear Paige.

"Hannah, that's enough," she orders. I give her a surprised

glance. "When have we ever told people they can't hang out with us or experience our amazing fandoms?"

Hannah throws a hand in my direction. "Come on, Paige, she's—"

"Yeah, I know. She's Cameron Bright," Paige interrupts. "She's done shitty things. She's not perfect. Who is? *We've* messed up, each of us. Grant cheated on you, and we hang out with him. No offense, Grant." She darts an apologetic look in Grant's direction.

Grant shrugs genially. "None taken."

"I'm not blameless, either. I blew off trivia night to go to a party held by a spoiled cheerleader I've never talked to and hooked up with piece-of-shit Jeff Mitchel."

Hannah goes quiet. In her expression I watch resistance collide with understanding.

"If Cameron wants to experience *Rocky Horror* for the first time in her life," Paige continues, "I'm not going to say no."

There's a long pause. Everyone stares at Hannah, waiting. I don't dare move, not wanting to draw attention to myself. I'm kind of unable to believe Paige stuck up for me like that. Even if Hannah kicks me out and I completely fail in my goal for the night, it will have felt good to have heard Paige say what she did.

Abby speaks up hesitantly, her voice cutting the uncomfortable quiet. "Hannah, you did say it would be better if we had a couple more people in our group for the costume contest."

Hannah turns toward Abby. I watch her take in her friends, the way Charlie's pointedly concentrating on picking a thread from his costume and Abby's folded her arms like she's made up her mind. Even Grant doesn't meet Hannah's gaze. Finally, Hannah faces Paige, not sparing a look in my direction.

"Fine," Hannah says. "She better have a good costume."

Turning her back to me with thorny deliberateness, Hannah collects her costume from the floor and goes into the closet to change. I mouth a *thank you* to Paige, who gives me a wink. "Grant!" she says. "Corset time." Grant dutifully gets off the desk and follows Paige into the bathroom connected to her room.

"There's another bathroom in the hall," Abby offers.

"Thanks," I say gratefully.

I wander into the hall and find the bathroom. Closing the door, I place the costume on the floor and release an even breath in front of the mirror. I didn't realize how nervous I was until now.

I've never had to try to impress my classmates, to win them over. I've never known how it feels to *want* them to like me. With Paige and her friends, it's different. I want them to talk to me, to include me in their unusual interests. To not hate me.

I want to be their friend. Not for my amends list, not for Andrew. But because I like them.

They're not that different from my friends, I'm realizing. They're knowledgeable about their passions and fiercely devoted to them, and they won't take shit from anybody. The main difference—other than taste in clothes, movies, and pretty much everything—is the willingness of Paige's group to invite others into what excites them.

I check my phone. No messages.

I put on my costume, the woman's tux I took from my mom's box with a hideous glittery orange cummerbund I picked up from Party Central a couple days ago. I don't care how ridiculous I look. I only want to look good enough to help Hannah win the costume contest. There wasn't enough time for me to find the components for a lead character's costume, but I think I pulled together a pretty decent Transylvanian, one of the background ensemble I found in a couple images.

Nervously, I glance at my phone again. It remains black, and I begin to worry my plan's going to fall through.

I open the bathroom door and walk in the direction of Paige's room. I'm nearly there when I catch sight of a door cracked open—revealing Brendan. He's at his desk, working on the computer, predictably.

I knock. Without waiting for him to invite me in, I push the door open and barge into his room. Brendan swivels in his desk chair, his eyes widening when they find me. *"Cameron?"* His voice comes out an utterly charming squeak.

I close the door and walk brazenly over to the one open place where I can sit in his room: his bed. I gesture to what he's wearing, corduroys and a RAVENPUFF shirt. I feel a small swell of pride that I understand this one. I'm pure Slytherin, obviously. "You definitely can't wear that to *Rocky Horror*," I inform him.

Brendan's composure is far gone. His eyes dart from me to his pillows. I get the feeling he's completely unprepared for having a girl even remotely *near* his bed.

"I'm not going," he gets out eventually. "I'm surprised you are."

I shrug, surveying his room. It's not neat, exactly. It looks closer to uninhabited, like a model of a teenage boy's room constructed by a set designer with a shoestring budget. His desk is uncluttered. His bookshelves hold only textbooks and a row of novels. Two video game posters hang above his bed, *The Last of Us* and *Uncharted 2: Among Thieves*. In the corner of each I notice a logo with NAUGHTY DOG in heavy font and a red paw print.

"I'm not going for the movie," I say. "Honestly, it looks awful." The instant it's out of my mouth, I regret wording my opinion that openly. But when I look at Brendan, I find his lips curving upward humorously. "Paige says it's really about the rituals, not the movie," I go on. "I'm a bit nervous for the virgin-sacrifice part, I have to admit." I read about it online. Everyone who's never been to *Rocky* before gets forced into some kind of public humiliation. "But, hey, I'm already dressing up and going to hang out with a bunch of teenagers in lingerie in public. Can it really get more embarrassing?"

Brendan laughs. His posture relaxes a little. "You have strong opinions on stuff."

I stiffen, suddenly anxious. "I—" I falter. "I wasn't trying to insult Paige's event or whatever—"

"Don't worry about it," he says lightly. The anxiety rushes from me as quickly as it came. "It's cool. Having your own opinions, I mean. I like it." He smiles, and I find myself studying how it brightens his face in a way I never noticed. "Except when it's about how gross Barfy Brendan is," he adds.

"Was," I hastily amend. "You're not gross now. Not at all."

I blush when I say it. I don't know why.

"Engrave that on my tombstone," he jokes. I laugh, relieved he's broken the emotion of whatever *that* was. Brendan goes on. "Speaking of teenagers in lingerie—"

"Now that's a promising lead-in," I cut in.

Brendan grins. "You're dressed modestly for *Rocky*. I've had to watch Grant walk around in a corset and underwear and my own sister with her shirt upsettingly far open. Yet here you are in a tuxedo."

"This is Hannah's night," I say earnestly, ignoring the possibility he's suggesting he wishes I were wearing less. His face reveals nothing. "I didn't want to make it about me."

"About how hot you are, you mean," Brendan replies.

My eyebrows spring up. "So you admit it!" I can't ignore the thrill that runs through me, and not just because I've caught him after he's been trying to cover it up.

But Brendan shrugs, unfazed. "It's an objective fact, Cameron," he says easily.

I reach for words and come up empty. It would be cavalier coming from anybody, declaring I'm objectively hot. I'm doubly in disbelief because it's *Brendan* coming right out with it instead of dancing around the idea like he's done in our texts.

Before I figure out what to say, the door flies open and a tall man walks in without knocking. "1540, Brendan?" he says. This must be Brendan and Paige's dad, I assume from his gargantuan height and curly brown hair. Noticing me, he spares me a glance but continues like I'm not here. "You had a perfect score on the PSAT. What happened?" he interrogates Brendan.

I cut Brendan an impressed look. 1540 must be his SAT score, which is way higher than I scored.

But I read defeat on Brendan's face. "The Beaumont college counselor said 1540 is definitely enough for MIT," he says.

"I don't care what's *enough*," his dad returns. "I know you're capable of getting a perfect score. You demonstrated it on the PSAT. You know how many more scholarships you could earn with a 1600." He walks to the door. "You'll retake the test in December," he says, his hand on the knob. There's no hint of a question in his voice.

I study his uncompromising expression. Brendan's dad is definitely handsome, for being dad-aged. The hard line of his jaw, his straight and narrow nose. They're Brendan's features, drawn by years of responsibility and sharpened with an edge of cruelty. It's what sets them apart from his son's. I prefer Brendan's, kinder and gentler. I hope they stay that way.

"I have a heavy course load this semester," Brendan protests. I understand what he's not saying. He has the video game contest coming up, and either his dad doesn't know or Brendan's wise enough not to bring it up. "I don't have the time to study right now," he continues.

"Well, you might if you didn't spend your time playing video games," his dad shoots back. "If you'd studied enough the first time you took the test, we wouldn't be in this position. Say good-bye to your guest"—he nods in my direction without looking at me—"and spend the afternoon working on critical reading."

Brendan nods. I don't know if his dad catches the way Brendan's jaw tightens, like he's biting back a refusal.

Mr. Rosenfeld's voice softens, if only slightly. "I'm just trying to help you achieve everything I know you can," he says like it's a compliment and walks out of the room.

I hear Brendan exhale—in relief or frustration or both, I can't tell. Part of me doesn't want to look at him, in case he's embarrassed or wants time to himself. I felt my insides twist hearing his dad belittle Brendan's interest the way I did when we first talked. Not just from the unfairness of what Brendan's dad said but from guilt over my own words. What I said—*mindless video game*—would have reminded him of criticism he probably hears over and over when he's home. No matter how hard Brendan works to hide his interest in computer games, his dad probably picks up on the smallest signs and never lets them go. I know what it's like to have your dad's voice echoing in your head, wishing you could shut it out and failing.

"Sorry about that," Brendan says stiffly. He reaches for the SAT prep book on the shelf over his desk.

"It's okay," I say. Then before I know it, I hear myself add, "When I sent my dad my scores, he only said he'd hoped I'd get at least twenty points higher than I did, what with where he pays for me to go to school."

Brendan's eyes find mine. "When you sent—" he begins delicately, thinking. "Does your dad not live with you?"

"No. He lives in Philadelphia," I reply, feeling how weird it is to say it out loud. My friends barely know my family situation, and they've known me for years. I'm definitely not the *hi-nice-to-meet-you-here's-my-autobiography* type of person. I don't want pity, sympathy, preferential treatment. I haven't wanted to confide in anyone new. Not until now. "He and my mom never married. I've never lived with him. He only visits when he has business in town, which is, like, once a year."

Brendan watches me for a long second. "Your dad sounds like a dick."

He says it so evenly, so thoughtfully, I feel a laugh nearly escape my lips. The joke lifts a little weight from my chest. "Yeah, I guess he kind of is," I say. "He and your dad would probably get along."

Brendan gives a short laugh. "They would," he agrees.

"But really," I go on, "that was bullshit, Brendan. A 1540 is amazing, and *The Girl's a Sorceress* is too. Which is why"—I get up from his bed and walk to his desk, where I grab the SAT book and return it to the bookshelf—"you should blow off studying and come to *Rocky Horror* with us."

His expression's conflicted, but I can tell he's intrigued. "I can't do that," he says grudgingly.

"Of course you can," I urge. "Tell him you're going to study in the library and come witness my public humiliation. Virgin sacrifice, remember?"

Brendan chews his lip. "I don't even have a costume."

I smirk. I have exactly what I need to end this discussion.

I found *it* in Party Central and bought it on a whim just to see Brendan's reaction. I had no idea how perfect an opportunity he'd give me. I reach into my bag and pull out a shiny gold Speedo. I fling it onto Brendan's lap.

His mouth drops open, but before he can get out a reply, I feel my phone vibrate. I check it quickly. *Finally.*

"I'd like you to be there, Brendan," I say, walking to the door. I throw a meaningful look in the direction of the Speedo before I leave the room.

Twenty-Six

I RUSH TO PAIGE'S ROOM. THE DOOR'S open, and everyone's nearly in costume. Grant's in his corset, which has a new trim of lace. Abby's French-maid costume is perfect, just like the pictures I saw online. Charlie's vaguely disturbing in bloodstained operating-room scrubs with a pearl necklace. Everyone turns to me when I burst in the doorway.

"Come outside with me," I say quickly. "I have a surprise."

Nobody budges. Paige eyes me skeptically. Not exactly the reaction I'd hoped for.

"Trust me," I tell her.

Paige hesitates. I can't exactly blame her for doubting my intentions. I keep her gaze, throwing sincerity into my expression.

"Well, I'm curious," she finally says and walks to her door. Relieved, I wait while everyone else files past me into the hall. Even Hannah, who cuts me a suspicious glare.

I follow them out the front door, where a yellow van waits in Paige's driveway. I walk to the van's rear doors. "I was told there would be a costume contest tonight," I tell the group grandly. "Obviously, we have to win." I steal a glance at Hannah, whose brows, I'm pleased to find, have furrowed in confusion, not anger. "And no look could be complete without the perfect hair and makeup."

I throw open the doors with a flourish, revealing Elle. She sits at her mobile vanity, surrounded by racks upon racks of wigs and makeup, brushes and mirrors. Her "Elli" logo is painted on one wall, pink lips dotting the "i." In front of her she's taped up pictures of every *Rocky* character.

Everyone leans in for a look, impressed. Even Hannah's mouth drops open.

Elle watches them a little haughtily. "Who's first?"

Without hesitating, Abby climbs into the back of the van.

Elle gives her costume a once-over. "Magenta." Elle purses her lips, her eyes flitting to the corresponding picture on the mirror. "Fun. Great wig. Now, everyone out," she announces, waving her hand with a diva's drama. "I need space for my art." Everyone steps back, and I close the van doors.

I rejoin the group and find everyone chattering excitedly. I hear Grant, relieved, confessing he would have definitely screwed up his Frank-N-Furter makeup on his own. Charlie eyes me approvingly. "Cameron, this is awesome," he says. I nod demurely, inwardly pleased. Only Paige watches me with something less than gratitude.

She looks skeptical, even distrustful. I know what she's thinking. She already figured out I have an ulterior motive in Andrew. She's the only who knows that everything I'm doing here—coming to *Rocky*, bringing Elle—is part of a plan.

It hurts, not unexpectedly. I don't want Paige to be wary of everything I do for her. I want her to enjoy this. I want us *both* to enjoy this.

I pull her away from the group. "Everything okay?" I ask.

"Everything's fine," Paige says lightly. "I know you have an agenda here, and what you've put together here *is* really cool. I do appreciate it," she goes on. "I just hope you understand we're not just pieces to push around in whatever game you're playing." She gives a sad half smile. "When all this is done, I'd hate to have reason to think you're nothing but a cruel popular girl."

"I don't want you to," I reply quickly. "Look, I wouldn't be dressed like this, spending my Halloween watching the world's weirdest movie, if I didn't really want to."

Paige nods, and I'm hit again with the rush of nerves I felt sitting on the bleachers. I *don't* want to disappoint Paige. I genuinely enjoy hanging out with her, and that won't change regardless of whatever happens with Andrew and my amends list.

Pushing away questions of Paige and my project, I rejoin everyone by the rear of Elle's van. Every time one of the group climbs out of the mobile makeup studio, we cheer. We're loud enough I'd worry about the neighbors complaining if the block weren't full of running and screaming trick-or-treaters.

Elle transforms the group into perfectly powdered and glittering creations. When Grant emerges unrecognizable in his Frank-N-Furter costume, I catch Hannah's open admiration. Gawking in Grant's direction, she nearly stumbles climbing into the van.

Hannah's the final one of the group without her makeup, other than me. Not wanting to disturb Elle's process, I wait twenty minutes before I join them in the van. Hannah sits in front of Elle's mirror in bright red lipstick and a short red wig, her face powdered white. Elle, checking the picture on the mirror of Hannah's character—Columbia—for comparison, is drawing thin eyebrows over the patches she's used to cover Hannah's real eyebrows. Her reflection perfectly matches the picture of Columbia. It's uncanny.

Hannah doesn't acknowledge me when I walk in. But she says to Elle, "It was really cool of you to come out here for us."

"It's nothing." Elle waves the comment away with her pencil. "Besides, I got content out of it. Grant's the first guy to agree to be on my channel." Even under the heavy powder, I don't fail to catch the blush that colors Hannah's cheeks when Elle mentions Grant.

Hannah's eyes find mine in the mirror. "And it was ... nice of you to organize this, Cameron," she says. "Thank you." Even though she's grimacing, her voice grudging, her gaze doesn't waver.

I nod. I give Elle an indicative glance, which she catches, putting down her pencil. "I have to go wash my brushes," she says casually. She leaves the van, and it's only me and Hannah.

I rush into the speech I've prepared in my head. "Hannah, I know you said you don't blame me for what happened with Grant. That's not the point. You deserve an apology. What I did to you and Grant was wrong."

Hannah watches me in the mirror. "It's ... Thank you," she says uneasily. "It really is Grant's fault, though."

"I know," I say quickly. "I'm not taking responsibility for what he did. I'm not telling you to forget what he did, either. But, Hannah, do you still like him?"

Hannah's eyes drop.

I don't want to waste this opportunity. For the first time, she's listening to me. "If you do, consider forgiving him. Not for him, for yourself. Because *you* deserve it."

Hannah's gone quiet. I wait. There's nothing else I wanted to say. It's her decision now. And if she says she'll never forgive him, I'm not going to push them back together just to feel better about myself. Between Hannah and Grant, she's the one I wronged worse. If Grant doesn't get what he wants—getting back together with Hannah—he's going to have to be okay. Hannah's wish is worth more. I *know* she has feelings for Grant, but she could tell me right now she's not interested, and I'd say nothing more.

Hannah waits a long moment.

"Do you think he's changed?" she finally asks. Her voice is choked with tears.

I open my mouth, then close it. Hannah directly requesting my opinion on Grant isn't something I'd expected or planned for. "You know how Grant is. *Who* he is. He's a good guy," I say, feeling it genuinely. "He made a mistake with me when he was sixteen. We're teenagers. It's practically a requirement we make mistakes. He's never even looked at other girls since he cheated." I consider softening the word choice, dancing around the "C" word, and decide not to. Grant did cheat, and I'm not trying to get Hannah to forget it. She asked for my honest opinion, and if there's one thing I have to offer, it's honesty.

"Well"—Hannah gives me a pointed look—"he hasn't talked to me in weeks. Not after you started coming to Mordor."

I weigh her words, realizing . . . *shit*. I groan. "I'm an idiot. I'm sorry. Again," I add.

Hannah's eyebrows furrow, and I'm afraid she's going to screw up the patches Elle put on. "For what?"

"I told him he was coming on too strong," I confess, "and he should chill a little, give you space. I see now how that looked," I say regretfully. "I promise it's the last time I'll ever interfere in your relationship."

I'm expecting Hannah's ire or accusation. Instead, her expression only remains confused. "You guys talked about me?" she asks.

"Hannah," I say. "I know for a fact Grant would *gladly* talk about you to anyone who would listen. Grocery-store clerks, haircutters, whoever. It's a little annoying, actually. But sweet." I walk to the windows in the van's rear doors. "Look at him."

Hannah gets up from the stool and joins me. I point out the window. Grant's on the sidewalk outside, in a corset and high heels in broad daylight, parading in front of Paige's house and tunelessly singing "Time Warp" to himself. Every time he gets a word wrong, he curses to himself.

Hannah laughs, and for the first time she doesn't hide the smile Grant brings to her face.

"I'm not telling you what to do. It's just . . . he's obsessed with you," I say gently. "If a guy were ever willing to go to such embarrassing lengths for me, wouldn't I be an idiot for ignoring him?"

Her eyes remain fixed on Grant, who's now chasing his lyric sheet down the sidewalk and into the neighbor's hedges. Even I have to admit it's adorable.

"You know, Cameron," Hannah says, "for once, you might not be wrong."

Elle finishes off my makeup with a bright orange wig to match my cummerbund. I'm hideous. It's perfect. While she's packing up her collection of brushes and fake eyelashes and eyeliners, I thank her again for coming.

"No problem," Elle replies, climbing out of the van. I follow her to the driver's side door. "Are you going to explain what exactly you're doing with these people?"

I pick up the edge in the way she says "these people." When I texted Elle the idea of helping with *Rocky*, explaining how she could use the content for her channel, I'd waited for her reply with a kind of nervous excitement. Not that I expected she and Paige would become besties, but I'd hoped the event could bring together the two weird, incongruous halves of my social life. Elle had replied only, *ok. Where and when?* Which was indecipherable, but better than nothing.

I search her expression, but she's fixed her features in an unreadable mask. She gets into the driver's seat and closes the door hard. "Is there a problem with me hanging out with them?" I ask hesitantly through the open window.

"I don't care who you hang out with," she says sharply. "I don't care if you have a whole group of new friends." She darts a judgmental glance in their direction. "I just hope you remember I'm your *best* friend."

"Of course I do," I reply, caught off guard.

"Good," Elle says. "If this is because you've got the hots for Charlie Kim or BB or some other . . . socially challenged guy, I want to know first. Not Paige."

"Brendan," I correct.

"Really?" Elle's eyes widen. "You're into BB?"

"No, I—" Flustered, I fumble for words. "It's—I'm not into Brendan. I just call him Brendan now. The nickname I gave him, it's stupid."

"Huh." Elle narrows her eyes. "Well, okay. Brendan."

I smile reassuringly. "I'd tell you if I were into Brendan, or anybody new."

She eyes me, and my smile fades. Normally, now's when Elle would look pleased or haughtily joke about her unfortunate hookups with Elijah from marching band. Instead, she's stony, scrutinizing. Something's still off.

"Hey," I say, "would you want to come with?" I ask, nodding at the cars. "We could hang out."

"With them? No thanks." She turns the key in the ignition. "Have fun, though," she says. She pulls out of the driveway, leaving me to watch her taillights recede down Paige's block. I bite my lip, torn. Finally, I decide I can't worry about Elle tonight. I have a night of ridiculous costumes and virgin sacrifices to survive.

While Paige and Charlie haul a cooler out the front door, I walk to Paige's car, where Abby waits in the passenger seat. I gingerly climb into the back, careful not to disturb my wig or costume. I have to push aside piles of homework and a pair of mismatched Converse, and I can't help cringing. One of these days, I'm going to give Paige's car—and room—a good top-to-bottom organization.

"I can't believe it," Abby says under her breath.

"What?"

She points to the car in front of us, by Paige's mailbox and the trash cans lined up on the curb. I look. Grant sits behind the wheel, Hannah in the passenger seat next to him. Grant says something, and I watch Hannah laugh.

"Hannah *volunteered* to go in Grant's car," Abby says. "Either she really hates you or something's going on with those two."

Twenty-Seven

NIGHT IS FALLING WHEN PAIGE PULLS INTO wherever we're watching this movie. We pass manicured lawns and wrought-iron gates, and then what I realize are gravestones. "Wait," I say, startled. "We're watching the movie in a *cemetery*?"

Paige glances in the mirror. "Did I not mention that?" she asks coyly. She parks the car. "The Hollywood Forever Cemetery hosts the greatest, weirdest screenings."

I get out of the car, awestruck. Into the cemetery file hundreds of costumed Columbias, Magentas, Riff Raffs, and Frank-N-Furters, and with them people in wild costumes I don't recognize. It's a parade of neon-colored wigs, fishnets, and *elaborate* underwear. They walk toward the palm trees ringing the cemetery, heading for the open lawn where picnic blankets carpet the ground. Near the tombstones and mausoleums, people pose for pictures in their costumes. On the far end is a high, white wall, projected onto which is a pair of ruby-red lips.

"It's . . ." I falter, not finding words.

"I know," Paige says, smirking.

Grant's car pulls in next to ours while I'm watching a row of particularly perfect Frank-N-Furters walk into the cem-

etery. From the way they're handling their six-inch heels—
way better than I ever could—I figure they're probably
professional drag queens. A car door opens beside me, and
distantly I'm aware of Charlie, Grant, and Hannah climbing
out, and then a fourth person—in a shiny gold Speedo.

I whip my head around so fast my wig nearly falls off.
Brendan?

He stretches, his back to me, and I unabashedly gape. Besides the small and *very* tight Speedo clinging to areas I consciously try not to think about, he's essentially naked.

I focus on his neck. That's safe, I rationalize to myself. I've
seen his neck before. But then there's the spot where his neck
meets his shoulders, and—*wow*, he has great shoulders. From
there it only gets worse. His back is broad, not muscled exactly, but nice. Really nice.

Grant calls Brendan over to the trunk, and he turns in my
direction. I try to blink, to close my eyes, but it's possible I
no longer possess eyelids. There's nothing but Brendan all
the way down to the line of gold encircling that place on his
hips below his navel. Mercifully, my gaze doesn't stray lower.

Brendan pulls a cooler out of the trunk and heads for
where Paige is holding down our spot. On his way, he tosses
me a wink, and suddenly I'm incredibly parched. He looks
like Benedict Cumberbatch's younger brother, and I have no
idea what to do with that information.

Hannah comes up next to me. "Are you going to help?" she
asks, a note of amusement in her voice. "Or just gawk?"

"What?" I sputter. "I wasn't—"

Hannah giggles. "It's okay. He does look good." Brendan's

reached the picnic blankets, where he's bending down to put the cooler on the grass.

Bending *over*.

"I'm going to go unload the car," I say decisively.

I focus on collecting the shopping bags of candy from Paige's car. Red Vines, Mike and Ikes, Milk Duds. I'm entirely unready for even casual conversation with Brendan. I'm definitely not ready to unpack what he's doing to me in the Speedo I had no idea I was incredibly unwise to suggest he wear.

I busy myself with whatever will buy me time before I face Brendan. I arrange the sandwiches on plastic plates. I put out everyone's napkins and plastic cups. I walk to the trash can with the sandwich wrappers *extra slowly*.

But finally, when I'm eating a turkey on rye on the blanket while everyone else takes photos with other Riff Raffs and Franks, Brendan drops down beside me with a plate of roast chicken. I gulp and come close to choking. I'm expecting a joke or a pointed comment. God forbid he ask me how he looks.

Instead, when I give him a quick glance, he's watching the crowd with wonder or bewilderment or both. "This is . . . insane," he breathes. I can tell it's a compliment from the way he says it.

"It is," I say quickly, glad to avoid the subject of *his* costume. "Everyone put an unbelievable amount of effort into their costumes. They look awesome. Not as good as us, of course," I add.

"Of course," Brendan says. "For real, though, I can't believe how *hundreds* of people still make costumes and dress up, and this movie came out in the seventies. I could die happy if even one person cosplayed for one of my games." I watch him looking wistfully at the crowd, and I feel a grin playing at the corners of my lips. He's cute when he's expressing geek dreams.

I blink the thought away. This Speedo's obviously warped my thoughts beyond rationality.

"Thanks for inviting me." Brendan turns to me, his eyes bright. "I'm glad I got to be here. To experience this." He throws out a hand toward the field of brilliantly colored cos-tumes.

I feel a burst of courage, and the words are out before I can contain them.

"*I'm* glad I got to see you in your costume."

Brendan beams. He reclines on the blanket, revealing the long, pale stretch down to his waistband. I roll my eyes, but I'm blushing under my makeup.

"I didn't think you'd wear it," I say challengingly.

"I know," Brendan replies. "It's why I had to. I can go change, though," he adds hastily.

"God, no." *Wow*, I really need to work on controlling this honesty thing.

Brendan raises an eyebrow. I dart my gaze from his—and then turn back to face him, because why not? I'm popular, and Brendan's a junior. I have the high ground here.

"Like I said," I drawl, "definitely not gross now."

Brendan props himself up on one elbow. And without a word, he runs his eyes down the length of my figure very deliberately.

Brendan Rosenfeld is checking me out. When his eyes return to mine, I feel a flush inch up my cheeks.

"Hey," he says suddenly. "Have you ever been to Grand Central Market?"

I fumble for words. "Um, no. Where?"

"It's a place I think you'd really enjoy," he says. "Could I take you? Next Friday?"

"Yeah," I say unhesitatingly, then catch myself. Did Brendan just ask me on a date?

Did I just accept?

Before I get the chance to clarify, Grant comes running up to our picnic blankets, followed by a giant dude dressed as Columbia. "Stand up, guys," Grant says excitedly. "Let him see our costumes." Everyone rushes over and lines up for the judge, including Brendan, and the moment's gone. I follow the group, straightening my wig.

We hold our breath. The Columbia scrutinizes every inch of our costumes.

His eyes linger noticeably long on Brendan's Speedo. Finally, he nods approvingly. "Okay, all of you can come up onstage for 'Time Warp.'" Everyone cheers. Hannah's fully freaking out, clutching Paige's arm and hyperventilating. The Columbia continues, "Line up when Brad—"

"Asshole," someone from the crowd yells.

"—and Janet—"

"Slut," someone else yells.

"—ring the doorbell," the judge finishes. "You know when that is?" Everyone nods enthusiastically except me and Brendan. When the judge walks off, Hannah squeals and flings her arms around Grant, who throws me a grateful, and exhilarated, look.

We wait for ten minutes on the picnic blankets until it's time for the movie to begin. There's a chorus of cheers when a Frank-N-Furter, who's a dead ringer for Tim Curry himself, takes the stage under the red *Rocky* lips, holding a microphone. He welcomes the audience and starts giving safety instructions.

But my mind's on Brendan. On whatever this Grand Central Market plan is. I honestly don't know if I want to go on a date with Brendan. I definitely don't *dislike* the idea. I remember the way he looked at me, the times he's made me laugh. He's unpredictable, with his wry humor and his texting and his tendency to surprise me, like how he showed up here in the first place. In his costume, no less.

I steal a peek at him sitting beside me. His eyes are fixed on the stage, his features shadowed in the nighttime. I wonder what he's thinking. I wonder if he's thinking what I'm thinking.

There's something between us.

I don't know if it's real, and I'm trying hard to deny it. For one thing, he's Brendan Rosenfeld, until recently Barfy Brendan. He's a junior and an outcast. I go two years without a boyfriend, earning a reputation for rejecting every guy within flirting distance, and now *Brendan's* making me lightheaded? For another thing, there's Andrew. It's Andrew I've liked for a year. If not for him, I wouldn't be here in the company of a group of costume fetishists. He fits into my life, into every one of my plans.

Brendan Rosenfeld fits into *none* of my plans. I have no reason to let him distract me.

Yet here I am, distracted.

The announcer's voice yanks me from my thoughts. "Now, virgins, where are you?" he bellows. Grant and Abby instantly point at me, grinning broadly. I'm too caught up in my head, too frazzled by Brendan next to me to react. The announcer goes on, his voice dripping lasciviously. "The long wait is over. I'm glad you saved yourselves for tonight. For *all* of us." He winks theatrically and receives hoots and cheers from the crowd. "Don't worry, I'm not going to force you up here for some ignominious humiliation," he says.

The audience groans. I heave a breath of relief.

"No, I have something even better planned." My nerves return with an unpleasant tingle. The Frank-N-Furter struts from one end of the stage to the other. "As is customary with anyone's first time, there was someone special enough or just plain hot enough to get you to hand in your V-card. I want you to find that special someone," he continues. I think I catch Brendan dart a glance in my direction. "And with consent, of course," the announcer says, "I want you to thank that person for popping your *Rocky* cherry . . . with a kiss."

The crowd howls, but I hardly hear them. My eyes find Brendan's, both of us frozen in uncertainty. Technically, I brought him here. I can't tell if he's going to go in for the kiss—which is when I realize I want him to. I want to find out whether whatever is between us is real.

I start to lean over, closing the charged distance separating us.

"Well, Bright," I hear over my shoulder. Paige plops down onto the blanket between Brendan and me, turning to me with a smirk. I blink. "I'm the one who brought you, right?" She's smiling slyly, and I want nothing other than for her to go away. But the window is shut between me and Brendan. If I were to reopen it, I'd lose the easy pretense of the *Rocky* ritual. I'd be kissing him for real.

I recover my composure. "I'm willing if you are," I tell her. Paige shrugs. "Why not?"

Without a moment's pause, I lean forward. Paige does, too, and just like that I'm pressing a big, dramatic kiss to her lips. I feel her swallowing a laugh, which of course makes me bite my cheek to keep down one of my own. It's not an unpleasant kiss. It's just, it's *Paige*, and it couldn't be more platonic. Abby whoops and Grant applauds, while Charlie collapses in stitches. Finally, Paige and I pull apart when we can't hold our laughter in any longer.

I catch sight of Brendan half covering his eyes behind Paige, and I can't tell if he's relieved or disappointed to have dodged the virgin sacrifice.

"Thanks for that, guys," he groans. "I get to see Cameron Bright make out with a girl, and it's my sister."

It's not long after the movie begins that I come to realize everyone's following some unwritten script. Every time the character named Brad walks on screen, everybody yells, "Asshole." They throw rice for the wedding scene, and they break out water guns and newspapers when Janet and Brad get caught in the rain.

I'm swept up in the rituals. I yell obscenities with Hannah and Paige, I dodge Grant's water gun. I have no idea what's going on—I can hardly follow the plot—and I don't care.

We run on stage for "Time Warp." The dance is easy enough that I learn it right then and there from watching my . . . friends. Because that's what we feel like now. A jump to the left. A step to the right. I laugh until my sides ache when Brendan swivels his hips to the music. He catches my eye and grins, his gestures growing more exaggerated the longer I laugh.

When the song ends we run off stage, clutching our wigs and sweating in our sequins despite the chilly night air. Grant collapses onto our blankets, flinging his four-inch heels off in time to catch Hannah, who crashes into him, laughing. Paige and Charlie pile on, and I drop down beside them. I'm winded, but more from exhilaration than exertion. Like I've just placed first in a race and could run for miles more.

Abby passes me a bag of Hershey's Kisses. I take three and pass the bag to Brendan, who checks the ingredients before pouring out a couple. I give up on watching the film, finding the audience way more entertaining. Groups dance in the aisles, a Janet races by and throws us a handful of glow sticks, the performers on stage perfectly mirror every action in the film. And it's wonderful, weird magic. Paige and Hannah were right.

I notice Brendan shivering in the middle of the film. He's pulled his knees into his chest, his chin chattering.

"Do you have a jacket?" I ask. Even in the dark I can make out the goose bumps on his back—his *very exposed* back. I try not to look too long.

"I'm fine," he replies, flashing me a confident look. "I don't want to ruin my costume."

I roll my eyes. "There's another blanket in the car. I'll get it." Before he can protest, I weave my way through chairs and picnic baskets to the parking lot. I pass a mausoleum and catch a glimpse of red against the gray stone. I turn, nearly tripping on a discarded water gun.

It's Hannah. Hannah *and* Grant. Her red wig shines in the dull light as she pulls Grant against her. He brings his lips down to hers, his eyes filled with open wonder and something so yearning I have to look away.

I hurry my steps, not wanting to disrupt them, and grin the whole way to the car.

Twenty-Eight

I GOT THREE HOURS OF SLEEP LAST night, *maybe*. I should have made progress on my *Taming of the Shrew* term paper, but after walking through my door at two in the morning, my face flushed and heart racing, I could only lie in bed and stare at the ceiling as I relived the night.

I've been reliving it all day since.

We're outside today at our usual table for lunch, but the marine layer hasn't quite burned off yet, and the sky is still a dull gray. Brad had a mock trial meeting to lead during lunch, so it's just Elle, Morgan, and me. I have my notebook out on the table, and I'm trying to outline my English paper, but the question of Brendan keeps me distracted.

I've worked the problem over every waking moment, with zero progress. His invitation definitely felt like a date—

"Cameron?" Elle's voice cuts through my thoughts. "Are you listening?"

I look up. Elle's eyes are hard, her lips pursed in annoyance the way they were in Paige's driveway. "Sorry, um, just really behind on this." I tap my notebook, knowing full well Elle's noticed I haven't written a word since lunch started. Even so, I try to muster a studious, somewhat stressed expression.

Elle grabs my notebook out from under my pen. "'Katherine, the Villain Reeducated'?" She reads aloud my current title, her voice heavy with derision. "You're *not* submitting this," she declares.

Scowling, she flips through my outline. I'm not sure if she's truly offended by the topic or if she's taking out her anger that my head was elsewhere after I spent the night with Paige and my new friends. Probably both.

"Katherine's the victim, not the villain," she concludes, then rips the pages out of my notebook.

I gape up at her. Elle's always been decisive to the point of demanding, but she's never treated *me* this way. This isn't about the paper. It's about what she said last night. "Elle, come on," I get out before I notice the change in her expression.

Her eyes fixed on the page now open in the notebook, her features have gone rigid with anger. For a moment I'm blank, uncertain, wondering what outline she could possibly be reading, what essay idea I've had to fill her with fury—

And then I remember what notebook she's reading. What page.

I stand sharply and make out my amends list. I grasp for it, but Elle keeps it out of reach as she reads.

"What is this?" she asks, her voice unnaturally soft. *"Paige Rosenfeld, for calling her pathetic—fix things with Brendan. Brendan Rosenfeld, for giving him the nickname that allegedly ruined his life . . ."* I watch her eyes skip farther down, knowing what's coming and unable to stop it. *"Leila,"* she reads, her hand shaking, *"for being cruel about her relationship with Jason—tell her the truth about what her boyfriend did behind her back."* Her eyes return to mine, furious again. "You *told* Leila about me?"

"No, Elle, listen," I hurry to say. "It's not what you think. It was after you'd ended things with him. I told Leila that he cheated. *Not* that you were involved."

Elle huffs a laugh. "Just because you didn't use my name doesn't mean you weren't gossiping about my private life. And for what? This stupid list?"

I flinch from the bite in her words. Morgan recoils behind me, averting her gaze. "It wasn't gossip," I protest. "I was trying to help Leila—to make things right." I want to continue, to explain how this isn't about her. How I'm trying to correct my own wrongs. But Elle sets the notebook down, unnervingly calm, and my explanations catch in my throat.

"Make things right?" she repeats. Her cheeks flush, her eyes sharpen. "How is it *right* to betray your friends? You know"—she gestures to herself and Morgan, who doesn't look up from her plate—"your *real* friends? The people who've cared about you for years? Not the losers you hang out with now," she spits. "They don't even like the real you. Only the timid version of yourself you've created to convince Andrew you're not a bitch."

We've drawn the attention of the tables nearby. I feel them watching us, hear their wary whispering. I should defend myself. I should tell Elle she's wrong. But I can't—not when she's voiced the fear I've been forcing down.

"I'm just telling you the truth. *Somebody* should," she continues. She knows she's hit a nerve. I hear the venomous determination in her voice. "I noticed right away. Ever since Andrew humiliated you, you hardly speak your mind, worried you're going to offend someone and live up to what he called you." She nods to the list open in my notebook. "I had no idea how far you were going, though. It's all for Andrew, isn't it?"

It's not. The words are there, ringing in my head, but I can't get my mouth to work. My best friend is looking at me with disgust and disappointment. Suddenly I'm my mom, and it's easier to let my dad yell than it is to fight back. Because with someone who cares about you, who really knows you, you shouldn't have to defend yourself.

Elle picks up the pages of my essay. "Katherine's not the villain of the play. It's the people trying to change her," she says with finality and turns like she's just going to sit back down and finish lunch.

The dismissal unlocks my voice. Words I've wanted to say for weeks rush out, harsh and without thought to the damage they'll do. "I suppose I should be like you, Elle. Right?" I abruptly pick up my bag. "I should take whatever I want, from *whoever* I want, and not care who gets hurt, as long as I'm happy." The carefully constructed walls I've built crumble. "You know, being yourself isn't permission to be a terrible person."

Elle's eyes widen. I turn and walk away.

Twenty-Nine

I DON'T MAKE IT OUT OF THE courtyard before my stomach knots.

This whole month I've done nothing but try to repair relationships. I've fixed things with people I hardly know, found parts of myself I never expected. Yet now I've managed to wreck my closest friendship. Elle *was* out of line, but that doesn't justify what I said. If there's one thing I've learned from my reinvention, it's that there's no excuse for cruelty and that everyone—*everyone*—deserves an apology when wronged.

I walk through campus without a destination.

I've watched my every word, my every action. I've held myself to strict standards. It wasn't enough. I've ruined a friendship, I'm no closer to Andrew, and Elle was right when she said Paige might not actually like the real me. I don't even know why I'm doing this anymore—whether Andrew's really the goal or whether this is for me, to be friends with the people I've begun to respect.

And then there's Brendan. I don't know how he fits into all of this—haven't allowed myself to consider it.

Without ever deciding where I'm going, I find myself outside the robotics room. Paige walks out, her head, as promised, completely shaved. It doesn't look totally terrible. I guess she was trying to convince Brendan to come outside. She sees me and starts to smile, then worry fills her eyes.

"What's the matter?" she asks. I know I must look harried, wild even, like I've fallen through what I thought was solid ground.

I pace in front of her, my thoughts racing too quickly for me to stand still. "I'm tired of holding myself to everyone's standards," I reply. *Andrew's, Paige's friends', my friends', my father's.* I'm tired of planning meticulously to fit my life into everyone else's expectations. "I do everything I'm supposed to, and still I fall short." I stop suddenly, facing the robotics room door. "It's time I figured something out for myself." Time I went off-script. I glance up at Paige, determination pulsing through me. "I'm going to kiss your brother," I conclude.

Paige begins to laugh, until her expression changes to openmouthed astonishment. "You're not joking," she says.

"Nope," I reply, expecting her to object.

Instead, comprehension slowly settles on Paige's features. She opens the robotics room door for me with a dramatic flourish. "Well, don't let me hold you up."

I walk in, fueled with purpose, ready to—

I falter just inside the doorway because the room's not empty. Of course. The one time I'm counting on Brendan to have hidden himself from human contact, the room is half full of people. There's a group of what could possibly be the robotics team working on a collection of circuit boards near the front of the room. Brendan's in the back, helping Patrick Todd with homework.

I hesitate for a heartbeat. But I'm not going to let myself lose my nerve just because there are people watching. I walk forward, right to the back of the room.

I'm not doing this for my list. I'm doing this for me. Because letting the opportunity vanish under the stars at *Rocky* was a mistake. A mistake I need to set right.

Brendan doesn't notice me come up behind him. I tap him on the shoulder. He turns, and finding me he smiles. "Hey, Cameron," he says.

"Hi. I need to ask you something," I tell him.

"Okay." He waits, expectant. I nod to a corner of the room, and his brow furrows. "Give me a second," he says in Patrick's direction and follows me toward an empty desk.

I turn to face him when we're a comfortable distance from everybody else. There's a question on his lips.

Before he can ask it, I'm pulling his waist to me and kissing him.

I'm dimly aware of the room going quiet, and I don't care. I *have* to know if whatever's between Brendan and me is real or just a crazy figment of my imagination. His surprise settles, and he kisses me back, and heat hurtles from my cheeks down my spine. His hands find my waist, his fingers brushing my hips, pulling me closer.

And I have my answer.

Flooded with feeling, I lean into him, my hands bunching in the hem of his shirt. His lips press against mine, uncharacteristically demanding. From underneath the currents coursing through me, a thought slips to the surface. I want more of him, much more. But we're in the robotics room.

I wish we weren't in the robotics room.

The thought forces me to drag my lips from his. Brendan's out of breath. He opens his mouth, confusion and astonishment in his eyes.

I don't give him the chance to ask whatever he's about to. "Cool, bye now," I stutter smoothly, then walk past him. Ignoring the hushed laughter following me out, I throw open the door and head into campus, not knowing where my feet are taking me.

I walk down hallways and through courtyards until I duck into a bathroom. I need time and quiet to process what just happened. In the stall, I close the door and lean against the wall. I kissed Brendan *because* I didn't know what to expect, and yet the kiss was outside everything I'd ever expected. My finger traces my lips, still singing with sensation.

Part of me wants to go right back to Brendan and hear what he was about to say. But part of me doesn't. Because if I go back in there, Brendan could be thrilled. He could welcome the possibility of us with open arms.

But he could not.

I know he kissed me back. I could feel how he wanted me. But does he want *me*? Is it just because I'm beautiful, blonde, and popular? Is it too much to imagine he could want to date me, Cameron Bright, for who I am—who I really am, beneath those things?

The questions begin to change, keeping me pinned to the bathroom wall, warping into unbearable images. Scorn in Brendan's eyes. Him pushing me away. I can practically hear his rejection, how he'll tell me no matter how beautiful he finds me, he couldn't possibly care for real about a person like me.

A bitch.

I have no reason to expect giving myself to someone would go any differently this time than it did with Andrew. That's the honest truth. I never open myself up to people like I did with him, and it couldn't have hurt worse. The memory hasn't faded, the bluntness of his voice, the bite of his words.

I close my eyes, an image forming of Brendan calling me a bitch, wondering how I could ever think he'd want me that way, walking out with the disgust in his eyes that Andrew's held, disgust I'll never forget.

I couldn't bear if it happened again. Not with Brendan.

And then there's Andrew. He's been my goal while I became friends with Brendan and Paige, while I went to *Rocky* and did things I never thought I would. I've changed for him. If I give up Andrew and trying to reinvent myself, who will I be? Will Brendan even want that girl?

The questions keep me prisoner here until the bell rings for class.

Thirty

I RUN AFTER SCHOOL, MY HEAD A whirlwind. I ditch my phone in my room, wanting to avoid the barrage of texts and calls I anticipate from an irate Elle, and probably Morgan, too. I've watched Elle in arguments before, and she's as persistent in disagreements as in everything else. She won't let a fight drop when she feels wronged.

I hit the hill near my house, not yet feeling the pain of exertion. The entire run, the kiss with Brendan plays on repeat in my head. My lips haven't forgotten the feeling, though I almost wish they would. I know I have to face him, and when I do, I'm going to have to decide whether to put myself up for rejection again and whether I'm ready to give up everything I'd planned for with Andrew.

I finish my run in under an hour and head up to my room. Glancing in the mirror, I notice I've somehow ended up with a sunburn in November. I pick up my phone, preparing with heaviness in my stomach for strings of angry texts and voice-mails.

Instead, there's nothing.

The weight drops from my stomach, leaving only empty dread. It's worse than a bombardment. Elle's written me off completely, not even caring enough to respond. I hesitate, considering texting her and trying to work things out. But it's obvious she wants nothing to do with me. It'd probably only piss her off worse if I reached out.

I drop into my desk chair, half hoping the colorless carpet or the paint-chipped walls will swallow me up and I won't have to worry about this. I might have just lost my oldest, closest friends. Next to the question of whether I'm ready to give up Andrew, it's another huge piece of my life from which I'm untethered, and I'm drifting.

I want to text Brendan about the fight with my friends. I need a person to confide in, to reassure me and help me remember who I am without them. To keep me from drifting too far. But it's not fair to talk to Brendan without giving him an explanation for the kiss. Even if I don't know if I'm ready to open myself up for rejection, I can't pretend the kiss didn't happen. Besides, I'm more than a little curious how he's feeling about it.

I unlock my phone and stare at his name. Finally, I write a text.

> **About this afternoon . . . I'm sorry I basically attacked you in the robotics room.**

Right away my phone vibrates. He's calling me.

Panic races into me. Who actually *calls* people? In my experience, it's only people who want to yell at me.

I pick up.

"Undoubtedly your most unnecessary apology ever," Brendan says before I get a word out.

I grin, relieved. "Yeah?" I ask.

"Yes," he says. "I'm sorry if I was weird or whatever . . ." he continues.

"Now who's apologizing unnecessarily?"

"Really?"

"Yes. Really." I hope he hears the conviction in my voice. "You know," I say, climbing onto my bed and crossing my legs on the comforter, "you're not a bad kisser, for someone who spends every waking moment playing and working on computer games." Feeling a flush in my cheeks, I pluck at a feather protruding from my pillow. "You're a good kisser. A really good kisser."

"Cameron," he says, gently teasing, "you can give me your honest opinion."

"I always do. You know that," I reply.

"I guess you do," he says, his voice edging from playfulness to something softer, something intimate. "Excuse me while I go into cardiac arrest," he adds, and I laugh.

"You're not going to tell me *I'm* a good kisser, then?" I nudge. "I'm hurt, Brendan. No, *scandalized*."

"Don't you already know?" he returns quickly.

"I don't, actually. It didn't exactly go well the last time I kissed someone." I pause, reconsidering. "Wait, the last person I kissed was Paige. That went pretty well."

"How well?" Brendan asks. "Wait, never mind. Never tell me. Definitely never tell me who was better, me or my sister."

"You're dodging the question," I remind him. "You haven't given me a real answer on whether I'm a good kisser." I'm flirting more shamelessly than I'm used to, trying not to betray my nerves.

There's a long pause. Whatever he's about to say, he's giving it real thought. I wait, unmoving, and feel everything in me narrow in on the quiet on the other end of the phone. "Even though I have no experience whatsoever and I'm entirely unequipped to judge comparatively," he finally says, "I am one hundred percent certain that you, and that kiss, are unparalleled."

Warmth spreads from my chest to the grin I feel forming on my face, rushing to the ends of my fingertips. I'm not afraid for Brendan to know how I feel. I *need* him to know. "You don't have to reevaluate? Reassess? Confirm your first impression?" I ask playfully. *Now? On this very bed?*

"No confirmation necessary," he says unhesitatingly.

My smile slips. It's kind of a compliment, I guess. I thought I was pretty obvious about what I was suggesting. I would've expected him to jump at the chance. Brendan has zero experience, I remind myself, and it's an established fact guys can be clueless when it comes to hints and come-ons.

I'm about to encourage him in terms a little more explicit when he speaks up. "I know I said I wasn't interested in you helping me with my social life at school, but I'm glad you didn't listen," he says. "I honestly didn't think it would work, or that I'd care even if it did."

I blink, not following.

"But it did work, and . . . it's really made things better.

People have started treating me differently since we kissed," he goes on.

"Um," I say fumblingly. "How?" I don't understand why we're talking about this instead of flirting.

"Well, no one's called me BB since, and I can just tell they see me differently. People make eye contact with me in the halls, you know? They say hi to me. I'm not a loser. I'm someone Cameron Bright kissed."

The horrible realization drops onto me, and the air rushes from my lungs. He thinks I kissed him because I'm still trying to turn him popular. But it wasn't that. Not at all. I did it because of what I feel for him. But it wasn't real for Brendan. If he can't even consider that it might've been real, I have to think he feels nothing for me. I'm not even a possibility.

I'm just the girl trying to make up for the shitty things she did.

"I don't know how you predicted kissing me would reverse six years of being a nobody," Brendan says. "It did, though. Thank you."

"You're welcome," I say, my voice hollow.

"Hey, I've got to go study. My dad's walked by my room three times with increasingly pointed glares at my SAT book," he says with a laugh, obliviously chipper. "We're still on for Grand Central Market Friday, right?"

The mention of our plan hits me harder than I would've expected. Definitely not a date, then. I don't know how I convinced myself otherwise. I want to cancel—except I can't without explaining why.

"Yeah. Friday," I repeat as if his words have echoed through me, leaving nothing behind.

In an hour, I've showered from my run after school and am working on my *Shrew* paper when there's a knock on the front door. I hear my mom greet Deb, and I remember it's Monday. I was going to run with Andrew today. I completely forgot, caught up in the drama with Elle and now the jarring conversation with Brendan.

Guiltily, I walk into the hallway, damp hair hanging over my shoulder. Andrew catches sight of me past his mom, who's chatting excitedly with mine.

His eyes linger on my wet hair. "Guess we're not running today," he says, the dimple in his cheek dancing with amusement.

I reach for a witty reply and find nothing. "Yeah, sorry," I say instead. "Do you want to do homework?"

The humor fades from his expression. "Sure." His voice is light with what sounds like forced nonchalance.

I return to my room, feeling frustrated and off-kilter. He follows me, and for the next half an hour, we work halfheartedly on homework. In an effort to act normal and not like a totally distracted zombie, I ask him how his first game went. When we head to the dining table for dinner, the Chinese takeout my mom picked up down the street, I try for the thousandth time not to think of Brendan. It doesn't work, and for the entire meal he, and the kiss, and the horrible phone call we just had play on repeat in my mind. I utter only a handful of words, and in an hour, Andrew and I are back in my room.

Picking up my copy of *The Taming of the Shrew*, I flip unenthusiastically to act 3. I really have to finish a draft of this essay.

"What are you writing about?" Andrew asks, nodding at the book in my hand.

I blink, fighting to remember exactly what I am writing about—to remember anything except Brendan's hands on my hips, pulling me closer. "Katherine's character arc," I get out. "You?"

"I don't know," he replies thoughtfully. "Maybe the role of wealth in romance and marriage."

I nod, not having anything more to say, and return to the play. Neither of us speaks for a few minutes. I will myself to focus on Kate resisting becoming Petruchio's bride.

"Did you have fun at *Rocky*?" Andrew asks out of nowhere. "Paige told me she had a great time and that you brought Elle to do everybody's makeup."

It throws me that Andrew's bothered to ask another question. I'm really not in a talkative mood, and usually Andrew isn't either. I don't understand what's gotten into him, why he's picked today to play twenty questions instead of doing our homework in peace.

"It was fun, yeah," I say hesitantly, hoping he'll take the hint.

"I think it's really cool you went," he says, *not* taking the hint. "I didn't know you liked stuff like that. People at school pretty much refuse to try new things. I just think it's awesome you're different from them."

"Um, thanks?" I guess it's a compliment.

"Hey"—he closes his Calc book eagerly—"do you want to take a study break?" From the practiced way he asks, I get the feeling this has been his plan all night. "We could watch *Sherlock*?"

"No," I say quickly. I definitely cannot watch an actor who bears a significant resemblance to a certain video game programmer I'm desperate *not* to think about tonight. Andrew's eyes widen, and I realize how harshly I just refused. "I just can't take a study break right now," I add hurriedly. "I'm really behind. Next week?"

He nods, satisfied. I return to *The Taming of the Shrew*, my thoughts tilting precariously. *What is wrong with me?*

Weeks ago, I would have jumped at the chance to do literally anything with Andrew. Now, I'm a confused, preoccupied mess, while he's going out of his way to be friendly. I have him right here, and yet I'm trapped in my own head, reliving Brendan's kiss and its consequences. He's messed everything up.

No, *I've* messed everything up.

Thirty - One

THE NEXT DAY, EVERYTHING'S DIFFERENT.

In the halls I catch glances in my direction and hear furtive whispers. There are a couple repeated words. *Brendan, robotics room*. When I pass a group of girls near my locker, they erupt in hushed giggles.

In Ethics, Morgan gives me only a timid look I don't know how to interpret. I guess it's better than the complete texting moratorium of yesterday. No luck with Elle, though. When I try to catch her eye in between classes in the morning, she determinedly ignores me. I have to bite my cheek to keep from saying her name out loud in the locker hall. I wonder if she'd ignore me then.

I know I hurt her yesterday, but under the remorse, I feel a new current of resentment. Why do *I* have to apologize first? She hurt me, too.

I'm outside English, following a few steps behind her, when I hear someone make an exaggerated smooching sound to my left. It's undeniably meant for me. I'm ready to let it roll off me the way I have every other Brendan-related joke and whisper today—except this time, I catch Elle give a small smirk and chuckle derisively.

It's the final straw. I'm done letting her ignore me.

"Excuse me?" I say, rushing to meet her in the doorway while everyone's walking to their desks, unpacking their things, and talking in the pre-class minutes. "Do you have something you want to say to me?"

She looks me over, her eyes cool, then dismisses me with a shrug. "Not at all."

I block her way to her desk. "You've never been one to hide your opinions before. Why start now?" My heart pounds painfully. I know whatever she says next won't be pleasant, but it'll be something. Something that proves I'm not nothing to her.

"Okay," she replies snidely, her voice low enough not to be overheard. "You're right. I think what you did yesterday is disgusting. I remember the entry for BB on your list, and it repulses me that you'd use your body to accomplish a goal like that. You wouldn't even consider dating two months ago. Look how far you've come."

Even though I know we're in a fight, I didn't think Elle was capable of thinking that of me. I falter in the doorway long enough for her to fire me one final glare and walk past me into English.

I recover my composure and follow her in. There's no way she's getting the final word.

But before I have the chance to reply, the bell rings. I'm caught halfway to Elle's desk. Clenching my jaw, I retreat to my seat while Kowalski walks to the front of the class.

"I want to turn our discussion to the ending of the

play," Kowalski says. "Namely, to Katherine's final mono-logue. I imagine a number of you have strong feelings on the speech"—her eyes flit to Elle—"and in the interest of a varied discussion, I'd like you to pair up and discuss your thoughts before we reconvene."

My hand shoots up, and I don't wait for Kowalski to call on me. "Elle and I want to be partners," I say unhesitatingly. Out of the corner of my eye, I see Elle's eyebrows rise.

"Okay, Cameron," Kowalski says with a funny look. "The rest of you, feel free to choose your partners without inform-ing the rest of the class."

There are a few chuckles, but I don't bother to be embar-rassed. This is perfect. Elle's either too thrown to protest or she doesn't care enough to explain to Kowalski.

I gather my things and join her in the desk beside hers. She refuses to look at me, her expression tight and furious. Undeterred, I stare her straight in the face while I unpack my *Taming of the Shrew*.

I'm about to speak when Elle preempts me. "Anna," she calls out. "There's an odd number in the class. Come work with us." I blink, turning in my chair to find Anna Lewis alone at the front of the room while everyone else has part-nered up. I can't help noticing Paige and Andrew sitting to-gether in one corner.

Anna joins us, looking like she knows she's stumbled into something unpleasant but doesn't want to incur Elle's wrath by refusing. "Okay, um," she says, her voice high, evidently eager to get the discussion going. "I think Kate's final speech is kind of messed up. She's saying your husband is your *sovereign*, like your king, and you have to devote your entire life to"—she flips the pages, looking for the line—"placing your hands below your husband's foot."

"Imagine," Elle utters without a pause, her voice low, "going to humiliating lengths just to please a guy."

I hold my tongue. Elle has no idea what she's talking about. What I did with Brendan—*with* Brendan, not *for* Brendan—was far from humiliating.

I bury myself in my book. Focusing on the words is the only possible way I'll get through the period without an outburst. Anna's not wrong. Kate's final monologue is horrendous. *I am ashamed that women are so simple,* I reread, *To offer war where they should kneel for peace.* I cringe.

"Yeah," Anna replies quickly, obviously eager to keep the conversation on Shakespeare. "I just don't get why Katherine would completely give up on herself, though. Like, Petruchio's not that great. He's kind of a jerk, honestly."

"Because he abuses her and sleep-deprives her!" Finally Elle's glare snaps to Anna, who visibly flinches. "He intimidates her into obeying."

A woman moved—"moved" meaning angry, I find in the glossary—*is like a fountain troubled, Muddy, ill-seeming, thick, bereft of beauty.* I keep reading, feeling my pulse quicken with anger.

And I don't know whether it's out of a compulsion to be combative with Elle or what, but the next moment, I hear a word escape me. "No," I say sharply. Elle's gaze flits to me, poisonous. I go on. "No. It's not only because Katherine's intimidated by Petruchio. Does this speech feel intimidated to you? It might've begun with physical abuse, but along the way, Petruchio no longer needed to frighten Katherine. Because he got her to do it herself. He taught her to believe there's no alternative to helplessness and obedience." I point to the lines I'm reading. *Now I see our lances are but straws, Our strength as weak.* "She's been taught that this treatment is the way of the world and there's nothing she can do to change that."

Elle's eyes are finally on me, but impossibly, my thoughts have left our fight. They're racing too quickly for me to concentrate when Elle turns back to Anna and continues the discussion.

I thought I was in control when I decided to "tame" myself. But what if I wasn't? Andrew is a good guy, a guy I care about. He's not Petruchio, and I'm not Katherine, giving up her will for a guy she detests. I've never been starved or locked away. But in ways I never knew, his words crept into my head and convinced me I needed to prove myself. I believed I was *improving* myself in order to get what *I* wanted. But the hardest kind of control to break is the one you don't know is there.

Now I know. I'm done with my list. I'm done with "taming."

Kowalski's voice interrupts my thoughts. "Everybody return to your desks, and we'll discuss as a class."

Anna practically falls over in her eagerness to leave. I stand up, looking down at Elle. "You know," I say softly, "I didn't kiss Brendan because of Andrew. I kissed Brendan because I like him."

Elle blinks, but she says nothing, and I return to my desk.

When the bell rings for lunch, I don't bother going to our normal table. I definitely don't want to go to the robotics room, not ready to face Brendan after yesterday. Instead, I catch Paige walking out the door. "Hey," I say, "can I sit with you guys today?"

"Um." Paige eyes me quizzically. "Yeah, definitely." We walk through the hall. If Paige notices the stares and stifled laughter my presence elicits, she doesn't react. I guess she might be used to it. But when we're walking into the dining hall, she asks tentatively, "Do you . . . want to talk about whatever's going on with Elle?"

"Not really," I say quietly.

Paige nods. We join the line into the kitchen, walking up behind Grant and Hannah. They've obviously decided to publicize their new relationship to the entire world, and they're presently treating the food line like a parking lot past business hours. They're unable to keep their hands off each other. Grant whispers in Hannah's ear, and she giggles and blushes brightly. Paige gives me a dry look. I force a commiserative shrug in return.

I want to be happy for Grant and Hannah. I *am* happy for them. It's just, watching them together, I can't help wondering if I'll never have a relationship like that. If I'm not good enough. Early indications have not been promising.

Paige must notice my expression, because she turns to Hannah. "Can't you guys just go hook up in the instrument storage room like everyone else?"

Grant looks at Hannah like he thinks that's a wonderful idea. Hannah, however, withdraws from his arms. "We'll keep the PDA under control. Promise," she says, the blush not having faded from her cheeks. Grant pouts behind her.

I give Paige a grateful glance, feeling my chest warm. I still have her, which is worth a lot.

We find the rest of the group once we've gotten food. I join Abby and Charlie, while Grant sits on the opposite bench with Hannah and Paige.

"Guess who's not having lunch alone in the robotics room today," Paige says, biting into her panini.

I brighten. "Brendan's coming?"

"No, a couple guys from his chemistry class invited him to eat with them," Paige answers cheerfully.

"Oh." I deflate. "Wow. Has he ever done that before?" I have a good guess what their topic of discussion will be.

"Nope," Paige says. "It's thanks to you, of course."

"You've made him a legend," Charlie says next to me. "Everyone's talking about how he must have mad game if he got *you* to kiss him." He's looking at me like he wants me to confirm. And I can't deny, Brendan does have unexpected game, but it's not something I feel like discussing right now.

Hannah cuts in. "Are you guys, like, together?" she asks

conspiratorially. Unsurprisingly, Hannah's been downright congenial to me since *Rocky Horror*.

"Oh, no." I iron casualness into my voice. "It wasn't like that."

"Well, good," Abby says. "Because I heard three girls talking about wanting to ask him out."

I flinch and hope no one notices. Three feels like an awfully big number.

"I heard he gave his number to a sophomore cheerleader," Grant chimes in.

And that's all I can take. Abruptly, I get up. "I just realized," I say hurriedly, "I have to talk to Mr. West about the Computer Science final." I feel queasy. Without bothering to pick up my food, I leave the table.

I'm a complete idiot. Brendan could never want me. How could he, after everything I've put him through? He wants a *nice* girl—a sophomore cheerleader.

Wandering into the sunlit courtyard, I don't get far before I hear someone calling my name. It's Andrew. He's jogging to catch up with me. "Hey, Cameron," he says, like he's trying to be casual, but I detect a note of urgency in his voice. "Can we talk?"

"Um, yeah," I say distractedly and wait.

"In private?" Andrew prompts.

"Oh, um. Okay." I follow him to a classroom, and he holds the door open for me.

The door's hardly shut when he starts speaking again. "Winter formal's coming up," he says, his voice jarringly loud in the empty room. I recognize nervousness on Andrew. The way he bunches his shoulders, the way he rubs his knuckles uneasily. "I was hoping you'd be my date," he finishes.

I feel my eyes widen. Images flit through my head. Arriving at the dance on Andrew's arm, placing my head on his shoulder while the music plays.

I've fantasized about that night. I knew how I'd style my hair swept off my shoulder, knew what a figure Andrew would cut in the navy blazer he got for his sister's graduation. I knew it would be perfect.

"Why now?" I ask suddenly.

Andrew blinks, obviously not expecting the question. "What do you mean?" He fidgets with the straps of his backpack. "I'm sorry if I should have planned something more romantic—"

I shake my head. "No. Why do you want to go with me *now*? What changed your mind about me?" His conversation last night, his unusual friendliness, I now realize, wasn't friendliness at all. He was flirting, and I was too distracted to pick up on it. I study his features, trying to recall the way I obsessed about the dimple in his right cheek, the flecks of green in his eyes, the gentle arch of his brows.

His hands relax. "I know you've been trying to be nice to Paige. Then you got Grant and Hannah back together, and, well, I noticed. But when I heard what you did for Brendan yesterday I saw how committed you are—how hard you're working."

I have to hold in the laugh that bubbles in my throat. What perfect irony. Weeks of strategizing, and what ends up catching Andrew's attention is the one act I *didn't* do as part of my reinvention—the reinvention I just gave up. I'm marveling at every way in which that kiss backfired when I notice Andrew leaning in, his lips nearing mine.

I pull back, surprising myself. It's so quick I don't have time to think about what I'm giving up, what fantasies or long-formed plans.

Yet the moment I draw away, I know how right the choice was. I never considered how long it's really been since I've fantasized about that perfect night with Andrew. A while, I guess.

I can tell the rejection surprises Andrew, too. His forehead creases, and his eyes narrow. "I thought you wanted this," he says, his voice more baffled than vulnerable.

"I did," I reply, searching my own feelings. I can't deny Brendan's changed things. But even without Brendan—because honestly, I've no reason to hope *that* will turn out—I can't convince myself to want what I used to with Andrew. "It's just . . ." I say finally, "I don't think you like *me*. Only the girl you think I've become."

I remember what Andrew said about *The Taming of the Shrew* in class. How it was a good thing Katherine was compelled to change. I had grabbed on to his words like driftwood from the shipwreck of my apology to Paige. But I know how wrong they are now. Katherine has a husband by the end of the play, and she's better liked, but she's not herself. She's only who Petruchio tames her to be.

And in an unpredictable rush, I'm angry. I'm angry my plan *worked*. I've won Andrew, but he only wants me because I've twisted myself into a new shape. I can admit that because of Brendan—of how I could've felt for Brendan. I liked him in a real way, and I wanted him to like me in a real way, too. It's exhilarating, and crushing.

With Andrew it wasn't that. From the very beginning, for both of us, it was never real. Andrew's the guy who worked on paper, who represented everything I thought I wanted. Everything I told myself I wanted. If there's one thing I've learned from kissing Brendan—other than how nerdy junior boys can be unexpectedly proficient kissers—it's that you can't pick or predict the person you'll fall for. You can't figure it out with a list or a plan.

"If we were meant to be together, you wouldn't have wanted me to change first," I say, hearing a charge in my voice.

"Cameron, I don't know what you're talking about," he says, sounding urgent. "I've always liked you."

"No, you haven't," I reply, not hesitating. The thoughts fit together in my head with perfect clarity. "You liked the idea of being with Cameron Bright. But when you had the chance, you realized you wanted someone else. Someone nicer. I'm not that person, Andrew," I declare. "I'm done hiding my opinions and not being honest."

Elle's words ring in my ears. I haven't forgiven her for the way she delivered them, but she wasn't wrong. I've apologized and done things for people just to please Andrew. Of course he'd like me for that. But those things didn't come from me.

What he likes is only what I tailor-made for him, wrapped up in a pretty bow. In trying to be better than my mother, I've made exactly her mistakes. I've given away pieces of myself in desperation to be with a guy with whom it'll never work out.

"You want me agreeable, and even-tempered, and . . . tamed," I tell him. "I won't be."

"When did I ever say I want you tamed?" he interrupts me indignantly.

"Remember what you said about Kate in *The Taming of the Shrew*?" I go on. "You said it was a *good* thing she was tamed by the end of the play. You said she was a better person for it."

Andrew's watching me in undisguised surprise. "Yeah," he says gradually. "I was talking about *Kate*. In *Taming of the Shrew*. A play."

I falter, his words catching me off guard. He has a point, but . . . "You called me a bitch, remember?" I ask, grasping for the point.

Andrew winces. His eyes grow confused, as if he can't understand how such a short word can have such power. Because of course he can't. "I—" he says and swallows. "Yeah. I did. I apologize for that, Cameron. It was wrong of me. You were horrible to Paige that night," he reminds me, not that I need reminding. "But I know you're not really that person. I needed time to forgive you for what happened with Paige. I respect how you apologized and were cool to Paige's brother. I never needed you to change who you are, though. I wanted you before everything with Paige, and I want you now."

It's exactly what I wanted to hear. It's everything I wanted to hear. And it's not enough.

"I don't think you do, Andrew," I say decisively. "I don't blame you, but I can't be the girl you want. I'm going to say the wrong things sometimes. I'll apologize when I do, but it's *going* to happen. I know there are people out there who are gentler, or more open-minded, or have more discretion than me—wonderful people. You want one of them."

It's unbelievably freeing to admit. I'm really, genuinely over Andrew. Not just Andrew himself but the idea of him, of the relationship I've worked toward and worried about and driven myself crazy for. I've defined myself for my entire life by my goals, my accomplishments. Recognizing there's nothing to this goal other than proving I don't let my dreams pass me by, I feel weightless.

Andrew opens his mouth, but I'm not finished yet. This isn't only about what he wants.

"I'm not the girl for you, and you're not the guy for me." I nearly smile as I say it.

Andrew closes his mouth, his rebuttal forgotten. I watch his expression shift from apprehension to acceptance and then agreement. He nods, his eyes on mine, and whatever this thing was between us is finally ended.

I could stay, could try to mend the frayed edges of our friendship. I walk to the door instead. There's no need to draw this out. If he thinks I'm rude for walking out, fine. I don't care what Andrew thinks. Not anymore.

I open the door and pause. "You already know nice girls," I

say from the doorway. "Girls you have real friendships with."

He looks puzzled. I push down the urge to put my opinion gently. I won't be doing that any longer.

"Andrew, don't be an idiot," I tell him. "There's one girl we both know who's nothing but accepting. She's kind and generous, and she would never do anything to make someone feel bad. You actually talk to her, too, which, by the way, is what people do when they care about someone." His confused expression only deepens. I don't restrain the frustration from my tone. "You tell her about what's worrying you on the team. You get lunch with her after pep rallies?"

He jolts a little, realizing who I mean.

"Bye, Andrew," I say and walk out the door.

Outside, I roll my eyes with weeks' worth of pent-up sarcasm.

Thirty-Two

I'VE AVOIDED BRENDAN FOR THE ENTIRE WEEK. For one thing, I definitely don't want to hear him detailing his plans with whatever sophomore cheerleader asked him out, and furthermore I'm nervous he'll realize the kiss was for real, and he'll be horrified. It hurt enough he assumed the kiss was a stunt. I couldn't take outright rejection.

But today is Friday, the day I agreed to go to Grand Central Market with him. Which means I can't avoid him any longer.

Unless I can come up with an excuse. I finish my sit-ups for the cross-country workout—frustratingly, not a run. I really needed the wind on my face and the pavement under my feet to help me come up with what I'm going to tell Brendan. I get up, grabbing my water bottle, and head for the locker room. I could fake food poisoning, I guess. Or an assignment I forgot. He'd understand.

I round the corner, and there he is, leaning on the wall next to the locker room. For a moment, I forget my excuses, and I'm only watching him exchange nods with a couple people passing by. Worse, he looks *good*. Objectively, there's nothing new about him. He's still too tall, with curly hair that's a little too long. But kissing him has made me painfully aware of all the *really* obvious ways in which he's hot. His, dare I say, chiseled jaw and warm eyes. His nonchalant posture, as if he doesn't care about impressing anyone. His smile, open and genuine.

Just more reasons I can't go through with this.

With a deep breath, I walk up to him, thinking of my excuse. "Hey, you ready?" he says before I can speak.

He glances up, and our eyes meet.

The excuse dries up on my tongue. I'm voiceless with the realization of how much I hated not talking to him. "Yeah," I say, finding words. "Just give me ten minutes to clean up. I apologize in advance if I stink."

Brendan grins. "I mean, it's every guy's nightmare to be one-on-one with a sweaty Cameron Bright."

"You'd be surprised," I mutter, walking past him. I'd thought he was flirting with me when he said things like that. Now I know he's not.

Thirty minutes later, I'm showered and we're halfway to downtown. We're in my car, and Brendan's reading me directions from his phone in the passenger seat. I'm trying my hardest to not be awkward, to pretend there's not this new place in my heart for him. Brendan's certainly not acting differently. I just have to force myself not to look at, think about, or remember the feel of his lips.

Easy.

Focusing on the road helps. But for the first time in Los Angeles history, there's no traffic, and we hit every green on

Wilshire Boulevard, a street I thought I could depend on for endless bumper-to-bumper purgatory. I'm dreading our arrival. I don't know how to act on this decidedly non-date, and the question has me on edge.

Before I'm prepared, we're entering downtown. Of course we find parking immediately. On the street, too. We don't even have to use one of those inconvenient eight-dollar public parking lots with peeling paint on the fences. We get out of the car in front of a cheap electronics store, the cluttered, nondescript kind with ten-year-old cell phones and blinking lights in the windows. I'm about to force a conversation when Brendan's phone pings with a text. While we walk, he types a reply, grinning.

"Is that Paige?" I ask, curiosity getting the better of me. "Say hi for me." I try to keep my voice disinterested and fail.

"No, it's Eileen Roth," he says. "Do you know her? I started tutoring her in Computer Science."

"Eileen doesn't take Computer Science."

He looks up, a hint of wariness in his eyes. "She's doing independent study. She wants to take the AP exam without being in the class. I didn't know you kept tabs on random junior girls' schedules, though."

I bite my cheek, fighting the irritation gathering in my chest. I know I should drop it. But the words fly out of me before I can contain them. "Come on, Brendan. She's flirting with you."

He blinks, bewildered. "No, she's not. We're just scheduling a tutoring session for Saturday night at her house . . .

Ah." His eyes widen with understanding. "Clearly, I'm bad at interpreting signals."

CLEARLY, Brendan.

We're walking past rows of mirrored skyscrapers with escalators and marble staircases in their street-level lobbies. "What are you going to do?" I ask, no longer holding the impatience from my voice.

"Do?"

"Are you going to this 'tutoring session'?" I form air quotes with my fingers.

He drops his eyes. I'm certain it's because he knows I like him and he doesn't want to hurt my feelings. "What do you think I should do?" he asks delicately.

"I don't know, Brendan!" I can't believe this. We haven't even gotten to the place for this not-date, and already we're discussing Brendan's *other* romantic prospects. "If you like her—if you want to hook up with her—then go. It's none of my business."

We round a corner cluttered with bicycles. "Did I . . ." He begins again after a pause. "Did I piss you off somehow?"

"What could you have done to piss me off?" I fire back.

"I don't know," he replies. I wrack my brain for ways out of this conversation while Brendan ushers me into the warehouse-looking building on our left, under an open metal garage door.

Whatever I was about to say, it's instantly forgotten.

I find myself in the front of a huge, high-ceilinged room crammed with tiny restaurants, food counters, and people. I'm overwhelmed. Not only by the smells and sounds—the hot, baked aroma of egg-biscuit sandwiches, the sweet-sour spice of Thai noodles, the clatter of cooking pans and sushi knives—but by the signs, the lights, the letters. While hipsters holding gelato cups and old women carrying fresh bread pass me and Brendan, I study the rows of dozens of vendors packed into the warehouse, noting my favorite details. The fishtail logo over the sleek, modern seafood stand. The trendy coffee shop's handwritten menu. The bold red-and-white lettering of the *pupuseria*—whatever a *pupuseria* is.

Brendan's voice is gentle beside me. "It's great, right? I knew you'd love it."

"It's amazing," I breathe. I walk into one of the aisles, pulling my phone from my bag instinctually. I begin to take photos, then turn, finding Brendan watching me, smiling softly. I feel my breath catch. Everything about this feels like . . . not a not-date. It has me beginning to question if it might be more.

"Paige showed me one of your designs," Brendan says, walking up next to me. "You're really good, you know. Like, professional."

"It's just a hobby," I hear myself say automatically.

"It could be more than a hobby," he insists. "If you wanted."

For the first time, I don't shake off the thought. I've enjoyed design, I've just never let myself wonder if it could be more. I've kept myself focused on Econ, on the path that would lead me closer to my dad's life. I didn't want to consider other paths, other places I could go. I didn't want to consider whether other things could fit me better.

But here in this place, with Brendan looking encouraging

beside me—looking like he believes in me—I'm considering it.

It would mean giving up the connection to my dad I'd hoped and planned for. It would mean giving up a world of chances to be closer to him. I don't know if I'm ready to do that.

"Do you want to get food?" Brendan asks.

I'm suddenly starving, at the mercy of the incredible smells surrounding me. "Wow, yes." I put my phone away. "Is there anything you can eat here?"

Like it's nothing, Brendan takes my hand.

"Let me show you. It's on me," he says.

I don't remove my hand. I follow him into the market, wondering for the second time what this is to him. He was just talking about going over to another girl's house, I remind myself. But the way my hand feels in his, I'm having a really, really hard time convincing myself this isn't a date.

Thirty-Three

AN ENTIRE WEEK GOES BY WITHOUT CLARIFICATION on the date-or-not-date question. Brendan took me to his favorite place and bought my dinner. He was perfectly friendly, but only friendly. He tried to explain *Game of Thrones* to me, and we placed bets on Paige's next hair color once she grows enough back to dye it again. He didn't take my hand again.

Things were normal at school, or whatever this new normal is. I had lunch with Brendan in the robotics room once while he worked on his game. Elle continues to ignore me, and I've given up trying to engage with her.

It's Friday night, and I'm for once eagerly anticipating an entire weekend alone in my apartment. I don't have a single social obligation, which admittedly is because I've managed to alienate my friends, reject my only dating prospect, and propel my crush into such new heights of popularity he's sure to have dozens of plans from which to choose.

I force the thoughts from my head. I'm not wasting the weekend on self-loathing and other useless emotions.

I could hang out with Paige. But she's picked up the vexing habit of dropping casual references to Brendan, and I'm not interested in hearing about his wonderful weekend plans or what he's probably doing with Eileen Roth. In the midst of a completely ordinary conversation yesterday—or as ordinary as Paige is capable of—about why I "need" to watch some show called *Boys Over Flowers,* she just *had* to mention that Brendan got a ride home with someone else yesterday, thereby giving her *Boys Over Flowers* time. He and I haven't talked about whatever he's doing in the dating realm after our awkward conversation outside Grand Central Market.

Every time Paige says his name she gives me this curious look. I don't know if she wants me to demand information or break down in tears or what, but I get the feeling she might be the only person—other than Elle—who knows the real reason behind the kiss, and now she's torturing me until I admit it. As if admitting it would change anything. It would only put Brendan in the position of having to reject me.

Regardless, knowing Paige, if I texted her she'd probably invite me over to witness firsthand whatever date Brendan will be on. Not something I need visual evidence of.

I kick open the door to our apartment, ready to collapse on the couch and watch something mindless and without even a trace of romance—Animal Planet, I think—when I'm stopped short by the sight of my mother wearing my old Homecoming dress.

It's a little too small, especially in the chest, and the length's shorter than acceptable for a work event. Her curled hair bounces down her back, and her eyes are painted gold and brown in a way that's pretty if a little ostentatious. She's pulling on a pair of very high strappy stilettos.

I'm almost afraid to ask. "Where are you going?" I say from the doorway.

"Oh, hey, Cameron," she replies brightly, fluffing her hair in the mirror next to the window. "Is it okay if I borrow your dress?"

I consider asking her to change, but she'll likely wave away my request with a muttered *It's just a dress, Cameron.* It's not the point anyway. I drop my bag on the kitchen counter and face her. "Where are you going?" I repeat.

"PTA meeting," she answers brightly.

I let out a relieved breath. As long as she's not going to a work function. I drop down onto the couch and reach for the remote. "Since when do you care about the PTA?"

"Since Deb texted me that your father is on campus talking to the board."

"*What?*" I twist around. I was on campus an hour ago. It doesn't seem possible my dad and I were in the same place and I didn't know.

Mom checks her phone and stows it in a sparkly gold clutch. The magnitude of her outfit choice hits me. She's dressed like she's going to a bar or a high school reunion— somewhere old people try to pretend they're twenty-five— not a PTA meeting at an elite private school. I know what those parents will be wearing, and they won't look kindly on my mom for treating our illustrious campus like a singles' night.

"There was some donors' meeting, and now the board is staying to sit in on the PTA meeting," Mom replies, unaware of whatever expression of horror I'm wearing. She grabs her keys and heads for the door. "I'll see you later tonight. Maybe," she adds with a wink I immediately try to obliterate from my memory.

Dad's here.

I'm out of my seat before she's reached the door. "Wait. I'm coming, too."

Mom's mouth twitches into a frown. "Cameron, I don't think students are typically invited to these."

I level her a dry look. "Are you even a member of the PTA?"

She meets my gaze, then holds open the door. "Point taken."

Mom starts collecting raised eyebrows and backward glances before we're out of the parking lot.

To her credit, she doesn't wither. Not even when a group of mothers in pantsuits and perfectly coordinated yoga outfits smirk and whisper as we walk by. I don't have the mental capacity to worry about it.

Dad's here.

Dad's here.

Dad's here.

The thought is an eclipse. Everything disappears behind it. We walk through campus, following the PTA signs pointing us toward the library, every step bringing us closer.

I try to remember when I saw him last. The beginning of summer, I think. He came out for a week, and we had dinner downtown and discussed my future. He mentioned his firm's internship and told me I'd only be eligible if I took an advanced economics course. I grasped on to the idea. I knew it was the closest I'd ever receive to an invitation to be part of his world.

He and my mom didn't get along that trip. I look at her now, how she's brimming with eagerness at the outside hope of a date with him. She cried for three days when he left in June, and it's as if all of that's forgotten, swept aside by something as small as the mention of his name in a text message from Deborah Richmond.

Then again, the last time he and I spoke he told me I was pathetic, and here I am, stupidly excited to see him again. I guess my mom and I have that in common.

I don't expect our relationship will be any different this visit. I can almost guarantee he won't be kind to my mom in front of the school's donors. He probably won't be kind to me, either. Maybe if I get the internship, get into UPenn, maybe then he'll see me for who I am.

Still, he's my dad, and he's here. I can't help hurrying my step.

We walk into the library, packed with parents and teachers.

I pick him out of the crowd immediately. His hair is immaculately cut, if grayer than I remembered. He's in a small group with the headmaster and a couple members of Student Government. Brad's there, to his right. Dad holds himself higher than everybody else. He's not taller than the rest of them, he just has a way of elevating his posture and squaring his shoulders in his perfectly tailored suit.

My mom grabs a seat directly in his eyeline. I know her

play. She's going to pretend she's here for the PTA meeting, just like usual, and running into him—dressed the way she is—is a coincidence.

I don't care about her plan. Unhesitating, I walk forward toward where he's talking with the group. He says something, and everybody laughs, which throws me for a second. There are plenty of things I know him for, but humor's not one of them.

I get a couple steps closer, and Brad notices me. "Hey, Cameron," he says, pleasant surprise comingling with curiosity in his voice. I guess that answers the question of whether he's giving me the silent treatment like Morgan and Elle.

Then my dad faces me. I falter for words. He grins, a grin he's hardly ever given me, warm and intent. It's incapacitating. The rush of emotions roots me in place. Surprise, well-worn wariness, and an awful, irrepressible strain of exuberance.

"Cameron!" he says, wrapping me in an unexpected sideways hug. "I'm glad you could make it." He smiles, and I catch the careful angle of his phrasing. It must sound to everyone else like he's invited me.

I can't help it. I mirror his smile despite the resentment mounting in me and the yearning that he *had* invited me.

The headmaster asks Lisa Gramercy a question. I face away from the group and say to my dad under my breath, "How long are you in town?"

"Not long," he replies. There's the terseness I remember. "I leave tomorrow morning." His eyes sweep the room, and finding my mom, he frowns. He pulls me a couple feet from the group. "What is she doing here? Why is she dressed like we're in a nightclub?" he demands.

It stings to hear. Even though I was just thinking something close, it's inexplicably worse to hear it from him.

"She's not going to make a scene, is she? The board's here. It's bad enough she's come dressed like this, but—"

Brad interrupts him. "Mr. Bright, the meeting's about to start. I'm sorry, Cameron," he says to me. "The headmaster said only Student Government can sit in."

I nod numbly. Brad cuts me an apologetic glance, and it's somehow worse that he understands he's ousting me from a rare opportunity to talk to my dad.

"Of course, Bradley," my dad says, and just like that, his generous grin comes back. "Weren't you interning with Whitestone last summer?" He faces Brad, and I'm cut off from the conversation.

"I was," Brad says. I remember him complaining every day over the summer on our group text about having to work with a venture capital firm when he wanted to go into law.

"Job like that for a kid your age, you're going places!" Dad claps him on the back. "We'll get coffee the next time I'm in town, discuss your career."

I blink sharply. He's never this friendly, not ever. I catch the way Brad's face brightens. He's only eager because he doesn't know who my dad really is, I remind myself, fighting down jealousy. I want to tell him it's fake, every bit of it—my dad's charm, his camaraderie, his attention to personal detail.

Or maybe it's not.

That's the thought I really don't want to be left alone with, to wrestle in the confines of my immaculate bedroom or out-run on the streets outside my house. That he's not dismissive of and too busy for everyone else. That it's only me he resents.

He and Brad head for their seats.

I grasp on to the one chance I have to remind him I'm worthwhile. "Dad, do you know when your company will tell me whether I got the internship?"

"I'm not in charge of recruiting, Cameron," he says distractedly.

I try one final time. "Well, do you want to get dinner when this is over?"

"I can't. I'm only in town for the night, and I have to get drinks with a couple clients." He takes his seat without even a backward glance.

I watch him, disbelieving. He could have pretended. He could have said, "Next time." I don't understand how he can invite a boy he hardly knows to coffee while he can't even *fake* wanting to have an evening with his own daughter.

Out of the corner of my eye, I see my mom working clumsily through the chairs, trying to get a seat closer to him. I remember the meeting's going to start in a couple minutes. I have to go, and it's kind of hard to breathe in here. I leave the library, not about to force myself to watch whatever plays out between the two of them.

The night is welcomingly cool, but it's not enough to ease the hurt fury roiling under my skin. I don't know what I expected. He can come to my school's board meetings, can chat up Brad and the headmaster, but he can't even spare me a minute, much less an evening. I wouldn't have even known he was in town if freaking Deb hadn't texted my mom. I hope Mom does make a scene. I hope she embarrasses him.

But it'll be different when I get into Wharton.

I recognize the faint voice whispering comfortingly into my ear. I hold on to the words. Unlike the night, they calm the bad blood coursing through me. If I can prove I'm like him—if I can get into UPenn and get a job like Brad's—my father will see me for who I am.

He has to.

Thirty-Four

I WAIT ON THE CURB IN FRONT of school, hugging my elbows in the November wind. I wish I'd driven myself here and could drive home. Instead, I have to wait, wondering how long my mom's going to linger in hopes it'll be different this time and it'll be a PTA meeting where he'll finally get down on one knee. She's imagining a Cinderella story twenty years late, my Homecoming dress for a gown and a library of parents and teachers for a ball.

I want to text her to ask whether she's going to leave the meeting early, except I know it'll be futile. She won't leave until Dad does. She *definitely* won't reply if she's preoccupied, or if I'm bothering her, or—

"Need a ride?"

I glance up from my shoes. In the school's semicircular driveway, with the engine running, waits a black beaten-up sedan. Paige peers out the open passenger's window, her neck craned from the driver's seat.

"What are you doing at school this late?" I ask.

Paige shrugs. "Didn't want to go home. Nobody was at Mordor because Charlie and Abby have chess club." She nods in my direction, presumably noticing my posture of cold-resistance. "I'm not going to wait here forever, Bright. You want a ride?"

I give school a backward glance. If I keep waiting I'll have to contend with whatever versions of my parents come out of there. My mom, flirtatious and triumphant or depressed and diminutive. My dad, cunningly charming or cold and distant.

I walk purposefully to Paige's car and open the passenger door.

"Thanks," I say, closing the door behind me. Paige pulls out of the parking lot. Neither of us speaks while she drives for a couple minutes on quiet tree-lined streets until she turns east onto Wilshire toward my house. Even though she's only driven me home once before, the night of *Rocky Horror*, she doesn't ask for directions.

"What were *you* doing at school this late?" she asks finally.

I face the window determinedly. I really don't want to discuss it. Even with Elle, I never went into detail about the particulars of my parents' relationship. There's no point. Being vulnerable would only open me up to unwanted pity and false reassurances and force me to wallow in my feelings. It's like crying—useless.

"My mom's at the PTA meeting," I say. It's not an answer, and I hope I've said it definitively enough Paige knows I don't want to give one.

We wait for the light to change, both saying nothing. I move my foot and bump something heavy on the floor. I nudge aside what I realize is a book, *America's History*, the junior-year AP US History textbook. There's a distinct possibility the book is Paige's and has remained in the passenger seat under the dash for a whole year, but it's probably Brendan's.

For a moment I'm grateful Paige was alone at school tonight and I don't have to contend with my feelings for Brendan, and then I realize what it means Brendan's probably up to.

"Where's your brother?" I ask masochistically.

Paige eyes me, on predictably high alert. "SAT tutoring," she says gingerly, likely planning how she's going to trap me into a confession of my ardent love for him.

"I can't believe your parents have him in tutoring—and on a Friday night—when he has a practically perfect score," I reply, determined to thwart her efforts. I remember their dad's expression while he lectured Brendan, his uncompromising demeanor, the way he appeared to believe it was to Brendan's benefit. I wonder if Paige got the same treatment. I can't imagine her, with her shaved head and her vampire posters, just going along with her parents' pressure. "Did you get a perfect score?"

She laughs derisively. "Of course not. I'm kind of flattered you think I'm that smart, honestly."

I furrow my brow. "Why do they have Brendan doing all this tutoring if they didn't for you?"

Paige goes quiet, her expression growing stony. I face the window again, understanding I've trespassed into territory she doesn't want to cover. It's none of my business if she doesn't want to discuss problems with her parents.

"Brendan's always been the gifted one," she says quietly. I turn back to her, having not expected an answer. Paige watches the road, a distance in her eyes. She goes on. "It was his kindergarten teacher who told my parents Brendan was special. The very next day, my dad decided Brendan was going to go to MIT, and I became the spare. It's not like he forgot I existed. I just . . . mattered less."

I nod. "You couldn't be enough," I say, hearing the echo of words that have run through my head a thousand times.

"Exactly," Paige says. We come up to a red light. She studies me for a moment, her eyes no longer distant. "I don't envy Brendan. I know he has it really hard, with my dad breathing down his neck every day while my mom says nothing. But I just wish that my dad would notice me, that he'd pay me a fraction of the attention he does Brendan, even if that attention is only him lecturing me and forcing me to study."

The light changes, and Paige returns her eyes to the road. We pass La Brea and Highland, a blur of streetlights and illuminated signs.

"It's why I screw off," Paige continues hollowly. "It's why I dye my hair, work on costumes until one in the morning, get shitty grades, and come home drunk from a nightclub where I hooked up with a guy I don't even like. Because I got into the same prep school as Brendan, and it didn't matter. I could get Brendan's GPA, Brendan's test scores, Brendan's college acceptances, and it *wouldn't fucking matter*. I get my parents' attention the way I have to."

I look at Paige, whose eyes remain on the cars crossing the

intersection in front of us. I knew what Brendan was going through with his parents, but Paige? I had no idea how much we had in common.

"Well, that's dumb," I say, my voice thick, "because you're awesome."

She laughs, wiping a tear from her cheek, and pulls up to the curb outside my apartment building. I glance up at my dark bedroom window, my hand on the car door. I want to acknowledge what Paige's confided in me. To tell her I'm touched she's allowed me to see this side of her and I won't betray her friendship—a friendship I'm grateful for every day. I open my mouth to thank her for what she's told me, for giving me more chances than I deserve, for being there for me when I didn't even know how much I needed her.

Instead, I say, "My dad showed up at school tonight."

Paige blinks, then turns off the engine and gives me her full attention. My heart pounds painfully in my chest. Telling her everything is terrifying, but I'm going to. It's the right way to show her she's important to me. And maybe her bravery has lifted my own. I take my hand off the door.

"Doesn't he live in New York or something?" she asks carefully.

"Philadelphia." I blow out a breath. "He didn't even tell me he was coming to town. My mom found out from a friend who saw him."

"Shit, Cameron. That's messed up." Her eyes are round, her eyebrows raised.

"It is, right?" I tentatively meet her gaze, genuinely needing her confirmation to believe it.

"Yes," she says deliberately. "It is."

Her words unlock something in me, and suddenly I can't get my own out fast enough. "It's just, he's not nice to my mom or even to me. But tonight, he was nice to everyone else."

"That's *not* your fault," Paige cuts in quickly. "People put on appearances in front of strangers. It has nothing to do with you."

I nod, unreasonably relieved to hear her voice what I'd been desperately trying to convince myself was true. I shift in my seat, facing her completely. "I don't know why, but I still try. I still show up hoping he'll want to see me. I send him my grades, my test scores—I do everything I can to talk to him. Is there something wrong with me?" My voice is quiet, but I force myself not to hide in the shadows coming through the window. "I know he's awful. I know it isn't okay when he calls my mom pathetic, but I still look at him and—and I want to be him. Because he's successful and he achieves his goals, and my mom . . . doesn't. It's why I'm such a bitch, I guess."

Paige's mouth softens with concern. "There's nothing wrong with you. He's your dad. *Of course* you want his approval, no matter what kind of guy he is." She pauses, and I think she's said everything she's going to until her lips curve lightly upward. "And you're not a bitch, Cameron," she adds.

I fix my eyes on the textbook on the floor, unable to meet hers. "But I am. Did you forget what I said to you at Skāra?"

"No. I haven't forgotten. You told me to find someone as pathetic as I am to hook up with," she says harshly, her anger from that night not completely faded.

"I as much as called you pathetic. I thought it, too. I have a dozen memories of my dad saying the same to my mom. I've watched it wreck her a little more each time. I *know* what an awful thing it is to hurl at someone, and I did it anyway." I raise my gaze to her. "I'm sorry, Paige. I really am. I would take it back if I could. You're a million miles from pathetic."

I'm the pathetic one. The thought is too heavy to reach my voice. Everyone knows it anyway, Paige especially.

"See?" Paige says. "Not like your dad at all, are you? Has he ever given a genuine apology like that in his life?"

The thought crumbles into a thousand little pieces. "No," I say, surprised. "I don't think he has." It sounds like such a small difference between him and me—just a few words. *I'm sorry.* But it's not small. It's actually really huge. I don't know how I didn't see it before.

"Besides," Paige continues, "you weren't entirely wrong. You were just saying something I didn't want to hear."

"No—" I try to protest, but she cuts me off.

"I hooked up with *Jeff Mitchel*, and I didn't even like him. It's why I was crying when I stumbled into you. I was disgusted with myself, with what a pathetic thing I'd done, and I was starting to wonder if it wasn't all just a big excuse. If I tell myself I'm doing it to get my parents to notice me, but really I'm just a screwup."

"You're not," I say quickly. "Not at all. Maybe—okay, definitely—hooking up with Jeff was a mistake. But no one's perfect, right?" She smiles, and I know she remembers the speech she gave her friends before *Rocky*. "I mean, if it'd make you feel better I could list all the mistakes *I've* made."

Paige's lips twitch. "That's okay. We can't sit here all night."

I pull an indignant expression, but Paige starts the car. "Wait, what are you doing?"

She drives back down the block without hesitating. "Your mom's not home, and we just had a major bonding moment." She steals a glance at me. "I think you should sleep over. Isn't that, like, something popular girls like to do?"

I laugh and settle into my seat. "I told you you didn't know anything about popular girls."

Paige raises an eyebrow. "Maybe. But I don't think you do, either. I think you're just you."

We sit in comfortable silence the whole drive to Paige's house.

Thirty-Five

I STARE UP AT PAIGE'S CEILING. HER room is dark, and she's snoring softly. I'm waiting for sleep, feeling peaceful in a way I could get used to.

It was past eight when we pulled into Paige's driveway. We ordered pizza—it felt fittingly stereotypical for a slumber party. Brendan didn't join us. I don't know where he is, and I didn't go looking for him. Paige forced me to watch three episodes of *Boys Over Flowers*, which ended up being nearly four hours because Korean TV episodes run over an hour each. While I didn't understand everything, I'll admit she wasn't forcing me by episode three.

Paige fell asleep pretty much immediately after we finished watching. It's two in the morning now. I get up and tiptoe to the door, wanting a glass of water.

But when I walk into the hallway, I can't help noticing an illuminated strip on the floor under Brendan's bedroom door.

I hesitate. I haven't wanted to tell Brendan the truth because I haven't wanted to face how uninterested in me I have to assume he is. It felt like worthwhile reasoning yesterday, even hours ago. Now, I don't know. I've told myself Brendan wouldn't fit into my life, but just because I haven't worked it out on paper doesn't mean it won't work.

I've been honest with everyone else in my entire life, even when it's to my detriment. If I'm not honest about my feelings toward Brendan I'm not just giving up the possibility of us, I'm betraying myself. If that honesty leads to getting rejected, then okay. I'm not afraid anymore, not after opening up to Paige about things I've never felt comfortable telling people close to me. Real friends like Paige accept me for who I am. I won't be alone even if Brendan rejects me.

I walk decisively to Brendan's door. Without knocking, I barge in, realizing a moment too late what a sixteen-year-old boy could be doing alone in his room in the middle of the night. Thankfully, Brendan's only writing in a bulky SAT book when I walk in.

He spins around in his chair, obviously startled. "I didn't kiss you to resuscitate your social life," I say, not giving him the chance to ask why I'm here.

His mouth works hopelessly to form words. "Cameron, it's the middle of the night. Why are you even in my house?"

I close the door and don't bother with his question. "I kissed you because I had to know what was between us," I inform him.

Confusion fades from Brendan's features, replaced by astonishment and finally something guarded. His voice is unsteady when he asks, "What did you conclude?"

"I have to admit something before I tell you," I reply. I

draw in a breath. I'm perched at the edge of a cliff, and finally I'm ready to dive. "You once asked me why I wanted to make amends for the things I've done. The truth is, I was doing it to become a better person." Brendan opens his mouth, but I hold up a hand, halting him. "And I wanted to become a better person so Andrew Richmond would date me."

Brendan's expression clouds over with hurt. "Wait," he says darkly, his eyes flashing, "our entire friendship, you were just using me to impress some other guy?"

I'm not going to try to talk him out of his anger. He's entitled to be angry. I'm here to bare everything in my heart, and I won't hesitate until I have.

"Brendan," I say forcefully. "Our friendship might have begun because of Andrew. But it was only that for about two seconds. Every time I talked to you after that horrendously bad first apology was because *I* wanted to talk to you." Brendan opens his mouth once again, and again I cut him off. "No, I have to say this. Last week, I got what I wanted. Andrew asked me to winter formal. And . . . I said no."

I watch Brendan's features while I say it, expecting incomprehension or even disgust. Instead, his face remains closed off, expressionless. I wait for him to say something. But this time, he's silent.

"I said no because of you," I continue. I feel the tempo of my heart pick up, my pulse pounding in the tips of my fingers. The words feel foreign in my mouth, even frightening. "Because when we kissed, I felt something real. Something I'd never felt with anyone, Andrew included. I think I was

feeling it for a long time. Of course, seeing you in your . . .
costume"—I glance toward the region on him I have in mind,
and I catch the flicker of humor on his lips—"helped wake
me up to my feelings. But it wasn't only that. It was the times
you made me laugh when I was upset, or when you told me
you liked and even wanted my honest opinions."

I walk across the room, closing the distance between us. I
feel electricity in my nerves.

"All my life," I say, "I thought love required hard work. It's
what my parents taught me." My dad's made me earn his love,
and my mom's chased it without ever reaching it. "But, Brendan, you've shown me it's the opposite."

I'm close enough now to touch him.

"It's not hard to be with someone you love. It's the most
natural thing in the world," I finish. He stands up, his eyes
locked on mine.

I lean in gently.

Brendan doesn't move away, and I kiss him.

Or, really, "kiss" isn't the word. I fold into him, fitting perfectly into the frame I once found unnaturally tall, running a
hand through his slightly too-long, wonderful hair. He kisses
me back, his arms encircling my waist and pulling me forward. It's like when we kissed in the robotics room, except
multiplied by a hundred.

Okay, now I'm thinking of kissing in mathematical terms.
The nerd is definitely rubbing off on me.

He's unhesitating. His hand runs up my back, his mouth
gentle and relentless all at once. I can't tell if I'm holding in

a breath or breathless. I wonder if every guy with no experience kisses like this or if it's just Brendan.

He withdraws, but his hands remain holding my waist tightly, not letting me go. "What's . . . happening right now?" His voice holds genuine confusion edged with exhilaration.

I press a kiss against his neck. "I just told you I want to be with you," I say, uncertainty tugging at my tone. "If you don't want to be with me, then I guess I'll go . . ." I start to turn away.

Brendan laughs, catching me by the elbow and pulling me back.

"You're joking, right?" he asks.

I don't say anything. Obviously, he's kissing me, which isn't nothing. But I just vomited my feelings to him in one long, acrid outpouring, and he's said nothing in return.

The humor fades from Brendan's expression, and he gently brushes a strand of my hair behind my ear. "I've been fighting feelings for you for a while, Cameron," he says. "Fighting because of what you did to me years ago and because everyone knows you're the unattainable Cameron Bright, and I thought I'd never have a chance with you. But it's been a losing battle." I've never heard this intensity in his voice, not even in our first conversation. His eyes, lit with perfect clarity, fix on mine. "I remember when I realized I felt this way about you. You were ordering Grant around in the library. And trying terribly, I have to add, to drop references to Link from *Zelda*."

"Don't you mean," I say, not suppressing a smile, "boy-Zelda?"

"How could I forget?" Brendan asks wryly. "I thought it was obvious how I felt when I asked you out on a date." Warmth swells in my chest. *It* was *a date!* "Then you practically encouraged me to hook up with Eileen Roth, and I got confused. I've been trying this week not to pressure you into anything you didn't want. But I've known what I want for a long time." His voice drops to a murmur. "Don't ever doubt this, Cameron. I'm crazy about you. *You*, with your fierce intelligence and extraordinary talent. You, with your uncompromising opinions. And I want you to know it. I'm desperate for you to know it."

I hardly even process his words. In the next moment, he's kissing me.

When I went for Andrew, I planned everything consciously, even calculatingly. I tried to find and design the perfect thing to say for every moment. Nobody's ever bothered to figure out what would be the exact right thing to say to *me*. What *I* need to hear.

Nobody until Brendan, who just did it effortlessly.

I draw us both toward the bed. Brendan follows, his lips remaining on mine. He breaks off when the backs of my legs touch the comforter.

"Cool, bye now," he says in a terrible imitation of me. His hands slip lower on my back.

Heat rises in my cheeks. "Oh, shut up. I panicked. I admit it wasn't my smoothest line." I speak haltingly, distracted by his touch crossing my waistband.

"No, it definitely wasn't your—" I cut him off with a kiss, having had enough of this teasing. "Mmm," he murmurs against my lips. "It's going to take my brain a while to accept this is really happening."

"That's okay." I climb onto the covers, pulling him with one hand onto me. "I've got time."

He holds himself over me on one elbow, dipping his head to press quick kisses to my lips. Each fires a spark through me. I bend my legs impulsively, instinctively, and he collapses into me, his hand running up my arm, his heartbeat racing to match mine. I can't catch my breath, but it's a delicious kind of breathlessness.

I feel a tremble in his touch, an echo of the nervous exhilaration flooding though me. Reaching up, I caress his forearm, and he grins into my lips.

He withdraws a fraction of an inch. "Do you remember," he asks, his voice a tender whisper, "when I told you there was nothing I could ever want from you?"

I do remember. I couldn't forget his vehemence during our first conversation, the wounded resentment in his eyes when he ordered me out of his life. I nod.

"Well, I was wrong."

"Oh yeah?" I run my hands up his chest, raising an eyebrow coyly. "What is it you want from me, Brendan Rosenfeld?"

He leans in, his lips brushing my cheek as he whispers in my ear. "Everything."

We wake to the routine sounds of Brendan's parents in the kitchen, footsteps and closing cabinets outside Brendan's door. We slept on top of the covers in our clothes, wrapped in each other. I don't even remember when we nodded off.

He tucks me to his chest, and I don't want to budge for the rest of the day. Possibly forever.

But instead, I whisper, "I should sneak back to Paige's room. I don't exactly think our relationship would go over well if your parents found out by walking in on us."

"We could risk it," he mutters, smiling sleepily.

I can't help a laugh. But reluctantly, I walk to Brendan's door. I pause with my hand on the knob, a thought leaping into my head, sunlight through an open window. "Brendan," I say, facing him. "Will you go to winter formal with me?"

Brendan beams. I can't remember a time he's looked this openly happy, and it's unbelievably endearing. It makes me want to ask him again, just to fix that expression on his face.

"Yes," he says. "Yes, Cameron. I'd love to."

I open his bedroom door, throwing a final smile over my shoulder.

I walk quickly and quietly down the hall to Paige's room. Easing the door open gently, I duck into the bedroom, where I'm relieved to find Paige breathing evenly under the covers. I slide gingerly into my sleeping bag.

I'm replaying the night, my chest full with the memory, when Paige speaks, startling me. "I knew it," she says, her eyes still closed. "I knew you liked him." She rolls over and fixes me with a triumphant grin.

I reach for a comeback. And for the first time in the history of my friendship with Paige, I come up empty.

"Wow," she says in undisguised astonishment. "You've got it *bad*."

I smile and roll onto my back, staring up at the ceiling. *Yeah, I do.*

Thirty-Six

I CHANGED MY OUTFIT THREE TIMES THIS morning, and I still have no idea if I picked the right one. What do you wear when you're going public to the Beaumont student body with your relationship with Brendan Rosenfeld while your friends hate you and want every excuse to scoff behind your back?

Not that what I'm wearing will matter to Brendan, of course. It doesn't even really matter to me.

The outfit's a distraction from this weekend. From the problems I knew—even while watching TV with Paige and taking refuge in Brendan's arms—I would come back to when I got home.

I found Mom sleeping on the couch in my Homecoming dress when I got home from Paige's on Saturday. Even though it was nearly ten, I didn't bother waking her up, but I had to resist the urge to throw the front door closed behind me. For the next day and a half, I endured her watery eyes and one-word conversations. Whatever happened with my dad, it wasn't good. She called in sick to work twice, and I know she's not getting to work on time today. It won't be long before she gets fired or quits.

I've kept out of her way. If I speak to her, I'll say nothing nice. I have nothing nice *to* say. I'll let out years of resentment, the bitterness that boils in me every time I have to watch her fall into familiar patterns with Dad. I know she was disappointed in her plans with him just like I was. But I don't understand why she can't or won't protect us from this person, this human wrecking ball who destroys us both every time we try to rebuild.

I have a full school day before I have to face her again, though—a day including Brendan.

I find him waiting on the front steps—waiting, I realize, for me. I've never seen Brendan in the morning. I figure he's usually in one classroom or another by now, and it fills me with an indefinable gratitude that he's come out for me. He's grinning already, and I feel a pang of frustration I can't put thoughts of my mom from my mind and concentrate entirely on this new thing between him and me.

I'm walking up the steps when two volleyball guys pass Brendan, cutting him quizzical looks. I notice the way his expression wavers, and he self-consciously shifts the straps of his backpack. "I wasn't sure if I should walk you to class," he says when I reach him. "Usually I pick up what I need for Computer Science from Mr. West's room—"

"Brendan," I interrupt, "do you *want* to walk me to class?"

He blinks. "Of course," he says after a moment.

"Then I don't know why this is a question."

Brendan's gaze wavers from mine. "It's just . . ." he begins reluctantly. "I'd understand if you don't want to be public about us," he says finally. "The only thing that's important to me is being with you."

His words throw me, until I put together the pieces—the way he dodges my eyes, the way he flinched from the jocks like a fugitive in plain sight. "You think I'm embarrassed to be seen with you?"

"Well . . ." Brendan half shrugs uncomfortably.

I take his hand, entwining my fingers with his. "You're wrong," I tell him. "So wrong I'm starting to doubt if you're as smart as everyone says you are."

Hesitantly, he smiles. We walk up the front steps, hand in hand. I don't fail to catch the glances from the crowd hanging out in front of the doors—including Elle, who's not openly stunned like the rest. Just dismissive. "You actually might be more popular than I am at the moment," I mutter to Brendan.

Brendan cuts me a curious look. "I am?"

"Elle and Morgan won't talk to me. Probably Andrew, too. Your sister's pretty much my only friend. Whereas I heard *you* had tons of girls trying to get with you last week." I nudge his shoulder.

"I guess you're right," he says brightly. "Wait," he adds, pausing with an expression on his face like he's just had an epiphany. "What am I doing here with you? If *I'm* the popular one, I should be taking the student body president to winter formal or hooking up with the captain of the dance team."

I shove him lightly. "Very funny."

"You think I'm joking?" He raises an eyebrow.

I indignantly yank my hand away, but he holds it tighter, pulling me to him and kissing me in front of everyone. I hear the murmur ripple through my classmates, and I don't care. I wrap my hand around his neck and kiss him back.

He draws away. "I *was* joking, you know," he says.

"Yeah," I reply breathlessly. "I know, dummy. Besides, half the school saw that. I think you're stuck with me now."

"Good." He opens the front door for me. "How should we tell the other half?"

I watch the clock in fourth-period English. For the first time in a while, I'm genuinely looking forward to lunch. I'm meeting Brendan in the robotics room, where he's going to walk me through the newest demos of *The Girl's a Sorceress*. Is this love, looking forward to video games?

Finally, the bell rings, interrupting Ms. Kowalski, who's spent the past five whole minutes reminding us our term paper is due right before winter break. I toss my copy of *The Taming of the Shrew* in my bag and rush to the door.

Morgan's waiting by the drinking fountain for Elle. I pass her, keeping my eyes determinedly averted.

"Hey, Cam, wait," I hear behind me when I'm at the end of the hall.

I turn, finding Morgan jogging to catch up with me. She's wearing a new pair of leather boots, and they click loudly against the tile. I say nothing when she stops in front of me.

"I—I heard about you and Brendan," she begins, her cheeks flushed. I'm not sure I've ever seen Morgan nervous before. "I just wanted to say I'm really happy for you."

"You . . . are?" I want to say more, but I can't decide if I'm mad at her for ignoring me for two weeks or happy she's speaking to me.

She tosses a look over her shoulder toward Kowalski's room, where Elle will be emerging any moment. "I'm not, like, choosing sides, you know. This fight is honestly really stupid, and I'm not getting in the middle."

I feel my eyes widen. "Sitting with Elle at lunch and not texting me is you *not* choosing sides?"

Morgan's lips twist into a frown, but she doesn't drop my gaze. "I'm sitting where I always sit. I can't control that you decided to move. And you haven't exactly been texting me either, you know."

The classroom door swings open, revealing Elle's shiny black hair. She looks for Morgan by the drinking fountain, then scowls when she doesn't find her.

"Look," Morgan continues, more hurriedly now, "Elle doesn't have a ton of real friends, and you . . . well, Cameron, you've made it pretty clear you don't need us. You have a whole other group of friends now *and* a boyfriend. I'm not going to abandon Elle, even if I do think this whole thing is idiotic."

"I still need you guys," I say quickly. It hits me then how *much* I need them. Elle and Morgan have been my friends for years. They understand parts of me I don't think Paige or even Brendan ever fully could. I like watching weird TV shows with Paige and joking about geekdom with Brendan, but I also like sitting in Elle's bathroom, learning how to line my lips, then going out to dance with her and Morgan to ridiculous pop songs. I don't think I need to choose between those sides of myself. Do I?

Morgan's expression softens. She opens her mouth, but Elle's impatient voice interrupts her.

"Morgan. You coming or what?" Elle asks, her arms crossed.

Morgan gives me an apologetic glance, then nods. "I hope you guys figure this out soon, Cam," she says before heading in Elle's direction.

I watch them leave, the physical ache of their absence worse than ever before.

Elle wasn't a perfect friend. Our friendship wasn't perfect. I know that now in a way I didn't before. But just because it wasn't perfect doesn't mean it's worth giving up on.

I've made enough apologies in the past few months to know when I need to make one more.

Thirty-Seven

I DRIVE RIGHT FROM CROSS-COUNTRY TO WEST Hollywood, where I proceed to hunt for parking for thirty minutes before finding a meter. Crossing the street, I take in the crowd of elaborately dressed twentysomethings congregated outside one of Melrose Avenue's many murals. The pink-and-white wall faces a patio with rows of folding tables holding stacks of T-shirts with intricate logos I don't recognize. A DJ spins hip-hop in one corner as girls in ankle-high Nikes and pristine makeup peruse the hats and jackets. Word only spreads for pop-up shops like this one on social media. I had to hunt surreptitiously for half an hour in Computer Science to figure out where I'm going.

I ignore the DJ and walk to the back, where an unmistakable yellow van waits. When a gorgeous model exits in fresh makeup, I catch the open door. Inside, Elle's cleaning her brushes.

She glances up, anger quickly settling on her features.

"You're following me now?" she asks shortly.

"I'll admit," I say, keeping my voice light, "I stalked you on Instagram to find you." Elle doesn't laugh, not that I expected her to. Her mouth remains a hard line. I pull in a breath, needing to say what I came here for. "Elle, I want to apologize."

She crosses her arms. "Added my name to your list, huh?"

"I have," I say evenly. "But not for Andrew. For you."

Elle says nothing. I know it's the closest I'll get to permission.

I continue. "You were right about part of what you said. I was wrong to change myself for someone else. No guy—no*body*—is worth that." Not even Brendan. If the only way for us to be together would be for me to change, I wouldn't. I'm done chasing people who don't want the real me. "And I admire how you don't compromise yourself or your goals. You never apologize for your ambition. I want to be like that," I admit.

It could be wishful thinking, but Elle's eyes might soften a little.

"But, Elle," I go on, "there's a difference between apologizing for who you are and apologizing for what you've done. I don't regret my decision to make amends for how I've hurt people. I don't want to change who I am, but I don't think trying to be kinder is necessarily the same as changing. I know it's a fine line. Sometimes I was on the wrong side of the divide between kindness and compromising myself," I say. "But sometimes I wasn't."

I watch Elle for even the touch of a reaction. Finally, she uncrosses her arms.

"Maybe," she says. She drops into the chair in front of her

vanity. "I understand what you were doing," she continues after a pause. "And I *would've* understood if you'd told me. But you didn't."

I lower my eyes. "I should have," I admit. "And I wanted to. But I just . . ." I pause, searching. "I just think you're untouchable. Unflinching. Completely *you*. I didn't want to get in your way, and I . . . thought you wouldn't care."

When Elle speaks again, her voice is even, but I know her well enough to hear the hurt that's replaced her anger. "You were my best friend, Cameron," she says quietly, and I don't miss her use of the past tense. It stings. "I would have cared. I *do* care. And you might think I'm *untouchable*"—she emphasizes it with momentary fierceness—"but I do depend on people. I depended on you." Her words gather force as she continues. "And you confided in people you hardly knew instead of me. You used the personal information *I* told you for your own agenda. Worst of all? You judged me. I've collaborated and encouraged and been there for you for years, and you decided I only use people for my own ends. My *best friend* determined I wasn't a good enough person to be a part of what she was doing."

"That's not—" I begin. But she's right. Everything she said is right.

And in a horrible lurch, I realize for the first time how the past few months have felt for Elle. How confusing and lonely they've been for this person I thought didn't care. How I pushed away the closest friend I had, who needed me more than I knew.

"I'm sorry," I say in nearly a whisper. "I'm going to fix this."

"Why? Just to ruin it again the next time you think I'm not worthy of being your friend?" Elle's voice finally wavers. "You can't fix betrayal with an apology."

I say nothing. My mind works furiously to bridge the impossible gap between us. Four feet that could be infinite, a lifetime's journey. Nothing comes, and I only watch her helplessly. Elle pretends not to notice, her eyes returning to the vanity, and begins rearranging her bottles of foundation with what I know is forced precision.

"Go." She speaks quietly and carefully. "Just go."

I have no choice. I force down the throb in my throat, nod once, and turn, passing a completely oblivious porcelain-skinned woman as she approaches Elle's van. I hear Elle greet her with YouTube-trained brightness, and for a moment I'm back in Elle's bedroom, excitedly positioning lights and watching when she hits Record. The thought is wrenching, nearly enough for me to turn back.

But I don't.

I won't force forgiveness on Elle. I've given enough apologies to understand the point is not to cross out the wrong, not to pretend it never happened. That's just the hopeful side effect. The point is only to let someone know they're worth your remorse. I won't push for more from Elle, though I desperately hope she forgives me. I really, really want my best friend back.

But it's her choice. Not mine. I have to be okay with that for now.

I thread through the tables of trendy merchandise back to where I parked. In the car, I have to calm my ragged breathing for a full two minutes—*inhale, exhale*—before I reach into my purse for my notebook. With a hand nearly as even as Elle's, I write a thin line through her name, the final on my list.

Thirty-Eight

FOR THE NEXT THREE WEEKS, I SPEND every lunch with Brendan, helping him beta test his game for the UCLA contest. In between being murdered by the sexy sorceress, I give him design feedback. Thanksgiving comes, and because my mom's on a cleanse, I go over to Paige and Brendan's. It's nice, nicer than I ever remember the holiday being, even if I catch Mr. Rosenfeld glaring at me twice.

I'm sitting in front of my mirror on the first Friday of December, straightening my hair.

It's definitely not the pre–winter formal ritual I envisioned. Normally, I'd be in Morgan's bedroom before a dance, trying on dresses from her endless closet and having Elle do my makeup. But tonight won't be the night I'd planned, and I'm learning to be okay with that.

I couldn't convince Paige to skip her annual Anti–Winter Formal Party. But Brendan's thrown himself into preparations for the dance with endearing enthusiasm, texting me about corsage colors and what tie he should wear.

It has me looking forward to the night in a way I'd never expected. I finish straightening my hair, permitting myself to admire my work in the mirror. I stand up, inspecting my outfit—my prom dress from last year, with the little rip next to the zipper.

I'm reaching for my heels when I hear my phone vibrate. I figure it's Brendan here to pick me up. Putting on one shoe, I glance at the screen distractedly.

It's not Brendan.

The sender line reads: *Bright Partners—Human Resources*. It sends a jolt through me, exhilaration or fear. My brain doesn't have time to decipher which. Without pulling on the other shoe, I hurriedly open the screen.

It's probably true that the contents of every important email ever sent could be understood from the first few words. This one, definitely.

From: human_res@brightpartners.com
To: c.bright@beaumontprep.edu
Subject: Summer Internship Program

Dear Miss Bright,
We have reviewed your application, and while . . .

Everything past "while" could be in hieroglyphics. I force myself to read every word anyway, feeling the hot flush rising in my face.

We have reviewed your application, and while we were impressed with your coursework and achievements, we received an unusual number of applications for this year's program from highly qualified candidates. Unfortunately, we could not offer you a position with our company this summer.

I read the email twice. Then a third time.

Without this internship, I won't have the chance to spend the summer with my dad. The thought registers only faintly in a corner of my mind, overshadowed by a realization I feel with a bite a hundred times deeper.

He rejected me. He rejected *me*. My dad knew I'd applied, knew I'd eagerly enrolled in Economics in the Entrepreneur's Market and requested a fucking *Economist* subscription for my birthday. He knew I wanted this. He knew I was trying.

And he rejected me.

With a shaking hand, I set the phone down. My stomach roils, and I feel like I'm going to throw up. Maybe it would help. Maybe this feeling is something I can force out of me over a toilet bowl. Cold sweat beads on my forehead, ruining the foundation I spent twenty minutes applying.

He doesn't think I'm good enough. Everything I did to please him—the courses I took, the grades, the hours I spent teaching myself—it wasn't enough.

It shouldn't matter. I told myself I was done trying to live up to everyone's expectations. When I kissed Brendan and turned down Andrew, I made the decision to do what *I* wanted. I hate Economics—why do I care that I'm spared a summer of spreadsheets and market projections?

But in the bottom of my stomach, I know why. Because it's my dad. If there's one person whose approval I should have, it's his. I understand he and I don't have a normal relationship. Years without visits, absent phone calls on my birthday, emails from his assistant—I've accepted that. But *this*? I know he pulls strings for colleagues' friends. All it would have taken was an email from him and I would have had that job. I would have been spending two whole months with him over the summer at his office.

But I'm not good enough. And if I'm not good enough now, I'm realizing I won't ever be. I've fought and hungered for his recognition. It's kept me going, driven me through hard classes and harder conversations with Mom. But the respect, the worth I hoped to hold in his eyes—I'll never have it.

I fumble for my phone. My thumbs dial out the number I know by heart before I've thought out what I'll say. I listen to the ring, realizing that with the time difference, he's probably in the middle of dinner. I don't care.

"Daniel Bright's phone," Chelsea answers after the third ring.

"Put me through to my dad." My voice cracks on the last word.

"Cameron?" she asks like she doesn't know exactly who's calling. "I'm afraid Mr. Bright's with a—"

"I don't fucking care!" I shout. My eyes are burning, but I clench them shut, trapping any tears. "I'll keep calling until you put me through."

The line goes silent for a moment. I'm sure Chelsea's used to cursing and yelling from Daniel Bright, but I've never so much as sent a passive-aggressive email to her in the past.

"I'm very sorry, Cameron. Could we—"

"*Listen* to me!" I interrupt her again. For a moment I feel bad for her. She's not the one at fault. But I call on the rotten, nasty piece of myself I'd thought was gone. "I'm not about to let some little assistant keep me from speaking with my own father." I breathe heavily into the line, the tightness only a run can dispel lodging in my lungs.

"One moment," Chelsea says softly. The phone beeps, then rings again.

"Cameron, this is completely inappropriate," my dad answers, his voice clipped in the way that always precedes a dismissal.

"How could you reject me from your own company?" I ask, the words exploding from my lips. "It's an *internship*. I'm not good enough to sort your mail and get your coffee?" *To be in your life?*

Clinking glasses, chatter, and low music fill the silence. "We have strict criteria for every position, internships included," he says evenly. "It's very competitive."

"I'm your *daughter*." It comes out a whimper, and I hate the sound of it. The desperation and vulnerability behind a sentence that should be little more than a statement of fact.

I think he hates the sound of it, too. His voice comes through harder, each syllable slapping the speakers. "Being my daughter does not make you qualified. Frankly, this call only confirms our decision."

Our. Not *their.* One tear slips down my cheek. I furiously wipe it away.

"Clearly," he continues, "you do not possess the professionalism we require. I knew you were spoiled, but this level of immaturity is disappointing, Cameron."

"Because I have to be professional every time I talk to you, right?" I say in a rush. I stand up, facing away from the mirror to hide from the redness in my eyes. "Because everything I do, every phone call—"

"This is exactly how your mother would respond." His words cut me to the knees, and I stumble to my bed. He pauses, like he knows how big a blow he's struck. Like . . . he's enjoying it. "Calling me to fix your problems because you couldn't put in the hard work on your own?" The knife of his voice becomes silken, patronizing, and low. "I've given you more than your fair share of opportunities. It is entirely your own fault you've failed to capitalize on them." The sounds of the bar or restaurant or wherever he is get louder, and I assume he's walking back to whomever he'd been in the middle of meeting when I called.

"I don't care about the *opportunities*," I spit down the line, every nerve in my body raw. "I just wanted a dad."

I end the call before he can hang up on me. It's not enough he's two thousand miles away. I throw my phone into the corner of my room, enjoying the heavy smack it makes against the carpet.

Something drips onto my chest, and I look down to find tears bleeding into the silver of my dress. My face is wet, my makeup ruined. Sticky clots of mascara pull at my eyelashes, stinging and itching my eyes. My breath comes in painful gulps, like I'm suffocating. I'd forgotten the feeling, it's been so long.

I don't reach for my running shoes. I don't stop myself.

For the first time in years, I cry.

Thirty-Nine

I TOLD BRENDAN I NEEDED ANOTHER FORTY minutes to get ready. By the time he texts me that he's outside, I've cried until my chest heaved with hiccups, iced my puffy eyes, and redone my makeup. I slip my heels on and walk outside, trying to recapture the excitement I felt for the evening an hour ago.

But I can't. I feel tired, like I've been sprinting uphill for years and my legs are too heavy to take one more step.

Paige's car is parked in the driveway, but Brendan's behind the wheel. He gets out when he sees me. "Wow," he says, his voice soft and reverent. "You look beautiful."

I drop my eyes from his, taking in his clothes instead. Pressed pants, blue button-down, and a perfectly knotted navy tie. His hair's slicked back with something. He looks handsome, clean-cut and adult. I muster a smile. "You look really great, too," I say, covering the ragged edge in my throat.

He walks to my side and opens the passenger door for me. I slide in and immediately observe that the usual clutter of textbooks, CDs, and junk-food wrappers have been cleared from the seats. The entire car is spotless and even smells like soap. It must have taken him hours to clean. The gesture is thoughtful and entirely charming and makes my heart plummet in my chest.

Brendan pulls out of the driveway and heads for the 10 Freeway. "So maybe I should have mentioned this before," he says, flashing me a nervous smile, "but I'm an exceptionally good dancer. Don't be intimidated when we get on the dance floor."

I stare out the window, his bright-eyed enthusiasm too hard to face. "I won't," I mumble.

I can feel his worried gaze on me. "That was a joke," he says carefully. "I'm a terrible dancer. You know that. Remember *Rocky*?"

I give him a quick grin, but my mind is a mess of my dad's words. *Disappointed. Failed. Immature.* Even if I get into UPenn—which I probably won't, but even if I did—my dad would still think those things about me. I'll never have his respect, no matter what I do. My whole life I've tried to impress him, to earn his recognition. Now that I know I never will, I don't even know what to do with my future. I feel worthless. Empty.

"Hey," Brendan says tentatively, "are you okay?"

I look up at him, his concerned expression and gentle eyes. Guilt turns my stomach. Brendan only came to winter formal because I invited him, and I'm treating him like crap. He's the best part of my life, the best person I know. I should be honest with him. But being honest would mean asking him to turn the car around, and I can't do that. I can't ruin the night he's been envisioning. Not after everything he's done for me.

And I don't want to be the spoiled and immature daughter who falls apart at criticism.

"I'm fine. A little tired," I answer, laying a hand on his arm.

"We don't have to go," he says quickly. I know he means it, too. He'd throw away all of his preparation and excitement if I asked.

"No, I want to." Going to this dance is the only thing that could distract me from the email in my inbox. If I'm not dancing with my boyfriend, I'll be alone and trapped with my dad's words. I need this.

"Okay," Brendan says after a moment. "But if something's bothering you, you know you can tell me."

I nod. I don't trust myself to hold it together if I start talking. Instead, I ask him how he got Paige to lend him her car. I listen as he recounts to me how he'll be doing all the research for her upcoming paper on British-US relations in the twentieth century.

It's forty-five minutes to Marina Del Rey. By the time we reach the harbor, I've hardly said two words. But I haven't had a nervous breakdown, either.

Winter formal's on Lisa Gramercy's family yacht this year. We pull into the Marina Yacht Club's driveway, the hedges trimmed with lights, and follow the line of our classmates' cars to the parking lot. The moment we park, Brendan bounces out of the car and rushes to open my door, taking my hand and steadying my step. I don't have to work quite as hard to force my smile then.

We walk through the gate to the dock, my arm in Brendan's.

The yacht is beautiful. The strings of decorative lighting on the deck illuminate the night, sending shimmering reflections onto the black ocean. People I know or vaguely recognize file up the walkway. Jeff Mitchel, his hand tastelessly low on the back of Bethany Bishop's gown. Leila Chapman and Patrick Todd. A group of sophomore girls, their voices loud and jittery with excitement and alcohol, each wearing a dress worth what my mom earns in half a year.

I find I'm clenching my jaw. Because it's too much. The opulence of it, the sheer wealth—I've gotten used to it in general, because it's unavoidable, but right now it feels like exactly what my dad said. Opportunities I squandered. Chances I wasted, or wasn't good enough for, to be successful like him and the families of my classmates.

Brendan and I board the yacht. He says nothing, but I know it's a thoughtful, generous nothing. We wander the deck, and I struggle not to dwell on how *amazing* everyone looks and how *wonderful* a time they're having. Not long after we board, I feel the yacht drift out from the harbor.

Finally, Brendan asks, "You . . . want to grab some food?"

His voice is tentative. He's trying, and I'm reminded he's being nothing but perfect while I roam the deck like a zombie. *I can do this.* I feel the chances of forgetting this pain for the night growing narrower every minute, but I can probably force myself to behave like a regular human being, if only for Brendan.

"Um," I say. I'm really not hungry. "Yeah. I'm starving."

Heart in my throat, I prepare myself to stomach salad or an appetizer. We join the buffet line, and I search for faces

I know, hoping not to have to talk to people. I can hardly handle conversation with Brendan. I recognize a few underclassmen from Brad's mock trial competitions. Morgan and Elle are at the buffet, half-full plates in hand. I turn, avoiding eye contact with them.

"What are you feeling like?" I ask Brendan, checking out the dinner options in the silver platters. Crab cakes, prawns, gnocchi in truffle butter. The rich smells are distinctly unappetizing, and I look away.

"Hey, Cameron." I hear a voice over my shoulder.

I turn to find Elle, who's outside the line, carrying her plate and watching me intently. It's the first time she's spoken to me in weeks, and honestly I'm too stunned to reply.

"I heard the Bright Partners decisions went out today," Elle says. "Will you be joining Brad this summer?"

I find my voice. "Brad?" I repeat dumbly.

"Oh, you didn't know?" Elle asks innocently, obviously aware I didn't. She's cold and goading, and I know she's still far from accepting my apology. "Brad applied for the internship a couple weeks ago, after your dad talked to him at the PTA meeting. He found out today he got the job."

I fight for a breath I hope will calm me. I can't think about this. I can't think about what it means that Brad got the internship and I didn't. I just need this conversation to be over. I know Elle wants to pretend to pity me, and I refuse to give her the chance.

I lie. "Yeah," I say with forced enthusiasm. "I got it, too."

"You did?" She sounds genuinely surprised.

Normally, I'd reply with snark or cynicism. I'd defend myself. But tonight, I don't feel worth defending. I say nothing.

"Of course she did," I hear Brendan say behind me, eager to have my back even though he doesn't know what we're talking about. I never told him about the internship. Surprised, I turn to face him. He's fixed his eyes on Elle determinedly. "Cameron's brilliant," he says with tossed-off confidence. "Anyone would want her."

Hearing Brendan vouch for me, calling me brilliant—impossibly, it hurts worse. Here's this boy I've known for just months saying things my father wouldn't in seventeen years. Things he'll never say. Of course, Brendan might think otherwise if he knew the truth.

"Congrats," Elle finally says, leaving Brendan and me in line. Morgan follows her.

I look up into Brendan's unwavering eyes. "Thank you," I say stiffly.

"Of course," he says, like it's the easiest thing in the world. "What's up with this internship, though?"

I put down the plate I didn't realize I'd picked up and grab him by the elbow. "I'll tell you later. I'm not hungry," I say quickly, not bothering to explain myself to his confused expression. "Let's dance instead."

Brendan follows without a word or a pause. I lead him onto the dance floor, not allowing myself to look back. They're playing an upbeat electronic song I don't recognize, and our classmates are a frenetic huddle of hands in the air and hips swaying. I pull Brendan toward me, beginning to move with the music.

He joins me, bobbing up and down a little off the rhythm.

He studies me, and I can't ignore the concern in his eyes.

Then, without any provocation whatsoever, he busts out an extravagant twirl and waves his arms in the air. "Am I doing this right?" he asks. He grins hopefully and swings his hips in a wide, outrageous circle.

And I can't help it. I feel the corners of my mouth twitch up for the first time this evening.

"Shake your hands more," I venture, daring myself to join in his carefree exuberance. "Like this." I throw my hands from side to side over my head, not minding that we're drawing glances now.

It's working, I can tell. I feel everything weighing me down begin to lift from me, letting me breathe.

"Of *course*," Brendan says. "How could I have forgotten?" He tosses his hands up, imitating me. A laugh escapes me involuntarily, and I hardly recognize the sound. Relief flashes across his features.

I grab his hands, the excitement gaining momentum in me. It's what I imagine the feeling would be like to lift off the ground in an airplane headed somewhere wonderful, weightless and anticipatory and exhilarating. We spin in a wide circle on the dance floor until I stumble over his feet and crash into him, loosening another laugh from my lips.

He catches me, righting me and holding me a little closer. "You're a safety hazard."

"Oh yeah?" I grin.

He grips me tighter. "I think I'd better hold on to you. You know, to protect innocent bystanders."

I rest my head on his chest. "I think you'd better."

In his arms, I'm finally *here*. With him. I feel like this dance, this room, this piece of the universe was reserved just for me. For me to feel wanted, and free, and okay. For a moment, the only things that matter are the way Brendan holds me and the way he gently kisses my forehead.

When we're out of breath and our feet hurt, Brendan brings me out to the deck. I'm struck momentarily by the view. We're farther out than I expected, the lights of the shore a glittering string of pearls in the distance. I can hardly discern where the sky ends and the inky roll of the water begins. The dazzling strings of lanterns on the deck warmly light the railing over the water.

I walk with Brendan to the edge and relax against the railing, my heart still pounding from the exertion. He collapses onto the railing next to me, half a laugh escaping him. I watch him, the night wind ruffling his curls, and find myself recognizing everything he is. How he came here tonight with me, how he made me laugh on the dance floor, how he defended me to Elle.

"You know," I say, looking out on the water, "you're not the guy I thought I knew before we were friends. You're . . . funnier, stronger, braver." I face him. "I'm grateful," I say, "and I'm sorry."

Brendan's brows join in puzzlement. "Sorry for what?"

"For my nickname. I know we've gone over this," I say when he opens his mouth, "but here with you now, I need to say it one more time. I'm sorry what I called you forced a wonderful, charismatic, honorable guy into the shadows."

I'm not expecting the way Brendan's face falls when I finish my speech. His eyes drift downward. "I haven't been entirely honest with you," he says. I feel a tremor in my stomach until he continues. "I . . . didn't hide away because of your nickname. It wasn't the best thing that ever happened to me. But I let it become an excuse. I used it to justify not finding my own friends, keeping myself closed away with homework and grades. I let it define me and told myself it was your fault. But I'm done doing that, Cameron, and it's because of you. I think it might be literally impossible to be your friend and not be inspired to be yourself. Be real. Be brave."

His confession throws me off balance. I say nothing, not really knowing how to contend with what he's just told me. But Brendan's not expecting me to reply. He draws in a breath to continue and stares deeply into my eyes.

Just like that, it's back. The tightness in my chest, threatening to choke off my words.

"Brendan, I don't—"

"I need to say this," he interrupts me earnestly. I itch to step back, but the railing holds me.

He takes my hand, and I want to tear free. I want to push past him and run inside. I want to disappear. Because I know what he's leading up to. From the flush in his cheeks, the tremor in his fingers, and the burning, *overwhelming* emotion in his eyes.

And I'm not ready to hear it. For a little while on the dance floor, I could lose myself in this terrible-turned-wonderful night. But the more Brendan says, the harder I fight the feeling I don't deserve this night—don't deserve *him*. I'm spoiled. Pathetic. I'm none of the things Brendan believes, and it's only a matter of time before he figures it out.

"I love you," he says. The words tumble from his lips and slip beneath the roar of the ocean. "I love you, Cameron," he repeats, louder this time.

For one moment the declaration hangs between us. His chest expands like he can breathe freely now that he's voiced his feelings. He smiles, and his entire face glows under the moonlight. I want to live in the moment forever, to stare at him and admire how beautiful he is inside and out while his words echo in my ears.

But his expression shifts. His brow furrows, his eyes dim. He's waiting for my reply. I open my mouth to say the words back, to smile and kiss him. It wouldn't be a lie. I *do* love him, and it's that realization that steals my breath and stays my tongue. I'm not good enough for him. It'd be better for both of us if I stop ignoring what I've known deep down since the day we first spoke.

"I—can't." I rip my hand from his and dash past him. Tears blur my vision, but I can't break down here. What I need is to run, but these shoes, this ridiculous dress, and miles of ocean are in the way.

I head for a bathroom. A slow song is playing on the dance floor, and dozens of couples hold each other, swaying like the sea beneath us. I hurry through the room, praying no one will notice me.

But in the narrow hallway, I stop short. In front of the restroom, there's a girl in tears, holding her phone to her wetted cheek.

It's Bethany Bishop. She doesn't notice me for a moment or two, and I overhear her conversation. "He went off with Kim Shepherd *in the middle of winter formal*. It's like I don't even exist." It's easy enough to guess what's going on here. Jeff Mitchel's never been an upstanding guy.

Bethany's eyes find mine. I watch her recognize me, then take in the tear trickling down my cheek, the dampness of my forehead. She hangs up hastily.

My stomach churns. At first, I think it's seasickness, but then I recognize it. The bitter, oily current coursing through my veins. "Bethany," I say with a familiar sneer. "You have only yourself to blame. I told you not to go for Jeff in September. Remember?" The cruelty comes back easily, blunting the pain in my chest and distracting me from my heartache. "You knew he could never care about you. You knew you were wasting your time trying to get him to like you. Now you're left with nothing, and it's your own fault."

It feels good. Even if I'm not only talking about Bethany. For a moment, I can breathe again.

I narrow my eyes. "You're pathetic," I say, dredging the words from the well of anger I've found deep in me.

Bethany's face crumples. I watch her eyes go glassy with a hurt she doesn't understand. It doesn't make me feel better— only different. But I can handle different. Guilt and remorse are more palatable than the empty sadness waiting for me.

They're old friends, the only ones who'll never leave me.

I want Bethany to lash out, to tell me I'm an awful person. A bitch. It's what I deserve. Hot and angry words. Hateful glances. Instead, her lip wobbles, and the fire fueling me falters. I turn before it can die out completely.

But the hallway's not empty anymore. Brendan stands in my way, pinning me between him and Bethany, who's now escaping into the unlocked men's room.

His expression is horrified, revolted, disappointed. His eyes find mine, and a crashing wave pummels my chest. He heard everything.

I have the insane urge to laugh, because he looks exactly like Andrew all those weeks ago in the nightclub.

Good, I think.

"Don't look so surprised," I tell Brendan. "This is who I am. The girl who called you Barfy Brendan. Nothing's changed."

Brendan shakes his head, and the muscles in his neck strain. "That's not true. I've seen the real you."

Now I do laugh. Because I know what he needs to hear. "You've seen an act," I say patronizingly, recalling his words in his bedroom weeks ago. Forcing the derision physically hurts, but I know what I need to do for him to forget me the way we both deserve. "You said it yourself, Brendan, remember? I used you." He flinches the way I expected, his eyes wounded. "I've been pretending to be someone I'm not to try to feel better about who I am. Only it wasn't for Andrew. It was for myself. This"—I gesture to the splintering thing between us—"it wasn't real."

The words hit him one after the other, and he shatters. I soak up the pain, letting it under my skin until I feel nothing else.

For years I've been terrified of ending up like my mother. I never knew what it'd feel like to become my father instead. Now I do.

I walk past Brendan. He doesn't follow.

Forty

MY STREET IS SILENT WHEN THE LYFT driver drops me off two hours later. I spent the rest of the dance locked in a belowdecks bathroom until the boat docked back in the harbor. I snuck off before anyone could find me, walked to the nearest bus stop, spent an hour on Los Angeles' terrible mass transit system, then called a Lyft when I was close enough to home that the fare wouldn't clean out my bank account.

I'm freezing and my feet are numb by the time I walk through my front door.

"Cameron?"

Every light in the living room is on. My mom's behind the kitchen counter, a cup of coffee in her hands like she waited up for me. That would be a first.

"How was the dance?" she asks.

I kick off my shoes, wincing when my stiff feet flatten on the carpet. "Great," I mutter, walking through the living room toward the hallway. The last thing I want right now is to be sucked into a conversation about whatever's keeping my mom up this late.

"I heard about the internship," she says when I'm past the kitchen. I still. "I think we should talk about it. Are you okay?"

I gape at her. She's never asked me that question before. Not when Dad didn't call to say he'd be in town before the PTA meeting, or when he ignored the birthday party invitation I sent him in third grade. I didn't think she even knew about the internship. My mind spins, searching for her motivation, something to explain her sudden interest in my feelings. Undoubtedly, it's connected to her relationship with him. She's got some new plan, some messy hope. I want nothing to do with it. I have zero interest in hearing how their love is "true" and "worth the hard work."

"I'm fine," I say. "I don't need to talk about this with you."

She sets her mug down with a sharp clack. "I'd like to discuss it anyway."

Her voice is oddly authoritative, but I'm not in the mood. "Yeah, no thank you," I say, walking to my room.

"I'm the parent here, and I—"

I whirl. *"You're* the parent? Since when?"

"Cameron," she says, low. A warning.

Not tonight. I'm not holding my tongue. Not now. This night has been a perfect storm of disappointments, and I'm tired of sheltering her from the truth. "Were you the parent when I was keeping track of our bills? When I had to find money for school supplies?" I step closer to her. "What about when you sat on the couch for days on end and I cleaned the house, did your laundry, made our meals? *When* were you the parent, Mom?"

Her eyes narrow. I'm not interested in whatever sorry excuse I know she's preparing. I'm done pretending my life is something I can fix with a list and hard work. There's no reason to hide how broken this home is—how she's run it utterly into the ground.

"The only time you are a *parent*," I continue, "is when it brings you closer to your ex. I know you've only kept me around in hopes of finally achieving your great dream of marrying my father. Admit it. You never wanted me for anything else." The accusations spill from me, fresh and furious, fears I've never voiced aloud. The heart of every doubt and insecurity that's ever weighed me down—that between the only two parents I have, nobody's ever wanted me.

I wait for her weak denial, her excuses, the explanations I've heard a hundred times before. She closes her eyes the way I've watched her do in dressing rooms, and I figure she's getting into whatever character she hopes will win my sympathy.

Instead, opening her eyes, she only leaves for the hallway.

I exhale a sigh. Unbelievable. She's an actress, and she won't even bother to play the part of the devoted mother. She won't even pretend I'm more to her than leverage with my father.

I walk to the front door, where I grab my running shoes. I don't care that I'm in my winter formal dress. I don't care that it's one in the morning and I have nowhere to go. I perch on the end of the couch, pulling one shoe on, disregarding my lack of socks and mindlessly doing up the laces.

Mom walks back into the room.

I keep my eyes on the laces of my shoes. Reaching for my jacket on the couch, I refuse to spare her even half a glance until she steps right up to me, shoving a small black box under my nose.

I pause and look up at her. Her eyes are a maelstrom, a combination of uncertainty and despair and even a little indignation. She gestures for me to open the box.

I do.

Inside is a huge diamond ring.

"He didn't want it back," she says. "It never felt right to sell it."

"What is this?" I ask, hearing the wobble in my voice. But I know.

"Your father proposed to me when I found out I was pregnant with you," she says, and the whole world tilts.

Realization rips through me, upending the carefully crafted order by which I've structured my life. I've always known my mother pined for a man who would never have her, that she was too weak to ever put herself first. They're truths that have shaped me in ways I don't like to admit, making me cynical, detached, skeptical of sharing my heart. I was wrong. About her. About everything.

"I wanted him, too," she continues. "I've always wanted him. You know that," she adds with a sardonic twist of her lips. "He wanted us to be a family. Which . . . is why I said no."

I feel a tear slip down my cheek. "What?" I ask softly, like this could all crumble if I speak too loudly. "Why didn't you tell me? I've been chasing him my entire life. If I'd known he wanted us to be a family, I wouldn't have had to."

"You would have chased him regardless. He's your father." Her expression shifts. The combativeness fades, replaced by something softer, almost wistful. "When he asked me, my only thoughts were for the baby I'd just learned about. You

327

were tiny, and yet you changed everything. He's a cruel man, and I knew that—I've always known that. I wanted to protect you from the father I knew he'd be, from the pain and disappointment he'd bring you. That's why I said no."

Tears continue to drip from my eyelashes. I'm breathless, frozen, too shaken to reply.

"It was the strongest thing I ever did," she says softly.

I stare at the proof in my hand. The proof that my mom tried, that she cared enough to give up what must have felt impossibly hard to abandon.

"I . . . haven't been that strong every day since," she continues. "I loved him even when I was saying no. Even when I knew what kind of man he is. I loved him for his charm, his intelligence, his confidence. When I no longer feared him being in your life, I gave myself over to those feelings. I know I'm far from perfect. I'm weak to love him. I'm sorry, Cameron. But"—tears run down her cheeks, and her voice trembles, buckling under the weight of her words—"I will always be grateful for that one moment of strength when he gave me that ring."

My mind begins reorganizing my memories, quietly and immediately. Every time my dad's ever called my mom pathetic, every time he's berated her choices—it was bitterness coloring his words over a rejection he couldn't fathom.

I imagine what my life would have been like if she'd said yes. Not the idealized version I've held on to—him coming to cross-country races or taking me out to dinner. The real version. The *honest* version. The pressure of his presence every day, the figure who'd dismiss me even if we lived under the same roof. It would be years of conversations like the phone call we had today. Years of constant contact with the cruelty I've instead caught only from a distance.

I drop the ring onto the end table, wanting nothing to do with it.

"You're the most important thing in the world to me," Mom says, and her words bring fresh tears to my eyes. But not the bad kind. Not the kind that drive an ache down your chest, that pull the breath from you and leave you hollow. They're the kind that release something long contained. "I know your strength doesn't come from me," she goes on. "But I'm proud anyway. Every day I'm proud."

Haltingly, she walks forward and wraps me in her arms. I'm too stunned to reciprocate. My arms hang limply by my sides. I never expected pride, never expected *love* from my mother. It's why I've sought my father's approval, why I hungered for the slightest sign he saw in me a daughter and not just a problem.

"I'm sorry for the mistakes I've made," she says, withdrawing. "I'm sorry for the times I haven't been the parent you deserve."

The apology unlocks something in me. I hug her fiercely, harder than I expected. "It's okay," I hear myself whisper. The moment the words leave my mouth, I feel a knot I'd never noticed unravel in my chest. And I realize I've had this backward, in a way. I've tried to fix everything in my life through apologies.

But it's not just about apologizing. It's about forgiving.

It's about forgiving my mother, and forgiving myself. Forgiving her for being unmotivated, for being uninvolved, for being weak. Forgiving myself for falling short of a standard my dad will never permit me to reach. Forgiveness is the release that washes the poison from my veins, the anger and envy I could never get rid of no matter how often I apologized. It's impossibly, beautifully easy. The only thing I have to do is forgive my mother and I'll have the parent I always needed.

I hug my mom until I feel new again.

Forty-One

THE NEXT DAY, I MAKE A NEW amends list.

The first item is an email to Chelsea, my father's assistant. I write her apologizing for being rude on the phone. One thing I know her day didn't need was a *second* Bright yelling at her.

Then I write Bethany Bishop a letter. I apologize for the horrible things I said to her on the winter formal yacht. And I apologize for every biting comment, every cruel remark I've said in passing. When I'm done, I look up her address in the school directory and drive the letter to her house myself.

I don't expect a reply. This apology's 100 percent completely not for me. Not for any goal or agenda and not to ease my pain and guilt. Apologies won't fix me, but they might go far in fixing the damage I've done to others.

I've just parked outside my apartment when I hear my phone vibrate in the passenger seat. The caller ID displays my father's office. I reach for the phone, preparing myself for whatever he's found to criticize now. For the first time, I'm unafraid. I don't care if I disappoint him. It's inevitable, and entirely empty. I'm going on a run with my mom tonight, and that won't change even if he's found a new way to reject me.

I pick up. "Hi, Dad." I hope he hears the ease in my voice. The confidence.

"Oh, um." Chelsea's voice comes through flustered. "It's not your dad."

"Right. What does he want?" I ask. I reach for my purse on the floor and reapply my lip gloss with one hand.

"I'm not—" There's a pause. "I'm actually not calling on behalf of Mr. Bright. It's just me."

"Oh." I didn't think my apology warranted a phone call unless—

"I got your email," Chelsea continues. "You really didn't have to apologize."

"I did," I reply. "It was wrong of me to yell at you last night."

"It's fine," she assures me. "I get it, the way that jerk's been acting. I mean, um . . . he's not . . ." she stutters, no doubt conscious she's just insulted her boss.

"No," I say, laughing. "He is."

Chelsea chuckles. "Well," she says, sounding relieved, "you had every right. I'm sorry he hides behind me. That's not why I'm calling, though." She pauses delicately. "I hope you don't mind, but I read the résumé you submitted for our internship and noticed your web design work. You're talented, Cameron. I took the liberty of forwarding your résumé to the design firm that rebranded our website a year ago. They have an office in Los Angeles, and I'm in touch with the CEO's assistant. He says they're looking for a summer intern."

I'm speechless. I hadn't even spared a thought for what I'd be doing this summer without the internship I'd planned for.

"If I've overstepped, please let me know and I'll retract your résumé—"

"No!" I blurt. It's not an internship that will impress my dad or bring me into his life, but . . . I don't care. I have my mom to be proud of me, to encourage me. The realization leaves me with that airplane-leaving-the-runway feeling again, weightless and thrilling. "Sorry. I mean, no, I'd like to be put up for the job. Thank you," I say sincerely.

"You're welcome, Cameron. Have a good rest of your day."

I cut in before she can hang up. "Hey, Chelsea?" I take a breath. "You've only ever been a conduit between me and horrible conversations with my dad. Just a voice on the phone. And, um, I wanted to introduce myself. Hi," I say, "I'm Cameron. It's nice to finally meet you."

I hear Chelsea's smile over the phone. "It's nice to meet you, too, Cameron. You know," she adds, "you're nothing like your father."

"Thank you," I say, knowing she has no idea how much it means.

Forty-Two

FRUSTRATED, I SCRIBBLE OUT ONE MORE LINE on the list I'm working on now. I've struggled for the past week to come up with ideas for how I'm going to apologize to Brendan. They're uniformly awful. From the obvious—*text him for the thousand-and-first time*—to the cringeworthy—*deliver a gluten-free cake with "Sorry I ruined your winter formal and was a huge jerk" icing*. Not my proudest work.

He's ignored my first thousand texts, of course. We're exactly where we began, with him hatefully pretending I don't exist.

Except now, I miss him every day. I'm not trying to get him back. I know he could never want the real Cameron Bright—not after what he heard. I owe him an apology, though.

In the meantime, I'm buried under the inevitable week-before-winter-break homework rush. I hole up in the Depths of Mordor every day to work. Today I *have* to figure out my *Taming of the Shrew* term paper. It's going horribly, of course. I could hardly focus on this stupid play even before the worst breakup imaginable.

Two hours and two rewrites of my opening paragraph in,

I flop back on Mordor's green couch, my book falling closed on my computer keyboard. "I'm never finishing this essay," I groan, rubbing my temples.

Charlie and Abby ignore me, playing their board game. But Paige, who's sketching early designs for her Comic-Con costume—a porg dress—glances up. "For Kowalski?" she asks.

After winter formal, Paige didn't hesitate to deliver a couple *very* direct speeches about how I blew it with Brendan, the best guy I could ever hope to find in my entire life. But when I told her what I'd been going though that night, Paige understood. I explained everything to her. Trying to win over Andrew, my "self-taming" plan—which of course she'd kind of figured out, other than the *Taming of the Shrew* inspiration. Now that I've definitely proven I'm not into Andrew anymore, Paige has stopped doubting our friendship. We both know it's real.

"Yeah," I say from the couch. "I've done, like, a hundred rewrites. I can't read this essay one more time."

Paige drops her charcoal. "Give it here, Bright." She holds out her hand.

"No offense, but you have a B-minus in English." I cut her a look. "I don't know if you're the one to help."

She rolls her eyes. "I was straight with you about your terrible UPenn essay," she shoots back. "I'll let you know if this one is trash."

I hide a smile. "Fine," I say, handing over my computer.

She starts reading, her expression growing serious. Her brows join in what first looks like puzzlement, then . . . worse than puzzlement. She sighs, she grumbles, she shakes her head at the page. My stomach sinking, I prepare to fight or discount whatever criticism she hits me with.

"'*The Taming of the Shrew* should be considered one of Shakespeare's tragedies, not one of his comedies. Katherine faces an impossible choice between being herself and ending up alone, or completely changing herself to find a partner,'" she reads from my essay, looking up with disbelief.

"Right," I say. "That's my thesis."

"That's bullshit," Paige declares.

Well, I won't pretend I'm surprised. "You read the body paragraphs, right?" I say weakly. "I think I supported my thesis well enough . . ."

"Cameron, you don't have to change yourself in order to be loved, or liked, or whatever." Paige watches me with careful concentration. I squirm in my seat, self-conscious.

"It's just an English essay," I say.

"We both know it's not." Paige's voice becomes gentle. "You're not really writing about Katherine. Is this why you haven't tried to win my brother back? Because you think you're like Katherine and you have to be a different person for him?"

I open my mouth, wanting to find a quick and decisive denial. But I don't.

"I know you think Brendan only liked a fake version of yourself. But it's not true," Paige goes on. "I've hung out with you for a while, Cameron. You're really no different. When you were with Brendan you weren't exactly the delicate, cuddly person you think you were pretending to be. You're biting and honest and funny, and it's awesome. I know Brendan liked that about you. *Likes* that about you." She raises her eyebrows emphatically.

I try to force down the hope I've done my best to destroy this week. But I feel the truth unfolding inside me. Paige is right. I *was* myself with Brendan. I was honest and open. It's why he liked me and why I liked him. Why I possibly loved him.

With that realization comes another, clenching and cold.

"I hurt him too badly," I choke out.

"Well," Paige replies, "then give one of those famous Cameron Bright apologies. You never know what might happen."

I feel doors and windows open in my head. I'll do exactly what Paige says. I'll put myself on the line. I'll fight until Brendan knows everything I feel for him.

"But first," Paige adds, "rewrite this shitty essay."

I take my computer back, grinning. "You're the worst, you know that?"

"Whatever," she says.

"*Whatever,*" I repeat like I'm pissed. But I'm not.

I'm grateful.

Before I can focus on Brendan, I have to rewrite my essay. For the rest of the week, I feverishly rework my thesis, reconfiguring my textual evidence. By the time I'm done, an unexpected feeling comes over me. I'm . . . proud of an English essay.

I retitle the paper "Katherine, the 'Villain' Mischaracterized." Then I proceed to crap on Shakespeare. But he deserves it. He wrote a bitch who's nothing but a bitch, nothing but the sixteenth-century version of a one-dimensional mean girl. Katherine is completely evil, giving audiences no reason to question whether her rudeness or her temper might come with good qualities, or even reflect them. He writes Kate off—into contempt, into comedy, into humiliation—instead of writing a woman who's complex and who changes on her own, respectably and without entirely erasing her personality. Who's both good *and* flawed, who can recognize and right her wrongs while not giving up her strength and independence. Who's kind without being weak, powerful without being awful.

And in brutish frat-boy Petruchio, who literally starves and beats Kate into submission, he gave readers permission to forget the real, cunning, invisible ways men tame "shrews." With judgment, with terminology, with effortless, biting words.

The Friday before winter break, I come home and hurriedly reread the essay one final time before I submit it to Kowalski. Without giving myself time to overthink the decision, I open a new email and write to Andrew. I attach the document and invite him to read my essay and to go on a run this week.

Andrew's a good guy. He's not Petruchio. But the way he judged me, the way he threw that word around, I want him to understand what it really does.

I hope this will be the beginning of a more honest friendship between us. I have a feeling it will.

I'm closing my email inbox when one unread message appears in the window. *Your Application to the University of Penn-sylvania.* I open the email, feeling an unnatural calm come over me, and read.

I got in.

I wait for the rush of relief, the explosion of triumph. They don't come. I read the whole email once, then twice, then a third time, trying to imagine myself under UPenn's stone arches and in wood-paneled lecture halls. I don't know what I expected to feel in this moment, but it wasn't nothing.

I wanted this. *I* wanted this. Didn't I? I told myself I did. I've told myself for years I'd be happy if I could succeed in my father's world, if I could earn a place close to him, if I could prove myself. Now that I'm finally accomplishing those things, I don't feel happy. I feel empty.

It's impossible to know whether I got in because my name is Bright and my dad's an important donor. I know it helped, but I didn't think I'd care. I thought I'd pounce on the oppor-tunity no matter how or why. Instead, I feel a near-magnetic repulsion, the instinct to avoid even the association of our names that the UPenn rep made.

Everything I did, everything I planned was to chase my dad. Knowing I have my mom, though—knowing I no longer have to chase him—I can finally stop running.

I can finally explore who *I* want to be.

Not who I'm pretending to be. The thought hits me like a punch. I've prided myself on being honest with everyone. With cheerleaders dumped by idiot boyfriends. With Elle when she's unreasonable, with Andrew when he's obtuse. With Paige, with Brendan, with my mom.

The only person I haven't been honest with is myself.

But now I have to be. It's the hardest form of honesty, but it's the most important. Not the endless criticisms my dad taught me.

Every Econ class I took pretending I cared what collateralized debt obligations and demand curves were. The *Economist* subscription I got from my dad. The conversation with UPenn's rep not even two months ago—they were lies. They were careful concealments of who I really am, a protective pretense profound and impenetrable enough I forgot it was there.

If I'm being honest, I don't want those things.

I close the email on my computer. Without thinking twice, I pull the UCLA Design and Media Arts brochure from under the notebook on my desk. Unfolding the brochure, I read the course descriptions, the curriculum, the opportunities for work with media and entertainment-industry companies in the city. I feel my heart quicken with a certain *rightness*. The feeling of finding what I didn't know I wanted. I can imagine myself in the classes and the computer rooms pictured, gazing for inspiration out the floor-to-ceiling windows onto UCLA's pine trees.

While I'm reading, Mom wanders into the doorway, holding a glass of what I recognize ruefully to be a juice cleanse— and in the other hand, a folded Eggo waffle.

I open my mouth to point out this incongruity. But I guess she catches the confused consternation of my expression, because she cuts me off. "I'm not doing a cleanse," she says, continuing sheepishly, "I just like the taste of the juice."

I close my mouth again. And because it's such a blissfully honest confession, I laugh. Mom's grin widens.

She's passing my door when she doubles back, a hand on the frame. "Hey, um," she begins. Her voice takes on an unfamiliar formality, even and hopeful. "Do you think you could design a website for me? A professional one, for acting?"

I drop the pamphlet. "Yes!" I don't hide my excitement. "Of course!" I've been telling her on our runs about the websites I've designed. She didn't really know I'd done websites before, which hurt, but, I reminded myself, she knows now. She's trying now.

She flushes, looking pleased. "I figured I could go on a few auditions. Why not, right? In between teaching, of course." She took a teaching job with the acting institute down the block. She got her first paycheck this week, and we celebrated with a dinner date Dad *didn't* pay for.

I nod, beaming. "I'm proud of you, Mom," I say, because honesty doesn't have to hurt. "Dad was really wrong about you."

"He's not as smart as he thinks he is," she says with a flippant shrug, but her eyes are glittering when she leaves the doorway.

I'm about to keep reading the UCLA pamphlet when I remember the box.

The box of my mother's costumes that I've hidden under my bed to keep her from throwing it out. I put the pamphlet down and crouch on the carpet, pulling the beaten cardboard box in front of me.

I heft the costumes into the hallway, my eyes catching on the jacket from my *Rocky* outfit folded on top. Placing the box in front of her bedroom door, I walk back to my room, remembering the wild magic of the night. The rituals, kissing Paige. Grant and Hannah, who post utterly adorable photos from Utah, where they're spending winter break with Hannah's family. Brendan in his ridiculous, wonderful "costume," and—

Wait.

I grab the UCLA brochure. *Why didn't I think of this before?*

Forty-Three

I'M SWEATING, HEAVY DROPLETS RUNNING DOWN MY neck, and dying to roll up the itchy fabric of my sleeves. The elaborately embroidered bodice clenches my chest uncomfortably, the edges jutting into my ribs.

I can't believe people actually do this for fun.

Of course, it *is* an amazing costume. It's Paige's handiwork, the product of a week spent studying the few images I had, designing, fitting, and shopping for fabric, wire, and the perfect buttons.

I'm the living replica of the sorceress from *The Girl's a Sorceress*. I followed one of Elle's Halloween tutorials for the makeup, a dark smoky eye and deep purple lips. It hurt not having her there in person, just the way it hurts every time one of our dance-party anthems comes up on my running playlists. And the hurt reminds me how what I'm doing right now might not work.

Walking through the UCLA sculpture garden, I feel the sun blistering my back. I'm really, really hot. Temperature-hot, that is. Although, I'm hoping I'm the other type, too. My costume is essentially a leotard with a long, double-slit skirt freeing my legs. Paige lowered the neckline to give it more décolletage and constructed a corset-like bodice with Gothic details. I have full sleeves and thigh-high boots—not ideal in the eighty-degree December afternoon. We don't have the luxury of seasons in Los Angeles, and the complete lack of cloud cover over UCLA certainly isn't helping.

I earn stares the entire walk to the Charles E. Young Research Library. Which I expected. I am, I would dare to guess, the only person dressed as a witch on this entire campus. Undeterred, I pull open the door to the convention center on the library's first floor.

For a moment, it's overwhelming. I underestimated the city's population of teenage video game designers. I walk past the booths, unable to avoid scoping out Brendan's competition. The entries range from the basic to the elaborate. *Doggos* appears to involve only controlling a pixelated dog to collect tacos. Others—*Red Mist, Zombies on the Moon*—feature stomach-churning, photorealistic gore. I find a couple of girls in one booth nervously watching a judge demoing *Wolf Warrior*.

And then I turn a corner, and there's Brendan. He's a few booths away, and he hasn't noticed me yet. He's explaining something to a judge, and I fall in love all over again with the eager intensity in his eyes, the perfectly unruly curl of his hair over his forehead. The cafeteria boss battle of *The Girl's a Sorceress* is up on the widescreen monitor over the judge's shoulder. Brendan unpauses the game, and I watch the computerized choreography I know well.

When the judge reaches over to play the demo, I catch Brendan's eye. His mouth drops open a little. I watch him take in my costume, heart in my throat with nervousness.

"So the game's open-world?" the judge asks, interrupting the moment.

Brendan clears his throat. "Um," he fumbles to reply. "What did you say?"

I wait a few paces from the booth, not wanting to interrupt his presentation. Brendan appears to recover his composure, giving the judge a long reply and demonstrating gameplay. Finally, the judge nods once, looking impressed, and leaves. For a moment, Brendan looks relieved and exhilarated, until his expression clouds and he searches the crowd for me.

I take a breath and walk up to the booth.

"I felt it was appropriate," I say, gesturing to the costume. "I do have a few things in common with the character. I'm blonde and intimidating, and I tend to do terrible things I really regret . . ."

Just then, as if the demo were listening, the sorceress viciously decapitates the hero's head. I wince.

Brendan's expression is hard. "What are you doing here, Cameron?"

"You once told me how much it would mean to you if someone cosplayed as one of your characters."

"You remembered that?" For a moment, he looks like he's forgotten he's angry.

"Of course I remembered," I say, hoping he hears the sincerity in my voice. "We were on the blankets in the cemetery. Waiting for *Rocky* to begin."

Brendan softens. But then, like he's remembering everything I said to him at the dance, his frown returns.

"Follow me," he says gruffly.

He leads me through the crowd, past *Wolf Warrior* and *Zombies on the Moon*. I catch more curious glances. We go out the front doors and into the sculpture garden, where Brendan finally brings us to an abrupt halt.

I don't hesitate. "Brendan, I'm sorry. For everything I said to you at winter formal, for the way I drove you away, for the girl you saw me become when I was cruel to Bethany."

Brendan huffs. "We've done this before. You don't get unlimited apologies, Cameron. I should have stuck to what I told you then. Stay out of my life," he says, his expression stern, but his voice wavers.

His hesitation is enough to give me the confidence to continue. "I will, once I've said what I came here to say. I need to explain what was happening with me the night of the dance. Remember the internship Elle mentioned?"

Brendan nods nearly imperceptibly.

"Well . . . I didn't get it. Which I know sounds insignificant. It just—it was with my dad's company, and I felt like if even he didn't want me, I couldn't be worth much of anything. I felt like I didn't deserve you. So I lied, and I told you we weren't real. I wanted to push you away because it's what I thought I deserved."

"I'm sorry about your dad," he says, his face rigid. "But you can't keep doing this. Going back and forth. *I* can't keep doing this. I went out on a limb when I fell for you, Cameron. A long, scary limb. I knew something was upsetting you before winter formal, and when I tried to get you to open up, you decided I wasn't worth it. I told you I loved you, and you told me we were a lie." His expression becomes vulnerable for an instant before his anger returns. "I gave you everything I could, and you treated me like you always have—like I'm just Barfy Brendan."

"Brendan, come on." I raise my voice, conscious we're garnering even more stares than I did on my own—an extravagantly dressed witch in a shouting match with a teenage boy. "Did making out with you every day count as treating you like Barfy Brendan? I know you have next to zero experience with girls, but it's time you get it through your head that I think you're cute—hot even, in a geeky way."

He blinks, and hope runs through me when I catch him struggling to suppress a smile. "I don't know if that's an insult or a compliment."

"Both, obviously."

Now Brendan lets out a small laugh. "You know, after all the apologies you've given, I'm not convinced you've gotten any better at them."

I rub my brow, feeling frustration creep in. "Well, I hope I'm better at declarations of love," I say, an edge in my voice.

Brendan goes entirely still.

I gather my thoughts, knowing I'm being given the chance to correct what might be the biggest mistake I've ever made. Brendan and I work when I'm unflinchingly honest—*because* I'm honest. What broke us was the one time I wasn't honest with him. The one time I wasn't who I really am. It's a mistake I'll never make again.

"It's come to my attention I'm not a perfect person," I say. "I most likely never will be. But I've decided that's okay. I'm going to make more mistakes in my life, and I'm going to apologize for them. If that's a problem for you—if you want me to promise to never mess up again, or if you just don't like the flawed person I am—then I would recommend you walk away right now."

I wait for him to do exactly that, for him to put his guard back up. When he does neither, I take a step toward him.

"I want to open up to you, too. I want to tell you more about my home and my parents, if you'll give me the chance. But right now, all I want to tell you is that I love you," I say with the force of every day I've spent in my room wishing I'd just told him when it counted, when I could've avoided tearing us apart.

Indecipherable currents of emotion run behind Brendan's eyes. My breath goes quiet in my chest. For what feels like the longest pause in history, he says nothing. Every passing second is a door closing inch by inch until finally the crack of light disappears.

I nod, schooling my features into understanding and my voice into evenness. I glance toward the library. "Okay. Good luck in there, Brendan." They're the hardest words I've ever said.

I begin to walk away. I'm a couple feet from him when I hear footsteps behind me.

Brendan grabs my hand, pulling me to face him. "You know," he says, "showing up here in that costume was really unfair."

The corners of my lips have begun to tug upward before I've even fully processed what he said. "I know," I say nonchalantly, not yet daring to hope. "I needed all the edge I could get."

"Unfair"—Brendan finally grins—"and the most thought-ful thing anyone's ever done for me."

My heart swells. I know it's ridiculous, the entire thing. I'm dressed in the costume of a freaking video game char-acter, professing my love to a boy I've only known—really known—for months. It's completely crazy. On paper, on the lists and spreadsheets that constitute my life, Brendan doesn't fit in. But he's upended every one of my plans, reversed every one of my expectations. Not just of him. Of myself.

I love him in spite of it. I love him *because* of it.

Brendan puts a hand on my hip, releasing a faint breath. "I never imagined this, not even in my wildest dreams."

I purse my purple lips. "You're saying you've never had wild dreams of me dressed up in some sexy costume—"

"Of you ever being in my life again," Brendan cuts me off gently. The joke dies on my tongue. "I couldn't bring myself to hope you'd ever want me, couldn't convince myself you ever had," he continues. "But . . . you're a hard person to pre-dict, Cameron."

You make me unpredictable, I nearly tell him.

"Can I speak honestly?" I ask instead, stepping up to him.

He smiles, irrepressibly. "I wouldn't have it any other way."

I lean in, tilting my chin up toward him. "You're an idiot if you don't kiss—"

He instantly presses his lips to mine before I can finish. And it's a dream come to life.

Four Months Later

THE THEATER IS TINY AND TOO HIP for its own good. The entire front façade is painted blue, with an Instagram hashtag of the theater's name in white on the bottom corner of the wall. To the right of the door, a mural features twin mermaids wearing the comedy and tragedy masks. It fits perfectly on Venice Beach's Abbot Kinney Boulevard, a haven for hipsters citywide.

I toe my sneaker distractedly on the curb as we wait for Paige, Brendan's hand in mine. I'm only giving up an afternoon to this theater because Kowalski promised us extra points if we went to a Shakespeare performance. I wouldn't have chosen *The Taming of the Shrew*, personally, but I lost a bet to Paige over her newest hairstyle. In return, she's forcing me to watch my *favorite* play because she thinks it's hilarious.

Pulling out my phone, I send a text to my mom confirming I'll be home in time for dinner. She's invited over her new boyfriend, a photographer who does headshots for the students where she works. I'm honestly really excited to meet him. My mom's been paying the rent on her own, and when my dad was in town in March, she didn't even try to contact him. I never told him I got into UPenn. UCLA has given me enough loans and scholarships that I don't need to go to him for tuition.

"Paige is never *this* late," Brendan mutters beside me.

He's wearing his Naughty Dog T-shirt, which I've noticed he's worn no less than once a week since he placed second in the contest and won an internship. His first day is in a couple weeks, right after the school year ends.

His hand tenses in mine. I look up and find Paige walking toward us, the reason for her lateness immediately obvious.

Her hand's clasped in Andrew's. There's an uncharacteristic exhilaration on her face.

Brendan groans. "Tell me they're not a thing."

I elbow him playfully. "Be happy for your sister."

When they reach us, they nonchalantly unlink hands as if we didn't just totally observe the giddy epilogue of what was probably a pretty epic makeout session. I give Andrew a teasingly raised eyebrow. "It took you long enough, dude." I've watched the unbelievably slow burn of Paige and Andrew for the past six months. The glances in class, the hangouts to which Andrew was first innocuously and then conspicuously invited, the precise seating order for movie nights and restaurant booths.

"Go easy on him, Bright," Paige says dryly. She winks, and her warning isn't enough to hide how obviously thrilled she is. Her cheeks are bright pink, in contrast to her newly platinum blonde hair—the hairstyle that lost me the bet. I didn't think she'd really go through with it, not with how conventional and stereotypical a hair color it is. But she did.

"We running tomorrow?" Andrew asks me.

"Of course," I reply easily. "I found the most brutal hill, if you're up for it." Andrew's eyes spark to the challenge. In the months since we decided we weren't right for each other, we've both made efforts to become real friends. He read my essay, and over coffee, we talked about the play and about us. Weeks later, he told me he wanted to ask Paige out but didn't know how, and I eagerly took on the role of matchmaker.

"Brendan?" Paige says, eyeing her brother. "Is there a problem?"

I turn to find my boyfriend badly covering a scowl. I exchange amused glances with Paige, while Brendan fidgets uncomfortably. "Isn't it a little weird?" he asks. "Earlier this year you walked in on Andrew and *Cameron* making out."

"I'm glad she did," Andrew says gracefully, wrapping an arm around Paige and pulling her to him, "otherwise this wouldn't be happening." He nods to Brendan. "And Cameron definitely wouldn't be dating you, either. If you think about it, you should be thanking me for making out with your girlfriend."

My eyes return to Brendan, who does not appear to appreciate this observation.

I thread my fingers through his. "Besides," I say, "I made out with Paige, too. That wasn't a problem." Brendan shudders exaggeratedly, and I leave the thought hanging, jokingly contemplative.

Andrew only laughs, opening the door to the theater.

They walk in, leaving me and an unamused Brendan, who rolls his eyes at me and pulls me inside like he's afraid of what I'll say next.

The lobby is packed. I recognize a few faces from school, including Morgan and Brad near an obnoxiously vintage concessions counter on the other end of the room. Morgan gives me a soft smile, which I return. Our friendship hasn't been the same since Elle, but we do hang out occasionally.

People begin to file through the heavy double doors into the theater. The play's supposed to start in a few minutes. "I'm going to run to the bathroom," I tell Brendan. "Save me a seat?" Brendan nods, his gaze still fixed protectively on Paige and Andrew. I roll my eyes and head for the bathroom.

Finding the bathroom empty, I hurry into a stall. When I come out to wash my hands, a harried brunette rushes in wearing a medieval gown she's somehow twisted halfway inside out. Startled, I stare.

"Said I was never going to do this again," the girl grumbles feverishly, struggling with her straps in the mirror. "But *no*. SOTI just *had* to have an acting requirement. This is ridiculous," she gasps, wrenching a piece of skirt from her waist.

"Um," I finally interject, "do you need help?"

For the first time, the girl seems to register my presence. Her eyes find mine in the mirror, and she doesn't look even a little embarrassed to have been caught talking to herself. "Could you go find the extremely hot Japanese guy with the great cheekbones waiting in the lobby?" she asks without hesitation.

I consider requesting a more helpful description until the

girl begins waging war on her straps once more, and I decide it's best not to interrupt. I return to the steadily emptying lobby, where I'm mildly surprised I can immediately pick out the boy she wants. He's wearing a well-fitting gray sweater and black jeans. While he leans on the concessions counter, he's writing with ink-stained fingers in a worn notebook.

I walk up to him. "Excuse me," I say, and he raises his brown-nearly-black—and very nice—eyes to mine. "You wouldn't happen to know a very unabashed brunette in a medieval dress who recently fled into the bathroom, would you?" I go on.

He grins, obviously finding this description amusing. "Do I ever," he says. "Why?"

"She's having a costume crisis," I reply. "She needs your help—urgently, it looked like."

He laughs, hard, and I feel like I'm left out of the joke.

"Thanks," he says. "I'll see what I can do."

I could go into the theater and wait with Brendan for the performance to begin. But I'm kind of invested in whether this girl's going to free herself from her tangled dress. I follow the boy into the bathroom.

The girl is contorted, craning her neck to see a knot of straps on her back. The boy pauses in the doorway. I notice the way his gaze drinks her in.

"This looks familiar," he drawls.

"Don't even start with me, Owen," she fires back, a note of humor in her exasperation. "This is entirely your fault."

"How, exactly?" The boy—Owen—replies. He glances hesitantly around the bathroom and, finding it empty except for the girl, crosses the room and begins straightening her dress, spinning her to face him.

"You're the reason I'm late." I catch the fondness in her eyes even though her words are accusatory.

"You're the one who, uh, insisted in the car we . . ." He blushes, and I do the same, picking up on why this girl who's clearly in the play was nearly late to her own performance. I wander to the sink and wash my hands very slowly, pretending I'm not eavesdropping.

"God help me," the girl chides, gently this time. "A year together and you still blush like the first day I flirted with you. No wonder I can't keep my hands off you." She runs one down his chest like she feels she needs to demonstrate. Owen throws a glance behind him, toward me. But the girl doesn't appear to care. "Of course, I might have more self-control if you hadn't surprised me and flown here from New York just to watch this sure-to-be-disastrous performance. The things a gesture like that does to a girl . . ." She gives Owen a meaningful look. "In conclusion," she says dryly, "your fault."

The amusement fades from Owen's expression, replaced by something softer. "I go to all your performances, Megan," he says. "And I missed you."

"You made *that* very clear in the car." Megan eyes him, flirtatious and goading.

Owen's cheeks flame brighter. I find myself liking this girl and her forwardness. I feel like we'd be friends. He gives the dress a final determined yank, and the fabric comes free.

Megan grabs Owen's wrist and checks his watch. "Crap," she breathes. "Carly's going to kill me, or force me to cast only freshmen in my next production. I don't know what's worse." She smashes a quick yet heated kiss to Owen's lips, then tears herself—a genuine effort, from what I can tell—from him and races from the room.

I'm left alone with Owen, feeling distinctly awkward for having overheard everything. "Sorry," I say. "I didn't mean to eavesdrop. I just, um"—I scrounge for a non-sketchy excuse—"I didn't know if you'd need help," I finish lamely.

"What?" Owen holds open the door for me. "Oh, no, Megan delights in embarrassing me with shameless public flirtation. It's basically how our entire relationship started." From the way he says it, I understand he enjoys her efforts just as much. "Sorry you had to be dragged into it. She really does have a shocking lack of sympathy for innocent bystanders."

"Don't worry," I say. "She's definitely entertaining."

"That's an understatement." He glances up at me like he's just remembered something. "Don't listen to a word she said about the play being a disaster. She's going to give a great performance. She always does. I'm taking a gap year to write plays in New York, and I spend every cent of the tips I get waiting tables going to her performances. And it's not just because she's my outrageous yet beautiful girlfriend."

"Who's she playing?" I ask, finding his compliments of Megan charming.

"The lead. Not that she wanted to, of course . . ."

Intrigued, I feel my eyes widen. "She's Katherine?"

Owen's eyebrows rise. "You're familiar with the play?"

"You could say that," I mutter.

"Well, you won't be disappointed. The Southern Oregon Theater Institute was going to put *Macbeth* on tour. But once the professors saw the depth Megan brought to Katherine in her performance, they changed their minds. I already caught the show at a college theater festival in New York, and it completely changed the play for me." His expression takes on a wistful quality, a faraway contemplation. It only makes him cuter. "It even got me thinking about writing a new play drawn from Shakespeare in which Katherine has her own reasons for remaking herself."

I nearly choke on a laugh. "Give me your notebook," I tell this young playwright who's probably barely older than I am.

Guardedly, Owen turns over his notebook. "What are you doing?" he asks protectively when I open the cover.

I jot down my phone number. "Call me if you want any character insight for your play," I say, handing back his notebook. "I had my own ill-advised self-taming project this year."

I expect him to laugh it off or politely decline. Instead, his eyes brighten. "Really?" he asks intently.

"Yeah," I say. The lights flicker, indicating the performance is about to begin.

"I definitely will," he says and heads for the doors on the right.

I enter the theater through the center doors. I hope Owen does call me, I find myself thinking. I'd like the chance to talk to him and this Megan.

I see Brendan's head poking up in the middle of his row,

inches taller than the rest. I edge down the row into the empty seat next to him. His gaze remains sternly on Paige and Andrew sitting in front of us.

"He better not just be with her because she's blonde now," Brendan grumbles. I laugh. "This isn't a joke, Cameron." He turns to me, exasperated. "He *has* demonstrated a penchant for blondes."

I school my features into sympathy, forcing down a laugh over how he's Not Handling This Well. "He genuinely likes her," I tell him.

"I don't trust him," Brendan replies resolutely.

I can't contain the laugh any longer, earning a scowl from Brendan. "Being blonde has nothing to do with it," I say patiently. "Think of us. We ended up together even though you told me blondes weren't your type."

He rounds on me incredulously. "You *believed* me?"

"Of course not," I say easily. "I just wanted you to admit it."

Brendan throws me a look, sweetly annoyed. "Very helpful."

I reach over and with two fingers tilt his chin to face me. "You're not just with me because I'm a blonde, right?" I ask, teasingly threatening.

The annoyance fades entirely from Brendan's expression. "No. Well, I won't lie, I might have spent a few freshman nights fantasizing about you because of it." I shove his shoulder, and he catches my hand to his chest. "It's *not* why I love you."

The lights dim. I lean into him and whisper, "Why do you love me, then?"

Brendan tips his head, pressing his forehead to mine. "Because you're smart and funny, understanding and opinionated, kind and bossy. You're a thousand things that make up Cameron Bright. You could never be just a type."

I grin, incalculably grateful to be nestled into this boy who says perfect things. "Exactly. And if Andrew doesn't recognize the thousand things that make Paige worth loving, I'll personally ensure he regrets it."

Brendan finally returns my grin. "Let's add 'a little scary' to your list of wonderful attributes."

I shrug. "Good thing you love me for it, because there are some things I'll never change."

"Better not."

He kisses me as the curtain rises.

Acknowledgments

THE OPPORTUNITY TO HAVE OUR WORDS PUBLISHED is a gift that—if *we're* being honest—never loses its wonder. We're grateful to everyone whose talent, encouragement, and friendship have brought us here.

First and foremost, thank you to our readers. We would not have this opportunity without you, and we express our gratitude with every word we write.

To our agent, Katie Shea Boutillier, thank you for continuing to champion the characters and narratives we want to write with precise guidance and endless enthusiasm. We'd be nowhere without you. To Dana Leydig, our editor, thank you for bringing this book to life with us from the beginning (even when the job called for dissing English class and Shakespeare . . .), and for inspiring us with your thoughtful, careful commentary. Oh, and for comparing Brendan to various teen movie and Broadway musical characters, which was the best.

Thank you to the Penguin Young Readers team for giving this book the perfect home. In particular, we're grateful to Katie Quinn and Tessa Meischeid for wonderful, innovative publicity helping this book find its way into readers' hands, and to Kristie Radwilowicz for our favorite cover art ever; and to Krista Ahlberg, Marinda Valenti, Janet Pascal, and Abigail Powers for thoughtful and diligent copyedits. To Kara Brammer, Caitlin Whalen, Felicity Vallence, and Friya Bankwalla, thank you for promoting our work and being wonderful humans.

Thank you to our friends in the writing community— Alexa, Bree, Bridget, Britta, Dana, Demetra, Farrah, Lisa, Mae, Marie, Maura, and Zach, we've loved celebrating and collaborating and commiserating with you amid karaoke, festivals, and Koreatown coffee dates. We're very grateful to the authors we've admired who have generously provided perspective on publishing and everything else—Julie Buxbaum, Sarah Enni, Morgan Matson, Kayla Olson, Romina Russell, Robyn Schneider, thank you for everything!

Thank you to the friends who encouraged us in the days when publishing was just a dream of ours, and who have continued to celebrate the ups and be there for the downs of our writing process. We love you.

To William Shakespeare, thank you for inspiration and for taking a beating in this book with grace.

Finally, to our families, thank you for valuing creativity and writing, for encouraging us to chase this dream, and for every fortifying word and excited text message that's come with this book. We owe you everything.

Turn the page for an excerpt from
Always Never Yours

"An utterly charming story of love, family,
heartbreak, and drama. I absolutely loved it!"
—MORGAN MATSON, *NEW YORK TIMES* BESTSELLING
AUTHOR OF *SINCE YOU'VE BEEN GONE*

Every guy she dates falls madly in love . . . just not with her.

EMILY WIBBERLEY
AUSTIN SIEGEMUND-BROKA

"An inventive, charming, insightful tale . . . Every page bursts
with humor [and] squee-inducing romance."
—*Entertainment Weekly*

ONE

"ALL THE WORLD'S A STAGE . . ."

Brian Anderson's butchering the line. I listen for the posturing and borderline mania Shakespeare intended, but—nope. He's doing some sort of half English accent and throwing iambic pentameter out the window.

"How about we stop there for a second?" I interrupt, standing up and straightening my denim dress.

"Just once, Megan, could we get through the scene?" Brian groans.

I shoot him a look and walk into the middle of the "stage," which for today is the hill behind the drama room. Our drama teacher, Ms. Hewitt—who everyone calls Jody—sent us outside to rehearse whatever Shakespeare scene we wanted. And by "sent us," I mean kicked us out for being obnoxious. I picked the hill for our rehearsal space because I thought the pine trees nearby would evoke the forest in *As You Like It*.

Which was stupid, I now realize.

"I feel like we're not getting what's going on in the charac-

1

ters' heads," I say, ignoring Brian and speaking to the group. It's only the four of us out here in the middle of sixth period. Jeremy Handler wears a hopeless expression next to Brian while Courtney Greene texts disinterestedly. "Orlando"—I turn to Jeremy—"is fundamentally a nice guy. He only wants to steal from the Duke to help his friend. Now, Jacques—"

I falter. A glimpse of green catches my eye, a Stillmont High golf polo. Biceps I have to admire peek through the sleeves. A wave of brown hair, an ever-present smirk, and *wow* do I want to go over and flirt with Wyatt Rhodes.

He's twirling a hall pass, walking unhurriedly in the direction of the bathroom. He's chosen a good bathroom, I notice. Roomy, with plenty of privacy because it's not near the locker hall. Perfect for a brief make-out session. I could walk over, compliment his impressive upper arms, lead him into said bathroom—

Not right now. If there's *one* thing that could keep me from flirting, it's directing the hell out of Shakespeare.

"Now, Jacques," I repeat, regaining my directorial demeanor.

"Come on, Megan," Brian interjects. "This scene doesn't even count for our grade. Jody doesn't give a shit. She just wanted us out of the room. And you know everyone's distracted."

I'm opening my mouth to argue that every scene matters when I hear a voice. "Megan!"

I turn to find my best friend, Madeleine Hecht, jogging up the hill, her perfect red ponytail bouncing behind her, freckled cheeks flushed with excitement. "I just left the library," she continues, breathless—Madeleine volunteers in the text-book room during sixth period. "And when I walked past the drama room I saw Jody posting the cast list!"

Hearing that, my actors drop their scripts and disappear around the corner, obviously on their way to the bulletin board at the front of the Arts Center. Not suppressing a smile, I collect the scripts.

I'm a director, not an actress, so the cast list doesn't hold the same thrill and terror for me that it does for the rest of the class. But this year, I'll be making my Stillmont High stage debut in one of the smallest roles in *Romeo and Juliet*, the fall semester play. I'm guessing Lady Montague or Friar John.

I wouldn't be, except it's my dream to go to the Southern Oregon Theater Institute. It's the Juilliard of the west, with one of the best directing programs in the nation. For what-ever reason, they require every drama student to have one acting credit on their résumé, a requirement I'm going to fulfill as painlessly as possible.

"Walk over with me?" I ask Madeleine.

"Duh." She quickly takes half the scripts off my stack, chronically unable to resist lending a hand.

Right then, Wyatt Rhodes emerges from the bathroom. I follow the lanky confidence of his walk, biting my lip. It's been six months since my last relationship. I'm due for my next boyfriend. Scratch that—*over*due.

"Wait here," I tell Madeleine.

"Megan—"

I ignore her, a boy-starved moth drawn to a polo-wearing flame. I'm grateful I spent the extra ten minutes brushing the inevitable knots out of my long brown hair this morning. I know I don't have Madeleine's effortless beauty, but I'm not *not* pretty. I guess I'm in the middle. I'm neither short nor long-legged. I have features not round, closer to round-*ish*. Mine isn't the body that comes with swearing off burgers or going running more often than every January 2.

Wyatt doesn't notice me, preoccupied with tossing his hall pass from hand to hand. I call out to him in a practiced and perfected come-hither voice.

"Hey, Wyatt." I gesture to his defined biceps. "Do the abs match the arms?"

Not my best work. I haven't flirted in too long. In fairness, it's kind of a high-school bucket-list item of mine to make out with a really, really nice six-pack, and the boy attached. Even in seven boyfriends, from athletes to drama kids, *nada*.

Wyatt grins broadly. I cannot believe I haven't hooked up with him yet. It's been obvious he's gorgeous for practically the entirety of high school, and this is far from the first time we've exchanged flirtations. He doesn't immediately come across as boyfriend material, but his hotness *must* bespeak a valuable interior. I can picture us now, having long, thoughtful conversations over cappuccinos . . .

"They do on the days I don't double up on breakfast burritos," Wyatt crows.

Okay, *short* conversations over cappuccinos.

"Today's one of those days," he continues. "But don't take my word for it." He eyes me invitingly, his voice unsurprised.

Not just because he's Wyatt Rhodes and he knows he's gorgeous, either. It's because I have a reputation for being boldfaced like this. Unabashed. Unreserved. It's no secret I've had seven boyfriends, and I'm not ashamed. Class Flirt is a title I've enjoyed every minute of cultivating.

I'm about to take Wyatt up on his offer when I feel a hand on my elbow. "Bye, Wyatt," I hear Madeleine yell pointedly. "We have to go to class." She drags me away from him, and in a low if not entirely unamused voice, she says, "What've we talked about, Megan? Wyatt Rhodes is on the no-flirt list." She considers a moment, adding, "He's number *one* on the no-flirt list."

"No, he's not," I reply. "Principal Stone is."

Madeleine gives an exasperated grumble. "Point taken. Wyatt's definitely number two. You put him on the list yourself, remember? After he asked in sophomore English what book Jane Eyre wrote?"

I nod grudgingly. "And there was the time he said *Furious Seven* was his favorite book on the yearbook survey."

"You're going to find a guy way better than Wyatt. Just give it time," she reassures me as we walk down the hill toward the Arts Center. "You don't think Tyler has any competition for Romeo, do you?"

Tyler Dunning is Madeleine's boyfriend. He headed off with a group of guys to rehearse *Macbeth* when Jody banished us.

"Of course not," I answer easily.

Tyler's a leading man in every respect. Tall, broad shouldered, with dark wavy hair—he's undeniably hot. He plays baseball in spring and still manages to score the lead in every theater production. Between his charisma and Madeleine's universal likability, they're the total "it" couple of Stillmont High.

"Who'd you audition for?" Madeleine asks.

"Lady Montague."

She wrinkles her nose. "Who even is that?"

"Exactly." I grin. "She's the smallest role in the play."

I'm expecting the crowd packed in around the bulletin board when we turn the corner. What I'm not expecting is how everyone goes silent. I feel eyes on me and hear whispers start to spread.

"You guys aren't being weird at all," I mutter, trying to sound sarcastic despite my mounting nerves. I know this silence. It's the silence of the un-cast, the scrutinized walk to the gallows of your play prospects. For the first time, I feel what my classmates must whenever a cast list goes up. My pulse pounds, nerves thinning my breath. I envision apologetic emails from SOTI, halfhearted tours of other colleges in winter. Even though I'm not an actress, I need this part.

I step up to the list, my pulse pounding, and intently search the bottom of the sheet where the smaller roles will be listed. *Lady Montague . . .*

I trace my finger to the corresponding name. *Alyssa Sanchez.* My heart drops. Alyssa was the obvious favorite for Juliet. Jody's not messing around. This was brutal casting.

Reading up the list, I don't find my name. *Friar John, the Nurse . . .* Unbelievable. Even after I explained my situation to Jody, she still screwed me over.

Then I reach the top of the list.

TWO

PRINCE: *For never was a story of more woe*
Than this of Juliet and her Romeo.

V.iii.320–1

"THIS IS A MISTAKE, RIGHT?" IN SECONDS I've fought through the crowd and thrown open the door to Jody's office. *"Juliet?"*

I hear something clatter to the floor. Jody's office looks like a yard sale of mementos she's kept from every Stillmont production. There are playbills, props, and even pieces of sets stuffed onto the shelves. What looks like a brass doorknob rolls in front of me.

Jody stands up from her desk, her chunky turquoise necklace rattling. "You're not happy," she muses, studying me through her bright red glasses. They stand out even brighter against her gray hair. "I thought you'd be happy."

I feel a heaviness settle on my shoulders. A nervous pit opens in my stomach. "This isn't a misunderstanding?" I ask weakly. "It's not Anthony pulling a prank or, I don't know, a typo from an incompetent freshman you asked to print out the list?"

"No, the incompetence is all mine," Jody says, a hint of humor in her voice.

"I auditioned for Lady Montague, not the lead of the play!" I barely keep myself from exploding.

7

She raises an eyebrow, unsmiling. "Well, you got the lead," she says, her voice level.

"Why? I don't want it. Can't I be someone else? Anyone else?" I know I sound pleading.

"You're just nervous, Megan." Jody crosses her arms, but her tone has softened. "Yours was the only audition other than Anthony Jenson's that demonstrated a true understanding of the material. I've seen you direct Shakespeare before, I know you understand the play. You're Juliet, whether you like it or not."

"Jody, please." Now I'm definitely pleading. "You know I only auditioned because SOTI has an acting requirement. I've never acted in my life."

"It's a learning experience. I'm not expecting you to win a Tony," Jody says.

"Well, are you expecting *Romeo and Juliet* to be a comedy? No? Then—"

"Megan," she cuts me off sternly. "You auditioned for the play. You got Juliet. You can take it or leave it, but I've cast every other role."

I know I have no choice—Jody knows it, too. It's already the end of September. This production's my last chance for an acting credit before college applications are due in December.

"This is not going to go well for you." I sigh in exasperation, reaching for the door.

⚐

I've taken one step outside Jody's office when I run into something solid and flat.

"Whoa," I hear above me.

Of course. I step back to find Tyler grinning down from the imposing height of six foot whatever. "Hey, Juliet," he says, his deep voice working on me in ways I sincerely wish it didn't. "This could be awkward, huh?"

It hits me suddenly. Tyler's Romeo. And I'm Juliet.

I quickly recover. "Nothing could be more perfect than the two of us playing doomed lovers."

He laughs and turns to face Madeleine, who's come up beside him.

It's not a big deal, but Tyler and I dated last year. Now we don't. He's with Madeleine, but I'm not jealous or resentful. In a way, I was expecting it.

Honestly, hating acting isn't the only reason I don't want to play Juliet. The other reason is, I'm not a Juliet. I'm not the girl in the center of the stage at the end of a love story. I'm the girl before, the girl guys date right before they find their true love. Every one of my relationships ends exactly the same.

Take Tyler. He's the only guy I've ever felt myself close to falling in love with, and he dumped me six months ago to date my best friend. But I'm okay, really. Everyone knows Tyler and Madeleine are meant to be. Besides, I'm used to it.

It started when I was eleven. I'd just proclaimed to Lucy Regis my undying love for Ryan Reynolds with the intention to marry him. The next day we found out he'd married

Blake Lively. Not that that was a real example. Just an omen of things to come.

The first boy I kissed, in seventh grade, passed me a note in social studies the next day informing me he was going to ask Samantha Washington to the Hometown Fair. They've been together ever since. Freshman year, my first real boyfriend ended up cheating on me with the literal girl next door, who, it turned out, was Lucy Regis. They just celebrated their third anniversary.

It's happened time and time again. It's not a "curse" or something stupid like that—it's just more than a coincidence. And it's why I couldn't possibly get into the head of Juliet, western literature's icon of eternal love. If the world's a stage, like Shakespeare wrote, then I'm a supporting role. Or hidden in the wings.

"You're not going to steal my boyfriend, are you?" Madeleine teases, wrapping an arm around Tyler.

"No, that's your thing," I chide without thinking.

Madeleine's face immediately falls, and I'm afraid she's going to cry for the hundredth time. When Madeleine confessed to me her feelings for *my* then-boyfriend, it took two hours of hugs and reassurance before the guilty tears ended. It's not like they cheated—Madeleine's so ridiculously thoughtful that she told me before she even told him.

And it hurt. I won't pretend it didn't. But I knew the pattern. I knew what was going to happen with me and Tyler. And I understood I'd only get hurt worse trying to fight the inevitable. Better to let the relationship end before I fell for him for real.

I rush to put a hand on her arm. "It was just a dumb joke, Madeleine," I tell her. "You two are perfect."

She smiles, relieved, and leans into Tyler.

"You guys coming to the cast party?" Tyler asks.

"Where?" Cast parties are a Stillmont drama institution. Drama's sixth period, but rehearsal can extend until 5 or 6 in the evening. For every production, the cast and crew choose one location for post-rehearsal dinners and parties. I'm just hoping it's not Tyler's house.

"Verona, of course." He grins like this is amusing.

I groan. Stillmont's an hour from the Oregon Shakespeare Festival in Ashland. It's not a coincidence we're one of the strongest high-school drama programs in the state, probably the country. When I'm not being forced to play the most famous female role in theater, I feel pretty lucky to have a teacher like Jody, not to mention the departmental funding. Unfortunately, however, proximity to Ashland has its downsides. Namely, an inordinate amount of Shakespeare-themed establishments. Verona Pizza is one of the worst.

Tyler doesn't hear, or he pretends not to. He looks down at Madeleine. "I'll drive you home after."

"But I have—" she starts.

"I know," Tyler interrupts, tugging her ponytail affectionately. "Your sister's ballet recital. I'll have you home in time."

I roll my eyes. Watching them together was the quickest, if not necessarily easiest, way of extinguishing whatever lingering feelings I had for Tyler. Now when I look at him, I honestly can't imagine dating him—regardless of how his objective adherence to certain standards of male desirability might *occasionally* affect me.

They smile at each other for a moment, looking like the contented lovers in erectile-dysfunction ads.

I'd hate them if I weren't happy for them.